MARTYRS' CONVENT

MARTYRS' CONVENT

JODY BRETTKELLY

For Kevin, who makes me laugh every day.

CHAPTER ONE

Notting Hill, London, England, June.

THE SUIT GOT me. Every time.

Oh, *yeah.*

I paused in the bathroom doorway in my robe, hair dripping, towel in hand, watching Declan. The shoulders of his pin-striped jacket strained as he bent over to pick up the tie I'd tugged off him last night. The back hitched up to show a luscious view of his hard, muscled arse and thighs.

I sighed. My kryptonite.

He straightened and turned to me. Slowly, he rolled his tie and tucked it into his pocket.

"Something I can help you with?" Raising his eyebrows, he gazed at me innocently.

He rested his hands on his hips. *Not* so innocently.

My chest tightened. God, this man. There was no one sexier. Because now I knew what lay behind the flat-front trousers and the white shirt, his clothes looking as sharp today as last night. He watched me blatantly ogling him, a half-smile playing around his lips.

The past three months had unwound like a movie montage of romance—walking Teddy, my Maltese mix, through misty London parks, hands in each other's coat pockets, snatching kisses as we crossed the road, a lust haze of dinners abandoned.

"Can you help me?" I repeated his question. "Maybe?"

Prowling up to him, I brushed my hands over his wide shoulders. He wore the suit on days he visited Parliament, part of his new job. Disillusioned with being an undercover cop on the drug team, he'd wanted to do something practical to help drug addicts by changing laws to fund new programs. His new role was as liaison between police, Parliament, and the community.

"Your suit reminds me. Sorry I didn't ask last night, but we were, um, occupied. How'd it go with ole Lord Pompiface?"

Declan shoved a hand through his short brown hair. He had drawn up a bill and was trying to get Lord Havistock in the House of Lords to present it. The bill aimed to tighten regulations at the ports to stop incoming drugs, build free treatment centers in towns wrecked by addiction, and fund resource officers in high schools.

"I like him. He's a good guy, and he's coming 'round. But it's slow work. A lot of lunches and drinks and listening to him complaining about his ungrateful Gucci-wearing kids."

I laughed. "Joyriding in Daddy's Rolls." Stroking his freshly shaven jawline, I shifted my voice into what hopefully sounded casual. "Did he say anything about that art theft at his castle?"

He playfully slapped my butt. "Nice try, Mata Hari." He turned a bit serious. "I need to be careful with him and the other politicians. I have to gain their trust. A few of those guys know I'm with you."

I slapped his butt back. "That rules out everything you hear about crime and politics." I was downplaying my desperation to not ruin the mood, but I was going through a serious dry spell at the newspaper. My fellow journalist, Sooz, whom I'd mentored for years, was kicking my butt, and word in the office was she had a huge story breaking in a couple of weeks.

"Surely you're not worried?" His green gaze clutched at mine. "Your big story was only five months ago. One of the most highly read articles for years." His pride pulsed into my veins, opening my heart to him even wider. My success was partly thanks to him. Back in my hometown in New Zealand, we'd pretended to be in a relationship so we could work together to expose a $100 million heroin ring. More importantly, I'd also solved the mysterious disappearance of my best friend twenty years ago.

"Newspapers are brutal." I shrugged. "You're only as good as the next story you're pitching. I don't have a next. Those two leads didn't turn up anything." He nodded, and I went to continue. "And Sooz is onto something big. I need job certainty and a better salary to guarantee I can pay rent for the whole flat. I'm too old for flatmates." I'd used the advance from my book about the case to help pay the rent so far. Declan opened his mouth, and knowing what he was going to say, I forged on. "I wish I had a setup like James's." He was one of our columnists. "He's given all the solid tip-offs, so he doesn't have to scramble for stories every month like I do."

Declan traced a finger under his bottom lip. "Your book comes out at Christmas—surely that's another point in your favor. Have you heard about the final edits?" He'd patiently listened from the other end of the sofa to hours of me proofreading my book out loud.

"They're coming. The editor's happy. To be honest, that's another reason I need a big story. I don't want people to think I'm resting on my laurels after the success of a story about the death of my childhood best friend. That feels wrong, as though I'm using her in a way. I want to have something new, be seen as a serious, current investigator."

I checked my phone. I'd put out a few feelers on a small police story, hoping it might be bigger than what it sounded. Nothing. My heart sank. There was only that one voicemail from yesterday afternoon.

"What do you think about this?" I pressed "Play." A strange rattle, bump, and clink filled the air.

"Ms. Joyson, I read your New Zealand heroin story. I have something for you. It's about Class A drugs shipping into London.

I'll call back tomorrow at four o'clock in the afternoon and let you know the details." A woman's voice. *Ms. Jaysn. Aye read…* her vowels were swallowed in a posh, old-fashioned way. I didn't want to be influenced by her accent, but she did sound sensible, and that made me less inclined to believe it was a hoax.

"Would someone call you with such a big tip-off?" Declan narrowed his eyes. "Wouldn't they want to meet?"

Bugger. Exactly what I'd thought. I groaned in frustration. "I thought you were going to help me get stories. What use are you to me now?" I joked.

"Fuck." He kissed the base of my throat. "How quickly she forgets." He lifted his head. "What about twice last night and once this morning?"

"Oh? What was that again?" I put a finger to my lips. "I might need a reminder."

"Well, for starters, this has to go." He eased open the tie around my waist and slipped the robe off my shoulders. As it drifted to the floor, he traced his fingers down my bare back. Mmm. My body swelled with anticipation. This was a discovery I'd made early on with him—there was something about being naked with a man fully dressed in a suit.

He kissed me sweetly, softly, then deep and hard. Pulling my bare hips to his, he walked me backward toward my four-poster bed swathed in orange organza. The sun blazed through the yellow silk curtains as we rolled onto the bed.

Ring, ring. I jumped. My editor's tone. On a Saturday? In a flash, I disentangled myself from Declan, lunged across the bed, grabbed my robe from the floor, yanked it on—not that she could see me—and answered the call.

"Morning, Isla. Felicity Barnfield here."

"Good morning." Breathless, I checked the clock on my bedside table: 7:10 a.m. My heart skittered. "Everything okay?"

"Yes." She paused. "Sorry to call so early and on a weekend, but I'm out all day at meetings, and an email will be sent out soon about some changes in the office. James Robinson is retiring. That means there's a salaried position going. That person will also be taking over his column, which, as you know, has a photo byline."

The ultimate accolade for any journalist, plus a pay raise and job security. My chest bubbled with excitement, and I grinned.

That person. Oh. My face fell. This was just a call to let me know I was a possibility.

Declan pushed to his feet and cocked his head.

"Wow." I smiled, trying to match my initial enthusiasm. "Thank you for considering me." I pushed the heel of my hand to my temple. Who was I competing against? "Would you feel comfortable telling me who else is being considered?"

"Sooz Cameron is also in the running. Sorry, I should have led with that."

My smile faded. That was completely different.

"The editors will meet and discuss, followed by the board. We will let both of you know our decision in two weeks' time."

I tensed, a knot squeezing tight in my gut. I had two weeks of working around the clock to find a great story.

"Thank you again, Felicity." I wrangled my voice upward. "This is exciting."

"Well, good. See you at the office."

We said goodbye and rang off.

I turned to Declan and told him the news.

Grinning from ear to ear, he folded me into a big hug. "Congratulations, you deserve it."

"I haven't got it yet." I squeezed the bridge of my nose, figuring out my next steps. Now I really needed a big story—soon. "Right. I need to get into the office."

Shimmying out of his embrace, I raced to my wardrobe. It came as a surprise even to me that it was flooded with color, all my old black and white work clothes in thrift shop bags at the back, waiting to be donated. I grabbed a striped tangerine suit and floral shirt. I used to dress only in black and white, just as I'd thought the truth was black and white. But back home in New Zealand, I'd discovered that opening my heart brought color into my life and the realization that the truth was more nuanced than I'd wanted to believe.

"Why aren't you more excited?" Declan was about to leave, but instead he watched, thoughtful to my frantic.

I raced into the bathroom to do my makeup. He leaned a shoulder against the doorjamb as I dabbed on mascara, trying not to poke my eye out.

"This is so bloody tough. Sooz is hardworking and talented. I want to support her, but I want this job for myself. It'll mean I can afford this flat on my own."

Declan moved closer and slipped his hands around my waist. "Save your rent money." He caught my gaze in the mirror.

Setting down my mascara, I went to object.

"I know we've talked about this," he said. "And you think it's too soon, but it's not. I want you to move in. You belong with me."

"I'd still need to pay you rent." I was putting off the discussion.

"Isla. I'm not looking for a roommate." His eyes softened. "I want us to live together."

I stiffened. I couldn't help it. Declan flinched. After our breakup, he'd taken months to realize he loved me and wanted us to be together, but once he'd made that decision, he was all in, heart and soul. And I loved that because I was committed too, and I couldn't think of a life without him. I twisted my mascara closed. But part of me wanted to keep my flat, that slice of independence.

Now panicked about getting a story so I could compete with Sooz, I grabbed my phone off the bed, sat down, and replayed the voicemail from yesterday afternoon. Fantastical, yes, but I wanted to keep an open mind. "Maybe she's calling again today to set up a meeting?"

Rattle. Bump. Clink, clink. I pressed "Stop." Then played it again.

"Is that what I think it is?" I asked Declan. Please let me be wrong.

"Is it the rattle of a door? The clink … coins?"

"It's one of those old red public phone booths, isn't it?" Frustrated, I punched into the mattress. "All my pay phone callers end up being conspiracy theorists, and the information never leads anywhere."

He reached for me and rubbed my upper arms. "Babe, you'll find a good story. I know you will."

I turned at the scratching at the door. "I've woken up Teddy. Better take him out," I said.

"Okay, time for me to disappear." Declan pulled his phone from its charger on the side table and pocketed it. Sometimes, his meetings were on weekends if that was the only time politicians could spare. "Let me know if you hear anything else about the job when you get into the office." He gave me a lingering goodbye kiss. "You know, I wouldn't have to go home and change if we were living together. We're spending at least an hour a day on this back-and-forth."

"Let's leave it a bit," I hedged again.

"But you *are* ready to meet Sephy?" His thirteen-year-old daughter was at boarding school, and though I was terrified of meeting her, I was nearly there.

"Yes, of course, after she gets back from the Europe trip with her class." My shoulders relaxed. That was a long way off. School hadn't even broken up yet for the summer.

"Speaking of, she has a test today." He grabbed his phone from his pocket. "I want to say good luck." He poised his thumbs to text her but jolted with a double take.

What was wrong? Adrenaline fired through my veins.

He viewed his text messages. "What. The. Fuck." His face was ashen, drained of blood. His breathing was shallow.

My heart racing, I put a hand on his back.

"Declan? What is it? What's happened?"

He scrolled down, focused only on his phone.

"It's Sephy's school," he answered finally. "There's been a big drug bust. Ten students have been expelled for holding. Marijuana, pills. And—what? Jesus, no. Fentanyl?"

He screwed up his face, incredulous. "What the hell is going on at that place? I'm calling her."

She didn't pick up. My heart constricted. Did this mean she was in trouble too? Though I'd heard that kids didn't bother answering phone calls. He texted her. She must have replied immediately. "Fuck," he spat out, then shook his head.

After some back-and-forth with her, he swore again. "Three of her friends have been expelled." He grabbed his briefcase. "I've got to get her out of there. I'm leaving to pick her up. She's coming home, and she's not going back."

I scooped up Teddy and kept pace with Declan as he strode through the living room.

"Shouldn't you call the school first?" I asked. "Find out what's happening. What's your plan when she gets home? Declan, I get that you're worried, but this isn't like you."

Fear flashed across his face.

"You're thinking about Sephy's mother, aren't you?" I asked.

Anguish tightened his mouth. He turned to fiddle with his briefcase, like he was blocking my question.

His response thrust me into a burning awareness. He was pushing me away again. Even though I'd asked about her several times, he hadn't wanted to tell more than what he'd confessed that one night during our investigation. Sephy's mother was part of the drug family he'd been investigating and had become his informant. He knew she took drugs, but not the extent. They got together, and when she got pregnant accidentally, she stopped using. She gave birth to Sephy and died of an overdose sometime afterward. I knew nothing more about the timing or the details. For someone so open, he was intensely tight-lipped about her. That hurt, but I figured he'd reveal more when he was ready.

"I'll text you later," was all he said as I opened the door for him.

"That would be great." I wrapped myself around him. His arms were stiff against his body. "Don't worry, we'll sort this out."

With a distracted nod, he headed out the door.

CHAPTER TWO

THREE FIFTY-FIVE IN the afternoon. *Tick, tick, tick.* Countdown to 4:00 p.m. My pulse thumped at the same pace as the antique wall clock at the top of the newsroom, my eyes dry from staring at it. I drove my pen into my notebook, ripping the paper.

Everything was hanging on this call.

This was my last chance. I'd gotten nothing from my call this morning to New Scotland Yard. I'd dug through all my contacts and researched cold cases and small police stories. I was out of ideas and resources. I prayed this woman was not just a conspiracy theorist.

4:00 p.m. This was it. My heart thumped hard against my rib cage. I glared at my phone, willing it to ring. Silence. My knuckles squeezed white.

Nothing. Maybe my phone wasn't— For the hundredth time I checked it was turned up for maximum sound. Yes. A sharp prickle scratched behind my eyes.

4:01 p.m. My phone rang. Unknown number. *Was this it?* Jangling with nerves, I jabbed "Answer" and pressed "Record."

Someone was breathing heavily on the other end. I could make out the thick metallic click of coins and the rattle of a door being closed—same as last time. But another sound brushed up against my eardrums. A buzzing? Or was it more like a ringing? It was a kind of reverberation.

"Isla Joyson?"

Ayla Jaysn. Those clipped vowels. Thank God. It was her—the phone booth woman.

"Yes, hello?" I said. "Who am I speaking to?"

"I'm the person who called yesterday afternoon."

Muffled voices intruded from behind her.

"I don't have much time. There's a shipment of Class A drugs arriving on a Norwegian ship called the *Fjord.* It's landing at Tilbury Port in Essex in eight days', next Sunday, three in the morning."

My fingers flying across the keys, I quickly researched Tilbury. My heart missed a beat. It listed that exact arrival. My whole body flushed with excitement. God, this could be a huge story. I was right to trust my instincts.

"How do you know this?" I asked.

"I can't say."

"Why not?" My head whirled with questions, desperate to keep her on the line, get her name, arrange to meet. I had to prove to myself that she was a credible source. As a trusted journalist, I could present this story to my editor without naming her, but I had to be certain of her identity and that she was reliable.

She caught her breath.

I jolted. "Are you okay? What's going on there?"

One voice rose above the volley of noise in the background. "Hey-hey." A rap on glass. "Hey-hey." Yes, she was almost definitely in a phone booth.

"Your brother," the man's voice spat out.

"Is someone else there?" If he'd heard her on this call, she could be in danger. My heart kicked into overdrive. "Are you okay? Are you safe?"

I crushed the phone to my ear to hear her short breaths rasp out.

"Please," I pleaded. "Tell me where you are so I can call the police."

"Don't call the police." Her words scraped with horror.

"Why? Why aren't you giving this information to the police?"

Now the male voice behind her was louder, angrier. "Your brother needs you," he insisted.

"I told the police the first time." Her reply was raced and slightly muffled. Was she shielding her mouth? Was she worried about that man overhearing? "All that happened was the shipment was offloaded at an earlier port. Do not tell the police. I'm trusting you to investigate this yourself."

"Are you suggesting there's an informant in the police?" That made it a much bigger story for me. It also meant she was in worse danger.

A door opened. Silence.

No, no, no.

"Are you there? Hello? Hello?"

I was almost yelling. I shot a quick look around the newsroom. A few of the weekend staff fixed me with concerned faces but I couldn't worry about that now.

I listened, holding my breath. Faint traffic noises seeped in, like she'd left the phone off the hook. I waited for the bang of a door being closed. No sound. Did that mean she'd been pulled out of the phone booth?

"Are you okay?" I called into the phone.

She was in trouble. I needed to go to her. But where was she? My gut turned over.

I should call the police. *But she said not to.*

How could I help her? My chest emptied, cavernous and cold.

I couldn't.

CHAPTER THREE

I WAS CONSUMED with the call and desperate to head out to Tilbury Port in Essex. But I'd already promised to help my best friend and old flatmate, Shakayla, that evening. She'd had a baby a week ago and was not doing well. On the forty-minute train ride to her house, I was clutching an armful of takeout from her favorite Caribbean place and a bottle of wine when my phone pinged with a text from her. *Please tell me you're on your way!* I set my bags down and replied with a thumbs-up.

Declan had texted too: *The eagle has landed.*

Me: *How's it going with Sephy?*

Declan: *Brilliant! JK. Not sure which is scarier, the ice-in-veins stare or the hand gestures. I've got her home, that's about it.*

The train braked with a screech, slicing an unnerving, juddering line through me. Sephy was home, and everything was about to change. She'd be there mornings, nights, weekends, and round-the-clock during school holidays. What would I even say when I met her? I didn't know any thirteen-year-old girls, and hadn't a clue what interested them. And if she didn't like me, what then? A colleague constantly complained about her life with stepchildren. Sephy was the most important person in Declan's life, and that was how it should be, but if she took a dislike to me, would our relationship survive it?

I didn't even know how to respond to Declan. I had to be careful commenting on her behavior since it could come off as rude or presumptuous.

> Me: *Least you've still got your health and GSOH.*
>
> Declan: *Yes, I keep making old-person jokes like that which infuriates her even more. Call me later when you're back from Shay's? I love you, babe.*

My heart melted. Seeing his *I love yous* in my texts never got old. And who would have thought I'd like being someone's babe? I started to type, *Love you and your big*— Shit, I couldn't text him stuff like that anymore. Sephy might see it. *Delete, delete, delete.* I typed a simple *Love you too.* Yes, much more family-friendly.

Another important text pinged from my publisher: *Confirmed you need to keep Jan and Feb next year free for the book tour. All of Jan in New Zealand.* The thought of being under the hot summer sun warmed me through. I couldn't wait. I was looking forward to seeing more of Mum and Dad. But this meant it was even more important I got a big story. I didn't want to arrive in New Zealand looking like I was resting my career on the investigation of the death of my childhood best friend.

A leafy walk from the gabled train station led me to Shay's little 1920s rose-wrapped stone cottage. Could I live here? Maybe. I imagined myself swinging a baby in my arms in the doorway. I'd already met little Marcellus Rolando le Nguyen, his first names from Shay's family and Bato's last name, when he was born. He was so sweet and pure and snuggly I couldn't stand it.

The wails of a baby rent the air.

I went to knock, but my hand passed through the open door.

Standing in the doorway was a tiny, pinch-faced woman in purple scrubs. Judy, Lactation Specialist, her badge read. She pulled on her trench coat, looking ready to leave.

"Never knock on the door of a new mum! You will wake baby. Is this din-dins?" She sniffed. "I hope there's no garlic in there? Or smelly cheeses. Or spices of any kind. And that wine will give baby a rumbly tummy. A breastfeeding mum needs the full support of her friends." She tutted, leaving me in no doubt I'd come up short.

I couldn't throw Shay under the bus by saying she'd ordered this. "The food's for me. And the wine's for me too."

She viewed me with pity.

"Only one glass, not the whole bottle," I added.

Inside, Shay was trudging across the living room floor in stained pajamas as Marcellus screamed bloody blue murder in her arms. This had been a stunning room filled with antiques from Portobello Road, reupholstered in beautifully serene fabrics designed by Bato. Now, every spare inch was covered in garishly colored plastic stuff for babies—holding, swinging, walking, feeding, and wiping babies. I'd gone shopping with Shay for months, and it looked like she'd ordered everything we saw.

"Isla. Thank God you're here." Across one cheek was a yellow streak. Was that … baby poop?

"Shay, how are you, love?" I dropped my bags and patted her shoulders tentatively, not wanting to jostle the baby into further fury.

She stared up at me, tears pooling in her brown eyes, which were hollowed underneath with dark circles.

"The baby hasn't slept in two days, so I haven't slept or showered in two days. Even when Bato tries to give me a break, I can't relax with all the screaming. I haven't even been able to get him out for a walk. I get everything ready, and he needs changing or feeding. My boobs are so sore I just want to hack them off. And how will I ever get back to work? If I hire a nanny, I'll be stuck if they don't turn up. If I put him in a nursery, he'll be sick all the time, and I'll have to keep him home. I'm well and truly fucked either way."

"Oh, Shay."

I gulped. This was the smelly, mucky, sleep-deprived reality of having a baby. Everything was different now. Sephy's home, Shay has a baby, and we're not just sitting around cackling over celebrity gossip and drinking margaritas anymore. Life just got very real.

I had to find a way to cheer her up, but hearing all this, I wanted to cry too. The responsibility she had for every second of this tiny human's life was terrifying. And she was stuck in this room. Not forever—logically, I knew that—but it was already starting to feel like it. My stomach churned over her loss of independence.

I wanted to offer to come and help every day, but I couldn't.

"When's your mother flying in?" I asked anxiously. She was coming from Jamaica.

At the mention of her mother, she let out an anguished sob and broke down into hiccupping tears. "Not for two whole days."

Marcellus started crying louder too. God, it all felt totally out of control. But enough of my feelings. I was here for Shay. I headed to the kitchen to set the food on the counter.

She followed me. "Please stay until Bato gets home," she pleaded.

"Of course. The scary lady at the door said you're not allowed the food I brought."

"Feck it. How could this get much worse?" Marcellus bellowed on cue. "Could he yell any louder?"

I winced. I couldn't imagine it.

"Bato feels rubbish for not being around. You know he's got that big clothing collab? He was up all night for this morning's deadline, putting the pieces together for the drop next month. The highlight of his career, and he doesn't have time to enjoy it."

"That sucks, Shay." I slapped my thigh decisively. "Okay. Tell me how I can help. First, I'm taking Marcellus from you."

I sat both of us down in the living room. By this time, he'd quieted. I slid him from her gingerly. She showed me how to hold him, supporting his head. He was so tiny and fragile. Please don't cry again. He let out a whimper.

"You have to stand up and walk," Shay said.

Don't drop him, don't drop him. Stiffly, my heart pounding, I creaked to my feet. He roused awake until he was back crying full force. Gingerly, I walked back and forth, alternating between making sure I didn't trip up and that he wasn't choking on his fury.

"Shay, put your earbuds in, have a shower, and heat some food up for yourself," I said, my eyes peeled on the tiny creature in my arms, red-faced with sobs. "I'll get mine later. Take as long as you want."

"Are you sure? You'll cope?"

"Look at me, so coping." I forced a smile.

With a new spring in her step, she climbed the stairs to her bedroom.

"Marcellus," I pleaded, rocking him. "I submit. You are totally in charge. You are king of the universe, no argument. Please take pity on me."

He must have taken my pleas to heart because, after ten minutes of walking him up and down, he fell asleep in my arms. Ah, do I possess the secret after all? This wasn't so bad, was it? Maybe I was a baby whisperer, and I was just finding out now. I went to lower him into his bassinet. As soon as my arms slightly dipped, he woke and gave me a furious look, opening his tiny mouth wide.

"Okay, little guy," I muttered quickly. "You win." Jerking to standing, I started pacing again. So, not the baby whisperer after all.

The stress made me wonder what it must have been like for Declan to manage this on his own. *Did* he do all this on his own?

When did Sephy's mother die? When did he take full custody of Sephy? I had no idea because he never wanted to talk about it. Being with him always felt like coming home and being wrapped in a warm blanket, but now I stared into a cold emptiness of what I didn't know about this huge, traumatic part of his life. The sharp ache made me question the certainty I'd felt about his love and our future.

I paced until Marcellus's eyelids fluttered close.

"Oh, little M, you are amazing," I whispered. He gave a little grunt in his sleep as though agreeing. Sighing over his finely-etched lips at peace, his tiny fingers, those toes that had yet to touch the earth, I saw him for the miraculous little creature he was.

Shay padded down the stairs, showered and dressed in a fresh set of pajamas. She disappeared into the kitchen and reemerged, her plate heaped with rice, plain flatbread, and salad with no dressing. Poor thing. She was obviously too scared to eat anything else.

She settled herself on the sofa.

"I'm a failure." She tore a piece off the flatbread. "But at least I'm a failure in fresh jammies."

"Shay." I gave her foot a careful nudge with mine. "Marcellus is the luckiest little guy in the world to have you as his mum. Give yourself a break. Look what you've done—the most amazing thing in the universe."

"What?" Shakayla asked, stabbing a forkful of dry lettuce.

"You literally squeezed something the size of a large grapefruit out of your vagina one week ago."

"Grapefruit," she scoffed. "More like a block of flats."

We burst out laughing, then covered our mouths. Marcellus did this cute grabbing-the-air thing, then settled back down.

"Ouch." She pointed at her crotch. "Everything hurts. I'm sure Bato thinks he's never going to have sex again in his life."

We covered our snorts. A little bit of the Shay-light came back into her eyes.

She took a forkful of rice. "Now. Please talk to me like a grown-up. Tell me about work."

"Well. I just found out this morning I'm up for a big promotion. It'll mean I'll be able to relax a bit. My job will be secure. Not that I can slow down or be complacent. Only issue is, Sooz is up for it too, and she has a big story in the works. So I need one." That made me think about the phone call again with new enthusiasm. I was intrigued by the mention of a possible police informant.

"Congratulations, Isla." She searched my face. "But why are you worried? Surely it's in the bag. You've got a big book coming out. That must count for a lot. Haven't you got an exciting PR world tour booked for January and February, including New Zealand?"

"The book's not coming out until Christmas. And when I go home, I don't want anyone thinking I'm resting my career on Janey's death. I don't want that story to be all that I have. I want to show I'm a serious journalist."

"I understand where you're coming from, I get it," she said. "Anything in the works?"

"I got an anonymous call today, a woman, about drugs coming into a port." I was trying to keep Shay in good spirits, so I needed to keep it brief. "It's a huge story if it's true."

"Sounds exciting. And what's happening with that dreamy boyfriend of yours?" She fluttered her eyelashes. "Is he still trying to persuade you to live in sin?"

I ground my teeth. "Yes. But there's a complication. There's been a huge drug bust at Sephy's school. Kids have been expelled, some of them her friends. When he heard, he drove straight to her school and picked her up. She'll be living with him full-time now and going to a local school. So I definitely can't move in at this stage. It'll have to be later. They need some space, and I'm totally unprepared to be a—well, what would I be to Sephy?"

She plucked at my sleeve. "Isla, don't hold off too long. I know you're worried about this next step, but you might be missing out on an amazing time together. Are you sure you're not just using Sephy as an excuse? Maybe she's fine about you moving in. And compared to this little guy, think how easy she'll be. She can walk around by herself, tell you what she needs, get herself fed."

A burst of hope lit up my chest. "Maybe. I'm meeting her tomorrow night, so I'll give you an update after that." I smiled. "Tell you the truth, I'm quite looking forward to it now."

CHAPTER FOUR

THE FOLLOWING EVENING, Sunday, at five, I stepped up to Declan's yellow front door. It hit me.

I couldn't just use my key and walk in like I usually did. I had to knock. The people inside were a family, and I was an outsider. But it was going to go okay … wasn't it?

His townhouse was in Shepherd's Bush, a sometimes gritty, vibrant old area half an hour's walk from my flat. Its yellow and blue hues—part of a pastel-colored street—lifted me out of any day. Today, my throat prickled as though I was wearing a rough, too-tight scarf.

I was anxious, too, because I'd cut short a frustrating day to be here on time. First, I followed up on some possible leads from New Scotland Yard. No luck. Then, I took a train to Tilbury Port in Essex and paced the metal fences. What on earth should I be looking for? The only way in was if I worked for a catering or cleaning firm, but there was no time to get a job with one. Finally, back in the office, I researched the Norwegian shipping company. It was an old, reputable family business that transported steel, food, and textiles—was any of that suspicious?

I had to focus on meeting Sephy. Squaring my shoulders, I knocked loudly.

Declan opened the door, looking exhausted and incredibly relieved to see me. He gave me a huge hug and kiss and led me in, his arm around me. Downstairs was an open-plan living room and kitchen that looked out onto a tiny garden. His parents had loaned him the money to buy a home when Sephy came to live with him full-time, and he'd paid them back through the years. It was decorated in warm neutral colors and very "him"—everything neat, clean, and in its place. Usually, until I walked in the door and messed it up.

But today, someone else had strewn clothes, bags, and notebooks all over. The person I guessed was Sephy lay sprawled on the sofa.

He kept his arm around me. "Sephy, I want you to meet Isla."

She grunted and kept tapping on her phone.

Declan rolled his head back and sucked in a give-me-strength breath. "Sephy, please put down your phone and greet Isla properly."

Sephy unraveled her long limbs and got to her feet, tall for thirteen, about my height, five foot seven. She had Declan's green eyes, but her dimples and straight, black, glossy hair must have been her mother's. She wore a holey cropped sweatshirt and big baggy jeans, the waistband folded over a couple of times, but still, the hems trailed on the ground.

"Hi, Sephy." I smiled and offered my hand to shake. I was stunned. Wow. Declan had a daughter. And she was beautiful. It was incredible. He'd had a major life experience, being a parent, that was an unknown world to me.

Sephy ignored my outstretched hand and looked at me. Up and down. Slow … painful.

Under her penetrating gaze, I shifted and squirmed and tried to flatten my mass of red curly hair. Why had I tried a cat eye with a blue liner without running it past Shay first? I'd dressed in florals, stripes, and paisley, which seemed fun at the time, but now I felt like a try-hard mess. My skinny jeans looked dated next to her cool, wide ones. She saw through me; my lack of confidence, the chinks in my armor, my inability to put an outfit together.

"Hi, Lisa," she said, shaking my hand.

"It's not Lisa," Declan said. "It's—"

He did a double take, then pressed his lips together, like he'd just realized she knew it wasn't Lisa.

"How *is* Lisa?" Sephy asked him sweetly. "I always liked her."

Cheeky. But kind of funny too. A bubble of grudging admiration rolled around in my chest. She'd subtly put me in my place. She was brighter, quicker, and sharper than I was at her age. And who was this Lisa woman anyway? Declan had never mentioned a Lisa. He'd told me most of the women he'd dated were very short-term, and he'd never introduced them to Sephy.

Declan's jaw set. "Obviously, I would not know, and you are being very disrespectful right now."

"*I'm* being disrespectful?" Sephy's eyebrows shot up. She threw herself down on the sofa and went back to her phone.

As she scrolled, I tried to think of questions I could ask her. What did thirteen-year-olds want to talk about? The only thing that came to mind was school and friends, which I suspected would infuriate her further, as she'd been unwillingly cut off from them. Seeing something on her phone, her face lit up. She swung her fringed suede handbag off the back of the sofa.

"Don't worry about me for dinner. I'm not hungry. Chamonix just texted. She's dying to see me. I'll be back around ten."

"Whoa, whoa, whoa." Declan held out his palm. "You're not going anywhere. You're staying home for at least twenty-four hours so we can talk and set some boundaries."

She flopped her arms over her head in protest.

"Dude. We talked all day yesterday and today. Literally, we have nothing left to talk about. You know I wasn't involved. And still you took me out of school. I didn't even have time to say a proper goodbye to my friends. Chammy lives around the corner. She doesn't even go to my school. She's a friend from preschool, you know that."

Declan shook his head. "You'll have plenty of time to catch up with her later."

Watching him being a parent like this, seeing this new side to him, I was impressed. He stayed calm and refused to get dragged into her arguments or match her energy. I didn't know if I could be that adult, rising above it all.

Sephy huffed. "Chammy just pointed out a major hole in this plan of yours to send me to the local high school. They're an urban school. They must have drug stuff as bad as my school. Maybe worse."

"We've talked about this," Declan answered patiently. "All my research shows private schools have much worse drug problems as the kids have more money." Sephy greeted this logic with a snort. "Also, you're going to be home after school, and I'm going to be more involved at home, at school, and out."

My mind raced, scrambling to catch up to the implications of what he'd just said. I tried to picture the daily impact on our relationship. I didn't plan to be here every night, but this did mean the three of us were going to be in this house together a lot. It meant no more date nights and definitely no walking around the house half-naked. Would he expect me to volunteer at her school, drive her around, help her bake cookies for fundraisers, supervise her homework? I tried to imagine myself on the PTA. Couldn't. I didn't know if I had the energy or the diplomacy. This was a huge change.

"What? Everyone will think I'm a baby," Sephy wailed. "Why are you being like this?"

"I'm being a parent." He gave a hopeful smile. "C'mon, Seph. Let's not argue. Let's just sit down and have a nice dinner together. I made your favorites—roast chicken and apple pie."

She seemed to waver for a second. Then her eyes went hard. "I told you I'm not hungry. If you're going to keep me a prisoner, I'm off to bed."

She turned on a heel, thumped upstairs to her bedroom, and slammed the door. *Oof.* The sound knocked through to my chest. I felt a little shaken.

Declan leaned back against the kitchen island and sighed.

"Well. That went well," he said. He smiled wryly and took my hand, rubbing his thumb over my wrist. "Isla, I'm sorry about her behavior. When she calms down, you'll see how great she is."

"She's been taken away from all her friends, I get it." When I was fourteen, I lost my best friend, and it was hard. Sephy shouldn't treat me like that, but I did understand. "It seems like she thinks you're overreacting. But she knows you feel this way because of her mother?"

Declan dropped his head and didn't answer.

"She does know about her mother?" I asked.

He put a finger to his lips. "No. She doesn't. I told her that her mother was killed in a car crash. That her mother didn't have any family."

"What?" My face froze with shock. I couldn't believe what I was hearing. Like another person was speaking.

He pressed his hands down in a shooshing motion. Pointing to his office across the hallway, he led me there and shut the door.

CHAPTER FIVE

ARMS CROSSED HARD against his chest, Declan paced the room. I sat on his old Chesterfield sofa, waiting.

"She started asking about her mother as soon as she could talk, and that's way too heavy a burden to put on a young child. It's not fair to her. I'm going to tell her when she's older."

"Declan, if you tell her, it will explain why you're doing this."

He shook his head. "It's not time."

Surprised, my hand flew to my chest. "When were you planning to tell her? When she's thirty?"

He glared at me.

I'd never seen him so angry. My journalistic nature was to keep prodding and pushing, but maybe this time I'd pushed too far. Doubt corkscrewed into my side. Should I apologize?

"Look, you don't understand the situation, so there's no point in us discussing this." His tone was very offhand. "I just wanted to make sure you don't raise the subject in front of Sephy."

My cheeks blazed at his stinging dismissal of me. And he was making me part of his lie. I gripped the arms of the sofa, trying to stay calm.

"You're right. I don't know anything about your situation or about Sephy. Why? You're so keen on us talking over everything, but you're so closed off about this."

"I can't tell you." His jaw clenched, and he turned away. "It's not—" His tone was final and still laced with anger, which might have been my cue to let it go, but I couldn't.

"How long are you going to keep this from me?" I said to his back. "Forever? I'm not allowed to know about this important part of your life and how Sephy came to be?"

He turned on me, his face blank as if to shut me down again.

My heart beat like rapid gunfire. Was this too hard a barrier to get past?

Maybe he saw that fear on my face. His expression softened, though pain still twitched in his jaw. He sat heavily in his desk chair. As he rubbed the wooden arms, I could see his hands were trembling. Staring into the distance, his breathing sounded high and shallow, like he was forcing himself back to a place he'd never wanted to return to. I saw what it cost him.

"I haven't told the whole story to anyone," he said. "Not even my sisters."

I nodded, not having the words to convey how I felt. "Thank you for trusting me" felt thin and too small.

"I finished university, then joined Criminal Investigations. One of my bosses saw something in me, and I was recruited into undercover. It was my first case, and I was determined to impress everyone and make my name. Then I met her, and everything came together."

"What was she like?" I asked softly.

"She was beautiful." His eyes held mine. "Well, you've seen Sephy."

I nodded and smiled.

"But it was more than just looks." His eyes glittered. "She was a bright light. Everyone was drawn to her."

He smiled into the distance like those were good memories. At the joy shining from his face, tendrils of jealousy wrapped tight around my ribs. I shoved away the emotion, ashamed of my petty feelings about a woman who'd died tragically.

"We had to work together closely, and I knew I shouldn't get into a relationship with her, but I was young and stupid and inexperienced"—he pressed hard against his forehead—"and completely fucking hopelessly in love. I fooled myself that the closer we were, the quicker we could bring her family to justice, which was true in a way."

He turned sideways in his chair, uncomfortably. "I knew she used, but I thought it was just at nightclubs on the weekend, what many twentysomethings do. She was sickened by what her family had gotten into, and we already knew that before we targeted her. Six months later, we made the arrests, and we relocated her."

Haunted and haggard, he shoved his fingers through his hair. "She broke it off with me, said she wanted to start a completely new life. I was devastated, but she said I reminded her of a time she wanted to forget. We set her up in a little house with a garden on the coast. She'd always wanted to live by the sea. She enrolled in teachers' college, and she seemed to be doing well there. She was clever and loved children and was the sort of person who collected friends effortlessly. One night, she called to tell me that she was pregnant with our baby, and she wanted to keep it. She promised she was not taking drugs. We kept in close contact from then on, and I took her to all her doctor's appointments, so I knew she was telling the truth.

"But soon after Sephy was born, she started going rapidly downhill. I moved in with her as a friend. She was very unhappy and felt isolated because she couldn't talk about her former life with anyone but me. She missed her family. Oh, she knew the horrible things they'd done while running their business, but they'd always treated her like a princess and lavished her with love, well, their kind of warped, narcissistic love. I felt totally responsible for the whole thing, as though I'd ruined her life. At the beginning, my ambition had reasoned that I'd got her involved for all the right reasons, and the ends justified the means. But none of that mattered when I saw her losing weight, so depressed she could barely get up in the morning, couldn't even brush her hair or change her clothes. This was someone I loved withdrawing from life before my eyes."

His face was drawn and tortured. "It became clear to me she'd used a lot more than I'd thought. I was so angry with myself. For fuck's sake, my job was to notice what people were hiding. Was I so besotted with her, so oblivious, that I hadn't seen what I should and gotten her help? She spiraled downward and couldn't pull herself free. One day I popped out, just to get groceries. I found her when I got back. She'd overdosed. There was a note: *I'm sorry.* Sephy was in the next room. She was only one month old."

I gasped. "Oh God." I touched his arm. "Declan, I'm so sorry."

Tears filled his eyes and slipped unchecked down his cheeks. Covering his face with his hands, he folded over, his elbows on his knees. Soon, his shoulders were racked with sobs. I laid a hand on his heaving back, desperate to say something to comfort him, but no words seemed right. He was always so together, but now I saw how he'd carried around this deep wound and blame for her death.

After some time, he raised his head slightly and wiped his face on his sleeve. I fetched some tissues and handed them to him. He took them silently and his red eyes sank back into his face.

"I can't tell Sephy that story," he said. "Don't ask me to do that."

Declan took a couple of minutes to get himself under control. Exhausted, he led me out of the office and into the kitchen.

I wanted to talk more, but he was turned away, his demeanor making it clear the conversation was over. Slowly, still without speaking, he checked the chicken and veggies and the pie in the lower oven. Normally, I would have offered to help, got out the plates and cutlery and set the table, but I sensed he needed something to keep his hands occupied.

After a while, he came and sat next to me on the sofa. He smiled, seeming lighter somehow—maybe it had helped for him to offload the crushing burden of this secret. But I sensed he wouldn't appreciate me pointing that out or suggesting he'd feel even more relieved if he told Sephy this story.

"Let's just have dinner and forget about this for an hour." He kissed a spot below my ear. "I missed you last night," he whispered. "We'll make up for it tonight."

My insides squirmed. The thought of being intimate while Sephy was in the house made me very uncomfortable. "Listen, I think I should go. Leave you two to have dinner together. It's way too soon for us to try this. And I don't think I should sleep over until things settle down."

"But I can't leave Sephy by herself, so I can't come to your place."

"Wait. Who's going to look after her tomorrow? It's Monday."

It was his big day at Parliament, the culmination of weeks of organization. He'd persuaded a group of ministers to meet with him and hear witnesses from the police, former drug users, and port workers. He hoped this testimony would prompt them to weigh in on the draft bill he'd drawn up, get behind it, and canvass other politicians.

"Oh shit. You're right." He slapped his forehead. "What am I thinking? I have to be in Parliament all day. I'll be totally out of contact."

He ran through the possibilities. His two sisters were a three-hour drive down the coast. They'd have to leave tonight, and anyway, they both had their own children to look after. His only option was calling an agency. Looking overwhelmed by the prospect, he started scrolling down a list on his phone, reading reviews.

My chest clutched at his obvious distress. I couldn't stand to see him like this. Hiring a stranger from an agency would create even more friction between him and Sephy. He'd been there for me, and tomorrow was an important day for him.

"I'll do it," I said. "I can work from here."

"Are you sure?" My answer was in his touchingly grateful smile. But I wasn't sure. He gave me a hug. "Isla, that's incredible, so generous of you, thank you." He rubbed his forehead against mine and gazed happily into my eyes. "This will be a great opportunity for you to get to know the real Sephy. My two favorite people spending time together."

Declan was such a sweet romantic. I gave him a wobbly smile, but a creeping disquiet made me grind my back teeth. I suspected she would not be happy about my looking after her.

He asked about my workday.

"What do you think about that call I got from the phone booth?" I asked, hopeful. It wasn't something I wanted to text him about, and we only had a chance to talk very briefly last night while I walked home from the train station. "It sounds like there's an informant in the port police."

He fiddled with one of the cushions. "I've worked with that team for nearly ten years. They're a great bunch of men and women. The best. I just don't see it."

"Could you make a few calls?" I covered his hand with mine. "See if anyone new has joined the team, someone who might need the money?"

"I can't, I'm sorry." He lifted his hand and scratched his cheek. His expression was guarded, his voice grated with irritation, as though he was disappointed I'd asked. "Part of the bill is working to tighten up laws in the ports. It helps the police, but they must trust me. Asking those kinds of questions would muddy our relationship. I can't be associated with this in any way."

I tried to tamp down my frustration. "But the team would want to know if there was an informant among them."

He frowned. "If you feel strongly there's something there, you should lodge a report through official channels. But to be honest, it sounds like a prank call."

I bit the inside of my cheek. I wanted to dig deeper, but I had no actionable information. Somebody must have seen her on the phone. But how did I narrow down which phone it was? There were two thousand phone booths in London alone.

His chest pumped up and down with shallow breathing. "Isla, please tell me you are not intending to turn up at Tilbury Port at three in the morning, by yourself? You must forget this. Or report the call to the police."

That was exactly what the caller didn't want me to do. If there was an informant in the police, they were the last people I should call.

And just in case this was a hoax, I did not want to send the police on a wild-goose chase, especially when I was trying to build up my credibility with them. The press officer, Sergeant Barb Dupee, gave no more information than asked for unless she knew you well. My former colleague and ex-boyfriend, Jack, for example, had long, informative chats with her and somehow got away with calling her Barbie. Although I'd helped crack a huge drug story that involved London Port, officially, I'd started on the crime beat only five months ago, and she seemed to be treating me with kid gloves. I was desperately trying to find a way to earn her trust. Reporting a call that wasted police time was not it.

Declan watched me, his brows drawn in worry. I knew him well enough to leave the subject alone.

But for me, this was not the end of it.

CHAPTER SIX

THE NEXT MORNING, Sephy stayed in her room when I arrived at seven. Declan seemed harried as he kissed me at the door. "Thanks again for this, Isla."

He ran up the stairs. "Bye, Sephy, I love you," he called through her closed door.

"Nope," she called back.

"Remember our agreement. Twenty-four hours at home."

No response.

I thought she might stay shut in her room until she was starving for lunch. But Declan was gone for only a few minutes when she padded downstairs and into the kitchen while I was making scrambled eggs and boiling the kettle for tea.

"Hi, Isla." She gave me a sweet smile. "How's it going?" She twisted her gray sweater shyly.

"Oh, good, thanks for asking, Sephy. Would you like some of these eggs? Or toast? A cup of tea?"

"Yeah. I'm thirteen."

"Sorry." Was it the eggs or toast or the tea that was not suitable? I had no idea.

She smiled apologetically. "But thank you for offering. Hey, I like your … sweatshirt."

I plucked at it. "This ole thang?" Good Lord. Did I just say that with a Southern accent? *Isla, shut up*. "Thank you. I like your jeans." This pair was even wider than yesterday's.

"Ta." She smiled at me, sparking a little light of hope that we might get through this day okay. Her face brightened even more, as though an idea had just popped into her mind. "Hey, listen." She leaned in conspiratorially. "Just thinking I might nip out to the market down the road to go shopping when it opens at nine-thirty. It's so close, I don't think it would be a problem."

Ha. I almost smiled. So much for my sweatshirt. I was so keen for her to like me, she'd hoodwinked me. And quite easily.

I realized I'd been trying to match her buddy vibe, lounging over the counter and dancing my shoulders. I needed to change my demeanor. Standing up straight, I prepared myself to speak firmly. "I heard your dad lay down the rules. Twenty-four hours at home."

She glared off into the distance, her jaw slack. "What is actually *happening* to me?" Her voice was deep and mournful. Throwing her arms into the air, she stomped off back to her room.

Calming myself by making a cup of tea, I wondered how I could have handled that better. I drew a blank. Maybe I'd done my best.

Eventually, I tamped down those thoughts, ate my eggs, and drank my tea, because I had to get to work. Back to finding that big story I needed. The timer on my phone went off. Nine a.m. I glanced at it. *Shit*. I've messed up. It was the Monday 9:30 a.m. press briefing at New Scotland Yard. I'd set the timer to walk there. Today of all days, I had to be there in person. But I couldn't leave this flat. Usually, I'd have sent Sooz and offered to share a byline with her, but that couldn't happen. I'd have to listen on Zoom, which wasn't great. Any questions I asked would be in the chat, and everyone would hear the answers, so my article wouldn't contain information fresh or different from any other newspaper.

At 9:30 a.m., I clicked on the Zoom link. Press Officer Barb Dupee stepped up to the podium. A tall, stern woman in huge glasses, she did her customary blowing upward at her bangs as though even her own hair annoyed her.

I noted all the incidents in shorthand, even though they were printed out in front of me on the screen. Like yesterday, nothing leaped out at me. Frustration burrowed deep under my skin, leaving me discouraged.

"And finally, a woman was found drowned in the River Thames near Parliament Square, following a routine dredging of the river last night." Barb's expression was pained. That wasn't like her. She was usually professionally blank-faced in delivering even the worst news.

"Her cloth shopping bag and one black sandal were found on the path. She was otherwise uninjured, and there were no signs of foul play. The logical conclusion is she leaned over too far, fell in, and drowned. She has been identified as forty-five-year-old Sister Modestia of Adjutor. She was part of a silent, cloistered order who live in Martyrs' Convent opposite Hyde Park Corner. The convent's Mother Superior said she'd left the convent that morning to do the grocery shopping. She was not wearing her habit. The Mother Superior said she must have decided to take a walk before doing the daily shop."

God, so sad, what a tragedy. The other nuns at Martyr's Convent must be devastated. I'd never noticed this convent, even though Teddy and I strolled through Kensington and Hyde Park every day and I knew that area well. Still listening to Barb, I quickly searched the convent online. A silent religious order opposite Hyde Park and amid a lively area of stores and restaurants? How intriguing. I'd never heard of it. I should do a story on it later.

I pulled myself back to the matter at hand—the poor nun who had died. How was she identified if she wasn't in her habit? Instead of typing my question into the chat, I waited until the conference had finished and put in a request for Barb Dupee to speak with me. Whatever answers I got from her would be exclusive. Not exactly a scoop, nowhere near, but even something small, differentiating my article from the many others, was a plus. Still, this was an opportunity to build a relationship with Barb, though I wished it were in person.

She muted her Zoom, and I watched as she talked to other journalists lined up. This was torture, wondering whether others were asking the same questions as mine. I pulled up the convent website and soaked in as much as I could. Built in 1903, the wide, redbrick building on a main road was remarkable for having a crypt containing relics of a few of the martyrs hanged on a nearby gallows centuries before. The convent was surrounded by grand garden squares, white mansion houses—some scruffy, some immaculate—bustling ethnic restaurants, and exclusive clothing stores.

Look at that. The convent offered rooms for overnight stays, described as private, silent retreats. Some nights even offered dinner. That might be a way to connect with the nuns and find out more about Sister Modestia. I'd book as soon as I got off the Zoom call with Barb.

When Barb was finished, she sat down and unmuted her Zoom. I thanked her for staying on and asked how Sister Modestia was identified.

"She wore a small cross with the order's insignia on it," Barb said. "We called Mother Superior, and she came and identified her."

"But if she'd left that morning, why hadn't Mother Superior called her in as missing? Also, why wasn't she wearing her habit?"

"I've already said Sister Modestia often took walks." A line of tension pulsed in her cheek.

That just didn't ring true. From the website, it was clear they were a cloistered, silent, contemplative order, the opposite of an order of nuns who were free to wander the city. "Apparently, there were times she didn't wear her habit because she didn't like the attention it drew. On a couple of occasions, she felt unsafe because of some comments made by young lads."

I'd seen and read about identifiable members of other religions being persecuted in London, but not nuns. Still, that didn't mean it never happened. Was the Mother Superior making this up about the boys? Or maybe those same young lads knew she was a nun, threatened her, and in her escape, she'd slipped over Victoria Embankment into the water?

"Where did she do her grocery shopping?"

Her answer took a minute while she looked through her notes. "Sainsbury's, just around the corner."

"But that's a long way from the Embankment where she fell."

"Ms. Joyson, this is the third time I've emphasized that the Sister liked to walk."

It was Ms. Joyson now. Oh, shit. Our relationship was deteriorating. She usually called me Isla. Even that wasn't the same familiarity she had with Jack, who she called "JK."

"The way she was found at the bottom of the river, the dredging. How often does that happen?" I asked.

She pursed her lips in agitation. "You could find this information online, and it's not relevant to the death." She sighed, resigned. "Apparently, there's a weekly dredging of the water and the silt. At sixty-six feet, the Thames is the deepest river in England, and without regular dredging, it would be full of rubbish." That was oddly specific, and I wondered whether she herself had asked that question.

I did a quick search. "The body would have risen to the surface two to three days later?"

She tsked. "Ms. Joyson, I don't think there's anything here." Her voice was cagey. "This morning, the Mother Superior was upset, of course, but she didn't push for further investigation. She was satisfied it had been properly looked into. That no autopsy was required. The bag and shoe left on the footpath indicate she slipped over the barrier."

"But is it conclusive?"

"Why are you dwelling on this? I hope you're not intending to present these nuns as an oddity or a curiosity, as if they are not people."

This prospect seemed to upset her. I took in her appearance. The base of her throat glinted. A necklace, maybe a cross? Was she a devout Catholic? Was I getting carried away because I was so desperate?

"No, I wouldn't do that." I clenched my hands. "Um, one other question."

"Yes?" She was exasperated. That trusting relationship I was determined to build with her was rapidly gurgling down the toilet.

"What was Sister Modestia's birth name?"

"This was her legal name. I think we can assume she renounced her past life. Given that the circumstances of her death were not suspicious, we didn't need to delve further." She thumped her file on her desk. "Now, if you will excuse me, I see on my phone I have a queue of other journalists to get back to."

My screen went black as she ended the session.

Bugger. That couldn't have gone worse. Now Barb thought I was a total pest. But this didn't feel right. So much was missing from her press release. Not that I thought she was lying, but maybe she was being overly respectful to the Mother Superior, obsequious even, accepting her assessments.

Once I got off the phone, I booked a room for the following night at the convent. I'd have preferred to go as soon as possible, but it was one of the nights they provided dinner, and I figured I might have more opportunities to talk to the other nuns.

I researched the name of the nun who'd drowned—Sister Modestia of Adjutor. Her first name could be either her baptismal name or a religious name she adopted as a novice. Her last name was taken from that of Saint Adjutor of Vernon, the patron saint of swimming. A tragic irony. Who named themselves after the saint of swimming if they couldn't swim all that well? Wasn't her drowning suspicious if she was a good swimmer and she wasn't injured during the fall? I sensed it was pushing it too far to call back Sergeant Barb to get her reaction to my reasoning.

If I was to investigate this properly, I needed a photo of Sister Modestia. I intended to show it to vendors along the River Thames and ask if they'd noticed her.

Where would I get her photo?

CHAPTER SEVEN

I RANG THE convent. A queasy swirl in my stomach reminded me that Sergeant Barb would not be happy about me calling.

"Martyrs' Convent, Sister Innocenta speaking."

I introduced myself. An uncomfortable rustle sounded from the other end of the phone.

"Mother Superior has instructed me to tell all journalists that the convent has nothing further to add beyond what we've conveyed to the police."

"I understand. I'm just wondering if you could possibly email me a photo of Sister Modestia? To go with the article? It allows us to know her better." I felt dreadful about not being honest with a nun, but I argued to myself that it was a sin of omission. And it *was* always more poignant and human to have a photo with an article.

She sucked in a breath. "I'm not authorized to do that."

"Adding a photo would be a proper tribute to a rare woman who devoted her life to prayer, rather than just this small, quite stark snippet."

She sighed. Maybe she knew I wasn't going to give up. "If you look on the website, Sister is on page six. She's part of the line filing into church. I didn't tell you that."

I felt good that I finally had something no other journalists did. But a sharp prick of guilt drove under my skin. She was trusting, and my bulldozer tenacity had broken down her defenses.

I pulled up the page. The photo was clear enough for us to use. "Yes, I have it. Which one is she, please?"

"Second from the front."

I found her and ran a gentle finger over her forehead. She was a striking woman, more handsome than beautiful, with high cheekbones, thick black lashes and eyebrows, and a square face. "Are you in this photo too?"

"Right behind her." A deep sadness drifted through her voice. I found her in the photo. Her cheeks were full and rosy, and she couldn't be much older than thirty. "I was always right behind her." She choked out a sob.

"Oh, Sister, I haven't even said how sorry I am for your loss. It sounds like you were very good friends with her. She seems lovely in this photo, very kind." Remorse drilled into my side because I'd been inconsiderate. And, honestly, I knew I was taking advantage of her.

"She was. I can't believe she's gone."

A church bell tolled behind her. The loud reverberations merged into each other.

"What time did she leave to go shopping every morning?" I asked.

She made a small noise, seemingly of hesitation.

"I imagine she went to Sainsbury's near you?" I pressed.

"Mmm. About nine, after morning prayers."

"What time did she usually get back?"

"Around eleven." Her voice was staccato with wariness. "It was just a few extras. We get a big delivery every week as well." A tense beat. "Why are you asking these questions?"

The church bells kept ringing, forcing more tension between us. I sensed I wasn't going to get her trust without being honest about why I was asking these questions.

"I don't understand why Mother Superior didn't call the police by, say, noon."

"I have to go," she said, upset.

Fear jabbed under my ribs. *I'm going to lose this story.*

"Hang on. Who's doing the grocery shopping now?" I asked.

The church bells were ringing wildly, like they'd gotten away on the bell ringer.

"I am." Her voice was shaky. "L-look. I'm definitely hanging up now."

"Can I meet you when you go shopping? I need to talk to you about Sister Modestia. I'm worried there's more to this."

"No, I can't. Look, Mother Superior is due back in the office."

"I have one more very important question."

Another bell rang. Then the reverberation. My nerves were so frazzled it felt like they were on the outside of my skin.

It sank in. This was the sound I couldn't identify on my phone tip-off two days ago. It was this reverberation after the bells rang. Did that mean the phone booth was near a church?

My eyes dropped to the *London A–Z* map book open on the kitchen counter. I'd just closely examined a page that showed where Sister Modestia had drowned. Now I noticed the map book was open at the location of the most iconic phone booth in London, famous because it was framed by the Houses of Parliament and Big Ben.

Oh my God. I stabbed a finger at the page.

Big Ben was right there.

The bongs from Big Ben were famously distinctive. They were even used on the television news at night. Maybe I'd heard the reverberations of Big Ben. Is that why she called at 4:01 p.m.? She hadn't wanted to give her location away? Or it could simply have been too noisy to speak while the bells went off.

The germ of a wild idea tickled at the edge of my reasoning. Was it possible? Maybe it wasn't a coincidence?

Could my caller have been Sister Modestia?

"One more question," I said. "Was Sister Modestia posh?"

She gasped. "Very. How do you know that?"

"I think she called me. Sister Innocenta, this means I have to speak to you."

"Who is on the phone, Sister?" a woman demanded in her background. She sounded like she was across the room.

"I'm not allowed to speak with you."

Interesting. That implied she knew something.

"Sister?" The voice was louder, closer, scolding. "Please hand the phone to me. You must tell callers, No comment."

"No comment. Thank you, and goodbye." She hung up with a bang. Disappointment twisted inside my chest. I hoped I still had another chance with Sister Innocenta. Maybe I'd run into her during my stay tomorrow night and persuade her to help me.

Rapid-fire, I typed up the story for my newspaper. For the picture desk, I zoomed into the picture of Sister Modestia on the convent website and cropped it. I snapped a page of the *London A–Z* map book, circling exactly where the Sister fell in. The picture desk would make cleaner versions. I needed to get to Parliament Square and ask if anyone had seen the woman in the phone booth and confirm whether my caller was the nun who'd died. I already had her picture on my phone—I'd show it to vendors on the square.

I could hear Sephy moving around in her room upstairs, obviously restless. It would do her good to get some fresh air and exercise.

Why not kill two birds with one stone?

CHAPTER EIGHT

I THOUGHT ABOUT calling Declan. But he couldn't answer. I was *fairly* sure he'd be fine with me taking Sephy out. Spending time together outside was better than her hiding out in her room. He might even be excited because this was a chance for us to bond.

I knocked on her bedroom door. No answer. I knocked again, and the door swung open. Sephy thrust her hands in her pockets and glared at me. Every molecule of her being radiated, *What fresh hell?*

"Hey, Sephy," I said brightly. "I was just thinking about what you said before. I need to take a break from work and wondered if you still wanted to get out of the house? I've cleared my schedule for a couple of hours. How about we take a stroll?" I didn't say all the way to the Thames, which could take us ninety minutes. What was I going to do if she refused? Sit here all day worrying about how many other journalists were chasing up this story?

She worried her bottom lip, like she suspected something was up, but couldn't quite figure out what. Unease crept along my skin as she surveyed me.

"Just to give you a break," she said cautiously. Making sure I knew she was doing me a favor.

An hour into our walk Sephy started dragging her heels. We were rounding the willow-draped lake at St James's Park. Through the trees rose glimpses of the enormous wheel of the London Eye and the roof of Buckingham Palace.

"Where on earth are we going?" Her jeans were too long, and she kept tripping on them. "This is *such* a long walk."

"But your dad says you do cross-country."

She gave me a baffled look as if the two activities were not remotely connected. Fair enough. I remember my dad suggesting I walk the cliff track with him in the mornings and thinking, *Why would I do that?* I promised we'd get a bus home.

The sun cut through the twirling mist, and I pointed out one of the famous pelicans who lived on the lake's island. Sephy skipped, a little bounce in her step. "So, Dad said you're a journalist. How do you get your stories?"

I felt flattered she was interested, though I remembered the sweatshirt comment this morning. Still, a little thrill buzzed through me. Maybe she *was* interested?

"Well, my job used to involve getting money back for our readers who'd been ripped off in some way. They'd lost their savings or their holiday or their house or their pension. After a couple of stories, I got a reputation as a consumer journalist who could get things done, and readers started contacting me. Or I'd get a call from a lawyer or a union officer or a consumer organization."

I smiled at her. "But now I do crime stories. So I go to the police conference at New Scotland Yard every morning." I could see the red phone booth on Parliament Square in the distance. A few tourists were milling around, waiting to take a photo inside. Excitement flushed through me because I was finally here and doing something about the story. "They give us a short rundown on what happened the previous night, and I follow it up with calls or try and speak to the victim."

She twisted her dark hair and considered that, her face scrunching up. "But how do you decide something is worth following up?"

"Good question. With any kind of journalism, it's a combo. There's the hard, boring work, like sifting through screeds of documents. Speaking to everyone on the block where the incident happened. And instinct. For example, you question an official, and their answer doesn't seem right, like they're covering something up."

"Ha." She picked up a stick from the ground. "Do you like it?"

"Most days. I hope I'm helping someone who can't speak for themselves."

"Hey. And you get to be famous." She used her stick to point at a red double-decker bus rolling past. On the side was an advertisement for my newspaper, featuring me and Sooz. Under each of us was a tagline about our most recent stories. Mine was "$100 million heroin ring uncovered. Book coming soon." But in the world of newspapers, my story was old news, and if Sooz got the promotion, I wondered whether they would bump me off the advertisement.

"Not really." I smiled ruefully. "Not the sort of fame most people want. During the investigation, you end up pissing off a lot of people. Even the people you're helping often get mad at you—the time you're taking or your line of questioning. You can become pretty unpopular. You never get used to it, but it's part of the job."

I clenched my teeth. Right now, it *was* the job. Clearly, Sergeant Barb wasn't too keen on me after this morning. How was I going to turn that around? Something else jabbed at my conscience. The way I'd pressured the young nun. And if I saw her tomorrow night, I had no option but to push her even harder. But she'd loved Sister Modestia. If her friend had been murdered, surely she'd support me if she knew I was trying to uncover the truth?

Sephy slashed her stick at the air and looked thoughtful.

"My whole life at school is about gauging how to make people like me, what to say, how to dress. It's kind of exhausting.

Just saying, Fuck it, I don't care what you think of me. I'm going to say and do what I need to; that would be a relief sometimes."

My heart ached for her. It was so hard to be thirteen. Also, should I pull her up on the swearing? Hmm. Pick your battles.

"That sounds hard, Sephy. I'm sorry."

She shrugged and threw away her stick, seeming embarrassed now that she'd confided in me.

Trying to make her feel more comfortable, I blurted out, "At least you get a whole summer off."

She went wide-eyed at me. "Dude," she scolded.

I grimaced. "Too soon?"

She gave a little laugh, sending a sparkle of glee into my chest.

"Your job is cool, though. I want to help people too. I think I want to investigate dodgy stuff, like you and Dad."

I felt uneasy at how I was presenting myself. Today I was thinking about how to save my career with a story, not how I could help someone. But the result would be finding justice for Sister Modestia, I argued. Sometimes motivations could be more complicated than pure altruism. If her information was true, I would help prevent a shipment of drugs into London, which might even save a life.

We'd arrived at the phone booth. It looked portentous, surrounded by the golden spires of Big Ben and the Houses of Parliament, where Declan was working. A queasy roll of sheepishness forced me to look away. Our excursion was harmless, but it might not be quite what he had in mind for today.

Sephy was drawn to a stall that sold trinket reproductions of the buildings around us. The owner cleverly displayed all the silly photos you could take with them for your socials.

"I'm just going to be over here, okay?" I told her. She couldn't know what I was doing. I was brutally honest with myself this time. I wasn't certain Declan would want her here. And I didn't want to ask her not to tell him. I wouldn't put myself in the middle of them like that. Also, I didn't want her to think I was reluctant to spend time with her, that I was ignoring her in favor of a story.

She nodded, distracted.

Turning my back to her, I discreetly showed the photo of the nun to a stall owner.

"Did you see this woman going into that red phone booth Saturday afternoon at four?" I asked.

No, she was too busy. She'd barely looked up all day. I asked three more stall owners, keeping a close eye on Sephy, worried she'd get bored and wander over.

The last guy had the largest stall. He wore a Beefeater hat and a London Tube T-shirt. His eyes lit up at the photo.

Bingo.

"Yeah, yeah, I saw her," he said.

"Fantastic." I couldn't believe it. I high-fived myself in my head, my heart rocketing out of my chest. I was getting somewhere. This wasn't just a hunch; it was real.

"She didn't have the nun's habit on, though. But she did have those bushy, unplucked eyebrows nuns have, know what I mean? Now women have those tatted eyebrows and false eyelashes—my wife, for one—so you notice it more. And the chopped hairdo. And big flat sandals, practical ones."

I was taken aback. "How do you remember so much about her?"

"Because when she walked past me on her way to the phone booth, she smelled of Christmas. And I do like Christmas."

"Christmas?" I said quietly, hoping he would catch on. His voice was loud, booming. It made me cringe. I fixed a friendly, encouraging smile on my face, but inside I was all nerves. *Don't let Sephy hear you.* I turned around to check on her. She looked up. *Damn.* A bead of sweat slithered down my spine. But surely she was too far away to hear? I swiveled back to him.

"She smelled of Christmas?" I asked again. "How?"

"Like that stuff you smell at midnight Mass."

I thought about that. "Frankincense?"

Maybe it had been burned at Mass that morning in the convent. Or maybe their chapel always smelled of frankincense.

"Yeah, yeah, that's the one. Anyway, she was waiting her turn. And then all these kids start pouring out of the phone booth. Must have been about twenty of them. She got in and started talking on the phone. I noticed this big geezer hanging around the back."

My heart galloped. Was that the man I heard talking to her?

"Interesting," I said. "You're very observant, you know."

He snorted. "Not what the trouble and strife says," he said, referring to his wife. I decided that was just the usual fatigue of being married. Unless he was trying to put one over on me, he was coming up with helpful details. "Anyway, then he says something to her. I heard a Russian accent, or Slavic, and she walks off with him."

The blood drained from my heart. That sounded bad. She must have been so frightened. God, I wished I could have helped her. This Russian must have been the guy who talked about her brother. Despite worrying about Sister Modestia, I felt a swell of confidence. My instincts were correct; I'd been on the right track.

"How did she look?" I didn't want to suggest anything that might put an image in his mind.

"How you mean?"

Now I did have to suggest something. "Did she seem afraid? Was he strong-arming her in any way?"

"She wasn't happy. But he didn't have his hands on her. She went with him willing, like."

Did she know him then, if she went willingly with him? Not that that didn't mean she wasn't in danger.

"What direction?" I asked.

"Toward the Embankment." He pointed toward the river.

My face fell. Fear rocketed through my veins. Oh my God.

CHAPTER NINE

"SHE IN ANY trouble?" The vendor stared at me. His face froze white. "Hey, wait a minute. You're not police, are you?" I shook my head. He looked even more frightened. "You're not with that fucking big Russian geezer, are you? You need to move, madam." He reached across me to the customer behind, who looked afraid too. "Can I help you?" The customer scurried off.

"No, I'm not with the police or the Russian guy," I said. "This woman called me from this phone. I was on the other end of the line. She asked for my help." He shook his head, totally confused. "Could you do me a favor? If anyone else comes asking about her, can you call me?"

I decided it was better not to give him one of my business cards because it might frighten him off. Instead, I wrote my number on a piece of paper and handed it to him.

Shaking his head, he reluctantly accepted the paper. "I don't like this, lady, not at all. And you just lost me a customer."

A tap nudged my shoulder. "Isla."

I swung around. Sephy. Oh no. How much had she heard? My stomach burned with worry.

"We better get going home," I said, moving her out of the vendor's earshot.

"It's a TikTok challenge," Sephy said.

"What?"

"Those kids in the phone booth he was talking about. It's a TikTok challenge. How many people can you squeeze into a phone booth. Hashtag Phone Booth Challenge. If you want to see this woman, we should look it up. She might be in the background."

My pulse quickened. "That's an amazing idea, Sephy. Could you do that?"

I watched over her shoulder as she tapped into her account and typed in *#PhoneBoothChallenge*. She scrolled through some videos taken of phone booths all over London.

"It's this one, see?" she said. It was the phone booth next to us. Big Ben and the Houses of Parliament were in the background. "We just need the most recent videos." She found one from Saturday and tapped the screen.

Sister Modestia was waiting behind the booth as the kids piled in. She was dressed just as the vendor had said. She peered around tensely, her shoulders curled as if making herself small.

"It's her," I said, touching the screen. "This is the one, Sephy. Thank you. Quick thinking on your part." Sephy beamed at me. We both watched until the video finished. "By the way, you didn't overhear our conversation, did you?"

"Just the last bit," she said.

Phew.

Before I could ask her what she was doing, Sephy tapped on the video, took a screenshot, saved it, and put the photo into Google search.

Up popped the article I'd written this morning about Sister Modestia's death. She shot me a curious look and quickly scrolled down the article. Suddenly, her head flicked up and turned in the direction of the Embankment where the Sister supposedly fell into the Thames. Her eyes widened and recognition landed on her face. *She knows something.* She was quick and bright, Declan's daughter, after all—the apple didn't fall far from the tree. I scanned her face even closer, a thick, leaden dread coating my insides as I saw her searching for connections.

"Isla. This nun—is she the woman who called you? What did she say?"

I felt a stabbing behind my eyes. "I'm just looking into the accident."

Sephy hugged her chest. I saw her face tick over as she put it together. "But you don't think she accidentally fell in, do you?"

"I don't know." I tried to look noncommittal. That was true—I didn't know.

She bit her lip. "Do you think she was … *murdered*?"

"What? Why do you ask that?" I thrust open my palms, like that was out of the question.

Sephy's eyes lit up, bright and keen. "Instincts, right? Something doesn't add up." She was repeating my words back to me, and I couldn't deny them now.

She spent the rest of the bus ride home in high spirits, chattering away about the true crime podcasts she'd listened to with facts similar to those of Sister Modestia's death. Despite the subject matter, I knew I should be happy she felt comfortable enough with me that she could let down her teen defenses and be enthusiastic. It was a big turning point for us. But my emotions were in turmoil because our bonding was for all the wrong reasons.

This was another terrible turning point in the case. Now I knew Sister Modestia was my caller, her death was personal. She'd picked me, trusted me. Had I let her down? Was she killed because that Russian man overheard her telling me about the drugs? I didn't call the police. But I hadn't known if her call was real, if she was credible. Still, should I have erred on the side of caution? Anyone who knew about a drug shipment was in danger.

If I'd called the police, could I have prevented her death?

Fighting my raging emotions, I thought through the logistics. If the Russian guy had walked her to the Embankment, that was only two hundred feet. Sergeant Barb said she was "otherwise uninjured, and there were no signs of foul play." So obviously, she had not been hit on the head or choked before being thrown into the river. If she was dead before she went into the water, the autopsy would show this due to the absence of water in the lungs. But there was no autopsy. The man who led her away was Russian, and they were known to have a strong preference for poison as an assassination tool. Did he poison her and push her in? The whole thing might have taken only five minutes. How could she have "fallen in" without someone seeing it?

And if I'd called the police, would they have made it in time? New Scotland Yard, the police headquarters where I walked to a press conference every morning, was just along the Embankment to the north. So, yes, they might have made it in time.

A horrifying thought burned in my blood. Do I have to accept some responsibility for her death?

But she'd asked me *not* to call the police.

I slumped low in my seat, the passing images of parks and old buildings blurring until my head whirled back and forth. I closed my eyes and took a swig of water from my bottle, waiting for the cool liquid to bring some clarity, but instead, the dry throb behind my eyes intensified. This was the sort of ethical dilemma that Declan was good with. He was exactly the person I needed, craved, to confide in.

He was the last person I could tell.

CHAPTER TEN

"WE'VE HAD *SUCH* a good day, Dad."

Sephy dropped the bread knife with a clang and threw her arms around Declan.

"Really? What did you two get up to today?" Declan hugged her back and beamed at us both. "Did you play board games?"

I was nervous when Declan arrived home at 6:00 p.m. I'd started making pasta, and Sephy was cutting up French bread and mixing garlic butter. But it looked like I had nothing to worry about.

Sephy stepped out of his hug, grinning. She was excited and lively, the way she'd been on the bus, a young girl rather than the teen I'd first met, alternating between screaming fury and eye-rolling irritation. Which was lovely, but I wasn't sure whether I should be worried. "Nope. We solved a mystery. We were investigators."

Declan's face fell a little, like he didn't know what to think.

I turned down the stove and kissed him on the cheek, trying to divert him.

"Hey. What about your big day?" I grinned at him. "Tell us everything about how it went in Parliament."

"No, I want to hear this." His voice was edged with caution, sparking anxiety in me.

"I was Isla's sidekick on her investigation," Sephy said. "We were hunting down this poor nun's murderer."

"*What*?" His eyes flashed from her to me, not knowing whether she was joking.

Triumphantly, she told him the whole story. Yep, and it turned out she'd heard all my conversations with the vendors.

He leaned against the kitchen island, clutching the sides. I slunk back toward the kitchen sink, my head bowed. Hearing it like this, it sounded like a different scenario from the one I had in my head. My shoulders stiffened as I braced myself for Declan's anger.

Declan turned to Sephy. "Could you give us some privacy, sweetheart? You're not in trouble. I just want to have a quick word with Isla."

Fuuuuck.

Sephy mouthed *Shit, sorry* to me and slunk up the stairs.

"You took Sephy on a job?" He jolted forward from the kitchen island where he was leaning and folded his arms tight across his chest.

I plucked at my sleeve, feeling defensive.

"It wasn't like that. Well, I didn't plan it out like that. I thought she needed to get out and get some fresh air. We were on a walk anyway, and when we got to Parliament, I thought I'd ask around. We were in a crowded square and she wasn't in any danger." Wasn't that honestly how I'd felt at the beginning of the trip? I couldn't have known about the Russian guy.

That made him fume.

"Is that true, though? This nun is dead. And I don't like the sound of that Russian. Isla, I don't want you taking her on investigations. Full stop. I didn't even want her leaving the house, and I thought that was implicit when I told her she was staying at home today, which you heard. And, frankly, I think it's time to take what you know to the police."

Okay, I *had* intended to take her on an investigation, but my hackles rose anyway. Where did he get off telling me to go to the police? I was tired of that line. He knew full well why I wasn't.

His face turned fearful rather than angry, and I hung my head, ashamed. What was I doing, haggling over the semantics of what I did, grasping for some, any, justification? "You're right, I did put her in danger. I'm so sorry."

He looked away. I fixed my gaze outside on the garden, not really seeing it. The two of us both breathing, upset, hurt, worried, was the only sound in the air.

In the glass doors' reflection, I could see him scrub a hand over his face. He touched my shoulder lightly.

"I'm sorry for snapping at you," he said. I turned to face him. "I was scared. Look, I know it's hard to stay home all day with her, especially when she's in a mood, but parenting *is* hard." He shook his head. "This is my fault—I shouldn't have put you in that position."

My gut emptied out. That didn't make me feel any better. Now I was considered too hopeless to be trusted with his daughter.

"Can I give you a hug?" he asked.

I nodded numbly. He closed his arms around me. That was the thing about Declan. He never sulked or stayed angry or irritated for long. But for the first time in his arms, I felt tense and miserable.

"Thanks for starting dinner." He rested his chin on my head and stroked my back. "You're going to stay and eat with us? Seems like Sephy is starting to come around a bit?"

I couldn't think. I stepped slowly out of his embrace, but the walls of the kitchen started closing in on me. I felt awful about so many things. I needed some air and to be by myself to think this over. I grabbed my handbag.

"I think I should go." I struggled not to show how upset I felt. "You stipulated twenty-four hours. It's already been that, and she's going to keep you to it, so it seems like you should start working this out."

Maybe I should make an excuse to cover my stay at the convent tomorrow night, but I couldn't think of one. No. I couldn't lie to him again. I'd just tell him. Tomorrow night. That would lead to more tension, but I had to accept it.

At the front door, Declan lifted my chin with his index finger. "Hey. Are we okay?"

I felt flat and depressed after the exhilaration of the sun-filled afternoon, like a fog had descended, seeping into my bones with a damp chill. I'd made progress on investigating Sister Modestia, and I'd gotten closer to Sephy, but I hadn't gone about it the right way.

I looked down. "Yes. I'm just mad at myself for taking her with me. I suppose I'm not used to being responsible for someone else." My next thought was unspoken. *And I'm not very good at it.*

I trudged down the tree-lined street, confused and upset. I'd been accountable for a teen. I was accountable to a partner. And I'd come up wanting. I'd withheld from Declan that I was very much pursuing this nun story and that I'd booked to stay at the convent tomorrow night. Accountability—using that word showed how wrong I was for all this. Surely you should *want* to tell your partner everything. You should *want* to take on responsibility for his child. Surely it should come naturally and give you joy. I wasn't the right person. I wasn't grown up enough.

And we'd been dating for only three months. Shouldn't we still be in the honeymoon phase? My friends at work said that phase lasted two years. They'd envied our bliss with more to come. Wasn't this way too early to be having so many complications and stresses? It wasn't just Sephy by any means. My job and his job meant we couldn't talk about either. When we did, it just created annoyance or disagreement. It was starting to feel like the time when we'd worked together for two weeks in New Zealand before we started dating. He was undercover and couldn't discuss any of his cases, which would have gone on to be a huge gap in our communication and meant that I couldn't get to know him better.

What was the answer? I was just about to round the corner when I heard someone call my name. I turned. Sephy jogged toward me, giggling slightly because she had to hold up the bottoms of her jeans so she didn't trip.

She came to a jump stop in front of me, breathless, her dark hair swinging, her cheeks pink from the exertion.

"Isla, I'm sorry I gave you away. I was just excited."

"No, you're fine." I waved as if it was no problem. "I don't want you keeping things from your dad. It was totally my fault. I should have thought it through properly."

"I don't know." Her green eyes sparkled, and her dimples deepened. "I had fun. Dad's just being a right pillock." She tapped me on the arm. "Well, see ya, Holmes."

I smiled. "Later, Watson."

CHAPTER ELEVEN

IF SISTER MODESTIA was pushed into the Thames in broad daylight, surely someone saw?

The next day, Tuesday, after attending the police press briefing, I walked ten minutes to the Embankment and filled the day showing Sister Modestia's photo to vendors, both the morning and afternoon shifts. Some had already spoken to the police. Unbelievably, it didn't matter whether they sold paintings of the sunset over the city or hot dogs—none of them had seen Sister approaching, falling, or being pushed over the Embankment.

I dropped off Teddy at Fleur's flat at 4:30 p.m., as I'd arranged earlier that morning. Fleur was my friend from home, and she'd stayed with me in London for a month. I'd enjoyed getting to know her in a different way from when I'd babysat her as a kid. She'd moved to another, more social flat around the corner because she wanted to meet people her age.

I hired a dog walker to take out Teddy three times during the day, but Fleur took him some evenings when I had meetings or was away. Thank goodness she often worked from home.

"Gidday, Mr. Teddy, you come for a playdate?" she asked. She looked more beautiful and happier every time I saw her, with her pixie hairdo and Bato's deconstructed blazers and ripped jeans that looked amazing on her rower's shoulders and six-foot frame.

"Sorry, Fleur, it's overnight this time," I reminded her. I planned to stay at the convent tonight.

"Oh, no worries, we love having Mr. Teddy for a sleepover, don't we?" Jack, her boyfriend and my ex-boyfriend, said from behind her. He baby-talked Teddy while Fleur made an amused face. Jack was a full head shorter than Fleur, which the old Jack would have hated, and was utterly besotted with her. It was still amusing and a little bit strange to see him with her. Why hadn't he been as lovable with me? We must have brought out the worst in each other. I was happy enough now to be able to reflect on this without angst, even with the new tension with Declan and worries about the story I was pursuing.

Before the convent stay, I needed to call over to Declan's place at 5:00 p.m. to see Sephy off. She was leaving in an hour for three nights on the coast with her aunt and cousins. Declan's sister, who'd come into town for a work meeting, was planning to pick her up, and Declan would collect her. He'd specifically asked if I could pop over before she left. I was going to have to tell him about my convent stay tonight. I felt worse because I suspected he'd organized Sephy's mini break partly so we could be together and talk things over.

I found Declan in his kitchen making spicy tamarillo margaritas, my favorite, and a fizzy, sunset-hued drink for Sephy.

Sephy was on a high at the prospect of hanging out at the beach with her cousins. And my whole body was vibrating with the hope that Sister Innocenta and I would connect, and I'd make some headway into Sister Modestia's death.

Sephy was making guacamole. Declan assigned me to fill the water pitcher. Sephy seemed to be doing fine, but Declan was searching for a better knife and bowl for her to use. I got out a water pitcher, and he exchanged it for another one.

The man was highly organized. He had a tool and proper home for everything, including a designated guacamole bowl and water pitcher, which was a bit persnickety sometimes, but I loved him for it. He was this way because he'd spent his childhood at boarding school and wanted a real home, and being away undercover for weeks and sometimes months only served to reinforce that. He took care of the things he'd chosen to surround him. My lips tilted in a smile, and my chest warmed as something occurred to me: just like he took care of the people he'd chosen to love.

I reached up to the cabinet and slid out what I thought were water glasses.

"Isla," Sephy said in a scandalized tone. "Don't you know those are the *outside* glasses?"

"Oh, God help me—you're right." I slid them back in.

Declan grunted and rolled his eyes.

"Now, hang on," I said in a teasing tone. "What happens if I take an inside glass outside?"

"What the?" Sephy dropped her avocado-cutting knife and gripped her hair with a wild face. "No. Don't do it, it's too risky."

I shook my head, forehead furrowed like a cheesy action hero, a glass held out like a talisman. "Someone must challenge his rule. Show the world that change can happen."

"I'm going out too." She slipped a glass from the cupboard. "You first. I'll cover you."

I eased open the double doors and peered out. "I think we're safe. He's not around. The covers are still on the furniture."

"And the squabs are safely stored in the squab cupboard." She gasped. "But could this be a trick?"

Both of us tipped our inside glasses tauntingly back and forth towards Declan. In slow motion, we opened the door to the back deck and crept around the garden, pretending to drink from the glasses.

"Okay, I see what's happening here," Declan said, hands on his hips, once we were back inside. He squinted at us. Beneath that mock annoyance, he was barely concealing his pleased smile. "Is this how it's going to go? You two poking fun at me every night?"

I raised my eyebrows with a questioning look at Sephy.

"Definitely my plan," I said.

"Ditto," she chimed in.

We collapsed into giggles, and Declan kept pretending to be mad at us.

A sensation I'd never felt before swelled my heart. Was this a glimpse into what our lives would be like if we were a family? It didn't seem so hard or complicated. It felt warm and easy and fun.

A sneaking dread crept up on me at the thought that I was keeping things from him. I still had to tell him about my convent stay tonight. I'd break it to him once Sephy left at 6:00 p.m.

"I'm excited to meet your sister," I said.

"My sister?" His eyebrows shot up. "Oh, God, sorry, Isla, in all this commotion, I didn't tell you. The plan changed. She couldn't make it up to London after all. I'm taking Sephy all the way down."

A six-hour car trip. Saved by the sister I'd never met. Now I didn't have to confess about the convent after all. I heaved an internal sigh of relief. But would he ask me to ride with him? A spike of panic was chased by a twinge of sadness. Only weeks ago, I'd have jumped at a long drive together, talking, laughing, listening to music. But now my only thought was, *How the hell do I get out of this?* I could pull the carsick card. He knew if I didn't sit in front, I would become terribly ill with motion sickness. Sephy might feel put out relegated to the back.

He grinned. "Would you like to come with us, Isla? Might be fun?"

Shoot. I would draw him aside and remind him I'd have to be in the front, and Sephy might be upset.

"Sephy, Isla gets carsick. Do you mind being in the back?"

She gave her one-shoulder shrug. "No worries. I like sprawling out in the back anyway."

Argh. I screwed up my face with feigned regret as I looked up at him. "Thanks for asking. Usually, I'd love to, but I have work to do. I'm on a tight deadline to find this story. I should pick up Teddy from Fleur's too. He's been there a lot in the past few days, and Fleur loves him, but I don't want to overextend his welcome."

He nodded but warily. My reply was a bit stilted and polite. He kept sneaking glances at me.

"I wish you'd bring Teddy over." Sephy flung herself over the sofa arm. "Dad, if you're going to make me stay home, it's only fair we get a dog."

Declan smiled. "We'll see."

At 6:00 p.m., Sephy dashed upstairs to fetch her overnight bag. I shrugged on my coat. I grabbed my handbag and my tote, which was stuffed with toiletries and pajamas for the convent stay, and work clothes for tomorrow.

"You've got all your things here," Declan said. "May as well stay."

"Oh, thanks, but there's a work thing I should go to." The convent was technically a work thing. I started toward the door and whispered so Sephy couldn't hear, "I've left my pills at home too." That was true. I'd have to take one tomorrow when I arrived home. That reminded me. When did I take it yesterday? My routine had been messed up. I couldn't remember.

I walked with Declan as Sephy hustled him out the door.

He looked dazed. "Everything okay?"

"Yes, of course."

"I'll text you." He seemed worried.

I wouldn't receive his messages. The confirmation for the room warned there was no Wi-Fi in the bedrooms or dining room, and they enforced a screen-free policy.

"I might not have the best reception tonight."

I wished I could be more specific, but I knew he'd tell me not to go, and to leave it in the hands of the police. If he found out about my plans, he'd be upset with me again and another disagreement would be inevitable. This tension was eroding the easy, fun us. I needed to gather enough information to prove I was doing the right thing and that would restore the old us.

He looked confused by my answer.

"Dad, let's go." Sephy pulled him toward the car. "Bye, Isla."

Declan's loving goodbye smile made my stomach twist. There was no time for him to question me. And that was what I'd been counting on.

CHAPTER TWELVE

"I'M MOTHER SUPERIOR. It is acceptable to address me as Mother." Her owl eyes blinked in a deeply creased face framed by the white wimple of her habit, which looked so painfully stiff it must have cut into her skin. She could have been anything between fifty and seventy years old.

"This is Sister Innocenta." The Sister nodded modestly. Her cheeks were rosy, as I'd seen in the photo on the website, and her face glowed under the light of the old wall sconces. Focusing closer, I could see it was a blonde peach-fuzz all over her face. This was what women looked like without the aid of waxing, makeup, and dermaplaning. I respected that. How freeing it must be—to slap on an inexpensive moisturizer and call it a day. Maybe they didn't even have mirrors.

Racing from Declan's house, I'd checked in late to my spartan white room at Martyrs' Convent, which smelled of soft lavender, sharp bleach, and … I breathed in deeply … yes, frankincense.

I was seated with seven other women at a long table in the refectory. It seemed like there were two mothers with daughters in their twenties, one mother austere and stern in a white blouse buttoned at the neck, the other with messy hair, smiling at me gently. Beside them, two women in their seventies looked meditative in white linen outfits and Zen necklaces. In the far corner, a tall, chic woman about my age in a voluminous black-and-white-spotted maxi with a huge bow at the neck, looked like she'd come straight from a photo shoot.

Well. What a crew.

Sister Innocenta kept her head down. It was hard to know whether she was avoiding my gaze or had been instructed not to look guests in the eye.

"We will bring you each a soup, main course, and pudding," Mother Superior instructed, hands folded over her chest. "We ask you to observe the rules of the order and not speak during the meal. Afterward, we will be taking questions about the order and our lives here at Martyrs', both spiritual and practical. We are actively encouraging women who are curious about a life in our order. Our numbers are depleted to the extent that we don't know if we can continue in this convent. We are—I wouldn't call it recruiting exactly—but we are open to interested young women." She nodded to the daughters. "Thank you. God bless, and have a good evening."

The stern mother looked proudly at her daughter. The messy, smiley mother looked visibly upset. I would be unhappy too; to release your daughter to such confinement, every minute devoted to prayer or chores, never to see them again. Like their lives had ended.

"Thank you, Mother," I replied. "Oops." I slapped my hand over my lips. Smiley Mum twitched a small grin, and Dotty Glamour smirked.

Sister Innocenta and another nun brought us pumpkin soup. I tried to catch Sister Innocenta's eye again, but she seemed to be avoiding me, even using the other nun to block her. Or was I being paranoid? Because she was in my range of sight, I focused on the other nun. She appeared middle-aged, but her arched eyebrows sat high on her face, and her skin was unusually smooth, her forehead shiny. She went to purse her lips, but she couldn't.

No. It couldn't be. Had I completely lost the plot?

Was her face … Botoxed? I was sure it was. Many of my female colleagues had it done, even some my age, so I was familiar with the extra-shiny, tell-tale signs.

She caught me staring and swept out of the room. Sister Innocenta finished up and followed her.

There must be an explanation, but I put that mystery to one side for the minute.

"A three-course meal—and the rooms are so clean," I loud-whispered. Seven pairs of round eyes fixed on me. "It must be hard for them to carry on given what's happened."

"Shhh." Stern Mum pressed a stiff finger to her lips.

Embarrassment flushed my face. I knew I was doing the wrong thing, but I had to plow on. "You know, the death of Sister Modestia. So sad. Did any of you know her?"

Loud shushing erupted from all around me, accompanied by more fingers pressed to lips.

"Does her death worry you two mums?" I asked. "Your daughters might be living here."

The door squeaked open. "Everything okay in here, people?" Mother asked pointedly.

We all nodded like a class of scolded preschoolers.

Once she'd left, the stern mother huffed in my direction as if my rule-breaking had tarnished them all.

Dotty Glamour's lips twitched like she was suppressing her amusement. She seemed like an ally. I shot her a teeth-clenching *yikes*.

Pondering what I should do next, I ate a mouthful of the pumpkin soup. Hmm. It needed salt.

I caught the eye of the stern mother who, would you know it, seemed to be guarding the condiments. How did the nuns conduct their daily lives without speaking? Maybe they chatted on the sly, slipping in a sneaky word here and there. How else had Sister

Innocenta and Sister Modestia become close friends? I pointed at the salt and mouthed, *Salt, please.*

She pretended not to notice. I pointed and again mouthed, *Salt, please.* She ignored me.

Finally, I mouthed *SALT, PLEASE,* so exaggeratedly I must have looked unhinged.

My ally's shoulders shook. The mother gave me a withering look, like asking for salt made me morally deficient. Reluctantly, in slow motion, she handed me the tiny glass saltshaker.

I salted my soup liberally and set the shaker down very close to my hand. Small of me, I know. It annoyed the stern mother even more.

My ally's shoulders rocked even harder as she looked to be holding in her mirth. Intending to let my laughter out, I dashed for the loo, went the wrong way, and ended up in the kitchen.

"Wrong door," Mother called sternly from the lime-green Formica counter on the left, where she and the other two nuns were plating the meals. I noticed a door at the far end. Did it lead to the rest of the convent?

"This way." Mother swished past me, thrust open the door to the refectory and pointed to the loo on the other side.

After returning to the table, I tried to behave myself during the main course and dessert, until it was time for questions.

The Botoxed nun and Sister Innocenta didn't reappear, just Mother. The guests mostly asked questions about the number of Masses in a week (every day), and how many hours of prayers per day (five in church, but they considered themselves in prayer every hour of the day).

I asked a few easy ones. How many nuns currently? *Fifteen.* Did you get your own room? *Yes.* What was full capacity? *Thirty.* I sighed. She was sticking to monosyllabic answers. Can family visit and have a chat? *This is a cloistered order, so no.* At that answer, the two mothers flinched and sucked in a breath.

I suspected I had one tricky question before she shut up shop. "I'm wondering about the day-to-day freedoms. Are the nuns allowed to just pop out, take a walk anytime they like?"

Mother's face froze. "We have sports games in our beautiful courtyard space. Exercise is all taken care of. Believe me, with all the cleaning and cooking, we are all exhausted at the day's end."

"I'm not really talking about exercise—"

"That takes care of the spiritual and practical questions." She shoved her hands into her wide sleeves and flattened me with her glare. "Speaking of exhaustion, everyone here looks ready for bed, as am I. So this is goodnight."

CHAPTER THIRTEEN

BACK IN MY room, I took a shower and waited for lights-out. I planned to snoop around. What was I looking for? Something, anything, to do with Sister Modestia, her old life, her new life, notes she'd left that gave a clue as to why she might have been killed.

The clanging from the kitchen seemed to go on forever. *C'mon, people, how about a bit of early to bed, early to rise?* They were nuns—surely they weren't binge-watching Netflix. To pass the time, I read a book of meditation techniques. One advised that once I was out in nature, I had to notice the plants and foliage but *not* give them names. Don't attribute words to what you see. *Just notice.* I tried to do it around the room but was bored within seconds.

It was a long two hours until it all quieted down just after 11:00 p.m. I crept out of my room, painstakingly putting one foot in front of the other down the stairs. *Creeeeaaak.* Shit. Old wood. In the refectory, I pushed open the door to the kitchen and ducked low. It was a large, very dated kitchen, but sparkling clean. No one here. I tiptoed across the floor to the back door at the end of the kitchen.

Through it, I found myself in a pitch-black corridor. I didn't want to light the way with my phone, so I waited for my eyes to get used to the darkness. I shuffled one foot at a time. A turn—where did this lead? Soon, I was standing at the side of a huge old freestanding stone wall. It must have been twenty feet high and fifty feet long. Astonishing. I edged forward to see the front. Carved into it was a massive scene of naked men and women at a picnic, drinking wine and eating fruit. Dangling penises brushed against round breasts and pert bums.

Voices cut through the silence. I dashed back around the corner.

Now, my eyes were adjusted enough to make out a row of rooms behind the wall. Seven of them. They seemed flimsy, almost prefab. Strange, the convent had fifteen empty nuns' rooms. Mother had just told us that. Why were they staying in prefab rooms?

Two nuns emerged from the first room, backlit. One thing was clear but puzzling—they were unbelievably young with firm brown skin, maybe even as young as Sephy. They even had that same shoulder-swinging way of talking. One of them whispered something, and they collapsed on each other, giggling like young teens.

First a Botoxed nun and now thirteen-year-old nuns? What the hell?

The next door opened. The two young nuns gasped and disappeared back into their room.

Another nun emerged—with a tall, bearded, good-looking man wearing green work overalls.

"Maybe we should stop?" He looked upset.

Were they having an affair? Sneaking around together?

"It's gone too far now." Seeming resolute, she shook her head and motioned forward. They hurried off. I had to follow them. At the end of the row of rooms, they turned and disappeared. I traced their steps to the end and peeked around the corner. I waited and watched them climb down an iron stairwell. The man keyed in a code and opened the door to a flash of lamplight and chaotic sounds of traffic. They both passed through the door to what looked like a busy back street.

A hand clutched my shoulder. I jumped out of my skin.

"What are you doing here?"

Sister Innocenta. She was red-faced with fury. "You are ruining everything. Do you want us *all* dead?"

"*Dead?* What do you mean? Are you talking about Sister Modestia? Please tell me what's going on in this convent? Let me help you."

"Get back to your room. Now. If you want to help us, forget what you've seen."

She hurried me back along the corridor behind the old stone wall. A small, hooded figure loomed at the end of it.

"Why are you back here?" a woman's voice boomed down the hall.

It was Mother.

We caught up to her. She looked steaming mad, her red cheeks twitching from grinding her teeth. "Sorry, Mother," I said. Better get Sister Innocenta out of trouble first. "Sister just told me I can't be here. I was only looking for a towel."

"We know you are a journalist, Ms. Joyson. Please don't lie so freely close to our chapel, the house of the Lord. There is nothing for you to find here. Come along." Without another word, she marched me back to my room and opened my door to find—a towel on my bed.

"Just needed one for my hair too." Was I persisting with this charade? Looked like it. She hadn't offered to get me another, but I rambled on anyway, like I was clueless.

Mother turned on a heel and left.

A few minutes later, there was a soft knock on my door.

"Sister Innocenta here."

I opened the door to the Sister presenting me with a towel, her young, round face flushed red. I thanked her and went to question her.

Before I got it out, she said, "I feel like you are looking down on us." I began to protest, but she calmly interrupted. "This is a beautiful life, and I chose to be here. So many people outside are searching for the peace we have here. Don't ruin this for us. We are trying to protect it."

A coil of shame wrapped around my torso. I *had* judged her and the other nuns for being misguided and I'd felt sorry for her and the rest of them for their cloistered life. Was that what she meant when she said I was ruining it? Ruining their spiritual peace? Was I imagining tension, conflict, and mystery where there was none? No, her words seemed more desperate, like it was something else.

"Sister, when you say protect—"

But she'd turned and was gone, treading with an eerie softness down the stairs. As soon as she left, I snapped the lock on my door and leaned against it, heart pumping. What should I do? Could I stay here all night? My throat seized up. I didn't feel safe—every instinct told me to leave. But something was going on, and I had to find out what.

So I stayed, jittery with adrenaline and nerves. In bed, I jumped at every bang and creak.

Who was that tall, bearded man? Were he and that nun having an affair? Did Sister Modestia find out about the affair? Is *that* why she was dead? But that didn't explain why the server nun had Botox done or why those other two nuns might only be teenagers.

Finally, the building went silent, but my brain filled with a shrill blast.

Sister Innocenta clearly knew something was suspicious about the death of her friend Sister Modestia, so why wasn't she trying to help me? Why was she doing the opposite—blocking me? What did she mean when she said, "You are ruining everything. Do you want us *all* dead? If you want to help us, forget what you've seen." Desperately, I tried to mentally catalog all the snapshots of dialogue, but the scenes flicked past faster than a card stack.

I shivered, my skin as cold as the old stone walls. What was going on in this convent?

CHAPTER FOURTEEN

"HELLO. YOU'RE NOT a nun."

A dry, deep voice with a hint of humor tickled my ears.

It was nine the next morning, and I was catatonic from so little sleep. I was leaving through one of the carved wooden double doors, intending to catch Sister Innocenta on her grocery shopping trip and worried about being late to the Wednesday police briefing at 9:30 a.m. I'd have to hail a black cab. The other guests were still lingering over breakfast, reading books as they ate since they couldn't speak. I knew Mother and Sister Innocenta would be watching me keenly this morning, so I'd dressed for work, packed, and taken my bag down to the refectory, ready to go. I'd had breakfast with the others, and once Sister Innocenta was out of the room, I'd gathered up my things and quickly left. I'd tried all the doors in the hallway to the exit, keeping a close eye behind me because I was terrified of being caught again, but they had all been locked.

I looked up to see who the voice belonged to.

Wow. Smirking at me was a huge, well-built man with glossy black hair. He wore a beige trench coat, dark jeans, and a roll-necked sweater, the sort of outfit you'd see in a catalog for expensive cashmere. He was holding a cluster of cloth shopping bags.

Beside him, Sister Innocenta shifted from one foot to the other. She gave an almost imperceptible shake of her head.

"Nope. No. Not a nun." I gave a silly giggle. Why was I so flustered? Because he was movie-star good-looking with high cheekbones, glittery eyes and full lips—a face you found yourself openly gaping at. I loved Declan, but I wasn't dead.

"Just spending the night in one of the women's retreat rooms," I said.

"What's it like there?" He took a step toward me. "Any wild parties we should know about?"

Sister Innocenta shuffled, embarrassed.

"No, just a lot of silent reading," I said. "And steamed veggies." That sounded rude and I smiled apologetically at the young nun. "The food was really good, very healthy."

A hint of a pleased smile ghosted her lips.

"So, you just hang out in your room all day and all night, no tours of the convent or anything?" he asked.

The nun caught my eye. She was tight-lipped. Did she want me to be the same?

"I asked about a tour. Even one without a lecture, because, you know, silent order. Definitely no tours."

"Not even a glimpse of the Grecian frieze inside? It's supposed to be exquisite."

The young nun cried out and pointed upward. I searched the sky for whatever had startled her and noticed the man was doing the same. But there was nothing but clouds, spires, and birds.

"So, the Grecian frieze?" he pressed.

Something furtive about the young nun's reaction made me wary of volunteering information to him.

"A Grecian frieze?" I squinted up at him. "What do you mean?"

"Well, this is hearsay. But apparently, it's a long, tall, freestanding stone wall with a depiction of a bacchanalian picnic."

Oh, he was talking about the wall I saw. Bacchanalian. I'd read that word only in books. It rolled off his tongue like he used it often, and he made it sound wonderful, like it was something you should definitely want to partake in. Did it mean the same thing as debauched? Not a question to ask a strange man in front of a nun. Too flirtatious.

"Unusually debauched for a convent." He spoke seriously, though the corners of his mouth twitched.

"Didn't even know they had one," I said. "But wasn't the convent built in 1903? Is it a reproduction?"

I checked the young nun's expression. She looked distressed. He'd been asking a lot of questions.

"Sorry, you are?" I asked.

"Oh, forgive my shocking manners. Cassius Devonport."

He offered a large hand, and I shook it. He held my hand for what seemed an extra second.

The name didn't ring a bell and yet, his face was familiar. Vaguely familiar, like he wasn't hugely famous, more like he was a bit actor in a popular series. But he had the face of a lead.

"Nice to meet you, Mr. Devonport," I said.

Sister Innocenta flinched. Was it the way I addressed him?

"Oops, is mister incorrect? Are you a doctor or something?" Or maybe a well-dressed priest?

He put a hand over both of ours. His top hand was bare except for one gold signet ring on his pinkie, intricately inscribed and with a ruby stone. It was one of those rectangle ones used as a seal for important documents in the olden days. I knew this random fact only because of Tabitha, my Home and Garden editor friend. Her insufferably condescending boyfriend, Peregrine, who thought of himself as an authority on decorum, wore one similar.

"No," he drawled. "Just a duke. Sorry."

"Oh." That made sense. He had the supreme confidence I'd imagined of nobility.

"I didn't have to study for seven long years to get my title. Simply born an average white male whose ancestors murdered the poor serfs for their land."

His reply was skewed toward someone who questioned titles and inherited wealth. Someone like me. I had to wonder whether he was pandering.

"Have we met before?" I asked. Though I'd have remembered that square face, those full-lashed eyes and strong brows. Out of the corner of my eye, Sister Innocenta squirmed. "Sorry," I said, turning to her. "I'm Isla." I held out my hand, but she just nodded and slipped her hands into her cavernous sleeves.

"How utterly rude of me," Cassius said. "May I introduce Sister Innocenta. I've volunteered to help her carry home her shopping, though she's wholly capable of doing it herself. This is a woman who scaled the Himalayas in her previous life." The nun glared at the ground and he sucked in a breath. "I shouldn't have said that. I'm sure she thinks I'm a blasted nuisance. But it's something I can do. I'm a huge supporter of these wonderful women and their devotion." He gave me his full attention. "Isla, I didn't get your last name? Funnily enough, you look familiar too."

Something occurred to me. "But if you're a duke, aren't you Church of England?" I asked.

He smiled at me, and it felt like the full force of the sun. This guy had an intense charisma, and when he turned it on, the flattery was overwhelming.

"Yes, our family is one of the few who snuck away from the Church, though they took pains to keep it secret."

We were interrupted by my fellow guests spilling from the entry doors and I was initially relieved at the slight respite from Cassius's attention. It was a lot of pressure being under his gaze. But then I felt annoyed and impatient because I wouldn't get to talk to Sister Innocenta now.

My ally found me and muttered under her breath, "Hey, Salt Wars, want to grab a drink sometime?"

The young nun used the opportunity to head down the busy road, her black skirts and long veil fluttering around her. Oh no, I'd lost her. What excuse did I have for chasing her? None, it would have looked very odd. Cassius followed, seemingly reluctantly.

As he walked away, he turned and gave me a lingering gaze. What did I do to deserve that? I was sure I wasn't flirty. Had I led him on in any way? No, I must have read his face wrong. His gaze was something, but not romantic.

"Smolder much," my ally said. "Jeez, you make a quick impression." So maybe I had been flirty with him? She turned to me and deadpanned, "Must be all the salt you eat. You monster."

I spluttered out the laugh I couldn't let free last night, and she joined in. She wore another magnificent outfit: a purple three-piece suit, a big white bow in her hair and chunky white loafers. We were obviously both heading to work, totes in hand.

I checked my phone: 9:10 a.m. I couldn't miss the police briefing again. I searched the streets for a black cab. Now Sister Innocenta had left, I'd given up on finding out more and I needed to have something to "work" on. I had to leave by nine-fifteen at the absolute latest to get to the police briefing on time.

"Why don't we swap numbers? Chin-Sun Han." She held out her hand, and I shook it. "It's Korean for 'the one who seeks truth.'" She quirked one eyebrow, and I wondered if she was telling me she knew I was hiding something. "Friends call me Sunny."

It would take only a second while I watched for cabs. She handed me her phone, open on a new contact screen, and I typed in *Isla, Martyrs'*. Until I knew what she was doing here, it was better she didn't know I was a journalist. I handed her my phone, and she followed suit with *Sunny, Martyrs'*.

"This is a bit old-school, but here's my business card." She took a sheet of thick paper from her briefcase and, fingers flying, folded it into an origami fortune teller, one of those paper games we made as kids. Inside, it was pretty and funny and clever, about what you wanted for your life or your career.

"Oh, how sweet." I slipped four fingers into it. "You have your own PR company."

"I do."

"What sort of clients do you have?"

I imagined it was designers. Maybe Bato knew her?

"A huge range. For starters, a big Catholic school."

I must have looked surprised.

"I know. I'm not the buttoned-up person you'd expect to do that sort of PR. I got the commission because, well—and this is not very British, because we're supposed to be ever so modest—I'm bloody good. But also because my mum is a bit of a clergical groupie."

I chuckled at the absurdity of her description, then slapped my hand over my mouth.

"It's okay, you can laugh. I do. Sometimes I feel like a naughty schoolgirl in the meetings, and I usually don't have anyone to cackle with me afterward. So, thank you."

"Is the convent another of your clients?" I spotted a black cab in the distance, driving toward me. My hand itched to fly up and hail it. I checked my phone: 9:15 a.m. I had to leave for New Scotland Yard right *now*. Should I wait for her answer? And I was very aware that next she'd ask why I'd chosen a convent stay. What the hell would I say?

"They were considering hiring me to pitch the retreat rooms as a story to journalists because they desperately need funds for repairs. An unusual night away for readers if a guided tour was included as part of the stay because these nuns have a life you wouldn't quite expect. They even play soccer—in full habit—in the inner gardens. It would make for some great photos. But the job faded away and I wondered why. I'm not someone who likes a 'no' or 'the job is on hold.' So, I thought I'd stay in one of the rooms and make another pitch."

Ooh. I let the cab fly by. She knew quite a lot about this convent. And why did the job go away? Because they were hiding something, and they didn't want her around asking questions? My brain was in turmoil. I was dying to ask more, but I also needed to make the police debriefing. And that question was coming, I could feel it.

"Why did *you* stay?" she asked. "I noticed you were interested in that nun who died. I only know what I read in the newspapers, but it sounded tragic."

Why was I staying here? Because I'd resented the Church since I found out what that horrible priest did to my childhood friend Kingi? It was true, but I had no wish to reconcile with the Church. Also, I hated to drag Kingi's name into this.

"I'd always wanted to check it out. And then my boyfriend's daughter came home from boarding school. I had to get away for the night."

I felt horribly disloyal, but her sympathetic expression told me she bought it.

"Hmm. If you're looking to replace your boyfriend, I suspect *someone*"—she nodded down the street—"wants to interview for the job."

"No, no, I'm very happy with— I shouldn't have spoken about him like that." He did make me happy, didn't he? The thought of Declan brought on a stomach-grinding mix of emotions, a softening in my limbs and heart, but also an ache in my chest when I thought of the future. It was simply that we were going through a tricky time, our careers opposing each other. I should check in with him. Last night I hadn't had time to look at my phone and now I wondered if he'd texted.

But for now, I had to get going. I was going to be late, and it was bad enough that Barb would witness that. Spotting a cab in the distance, I flung up my hand, smiling at Sunny, hoping it didn't seem too rude. I focused on the cab headed toward me.

"It's always nice to have a backup," she said lightly. She glanced around her. "You know who that guy is, don't you?" Her voice was a hush.

I looked at her. "A duke?"

She gave a half-nod, like, *That's part of it.* "The nun you were asking about? Sister Modestia? That's her brother."

My hand dropped.

CHAPTER FIFTEEN

"WHAT? REALLY?" I asked Sunny, not hiding my shock.

The corners of her mouth turned up like I'd confirmed something she suspected. "I don't know about you, but I slept horribly last night." She motioned down the street. "Would you like to grab a coffee, and we can wake up and chat?"

I glanced at my phone: 9:25 a.m. My windpipe constricted. Stay or go? I was going to miss the police press briefing. I'd have to pick up the press releases and call Barb back on anything that looked interesting. Two days in a row. It would seem like I wasn't prioritizing her, as if I was a bit of a slacker. But this seemed encouraging, a bird in the hand. A spark of anticipation ignited in my belly.

"Yes, I'd love to get coffee with you." I smiled enthusiastically. I prayed that what she knew about Cassius and Sister Modestia was worth missing the police briefing.

She took me to a place around the corner in bustling Queensway. Waving breezily at shop and restaurant owners, she greeted them in various languages. She obviously knew them, and I suspected, too, that she was privy to a few of London's best-kept secrets. The café was colorfully hung with photos of Türkiye and warm with rugs. In the back, older men smoked hookah pipes. A waiter showed us to a street-front table and took our orders. He returned with the food and served fresh coffee from hammered copper pots. It was thick and syrupy and startlingly strong.

"Was I right?" she asked after I'd taken a sip.

"One more of those and I'll be bouncing off the walls." I nibbled on my date pastry to soak up some of the caffeine.

"So, I know who you are." She spooned berries with rosewater and honey yogurt into her mouth. I waited for her next words. "C'mon. I'm a PR consultant, and my job is literally to know all the journalists in this city. Plus—let's face it you're on the side of a bus." She waved her spoon in my direction. "So, why were you talking to His Grace? Were you quizzing him about why he'd offered half a million for that Grecian frieze?"

My jaw dropped. "Half a million pounds?" I gaped at her, incredulous. "What's so precious about that frieze?"

She pressed a forefinger on the table. "That's to remind me to quiz you on what you were actually asking him. I use it when my girlfriend tries to wiggle out of a question."

I smiled at her insight. Good PRs had the same skills and instincts as journalists.

"Before she died, he was devoted to his sister and eager to donate money to Martyrs' to make her life easier." She took a sip of her coffee. "He said he wanted to take those roof repairs off her mind for a start. Sounds like they had a dreadful childhood. Cold, distant, physically abusive father, absent alcoholic mother. His sister pretty much brought him up. She was, by all accounts, a wonderful person. But the convent refused his offer of money. His sister said she'd taken a vow of poverty and didn't want family money funding the convent. But it didn't make sense."

The waiter appeared to ask if everything was okay, we thanked him, and I waited on tenterhooks until she continued. "The convent is desperate for funds to shore up the building, and it's not just the roof. He started to obsess about buying the Grecian frieze. Said privately that he knew it's not worth anything, but it was a roundabout way for him to donate. He was willing to pay five hundred thousand pounds as long as his workers do the removal."

My brain scrambled to make sense of her bizarre revelations. "What do you think?"

She winked. "What do *you* think?"

I had to make a snap decision without doing any research on her. She struck me as trustworthy, and between her and her mother, they seemed to have a deep knowledge of London.

"I suppose it depends on what this Cassius is like," I hedged. "What sort of guy is he?"

"He has a reputation for being ruthless and mercurial, but I've not seen that side of him. It seems he truly did love his sister."

"How old is this frieze? Where did it come from?"

"No one seems to know anything about the provenance or the age. There's also no record of whether it was built on-site. As far as anyone knows, it's pretty much worthless, just a huge hunk of carved stone with a naughty scene on it."

It seemed beautifully and intricately carved, though. How long had it taken to complete? Why did the artist or artists make it so big? And surely it wasn't commissioned by the nuns at the turn of the century? It wasn't remotely religious.

Dabbing a finger on my plate to get the last delicious pastry flakes, I thought hard. "I wonder if Cassius knows something no one else does about its true value?" My journalist friend Tabitha previously worked at Sotheby's, the fine art auctioneers, and might have a contact with some insight.

She nodded. "That was my first reaction too. Apparently, Cassius just says it will look beautiful in his garden. Which it would. Right by the maze."

"Half a million is a lot to drop on a garden ornament, albeit a bloody big one."

She laughed.

"So you've been to his place?" I asked. "What's it like?"

She stirred her coffee thoughtfully. "Tewksbury Castle? For the past two years, I've been my girlfriend's plus-one to his annual masked ball. I don't know him besides that. It's incredible, as you can imagine, a castle in the Cotswolds—that old golden-colored limestone, rolling gardens, an enormous swimming pool, fountains, magical views over a lake. Like *Downton Abbey* meets *Saltburn*, you know, that movie. But it was very crumbling grandeur, very run-down. Apparently, this year it was beautifully restored, so I'm dying to see it this Saturday evening."

"We'll have to meet afterward, and you can dish on the gargoyles and the fenestras, whatever those may be." I was disappointed that I was now forced to see her as a source rather than a friend, since I liked her. A constant push and pull in my life.

She laughed. "I'll certainly catalog all the bric-a-brac 'whattynotty' for you. Now, back to my original question—you can't get out of it now. Why were you talking to His Grace?"

I gave a little internal sigh of relief. She traded in information as much as I did. I used to live by my old editor's pronouncement, *You don't have friends, only contacts.* Spending time in my old hometown, I found that wasn't true, that building true friendships can help you in every way. But I was up against a deadline.

"Oh. *He* spoke to *me*." In fact, I wanted to talk to Sister Innocenta, but I wasn't sure I should confess that much. I had to hold back because there was a risk she might tell another journalist she knew better. But there was an issue, too, that came with not being totally up-front with her. She or her girlfriend might know more and be willing to share with me.

"Ha. If you wanted an invitation to the masked ball, I think it's yours." She grinned and nudged me. "Just saying. You could come with us. It'll be fun."

"Oh, thank you." I filed it into the back of my mind and pictured telling Declan. He wasn't a jealous person, but I didn't think he'd be happy about me heading off to a ball by myself. And I didn't want to. I'd get an invitation for him too. Though he was a bit more of a homebody than I'd expected of a former undercover cop who'd traveled the world for work, he was always up for new experiences, and he was a clotheshorse. This was a chance for him to air that tuxedo I'd seen draped in dry cleaner plastic in the back of his wardrobe. Mmm. I imagined he'd look *very* hot in that suit. The thought heated my whole body. "But seriously, I am happy with my boyfriend."

She tapped me on the forearm. "We'll do something else together then. I know this old bar that has a new absinthe cocktail."

I smiled at the thought of a friend who knew London like this.

"Yes, there's always a bar." She took a deep breath. "Hey, we both better get back to work. Stay in touch." We waved goodbye, but before I set off across Kensington Gardens for the office, I checked my phone for messages from Declan. It was 10:30 a.m. He still hadn't tried to call or text. Usually, we swapped messages at least every hour with silly emojis and jokes in between. Worried about his questions, I hadn't texted either. I sent a message.

> Me: *Looking forward to seeing you tonight. What's for dinner? Love you.*

I checked my phone ten minutes later at the entrance to work.

No reply.

It was gearing up to be a complicated, uncertain day, so I quickly texted Fleur, with a wrench on my conscience that I was imposing again, and asked if Teddy could stay on today and tonight. I organized for the dog walker to turn up to her house and take Teddy for his usual three walks in the park with his friends. If this kept on, Teddy might have to stay with his dog walker. I missed his little furry face so much it hurt. This was not how I wanted my life to be, but it was only temporary.

As soon as I got into work, I looked up Cassius online in both Debrett's, the register of all titled families in the UK, and Who's Who database. His older sister's full name was the same in both—Lady Beatrice Anastasia Octavia Aurelia Athena Devonport.

I discussed the news with my editor and emailed Cassius. I copied the exact press release from the police. "I understand this was your older sister? Could you confirm and talk to us about her?" I listed my work phone number and left a message at both his castle and work office in London.

A reply arrived immediately. "His Grace will not be commenting."

I called the convent. Another Sister, who did not sound like Sister Innocenta, answered. "We have already given you her legal name."

I emailed but the reply came back the same.

I talked to my news editor. Without any confirmation that Lady Beatrice Devonport and Sister Modestia were the same person, we could not run the story.

I texted Declan again. No reply.

CHAPTER SIXTEEN

THAT NIGHT, I went around to Declan's. I was jumpy and on my guard again. I expected to be quizzed about what I did last night while I was at the convent. I didn't have an answer prepared, intending to keep it vague.

Instead, we had a lovely dinner, like nothing was wrong. He was surprised I hadn't brought Teddy but didn't push it. Initially, it occurred to me it should have felt freer and back to "normal" without Sephy there. But after only a few nights of having her around, it felt strange not to see her. Maybe I was still nervous that he'd ask about last night.

Over homemade shepherd's pie—his specialty, as he lived in Shepherd's Bush—we talked about his trip yesterday to drop Sephy at his sister's. It was a long journey because the country roads were narrow, with high hedges on either side, so it was hard driving, but he and Sephy had a good talk, and she was very excited to see her cousins and learn how to surf. Now I was feeling like we were back to the old us, talking and laughing without walking on eggshells.

I asked him about the draft bill he was trying to get through. He seemed exhausted by the politicking to get people on board, constantly weighing whether he should give in to their demands for changes or promise something to get something. Did he ever think back to his undercover days and long for the risk and excitement?

It wasn't that he'd given it up for me, but I was part of the reason, and I wondered with a heavy heart, whether sometimes he resented me a little for it.

"Okay, enough of work." His eyes flashing, he pushed back his chair and, with a sexy half-smile, got to his feet. Rounding the table, he pulled me to standing. "Come upstairs; I've got something to show you."

"Now there's an original line." I crossed my arms and raised a flirty eyebrow. "Give me a good reason."

He grabbed me around the waist and tipped me over his shoulder. Smacking my bum all the way, he raced up the stairs.

"That's better than the gym," he wheezed out at the top of the stairs, both of us laughing.

"Bit out of breath, old man," I joked. Since I'd found out he was five years older than me, I'd teased him mercilessly. When our laughing died down, he looped his hands around my neck. The carefree joking of a moment ago vanished. Heat simmered in his gaze, and my pulse picked up.

He kissed me, and not the long, searching kisses we were sharing lately. *How are we? Are we okay?* No, this was pure oblivion as he pulled me in close, his lips and tongue playing with mine. He held my bottom lip with his teeth and released it slowly.

"Look on the bed," he murmured into my ear, his voice gravelly. It sent heat deep down and made my toes curl with anticipation. "I washed all the clothes you left behind in the past couple of weeks."

I laughed and sorted through the neat stack on the bed.

"How do you get the whites so white?" I asked.

"Tell you later." He grinned happily. "Now, don't be freaked out. But I did something else."

"Besides washing all my clothes?"

Leading me into his wardrobe, he showed me some hooks. "This one is for your long purple coat. I know you don't like the hem crumpling on the floor. And this hook is for your overnight tote. And these shoehorns are for your shoes."

I knew what he was doing, trying to make it comfortable for me to move in at any pace. My heart stumbled, touched by how completely open and certain he was about wanting to be with me. Gently, I took his hand. "Declan, this is …"

He furrowed his forehead, maybe waiting for my reply, but I couldn't think of the words I should use. He showed me the top two drawers in his dresser.

"I've emptied these out so you can leave things here."

I stared at him, my throat too choked to speak.

"What? Fuck." He rubbed the back of his neck. "It's too much, isn't it?"

I realized I hadn't been clear enough in expressing my gratitude. I didn't want this to lapse into yet another misunderstanding between us.

"You're never too much." I kissed him and ran my hands through his thick brown hair. "You are so good to me."

"Mmm." He traced his hands along the sides of my body. "Well, it's a present for me too. I bought a whole bunch of cane baskets for your files. They're hiding under the bed because I didn't know if that was over the top. And the pièce de résistance—" Releasing me, he reached under the bed and swung out a large hamper, a match for his one in the bathroom. "Your own laundry basket because you said you weren't ready for the dirty mixing."

"Ha." I opened the top, bent over, and, testing it out, reached deep into it.

He eased himself behind me, massaging my hips. "Argh. Could you do that again?"

"Happy to oblige." Slowly, to torture him, I straightened, grinding back into him. "Wow, you must be in heaven. I do know how you love a good basket shop."

He turned me around to face him and buried his face in my neck. "Yes, I spent a very pleasant hour with a cheeky pinot, scrolling through pages of organizing solutions."

"Why don't we take off all our clothes and throw them in our matching laundry hampers?" I suggested. "Just so they see some action tonight? Before you pass out. You must be exhausted from driving six hours last night and working all day."

His green gaze blazed. "I definitely want to do that. I'll just hang up your coat and tote and stack your shoes."

While he set up my things, unease chafed along my spine as I took a surreptitious look at his bedside clock: eight o'clock. I had to leave at ten thirty if I was to get to my surveillance position behind the convent at the time I'd planned. Last night, it was eleven when I saw that nun and her possible boyfriend leave through the back door. Where were they going? Was someone picking them up? It was a bit of a long shot, but I wondered whether a particular event happened at that time every night.

Today, I'd tucked my fire engine-red hair into a black hat, pulled on my old black coat, and walked up and down that back street. No one came in or out of the back door of the convent. What I also realized was that there was nowhere to hide while I watched the back door tonight. No café, no hotel. Not even an Airbnb to rent. That meant I'd have to crouch in the stairwell of one of the basement flats opposite. I'd scouted one that didn't have a streetlamp over it. Hopefully, the flat owners would keep their blinds down so I could wait unnoticed.

"So, how did your work thing last night go?" He glanced up from where he was slipping my shoes into the shoehorns.

My heart skipped a beat. *Blow.* I thought I'd gotten out of this. I was expecting to be quizzed, then wasn't. Now the topic was being raised again. I wasn't going to lie.

"Hmm?" I stared at my phone.

"Was it a police meet and greet?" His voice was light. "John and Andy there?" His friends. It was a reasonable question. When I'd been a consumer journalist, I could have gone to industry brunches, lunches, drinks, and dinners around the clock. But a police reporter didn't have the same social life, except for boozing it up in pubs with your competitors.

"Umm." Nope. I got nothing.

Holding my gaze intently, he stood up and cocked his head.

"It's just that in Parliament today, coming out of the House of Lords, His Grace Cassius Devonport, the Sixteenth Duke of Cheltenham, sidled up to me. Said he'd met my beautiful, redheaded girlfriend coming from an overnight convent stay. Then he slapped me on the back and said some other shit I'm not going to repeat about what I might be lacking."

Shame flamed my face. Inside my chest, my joy dissolved. I hadn't just been busted, I'd embarrassed him horribly. To make matters worse, he obviously didn't like Cassius.

Something else nudged me.

"How on earth did he find out I'm your girlfriend? I didn't give my full name."

"He's a well-connected arsehole who loves to have something on everybody."

"Holy hell, his contacts must be good to find that out so quickly."

Declan screwed up his face in disgust. "A network of vipers." He ran a hand along his jawline, drawing a rasp from his skin. "Why are you lying to me?"

"I'm sorry you had to hear it like that." I hadn't technically lied to him, but this wasn't the time to point that out. "Wait. Why didn't you ask me this at the beginning of the night? As soon as I came through the door?"

His eyes locked on mine. "I want you to know that you can tell me anything, that I'm here for you. You don't have to hide things from me. I want us to be open with each other."

His words were heartfelt and beautiful. So why did my stomach churn? He'd made it easy, and he'd made it hard. I did believe he wanted to be here for me, but also, I knew for a fact he didn't want me to pursue this story. I had to keep going to get the promotion. But also, I felt a deep responsibility to Sister Modestia. We were at an impasse.

His brow furrowed as he formed his next words painfully, carefully. "And I didn't want to start the evening off with conflict."

My head whirled as I plunged headfirst into a new certainty. Things had changed between us, and he felt it too. It had been so relaxed between us, and now every new scenario felt like a potential fight.

"So," he asked, "what on earth were you doing coming out of a convent?"

I fiddled with my hands. "It was one of those silent retreats. I saw it on the convent's website. It was a way to get into the convent to see where Sister Modestia lived, you know, the nun who drowned. I didn't tell you because you would have told me not to go."

He jerked his head back, annoyed at my accusation. Then he scratched his cheek slowly. "You're probably right." He sighed. "But I want to know you are safe, and I'll do anything to make sure you are."

"I'm not sure how we resolve this, but I want to be open with you too."

I talked about the overnight stay, excluding how I'd sneaked out during the night. Despite what he said, I was sure he'd be worried by how secretive the nuns were and what was going on in the rooms behind the Grecian frieze. He'd ask me again to take this to the police. How wild would this sound to someone who didn't know or trust me? "I think there's something odd going on in this convent because I saw a Botoxed nun, two thirteen-year-old nuns, and one nun who left with a tall workman." My rapport with Sergeant Barb would plummet to a new low.

I told him about meeting Cassius this morning, glossing over the looks he'd given me—what was the point in mentioning that? Anyway, I wasn't convinced he was sending signals to me. He could just have a naturally flirtatious manner.

Declan gave a disgusted snarl and sat down heavily on the bed, thudding back against the headboard.

"Of all people. Cassius. That fucking prick."

The force of his loathing sent goosebumps along my arms. I hadn't seen him like this before.

"How do you know him?" I sat at the foot of the bed.

He folded his arms tight, his hands balled into fists. "That guy I've been talking about in the House of Lords who is completely poisoning my ideas? The proud Tory, who says his priority is to protect business, in this instance, the shipping business. He says that, if anything, Thames Port should *loosen* the laws."

"*That's* the guy? Wow." I took a beat to sift through my conversation with Cassius this morning. "That's strange. That's not how he came across to me. He was very sardonic and dismissive of his title. Said—"

"Oh." He gave a bitter laugh and stared into space.

"What?" I climbed up the bed and got in front of him.

"He fancies you. He's clever. He knows you wouldn't be impressed if he tried the alpha duke shit he uses on other people. Don't go near that guy; he's bad news. Lord Havistock loathes the man, says he'll do or say anything to get what he wants." He shook his head, getting more and more upset, and scowled. "How did he look at you? What else did he say to you?"

His agitated tone made me study his face closer. A sudden realization dawned on me.

"Ha!" I wriggled triumphantly.

"What?" he asked.

I went wide-eyed.

"The man who is always so even-tempered, who barely gets ruffled, who is always so reasonable." I straddled him, a knee on either side of his hips, and gazed down at him. At the sight of his lips pressed together, I squirmed, gleeful. "Are you *jealous*?"

He traced a finger down my neck, inside my shirt and along the skin above my bra.

"Hmm. I could be if you like it," he said in a growly voice. He unbuttoned my shirt, slipped it off, and kissed my shoulder. Unhooking my bra, he removed it and groaned.

A hum in me started building, sweet and low. "Mmm, I think I do." A hard shift moved beneath me. "And, oh, what's this? I think you like that I like it too."

A laugh rumbled from deep in his chest. "Are you Dr. Seussing me or something? That's new." In one swift move, he flipped me under him, and holding my hands above my head, ground hard against me. "And I've got something new for you."

CHAPTER SEVENTEEN

IT WAS TEN thirty in the evening. Time to leave. Declan was breathing deeply, sound asleep. I hated to leave the safety and warmth of him wrapped around me like a very sexy body blanket, but I had to go now. Shamefully, I slunk out from under his arm and leg and slithered over the side of the bed. I tiptoed across the floor and grabbed my coat, handbag, and phone from its charger. I crept downstairs and quickly pulled on my clothes. After checking that the exit delay was activated on the alarm, I unlocked the door and snuck out, closing it quietly behind me.

Outside, the night was cold and clear; its serenity interrupted only by a few voices from people leaving the pub across the square. The moon and stars were bright and all-knowing, jabbing at my conscience, making me feel worse about sneaking out and leaving Declan in his orderly cocoon of a bedroom that he'd lovingly tweaked to make room for me. *Look at this beautiful man,* the moon seemed to be saying, *and look at what you're doing.* But he would disagree with my decision, fueling more tension and arguing. This was something I had to do to find out the truth about Sister Modestia's death.

Down the road, I called an Uber and was dropped off two streets from the convent. I wrapped myself in the old black coat I'd deliberately brought to hide in, pulled on my black woolly hat, and walked down the street that backed onto the convent. I turned toward the basement flat I'd scouted earlier today, opposite the convent. Huddled down in the stairwell, I waited.

I didn't know what I was waiting for or what I hoped to see. Still, I knew I was putting myself in danger even being on this road. Whatever was going on in that convent last night did not look right.

Wham. Clank. Loud sounds barreled from the end of the street. My whole body jumped in that direction. What was it? I couldn't see anything. No trucks. Maybe it had come from the park? I held my breath. Nothing else. I breathed again but shallowly and spooked. I rubbed my arms and curled back down, cramped, chilled, and on edge.

A scurrying sounded from above. I looked up to see a blur smack me on the face. My heart fired in my chest. I opened my mouth to scream. I felt claws, fur. *Get it off. Get it off.* I swiped at my face. It was already off. A cat bounded down the street. Just a harmless cat. My breathing started to ease.

I waited. It was nearly summer, but this was London and rarely balmy. An hour later, I was teeth-chatteringly cold. I needed an arctic sleeping bag if I was to stay here any longer.

A gasp of brakes rattled the air, along with the greasy smell of diesel. A big, dirty truck drew up. A man got out and used his phone. Hang on—was he the tall, bearded guy I'd seen coming out of the nun's room? A nun burst from the back door to the convent. Wasn't she the one who was having an affair with him? Following her were the two young nuns and three more behind them. They seemed to be fretting, maybe about leaving? The man hushed them.

"Oi. You." The voice came from the flat below. I looked down. "No sleeping in our stairwell." A young woman in sweats squinted up at me from her doorway. "Bugger off before I call my boyfriend."

"Shh, I'm hiding out," I loud-whispered. What was I thinking? That was a bonkers answer.

"What the hell? Jim!" she called.

Jim appeared at her side.

"Fuck off, or we call the cops," he yelled.

"Hey, you!" The bearded guy on the other side of the road yelled at me. He looked like he wanted to run over to me.

From below, Jim, the flat owner, bolted up the steps toward me. I threw myself upward and onto the footpath.

I checked the bearded man across the road. He lurched forward as if he intended to chase me. He hesitated. He glanced back at the women and then at me. Was he thinking he couldn't leave the women? He punched into his phone.

I sprinted to the corner and across the main road. *Paaaarp.* Argh. A black cab narrowly missed me. Crying out, I stumbled forward, wiping out onto the footpath. *Ouch.* I dusted off my hands. Blood beaded on my scraped palms. The knees on my pants were torn. Where to now? I could race to the nearest house, hammer on the door, and ask them to shelter me, but no one was going to answer the door to a stranger. Look at how that couple reacted, and I was just crouching in their stairwell. What about heading for the underground train? They could follow me.

I saw another man across the road getting out of his car. Coincidence? He opened the back door. A huge dog bounded out. I flew forward toward the entrance to Hyde Park. It was open until midnight.

"Stop!" the man yelled from across the road. The dog let out a bark.

I darted into the park and immediately got off the path to escape the beams of lamplight. I knew this park because I was here every day with Teddy. I zigzagged through the trees, past the fountains and the statue of Peter Pan, heading to the lake, the Serpentine. I couldn't hear the man or the dog but I couldn't stop to check.

Where to now? I couldn't sprint back to the main road—might run into him. Couldn't hide in the public toilets—the dog would sniff me out.

Water it was.

Ugh. Crouching low, I slid into the lake, trying not to make a sound. It was June, nearly summer, but the water was frigid and the outside air cold. I swam under the willows, where I was hidden. It was deep, much deeper than I'd imagined, and I had to tread water. It smelled so bad, like dog poop and rotten flesh. I gagged. I kept treading water, trying to keep my bag aloft, and I held my nose with the other hand.

"Fuck, where has she gone?" The man was close. A lone bark and a whimper. Hopefully the dog couldn't smell me anymore. But if they spotted me, I was sure both he and the dog wouldn't hesitate to dive in after me. I'd seen something they didn't want anyone to see. But what *exactly* was it?

A rustle, a grunt. It sounded like they were coming closer, but I couldn't see them. I hoped they couldn't see me either, but I couldn't be sure. A glint of light flickered in the darkness. The dog's eyes? Oh God. The rattle of its chain sent shivers up my spine.

"C'mon, boy, find her." An accent—what accent?

I held my nose and ducked under the water, bringing my handbag with me. I squeezed my legs stiff to sink low, pushing at the water with my one free hand to stay under.

My brain unwound a spool of fear. Was this what Sister Modestia felt when she was drowning? I imagined her terror at being trapped underwater, breathing it in, everything lost.

Argh. My thigh seized with pain—like it had been crunched in sharp jaws. I surfaced for a breath. Oh God, what is it? I shoved my hand down my sweatpants and felt something slimy on my bare thigh. I brought up my hand. Blood, lots of it. I've been bitten. Oh God. I screamed soundlessly into my closed mouth. An animal.

A rat? I slapped my hand over my mouth. I heaved and almost vomited into my hand. Could I hear the dog panting? I slipped under again. My mouth must have been open because I took a gulp of the water—slimy, filthy water. I gagged. I tried to think of blue sky, sun, air, nothingness. I surfaced and breathed deep, despite the slimy filth I tasted inside my mouth.

Eventually, the air was still, just a few honks of black cabs.

Back under. Count to ten. Up to the surface slowly. Still silence. I did it two more times. Silence. They must have gone. I waded out of the water, leaves, slime, feathers, and something hairy clinging to my limbs. Back on the grass, the feel and smell filled my stomach with bile. I threw up. I thought of the rat in the water—its ears, its tail, its whiskers twitching, creeping around me, sizing me up. Then opening its mouth and biting down on my leg. I jumped up and down, slapping at my arms and legs to get everything off. I pulled down my sweatpants. A red, raw bite mark pulsed on my thigh. I'd have to walk to the ER in Paddington and get that looked at. How would I explain how drenched I was? *Who the hell cares?* That was the least of my worries.

Fifteen minutes later, I trudged into Saint Mary's Hospital, dripping on the lino floor, filthy and smelling foul. I must have looked as horrendous as I felt, because I was immediately bumped up the list and rushed to a room out the back. Two policewomen interviewed me to make sure I hadn't been assaulted. I gave Shay's number as my person to contact because I worried that one of them might know Declan or know of him. It would be very bad luck, but not out of the question. How was I going to explain this bandage to him? Hopefully, by then, I could replace it with a very large Band-Aid, but still, what would I say? That I'd bumped into the side of a desk? They showed me to a shower, fetched me shower shoes, scrubs to wear afterward, and a blanket for my shoulders.

"I was running to get home quickly, and I tripped and fell into the water," I told the doctor when she asked me for the second time to explain how it happened.

She gave me a funny look. "But *how* did you fall in the water? Have you been drinking or taking drugs?"

"No, I was just very tired. I was working late."

Her jaw slack, she stared at me like she was trying to put something together. Did she remember me from the advertisement on the bus? I'd never considered myself famous, but this morning, Sunny knew who I was immediately. Thankfully, recognition didn't spark on the doctor's face. She wrote down my answer and turned away and wrote more, which probably meant she was noting that she didn't believe me.

A nurse with curly blonde hair and sweeping false eyelashes arrived to give me my shots. Spotting her long coral fingernails, I shrank back. How was she going to manage the needle with those nails? With a deftness that was mesmerizing, she had no trouble. Two hours later, after a thorough exam and a battery of tests, they'd treated the wound and given me all sorts of shots and antibiotics. My handbag was sodden; my phone unresponsive, but my credit cards were intact. I used the hospital phone and called a cab. Slinging a plastic bag containing my wet clothes and my handbag over my shoulder, I climbed into the back of the cab to worried looks from the staff.

Back home, I buried my phone in a bowl of rice, praying for it to be revived by morning, and took everything out of my wallet to dry. I put all my clothes through the wash, though I was certain I'd never get that smell out. It was three in the morning on Thursday. I had only a few hours until I had to get up. My throat hurt, my whole body ached, and nausea slugged at my head. I climbed into bed and coughed and coughed.

Scrambling out of bed, I looked down my throat in the bathroom mirror. It was red and swollen and I could barely swallow. I reached into the cabinet and measured out cough medicine. My contraceptive pills were sitting on the sink in a bright pink bowl. I kept them there to remind me. How many hours since I'd taken one? I tried to remember. Yesterday? No. The day before? My head swam. What was I doing the day before? I gave up. I popped one in my mouth, filled a glass of water to wash it down with, and tried to swallow while screaming in my mouth with pain. I needed something more than over-the-counter medication for my throat. I went online and made an appointment with the first doctor who would take me at eight in the morning. My eyelids heavy, I went to set my alarm. My phone pinged with a text, spiking my pulse.

At this hour?

I swallowed around the guilty lump in my throat. Was it Declan asking why I left?

It was a London number, unknown to me, but it hadn't been forwarded from my work phone. It was someone who had my personal number.

> *Hi Isla, Cassius here. We met outside Martyrs' Convent yesterday morning. I have a story for you. I'll pick you up outside your work tonight, Thursday, at six, and we can talk.*

My heartbeat stalled, my mind a mess of emotions. How did he get my personal number? The newspaper included my work number with every article I wrote, but not my personal number.

A story. It definitely wasn't a date. I had to make sure of that. He didn't even check whether the time was good for me. Maybe that meant it was such a good story he assumed he didn't need to, or maybe he was just supremely arrogant. Whatever. This was a posh bloke-about-town who knew people I would never encounter, privy to information I could never access, and I was a journalist desperate for a great story. He was the brother of a woman who'd given me information about drugs, then drowned, and the Russian man who'd come for her had said repeatedly, "Your brother."

I couldn't afford to turn him down.

Me: *OK, yes. Meet you outside my work at six.*

Professional enough? Maybe too unfriendly. I added, *Thank you for thinking of me for the story.*

Cassius sent a thumbs-up emoji.

Thumbs-up was not a flirty date emoji. Good, everything good.

CHAPTER EIGHTEEN

DRAGGING AND DRAINED, I arrived at work, disguising a limp from the still-pounding bite on my thigh. My throat felt so sore I couldn't swallow, and my head swam with nausea. At the doctor's appointment, she'd changed my dressing and given me stronger antibiotics, pain relief, and something for my sore throat, saying I should stay in bed for three days. When I insisted I had to get back to work, I did get her to admit that it wasn't infectious, so I wasn't being irresponsible toward others.

I wanted nothing more than to get a cab home and go back to sleep. But yesterday, I'd asked Sergeant Barb if I could have an introduction to one of the medical examiners at New Scotland Yard. I could tell she wasn't happy as I didn't have a specific case, just general questions. A text arrived from her as I sat down at my computer. She'd organized a meeting for this morning.

At Westminster Morgue, I was grateful for the intense cold of the basement office. Dr. Ashantay Adu greeted me, a bright flash of vibrant warmth amid her steel surrounds, her braids wound in a colorful scarf that complemented her wrap dress in an African print, worn under her white coat. The place smelled of formaldehyde, but anything was better than the reek of the Serpentine last night.

I explained that I'd only just transferred to the police beat six months ago, and I was keen to learn about the processes following a suspicious death.

"I've done some googling," I said. "It seems that no poison can be concealed longer than three days."

"You're right." An amused smile crept onto her face. "Sometimes, I wonder why I went to medical school."

I grimaced. "Sorry, I know it must be endlessly irritating to have people quote Google at you. So, if you get a request to analyze the body *after* the three days, you can find the poison?"

"Yes," she said slowly. "You're thinking about a specific case, aren't you?"

"Sergeant Barb—Barbara Dupee—said I couldn't inquire about a specific case without checking in with her first, so I'll just talk in generalities. What if the medical examiner and coroner have already declared the death to be, say, an accidental drowning, and not suspicious?"

I held my breath, scanning her expression, worried that I'd tipped my hand. I expected her to immediately know what case I was thinking of.

"An accidental drowning?" A light ignited in her brown eyes, and she made a slight sound in the back of her throat as she rolled her chair from the desk. Yes, it seemed that case had come to her mind. Was this good or bad for me? I watched her carefully. She seemed concerned, tapping her pen against her lips.

"You could bring forward new information if it raises reasonable doubt," she said finally. "This is very difficult to do. And the body has to be intact. Which means you must raise these doubts before the cremation."

Cremation.

My heart skipped a beat.

I hadn't thought about that. Once banned, cremation was now accepted in the Catholic Church, but the Martyrs' Convent's order was traditional and maybe the nuns even had burial plots allotted to each of them. Or would Sister Modestia be buried at her ancestral home? A question for Cassius. Another reason to meet him tonight.

That afternoon, back at the office, I signed up for another night at the convent. But as soon as my request went through automatically, I was informed of a glitch on the website and that the rooms were full and my payment had been refunded. *Blow.* I suspected I'd get the same response repeatedly from now on.

Frustrated, I resolved to uncover more about the Grecian frieze. My friend Tabitha might help. I found her downstairs in Home and Garden, which she headed, arranging Lucite chairs, wallpaper, and orange dahlias, most likely for a shoot. Her big blue eyes lit up.

"Hey, was just thinking about you." She adjusted her shiny blonde ponytail. "Do you want to stay at my parents' place this weekend?" We'd stayed a couple of times. They lived in a run-down manor house in a little hamlet in Gloucestershire. She was forever coming up with ways for them to make money, but they'd resisted, insisting on "muddling through," but they had finally acquiesced to some remodeling to accommodate her latest idea of a B&B with a difference. Must Love Animals—dating weekends for animal lovers.

"I'll have to check with Declan. Why? What's the occasion?" Oh, we couldn't go anyway because we couldn't leave Sephy on her own. I sighed. Declan was a bit of a homebody after years of being away undercover, but I felt too young to be staying home every night. This hadn't been an issue before, though I was starting to suspect Declan had been open to going out before because we were seeing London again, together. Staying home had meant staying in bed, but that wasn't going to be an option now.

"The masked ball. You're going too? I heard you're getting an invitation."

My eyebrows shot up. First Sunny had mentioned the ball, and now Tabitha. "News to me. Who did you hear that from?"

She tapped her lips. "Hmm. I can't remember. Well, let me know. Mummy and Daddy would love to see you, and we can all go together. Peregrine won't be driving up with me. He's traveling up the day before and staying with his parents." Her boyfriend, Peregrine, self-appointed arbiter of etiquette. On meeting, I'd found him amusing, and I got quite a good story for the Life and Style pages from him, but I tired of his constant correcting of the way I spoke.

I tried to gently shift the subject.

"By the way, obscure question out of the blue. Do you know anything about Grecian friezes? I know you interned at Sotheby's art auctions. I have a potential story that involves one, and I'm not sure of its significance."

Her eyes widened. "Grecian friezes? Hmm. I know very little about them. But I can introduce you to Ishani; she's wonderful. A whole bunch of us started together, but she stayed on, and now she's head of her department."

"Oh, perfect. I'd love an introduction."

"Of course." She tapped a message on her phone. I checked mine, which showed the joint text. "And I'll see you at work drinks tonight," she said.

I nodded. I didn't tell her I was planning to see Cassius. I didn't know if I should feel happy about meeting him or not.

I'd dressed this morning in an old-me black business suit and white shirt to keep things clear with Cassius. New me slipped on my shiny red kitten heels for some color. As soon as I left the house and stepped into the cab, I realized they made my limp worse. By the end of the day, though, the pain pills had started working. The nausea was still there. Maybe a slight reaction to the meds?

I left the office at six to meet Cassius outside. As I reached the front doors, I remembered what Tabitha had said. Tonight was our regular informal staff drinks, where everyone headed off to our local. As I pushed through the door, I realized about twenty other journalists, including Tabitha, were right behind me.

My gut plummeted.

Because there he was, for everyone to see. Hands shoved into the pockets of his brown tweed trousers—presumably it showed a shedload of confidence to wear a country suit in town—Cassius lounged against a vintage Rolls-Royce. Chauffeur driven. *What the fuck?* He smirked. Because, yes, I'd said that out loud. The small crowd of my colleagues leaving for drinks clustered around me. Murmurs of excitement rustled the air.

"Your Grace," Tabitha called from behind me.

My spine stiffened, horrified—this brought more attention to him. But it made sense for him to know Tabitha, and maybe my coworkers wouldn't notice he was there for me. My anxiety eased.

Cassius nodded. "Tabitha." He smiled.

I hoped they'd start a conversation and my colleagues would wander off. Just at that moment, Declan strode around the corner, flowers in one hand, a box in the other. He'd come to surprise me. His face was lit up, like he couldn't wait to see my reaction.

Oh God, he was going to be totally mortified. I knew exactly how this might look, even from a distance. Then a tiny molecule of hope formed in my chest. Or maybe it didn't?

The gifts he bore were testament to how entwined our lives had become, beyond the furtive first intimacies. I knew the box in his hand contained a single cupcake from my favorite bakery, plain vanilla with vanilla icing and sprinkles. *He* knew if he'd bought a whole box, I'd eat them all at once—what I liked, I loved, and I had zero impulse control. Afterward, I'd groan and moan on the sofa for hours, feeling horribly ill. So just one was best.

Declan stopped in his tracks. He'd seen us.

Cringing, I went rigid, not knowing what to do next.

Cassius opened the car door and beckoned to me so no one could possibly be confused about who he was waiting for. My stomach rolled over, and it wasn't from the meds. Was he taunting Declan?

Declan paced slowly toward us.

"Hello, mate." Cassius moved toward Declan, extending an open hand. I'd always thought of Declan as tall. I'd looked up to speak to him or kiss him. But he seemed slight and boyish next to Cassius, who was bigger and broader.

Declan had both hands full and couldn't shake Cassius's hand even if he'd wanted to. He was slack-faced.

"He's got a story for me," I explained. Declan slightly shook his head. I tried again. "We're just having a meeting."

The whole scenario was so awkward that even my journalist colleagues—who, let's face it, were all professional nosy parkers—sucked in a nervous breath and edged away.

To make everything worse, the traffic built up behind us, and cars and black cabs were honking their horns for the Rolls to move on. Panic filled my head. Either I had to bail on Cassius and let him—and his story idea—drive away or leave without talking properly to Declan.

"I'll see you at home," I said to Declan, my eyes desperately searching his, my heart tight and heavy. He said nothing. My legs like deadweights, I slid into the back of the Rolls. Cassius shut the door after me and got in the other side.

Miserable, I stared through the back window as we drove away. The work crowd had moved on, and Declan stood on the street alone. He strode up to the nearest rubbish bin, shoved in the flowers and the single cupcake, and walked away.

Cassius fixed me with his dark, brooding gaze as we drove past the black-and-gold wrought iron gates of Kensington Palace and its leafy park.

The car was unusually wide. He was sitting on the other side, but he took up a lot of room with some major man-spreading, his large brogue-clad foot resting on his tweed knee, his arm slung along the back of the seat, his long manicured fingers nearly touching my shoulder. He pushed a button in front of him, and the glass partition rolled up between us and the driver.

"What was in the box?" A gleam sparked in his eyes.

"One of my favorite cupcakes," I said.

He scoffed. "I would have brought you a whole box."

An intense protectiveness for Declan swelled through me. "He knows me better than that. I like just one."

I smiled to myself that Declan knew this. He must have been so upset to throw it away. A lump of shame lodged in my throat. Talking about him any longer felt horribly disloyal. I needed to get us off the subject.

My chest expanded with a breath. It was time to acknowledge Cassius's loss. "Look, I hope this doesn't seem intrusive, but I wanted to say how sorry I am about your sister. Someone told me your sister is—was—Sister Modestia. Such a tragedy." I needed to acknowledge I'd contacted him. "And—I'm not sure if you realized that I was the journalist who emailed and called you about that."

He lowered his eyes. "Yes, I saw your name. And thank you for not running that story. I couldn't bear the hypocrisy of condolences from people who didn't know her or me."

His words yanked through me like a serrated ribbon of steel. Now, I was in a quandary. Did I admit I would have run with the story if I'd gotten a confirmation? Would that put him off me? Make him rethink working together?

"Let's talk about her later." He glanced out the window.

I was covering up so much in the rest of my life, I couldn't add this too. Before I could second-guess myself, I blurted out, "I need to be honest. If the convent had confirmed the two women were the same person, I would have run that story."

He flinched, then shrugged. "You're just doing your job. Thank you for your integrity in admitting that. That makes me respect you more."

Phew. Interacting with him was like a roller coaster. I was thinking about having a drink when we got to dinner, but I knew I couldn't. The painkiller was starting to wear off. After a couple of minutes, I turned to him. "So, tell me a little about this story."

He nodded to the chauffeur in the front and lowered his voice. "This car is not completely private. Wait until we arrive."

"Where are we going?"

"I'm taking you to my club. Better privacy." His phone buzzed with a text, and he was distracted for the rest of the trip.

He could speak more freely at his club? That didn't make sense.

CHAPTER NINETEEN

"GOOD EVENING, YOUR Grace. Good evening, ma'am," two door attendants chorused as the chauffeur guided us from the car to the entrance of Toff's Club in Mayfair. Established 1750, according to a brass plaque on the wall.

In a flurry of three sets of arms, the chauffeur and the attendants reached to open the door for us. I got flustered and overwhelmed, but Cassius just put a proprietary hand on my back and sailed us past them with an unseeing nod. I paced faster to shake off his hand.

Seated in the dark-paneled dining room, I refused the gin and tonic Cassius offered me because I was on antibiotics and asked for just tonic, which seemed to disappoint him. While he was collared by someone he'd gone to school with, I clutched at my throat and rubbed the pounding bite on my thigh. The painkillers seemed to have worn off very quickly.

The man finally gave Cassius a hearty clap on the shoulder and nodded to me with a tight smile before he headed off. Cassius rested his elbows on the red leather arms of his chair and took a deep breath.

"Okay, the story. You know this club is being sued for systematically allowing the sexual harassment of staff by both other staff and patrons?"

My spine straightened. I wanted to be intrigued but the story had been done. Was there something else to it? Maybe he was just chatting.

"Yes, I remember the headlines. Awful. Is it true that staff here are all called Henry, regardless of their sex or real names?"

He nodded. "Tells you everything you need to know about this place. The club must have hired a crisis management firm, because we all received a letter saying the club obtained a unanimous vote to allow women to join. But I know it's far from unanimous. They haven't even got a majority, and I have copies of some very ripe letters from the members here to show it."

What? He had proof? My pulse thrummed in my ears, and I leaned forward, eager. This seemed like a juicy story. In the car, I did wonder why he hadn't opted to tell me this over the phone, especially as he was consumed by work. But I always preferred to meet contacts in person because you formed much closer bonds and got a chance to observe their demeanor when they parted with information.

After reaching into his briefcase, he pulled out a folder and handed it to me. I opened it. The pages were loose. The top page was the results of a survey on whether the club should allow women to join. Only thirty percent agreed. The hair on the back of my neck stood up. Oh my God, this was a great story. The rest of the papers were letters from members protesting the decision. I quickly skimmed them.

> *Hell will freeze over before I allow women in these rooms. Of course, women have their place, but not in a private club contributing to important discussions of state. Women are patently unable to have the sort of discussions about politics and business we partake in at the club. We go to our club to relax—how is that possible if the men are peacocking for the women's attention? Because that is women's only role. Our club*

is a refuge from the vulgarity of the world, which, of course, includes women.

This was a Social Diary story. A great one. It was not the big crime story I needed to successfully compete with Sooz, but the letters were written by men from a variety of occupations, including politicians and captains of industry, and it would hold the attention of my editor for a short while. "These are … God, I can't think of a word."

"*Revolting* might be a start." His upper lip curled disgustedly as he eyed the clutch of papers in my hand. I'd suspected on meeting him yesterday that he was pandering to me, downplaying his title and position, even embarrassed by it. I questioned that now. Tonight, he seemed genuinely appalled by these letters. But why was he willing to share with me? Why *me*? He must have loads of contacts at other newspapers, ones who were of the same political persuasion as himself. "Put them in your handbag."

I slid them into my handbag and anxiously checked around to see if anyone was watching or trying to listen in. No one was obviously doing this, but I was clearly more worried about the prospect than Cassius.

"This is a great story for the Diary pages tomorrow—thank you," I said.

He smiled slightly as he raked through his thick mane of black hair and brushed something off his jacket, unruffled and confident. Not even a hint of concern that his name would be mud with the men in this room he'd grown up with and with whom he presumably surrounded himself. I felt like my eyes were popping out of my head with incredulity.

"What?" He smiled a little, his amused eyes catching mine.

"Aren't you worried that when everyone reads the story in our Diary pages tomorrow, they'll remember you handed me some papers at the club? Won't you be in huge trouble?"

He grimaced and gave a lazy shrug. "Who cares if they kick me out? I'm happy never to return. I can't remember the last time I was here anyway."

Was he just saying that? Because the constant greetings since we got here indicated the opposite. "But so many people here know you. Pretty much everyone who's passed this table."

"Yes, because I'm a duke, and they're all sycophants who support the status quo."

He seemed to hate them all, and yet Declan saw Cassius as a titled prick who used his position to bully him. I took Cassius in, carefully cataloging his face and his expressions. Was he putting on an act for me? Did I need to get to the bottom of this contradiction? For a second, I was annoyed at myself for always wanting to dig deeper, which invariably led to untold complications. Why couldn't I just make life easier on myself—just take this story and run?

His lips quirked up. "This is why I like you. You remind me of my sister. You're honest, almost guileless. It's hard for you to hide your feelings. I'm aware you are skeptical of me, that you want to dislike me."

Shit. My heart sank. I wasn't doing a very good job of covering my emotions. I thought about contradicting him, but he'd just said he appreciated that I was honest. "Well, I have heard, um, reports."

He glowered with anger and slapped his hands on the armrest. "That I'm an arsehole? Yes, probably, when I need to be. Should I pretend I'm misunderstood? Fuck that."

His show of emotion sent a shudder of fear through me. Those flashing eyes and huge body tensed with rage were intimidating. But I willed myself not to show it. "You are honest too."

Visibly shaking himself, he went back to his watchful intensity, seeming annoyed by his temporary loss of cool.

"Sorry, not having a go at you," he said. But I noticed his hands gripped the chair hard. "I admire how you're prodding me, not letting me get away with anything. You're not just ingratiating yourself to me for the sake of a story. I like that."

The firelight flickered on his face as he served me one of his smoldering looks.

Beneath his steady gaze, I squirmed in my seat, self-conscious. Primly, I stilled my hands in my lap, not knowing what to say that didn't seem like I was responding.

My forehead felt damp with sweat, and I wasn't sure if it was the meds. The truth was that now I was in his debt. He might ask for something sooner or later. Sometimes, there was a little give and take, but I didn't want to feel he'd ask for something I was unwilling to give.

"That's good you like my interviewing technique," I said. "Because I do need to know—what's your motivation in giving me these papers?"

His demeanor changed, and he seemed guarded, his shoulders high, his elbows close to his side. "Don't some of your sources love the power of seeing their tip-offs published?"

"Yes, of course. But you have power already. Gobs of it."

His black brows shot up, and I thought he was going to castigate me for that. Instead, he gave a huge laugh, flashing his white, even teeth. I relaxed just for a second. It was hard to predict his reactions, but it was definitely better if I was honest with him about my reactions—that seemed to go down well.

"I've followed you for years," he said. "I trust you. And this lot"—he nodded around us, ignoring jaunty waves from every direction—"deserve their comeuppance. Every one of them reminds me of my father."

"That's a bad thing?" He seemed to want revenge for his father's treatment of him and his sister. It wasn't the worst motivation I'd ever heard, and at least I knew where he was coming from. He hadn't given me this story because he was worried about the staff or trying to right the wrongs of their admittance practices. It was more about exposing the men for the entitled women-haters they were.

His lips curled, sour. "It's not a good thing. A violent drunk when with his family behind the doors of his castle. But utterly charming when surrounded by his chums, and I'd outshot everyone. Which is why I became so good at all that hunting and fishing nonsense. To get his approval."

Was he sincere? He seemed tortured by this. As though he wanted me to understand him. Like he knew what Declan had said about him and he wanted to change my mind. But why? He must know I was going to write up this story.

"I'm sorry, that sounds so rough."

He ran a finger across his forehead. "It was."

"Did you have anyone who had your back?"

Happiness flickered in his dark eyes, and his lips turned up slightly at the corners. "Yes. My sister."

"Sister Modestia? Sounds like she meant a lot to you."

"Bea. Her name was Beatrice." His eyes pooled and he appeared on the verge of tears. "Yes, it's been a nightmare. We were very close. I loved her." His statement was so simple it was touching. His eyes went glassy. "She was a sister and a mother to me, brought me up. My mother was so terrified of my father that she just hid away and became very depressed. I was devastated when Bea went into the order because it meant I couldn't see her. I'd always imagined we'd live happily together at Tewksbury. When she told me she was going in, I even offered her the chance to start her own order in the east wing, plenty of rooms and a private garden. But she didn't like the idea. She was very independent and didn't want to be tied to the family inheritance, and I admired her for that, but I just wanted her to be around. It was a huge hole in my life when she left."

He appeared bitter and terribly sad, as if she was the only one he'd ever loved, and she'd left him. I took a second to process what he'd said, checking in with my first reaction. This was a part of our conversation where I didn't question his emotions. He deeply and genuinely seemed to care for his sister and made it clear she had been his lifeline.

"That must have been so hard," I said. "In a way, you lost her twice."

He jerked back in his chair. Had I said the wrong thing? But then he clasped his hands together, as if in prayer. He sat there like that for some time. I stared back at him, fidgeting, worried. Did what I say make him sadder, or did it explain his grief? He looked at me almost reverentially, as though I had such insight into him.

"Yes, yes, you're absolutely right," he said slowly. "I hadn't thought of it like that."

He leaned over the table toward me. "Look, I wonder if you can help me?"

CHAPTER TWENTY

OH SHIT. WAS this it? What he wants from me in return?

He tapped the table in front of him. "I think there was something going on in the convent that my sister couldn't tell me about."

I jolted inside and sat up straight. Had I given myself away? I didn't have a poker face. That did feed into what I'd seen: the nuns who didn't look like nuns, the strange comings and goings. Amid the clatter of cutlery and hum of conversation and waiters sweeping quietly across the room, arms loaded with plates of food, a side window of light beamed into my head. Was it possible that his sister was killed because of what Cassius suspected about the convent?

"What do you think is going on?" I asked.

"I don't know. It's just … my sister started clamming up on me when I went shopping with her. She seemed frightened of something or someone. And I think you suspect it too." He watched my face closely, but I didn't answer him because I wanted to hear what he knew and thought first before I gave away any information. "I've tried so many ways to talk to Mother Superior or any of the nuns. I can't even stay in one of their guest rooms to try and make contact. I noticed the day we met that you seemed to have some sort of connection with Sister Innocenta."

My skin crawled. Evidence he was watching me closely. There was scarce interaction between me and the Sister, and yet he'd detected what little there was.

"If you talk to her, could you let me know what she says? I try to help her with the shopping, but I can't go tomorrow." He seemed to be saying I should go. That was something I was considering anyway. I'd nearly given up, but now I had a refreshed determination to connect with her. At the same time, I didn't want him or anyone else to feel I was working with him or was linked to him. Not until I felt I could trust him fully. I was still wary of him, and I wasn't sure what it would take before I wasn't.

I nodded, not wanting to tip my hand by admitting I was investigating the convent. But I had to give him something.

"If I talk to her, I'll let you know," I said. "Also—I hope you don't mind me asking— when is your sister's funeral?"

His face turned genuinely angry and hurt. "I have no idea. The convent oversees all that." He sucked in a shaky breath. "I imagine I won't even be permitted to attend."

"Oh, that's awful. I'm so sorry; that just doesn't seem fair. I assumed the funeral would be at your place, and she would be … buried there."

His face fell into his hands, seeming overcome by the mention of a burial at his castle.

"I'm sorry," I said. "I've overstepped."

"It's okay." He raised his head to me. "I guess you're used to doing that in your job. Makes you a good journalist."

I swirled my tonic glass, willing the ice to melt so I had something to drink.

"Also, I have an invitation for you." He reached into his jacket pocket and pulled out a white envelope. "To my masked ball. I hope you can make it."

I opened the invitation and gazed at the beautiful card, tracing the embossed script with my fingers. I was taken aback, honored and flattered all at once. "Oh, thank you. Wow. It looks wonderful."

Then I checked the date. Saturday. It was Thursday today, which only left two days to find a dress. But that wasn't the problem.

The problem was that the drugs arrived at Tilbury Port in Essex on Sunday at three in the morning. I'd have to leave the ball about midnight to ensure I got to the port on time. That was doable, but I would have to carry a change of clothes and allow time to call an Uber. It was *a lot* of travel in one night. What did I think I could gain by going to the ball? That I might see something that gave me insight into Sister Modestia? Although, why would I? Sister Modestia hadn't lived at the castle since she entered the convent, and I wasn't sure if that was in her twenties or later. Still, Cassius was her brother, and I couldn't pass up an opportunity to understand him better.

I read the invitation properly: *The Duke of Cheltenham requests the pleasure of Ms. Isla Joyson and guest at the 40th annual Masked Ball at Tewksbury Castle, Gloucestershire. Dress: Black Tie.*

My name had been handwritten. He knew Declan and I were together, so why hadn't he included his name?

I tapped the card. "Someone has beautiful handwriting."

His lips quirked. "Ah, that's what she focuses on. Yes, my penmanship was exactly what I was hoping to impress you with," he drawled with a smile.

I wanted to make things clear between us. I worried that I may have given him the wrong idea. With a pang, I remembered the devastated look on Declan's face when I had left him on the sidewalk. And the way Cassius had rubbed it in.

"As you know, I have a boyfriend, so I'll bring him."

He shrugged. "It says 'and guest' on your invitation."

"How many people have you invited?"

"Five hundred, give or take."

"Bloody hell." I was gobsmacked by the numbers. I wasn't even acquainted with that many people, let alone have the first clue how to entertain and feed them or have the funds to finance such an evening. Pressing my lips, I held back a burst of laughter at one memory this prompted for me. Seven months ago, the morning after I met Declan, I didn't want to go to breakfast with him in case I got stuck with the bill. Financially, things had vastly improved with me, but this showed how many worlds apart I was from Cassius. He had a big life. Huge.

"How on earth do you cater for all those people?" I asked.

"Our cook is bloody amazing. He's done it every year for the four decades he's been with us, and his father before him. So he has it down pat. Well, *had.* Would you believe he's gone AWOL? Family stuff, I hear. Or maybe he's been taking nips of the cooking sherry, hard to know. So it's a new cook, cross fingers."

He nodded at a waiter standing in the corner. "Speaking of, shall we order dinner? They do an amazing steak and frites. Most of the rest is tarted-up nursery food, but it's still good."

"Thank you, but I need to get back to the office to write this up."

His face fell, his forehead creased. Worry clenched my stomach tight. Was I offending him by leaving? Maybe I should have stayed for dinner. Shoot, I'd messed this up. He could see my reaction as dismissive of him. He could make a fuss, ask for the papers back, and give the story to someone else.

"You're very professional. Work always comes first." He held out his hands as if framing my face. "Just means I picked the right person. Well, I'll just have to try and come up with another story, won't I?"

I would have worried if he'd added something like "and you'll definitely be having dinner with me next time." But he seemed mellow about it. Relieved, I gazed around and tried to soak up everything about the place without taking notes—roaring fireplaces topped with silver candlesticks and ancient leather furniture. The room folded around me like a stupefyingly soothing nightfall, with dark walls in hunter's green, midnight blue, and even a hideous brown that somehow worked.

I sneaked a look back at Cassius. He seemed different from the man Declan had described. Vulnerable and lonely and, by his reckoning, quite alone, considering his status. Why? Surely loads of women were interested in him? He was quite a romantic figure, sort of a large, brooding beast lost in his castle. Running a castle didn't interest me in the slightest—unless it involved lounging around a pool all day or wafting through the flowery meadows in a diaphanous dress, which I was pretty sure it didn't—but I was certain some women might like it or were even born to it. I didn't feel like he was bullying me or pressuring me, though his confidence was something I'd rarely witnessed, even in business leaders. And his moods changed very quickly. Did Declan have him wrong in any way? But I respected Declan's judgment. I couldn't trust Cassius yet, especially as the Russian man had repeatedly mentioned him: "Your brother."

"Feel free to text me if you need color." His lips turned up at the corners. "I think that's what you journos call it?"

"Thank you." I quirked my head. "By the way, I was wondering how you got my personal number?"

He put a finger to his lips. "*Did* I call your personal number? Hmm. I hadn't realized that. Apologies if that was a bit disturbing. You know, I can't remember how I got it. I've had it for a long time. Now I wish I'd called you earlier."

He'd had my number for a long time? That shouldn't be a surprise, as he had good contacts. Should that worry me, though? Tilting his head, his gaze ensnared mine, and he pushed out his lips slightly. *The smolder.* I couldn't mistake it this time. I pretended I didn't notice. I didn't want to take him seriously. I thought about having a giggle over this with Tabitha or Shay. Or my new friend Sunny.

He'd toed a fine line. His last comment was slightly suggestive but not inappropriate, which would have made me dislike him, especially after leaving Declan alone on the footpath.

Declan. I stood up, ready to go, and pulled my handbag over my shoulder, which was sore and tight. What had happened outside the office dragged a dark cloud over my excitement in getting this story. I needed to make things right with Declan. But I couldn't go to him now. I had a story to write.

CHAPTER TWENTY-ONE

"LOVE IT, ISLA, cracking story," the night editor said, back at the office. "Well done, you. Get a comment from the club ASAP. If everyone's left, we've probably got some home numbers. We want this ready to go first thing tomorrow morning. A perfect Friday story to get them talking."

There was no bigger thrill than to tell your story to your boss and watch them light up and give you their complete attention. To see her tell the picture desk and the subeditors who would write the headline and design the page, and have them turn to you, grinning, with a thumbs-up. In some ways, it was even more exciting than seeing it published in the newspaper the next day.

I moved to my desk.

Me: *I'm at work. I want to talk, but I have a story to write up and I'll be here past midnight. I'll see you tomorrow night after you pick up Sephy?*

Declan: *OK.*

Shortest reply he'd ever sent me.

CHAPTER TWENTY-TWO

IT WAS ONE in the morning when I turned the key to my basement flat. *What was that sound?* Couldn't be Teddy as he was at Fleur's.

My heart pounded in my throat. I'd been chased one night ago, so I was still on guard and twitchy. Our stairwell housed the rubbish bins. Was someone hiding in there? Taking a huge breath, I flung open the door to the rubbish bin enclosure. The light flicked on. Nothing. From above, a scooter whizzed by. Ah, that was what it was.

As I stepped over the threshold, a deep relief washed over me, then foolishness for being concerned. But wasn't my reaction normal under the circumstances? I swayed, not knowing what I should think anymore. I had to get to bed. I couldn't trust my judgment. My throat was feeling sore again, my wound ached, and I was exhausted from a long night working. I should focus on a sense of satisfaction that I'd written the story.

It was completely dark in my kitchen-cum-living room.

The air felt different.

Disturbed.

My feet froze to the ground.

Someone was in here.

Was it the man who'd chased me? My pulse pumped into a hysterical scream. How did he get in? Of course he could get in—he seemed like a professional.

My eyes adjusted to the darkness. I could make out a shape on my sofa. Sweat slid down my spine. I grabbed the doorknob to make a quick getaway. Dug in my handbag for my phone.

Then, the shape moved. *Get out of here, Isla. Go, go, go.*

My whole body trembling, I squeezed the door handle to leave.

I hit the light.

Declan unwound himself groggily. "Oh. I fell asleep."

"Shit, shit, shit, Declan. You gave me such a bloody fright." I pressed a hand to my thumping chest.

He sat up, blinking. "Oh, I'm sorry. I should have left a light on."

"Oh my God." I bent over, sucking in air, trying to get my breath back. "My heart. How long have you been here?"

"I don't know." He peered at me. "I was waiting up for you."

I stepped in front of him. Black shadows darkened his eyes, and his limbs moved slowly. He looked so tired and sad and it tore at my heart that I'd caused him this grief.

Breathing deeply, I readied myself to change tack. "Declan, I'm so sorry about what happened tonight, but—" I felt awful about leaving him on the footpath like that. I'd do anything to make it up to him. My phone buzzed. Despite my exhaustion, the sound jolted something. "Why didn't you text first to tell me you were coming?"

He bit the inside of his mouth. No answer.

That tripped my fuse. "Were you expecting to catch me out or something?" I demanded, angry.

"Well …"

"You *were,*" I said, furious. "You were expecting me to walk in with someone. Not just someone. Cassius." I dropped my handbag on the floor. "Honestly, how could you think that of me?"

Startled, he shifted back in his seat. He threw up his arms in frustration. "What do you expect?" He glared at me. "Last time I saw you, you were with him. And you had many opportunities during the day to tell me you two were meeting. You know how I feel about him."

I was offended that he didn't trust me. But still, I knew I hadn't been fully honest with him. I didn't have the moral high ground here.

"He gave me a good story tonight." My chin tipped up, my voice challenging.

"About a crime?"

I hesitated, defensive now. "A Diary story, not my beat. But it was a good one."

He twisted his lips. "Hmm. He gave you a story over drinks and dinner."

"I didn't drink, and I refused dinner. Even if he hadn't promised me a story, I still would have met him because he's the brother of Sister Modestia."

He eyed me, his face drawn and on edge.

"Besides the fact that you didn't tell me about going out with him, do you know how this looks? He is opposing my bill." He shot me a fiery gaze. "Not just opposing it, he's trashing it. He's trashing me and everyone who stands with me as weak and without substance, pandering to addicts. And you are seen going out with him on what looks very much like a date. It's just … humiliating."

My face and shoulders crumpled at his obvious anguish. I took a few seconds to think through what he'd said. Cassius was destroying Declan's new role and his reputation. Declan had just started this new direction in his career, and besides his impressive past in drug enforcement, his reputation was what sparked and fueled his fledgling relationships within Parliament. Those new connections were the key to gaining support for his bill. And I'd dented his pride by seeming to cozy up to his enemy, even though I knew that was furthest from the truth. But I hadn't told him about meeting Cassius, which made it seem like it could be true. I hadn't thought of my actions in that way—he'd changed my perspective.

I collapsed on the sofa beside him, keeping a distance because I sensed we had to talk about this without me trying to distract him.

"I'm sorry." I was, deeply. I clenched my teeth. I knew I shouldn't try to make *It could have been worse* excuses, but I couldn't help myself. "But no one saw. Well. None of your work colleagues know."

He leveled me with a look. "Isla. Half your newspaper staff was standing there. People who are literally paid to disseminate shit they'd just seen."

My hand flew to my mouth apologetically, as if trying to take back what I'd said. He was right. It couldn't have happened in front of a worse group of people. "Declan, honestly, when I saw you coming around that corner, I felt sick."

He gave a grunt of derision.

"That came out wrong." I backpedaled furiously. "I meant, because I knew what it looked like. And I would have given anything to replay that, and it just be the two of us." I sought out his eyes, craving any softening or understanding. "Any other day, I would have loved you to surprise me after work."

But he just closed his eyes and let his head drop against the back of the sofa. "God. You did all this for a Social Diary story."

That irked me. "A *great* Diary story. It keeps my name out there for readers who are thinking of calling in." I leaned forward. "I should have told you. I know you don't like him, and for good reason, but I think he might know something about the convent."

His hard gaze flicked back to me. "Did he try anything?"

"No, nothing, not even a hint of it. In fact, he said I reminded him of his sister. Who was, as we know, a nun. Those are *not* the words of someone who fancies me."

Declan dipped his chin, patently not convinced. He went quiet for a while.

"Much as I loathe to admit it, there's something he sees in you that I can see too."

That didn't sound good. "What do you mean?" I asked cautiously.

"I wonder if I can offer you what you need. Sometimes it feels like you're heading for a much bigger life."

A coil of shock wound through me. I'd never heard him admit to feeling inadequate before. He always seemed quietly confident, like he was who he wanted to be, and where he wanted to be. I went to object, but he used his usual hand motion to indicate that he wanted to explain more.

"Since I handed in my notice, I've been content being home. But it's unlikely I'll ever make much more money than I do. Unless I win the lottery, I'll be staying in my little house, and I won't be able to afford luxury holidays. I'm happy with my life. Really happy since I met you. And since Sephy came home, even though I know she's been a lot. But I wonder if I can offer you enough?"

My shock was cut with confusion. We'd fought about my job and how he wanted to keep us all safe. But this was about me wanting more than him, more money, more things, a more affluent lifestyle. My head was swamped, bewildered. Was this how I came off? I searched my memory for times when I'd whined about wanting any of these things, been bratty or grasping. But no, I couldn't think of a single instance. It was like he was talking about a different person. My confusion slowly cooled to dread. Was he saying we weren't essentially compatible? That we weren't going to make it? This seemed huge and scary, a pivotal moment for us.

My gaze roamed his face, searching for his meaning. "God, Declan, I don't know where this is coming from. I've never been about money. I don't know how you can think that about me. I wouldn't have gone into journalism if I'd cared about it. And I love your house. I mean, look at me; I'm still renting a tiny basement flat. You own your own place—you're way ahead of me. You've got your shit together, and you know what you want. I love that about you."

He turned his head against the sofa and gave me a small smile. "I haven't explained myself properly. It's not just the money. It's that Cassius can imagine you in his castle. I can see it in his face. Only so many people could do that life."

Shivering at the thought, I screwed up my nose. "I don't want that sort of status. God, I couldn't think of anything worse than living in a castle, having staff, being a hostess. I don't even love the lack of privacy that comes with being on the side of a bus, so I can't imagine having to greet five hundred people in one night."

He looked puzzled, probably at my mention of such a specific number.

I pulled the masked ball invitation out of my bag and handed it to him.

"Look, he invited us to his ball this weekend." I gave a disdainful shrug. "Short notice, I know, but let's go. Fuck him." Despite my fake swagger, I clenched my fists at my side, imagining Declan's reaction when the truth came out. I knew I wasn't suggesting this so Declan and I could have a good time, but because I needed to snoop inside Cassius's castle to find out why he wanted to get inside the convent, why he wanted that frieze, and if in any way he could be linked to his sister's death. It was ultimately for a story. And, as if reminding me of all my half lies, my already sore throat felt like I'd swallowed a grater. But telling him would provoke another argument. This was the last time I'd keep something from him. I just needed to do this.

"*And guest*," he spat out. "He hasn't invited me by name, arsehole." He tapped the invitation. "Fuck, and look, it's Saturday. I have a big meeting that afternoon—and it's definitely going to go on until at least eight. It's a two-hour drive to his castle, minimum. He knows I won't be there until very late. Maybe too late to even consider it." He rattled the invitation and pressed the edge into his furrowed brow, once, twice, three times, as if something occurred to him. He took a beat. "Shit. Now I'm wondering if he set up my meeting—it's with a couple of friends of his." He stared at me. "Is that too Machiavellian, even for him?"

A sinister chill crept up my arms. If Cassius *had* set this up, then having that premeditation, reach, and influence made me more frightened of him. But that fear also made me more determined to investigate, more intent to keep going, because it hinted at his ability to organize or be involved in something with dark and desperate motivations.

"Okay, so he's an arsehole," I said. "Come late, then. We'll present a solid front." I knelt in front of him, my hands on his knees. "A *dazzlingly* solid front. I think it will show your convictions. That you can deal with your enemies. Isn't that the strongest political position there is?"

That made him smile. "Okay, Churchill." He sighed. "Isla, as usual, you're just diverting my attention. A ball isn't going to resolve these issues we're having."

Issues? That sounded a little more official and serious than the way I'd describe it. As if undermining my slightly delusional under-the-carpet sweeping, my throat seared with an even sharper pain, reminding me of everything I hadn't told him. I cleared it, trying to ensure there was no scratchiness in my voice.

"But it's a *masked* ball." I shimmied my shoulders a little at him. "Which means you can bring your tux out of the back of the wardrobe."

"Again, I know what you're doing, Isla," he deadpanned. He went quiet for a minute. His lips tilted into a spine-tingling smile.

"That means you'll be in a mask too. Come here." He pulled me onto his lap with a growl. "I like the sound of that."

That gave me an idea. I didn't know if Cassius was involved in anything I was investigating, but I needed to use this as an opportunity to look around the castle. As well as wearing a mask, maybe I should hide my hair too? If anything like five hundred people were turning up, I had to have an anonymous appearance to mingle unnoticed.

"What will you wear?" he asked. Yes, he might be coming around.

"Shockingly, I haven't anything remotely suitable for a ball."

"Cinderella, get that fairy godmother and those little mice to start making your frock."

Mice, ugh. That reminded me of the rat that bit me. If it was a rat. My upper thigh throbbed harder at the memory, and I ran my hand over it. My face flushed at the thought that I hadn't told Declan about the whole incident. This was exactly what he was reminding me about. I would tell him, but it had to be another time. Tomorrow. The bite meant I definitely couldn't wear anything too short if I still had this ugly bandage on. The wound ached still. I wondered whether that was normal.

"Hey, let me buy you something," he said. "C'mon, we'll go shopping Saturday morning, take Sephy too. She'll be into it. If we are going to do this, let's dazzle them, like you say."

Usually, I would have loved the sound of that. But I needed to wear something where I could slip into rooms without being noticed. I'd order something ordinary first thing this morning.

He was insistent.

"I want to show Cassius what he can never have." His voice was steely and unapologetic, and his penetrating gaze sent flutters through my belly.

"Mmm, that's kind of hot." Surprised by my reaction to his possessiveness, I kissed him. He didn't deepen the kiss as he normally did, as if he'd used up all his energy for one night.

Me too. I fell against him. He put a hand on the back of my head and grunted but then went still. We were both so tired we didn't even have to discuss going straight to bed. He used the bathroom first, muttering something about so much medicine on the counter, and I muttered back about stocking up. Even through my weariness, I felt a sharp, bracing bash of reproach. I was still lying to him, and it tarnished all our moments together. But another disagreement would make things worse. He took off his clothes and rolled into bed.

I took my many medications and the pill, stuffed the meds into the cupboard, and switched out the bandage for a large Band-Aid, hoping the wound didn't start bleeding again. I normally slept naked, and wearing pajamas would be more suspicious. I slid into bed, a hand over the huge Band-Aid. He snuggled in close, his arm around my waist, oblivious to the bite. These small deceptions would end soon. I would tell him everything. That would be the last time I held anything back. I just needed more time. Calm washed over me at the relief I would feel. But right now, it was necessary.

CHAPTER TWENTY-THREE

WHEN I WOKE the next morning, Declan had already left to drive the six hours to pick up Sephy and bring her home. Sephy. I smiled. Surprise skipped through me that I was excited to see her and hear about her trip. I'd missed her.

Yesterday, my new contact at Sotheby's said she only had half an hour but was happy to meet at eight in the morning before her client meetings. That suited me, too, because I wanted to make sure I got to the convent by nine to try to catch Sister Innocenta leaving for the day's shopping. I knew I was being too hopeful about what this meeting would yield and tried to temper my enthusiasm. The truth was, I was hoping her analysis of the frieze would shed light on the rest of this story—Sister Modestia's death, why Cassius wanted the frieze so badly, and what the convent was hiding. That was way too much to expect of half an hour with a new contact.

I took all my medicine and gargled with the antiseptic the doctor had given me. My throat felt slightly better. But the bite was still sore, and when I switched out the Band-Aid for a bandage and cleaned it, it looked goopy and horrible. *Yuck.* Maybe it had gone septic? I had work to do today. It would have to be this evening. I made an appointment at an emergency clinic which had later hours.

I walked back into the bedroom to a barrage of pings. Uh-oh. I steeled myself for complaints about my Toff's story. My mind raced through what I might have done wrong. Names, dates? Couldn't be—I'd checked every word, which was double-checked by sub-editors. Was *all* of it wrong? Had Cassius or someone else falsified the papers? But we'd gotten a quote from the club. Not admitting it outright, but saying they were "concerned and reviewing the information." Which usually meant it was correct and heads were going to roll.

Reading my phone, I was greeted by a flurry of congratulations from colleagues and what we called a "herogram" from my editor. What on earth had happened? Between me filing the story and the newspaper edition coming out, clearly something extraordinary. This wasn't the normal response from my editor to a Diary story.

I pulled up the newspaper on my app. Oh my God. I gasped, and a rush of excitement brightened every part of me. My story was first on the front page, with a double-page spread inside. I guess I had underestimated the power of having your preconceptions about titled, powerful, and wealthy men confirmed. I scrolled down to the bottom. Already it had thousands of shares and five hundred comments. Furious, scathing remarks about the club and its members. A few "What's wrong with it, women have clubs too?" and "I belong to that club, and I have nothing against women, so don't put me in the same category" comments were beset by more vitriol.

The most comments I'd ever gotten on a story, let alone at this time of the day when the paper was just out. Despite how late I'd gone to sleep, I bounced around the room while I dressed to meet my contact.

I read the story again and hugged myself with glee. Amid my joy, icy tendrils of a new awareness laced eerily through me. This meant I owed Cassius. Big time.

CHAPTER TWENTY-FOUR

AT SOTHEBY'S, TABITHA'S art dealer friend greeted me in reception with a stiff handshake and a frosty face.

Oh no, what have I done?

Ishani Ali was my new contact, and I'd already pissed her off. Silent, she led me to her office, swishing elegantly in silk neutrals. I looked horribly out of place in clashing pink and orange—was that the problem?

Seated, she planted her palms on her shiny black desk. "Firstly, like most of London, I've seen your front-page story. Please tell me you're not doing an exposé on Sotheby's?"

Oh, I see. That explained her iciness.

"No, no, gosh, I never even thought about it." I hadn't. I was genuinely surprised to hear her suggest it. Though Sotheby's in New Bond Street was considered elite, dealing in art worth hundreds of millions, I wouldn't have put it in the same category as Toff's Club.

A sigh of relief escaped her red lips, and she smoothed her black hair, which she wore in a sophisticated bun. "Okay, but you cannot quote me or record me or rely on anything I'm about to say. I'm doing this as a favor to Tabitha, and she has vouched for you. Also, I don't want to know which convent your inquiry concerns, although I am very aware there is one only five blocks from here. As

I told Tabs, this is a stab in the dark. I need plausible deniability if this goes pear-shaped."

"I completely understand, and I respect everything you're saying. And yes, I would like this meeting to be confidential on both our parts. Please don't tell anyone I've met with you." This wasn't to build a rapport with her. If Cassius found out I was investigating further, he might completely shut me out. The nuns already seemed to have done that.

She glanced around her office, the dark furniture interrupted only by red peonies. "As long as you are not undertaking anything illegal, I can maintain confidentiality."

"I know too little about art to undertake anything illegal."

She gave a rueful laugh. "You'd be surprised."

My senses tingled. A hint of another story perhaps, but this wasn't the time to press.

"I can't offer any opinion about the black market for martyrs' remains if you've come about that?" she said.

I must have looked puzzled.

"The bones of the martyrs who lie in the convent's crypt?" she said.

Understanding dawned. "No, this is about a wall."

Though she'd clearly researched the convent, I gave the age of the frieze, built at least in 1903—or possibly earlier if it wasn't built on-site—as well as the dimensions, a description of its erotic theme, and how someone had offered to pay half a million for it if they could remove it under their own supervision.

"I need a photo of it." She raised an eyebrow. "Could that be arranged?"

"I will try." Maybe I could sneak in, pretending to make a delivery. That would involve a wig, a work uniform or overalls, and something to deliver. Doable, but to photograph the frieze, I'd need to deliver to the back door, which might make them immediately wary. Especially if the bearded guy loading the women into his truck was the one who opened the door to me. My best hope was Sister Innocenta, whom I hoped to see after this meeting. "But it's a contemplative order who don't welcome visitors except in rooms off to the side, so I'm not sure how quickly I can do that."

She rolled the fine gold chains around her neck. Now, she was starting to appear intrigued, her frostiness melting. "Okay, give me a minute," she said.

Silent, I watched her reactions closely as she flicked through a book on Grecian friezes and another on religious icons in London. I took in her office more closely for clues to her personality. Her desk was clear except for a black landline. She'd probably slid her laptop into a drawer to protect the identity of her clients. As I brushed lint off my now garish-looking trousers, I realized that despite her daunting chicness, she was consumed by the pages of her books—a nerd, albeit a fine art nerd.

She thumbed through a book on London's lost treasures. How fascinating. I made a mental note of the book. This would make another good article for the weekend magazine, something light and yet intriguing. It interested me, too, to see that she was consulting physical books rather than searching online.

"The wall and its frieze are huge, so likely they were made when the convent was built. Did you see any seams in it?"

I stared at the lamp illuminating her, trying to picture the wall. "I don't think so, though it was nighttime, and I'm hardly an expert, and I wasn't looking for any."

She frowned as if frustrated. "If it wasn't carved by someone important, why would they go to the trouble of hauling each piece through the door in order to put it together? Especially if it was so patently unsuitable for a convent."

I shook my head, stumped. "Yes, that's something I can't get my head around."

She glanced at her book. "But the same is true even if it was sculpted on-site by a nobody. Why create such a scene so out of sync with its surroundings?"

I sighed inwardly. More questions that neither of us could answer. I had to get something concrete from this to give me a chance to move forward. "How long would it have taken someone to sculpt?"

"A stone frieze, about fifty feet by twenty feet? One person, at the time the convent was built, might have taken a year or so. A team of say, ten, might take a month. But I can't think of an important artist of the Edwardian Era who carved scenes like that. That's if"—she raised a cautionary finger—"it was carved during that time."

"So you're saying it's probably not valuable."

She gave me an apologetic smile. It seemed as though she was starting to warm to me, and she was invested and wanted to help. "I can't see how it is."

"And yet it's such a huge thing to install in a convent or have commissioned. A massive undertaking, and it's not a tribute to God by any means. What do you reckon? Why was it installed?"

She tapped an immaculate red nail against her lips. Standing, she moved closer to me in her elegant silk pant-and-shirt set, which would have looked like pjs on me, and propped a hip on her desk. "We must use our imaginations." Her lips parted in a proper grin. One of her gray stilettos swung from her upturned toes. Her guard was down, and she seemed more my age.

"If the surface is not worth a lot of money, is there something inside that is valuable?" I suggested.

Ishani leaned toward me and grinned. "Ha. That reminds me of your story about the case in New Zealand. One anonymous person was willing to pay too much money for a run-down campground."

"Yes. We started to wonder if something valuable was either over the top, around or under it, like water rights, where its value would escalate."

She tapped her fingernails on her desk. "That was tragic. I'm so sorry about your friends, both of them."

"Yes, it was horrible." Even now, my eyes blurred with the memories of my best friend's death and the further tragedy that unraveled because of the cover-up. I paused and took a breath, regrouping before directing the conversation back to the case at hand. "So, are there diamonds or gold inside? Or underneath? But why create such a vast frieze? Couldn't you just stuff those diamonds or gold in a small art piece? And where exactly in the frieze are they?"

"Or it could contain a very valuable artwork. But how do we know where to start cutting into it?"

"Maybe there's a map or directive in the convent that indicates where the hidden treasure is."

"Or a riddle or a line in one of the books." Excited, she tucked a strand of hair behind her ear. It seemed she was beginning to enjoy herself. "For example, the treasure could be in a place least expected, like"—she threw up her hands—"behind one of the men's scrotum."

I burst out laughing.

She smiled. "You'd be amazed how often I have to use that word in my job."

I giggled some more. I pictured the wall and tried to count how many scrotums I saw. Best not repeat that, as we'd only just met.

She shoved her taupe sleeves up her arms. "Maybe this frieze is a result of someone with a very good sense of humor. We can't assume nuns in 1903 didn't like to have a good laugh. People always think of the religious as dour, but some of the ones I've met have been very silly and funny."

I liked that she was thinking of all possibilities, but I couldn't picture any of the nuns I'd met as silly or funny. Mind you, I'd met them in tense circumstances.

"But then this riddle must have been passed down through each generation of nuns. Where would we—I—even start to look?"

She shrugged. "I'm stumped. I'll do some more research on the scene depicted on the frieze, but I need a picture. I also need to know what the stone is. I wonder if any of the other members of the order around the world have this same frieze?"

"That's a good idea. I'll look into that. The nuns need money to make repairs to the convent. Apparently, they are quite desperate. If the wall contained something precious, surely they'd have taken a hammer to it by now? Because if there is a riddle or a map, then it must have been handed down to one of the current nuns. One of them must know where this treasure is."

Her desk phone buzzed. "Ms. Ali, His Grace is here." It was the voice of the receptionist.

His Grace.

My heart knocked hard against my ribs. Oh God. It couldn't be. There were only twenty-seven dukes in Great Britain.

It might be.

I had to get out of here. Now.

Ishani stabbed at a key to take the phone off speaker—she must have left it on accidentally—and picked up the handset.

"Just finishing up," she said. "I'll come and get him."

Sirens went off in my head. He couldn't find me here. How the hell would I explain it? I couldn't. He'd just mentioned the frieze to me and I'd pretended not to know what he was talking about. He clearly knew what Ishani did, so he would assume I must be inquiring about a statue or a frieze. He would know I suspected something about the frieze and therefore about him. He would cut me off. Maybe try to do what he'd done to Declan—make my name mud. The thought thrust a blade into my side. Last year, I was disgraced by that Fontaine story, and it took incredible amounts of hard work to recover my reputation through a big story and to get an editor to publish me. I couldn't go through that again.

He must be here about the frieze too. But why? Surely, if he'd offered £500,000, he'd already researched it?

Ishani rose, smoothed her already pristine pants, and adjusted the wrist of her taupe blouse, oblivious to the ragged, chaotic turmoil in me. "Yes, if they need money, then our theory doesn't make sense. Look, I'm sorry. I have a potential client coming in."

Where do I run to? Where do I hide? The bathroom was the only answer. I shook her hand. "Thank you so much for your time. Look, I just need to quickly nip to the loo. I'll show myself out."

Indecision flashed across her face. Staff working in this building must have been indoctrinated with strong security practices because they were dealing with valuable pieces. But she obviously wanted to make sure His Grace wasn't left in reception for too long.

"Yes, of course, down to the left." She walked me to the door, her high heels clipping the floors, and opened it. "I'm sorry, Isla. It feels like I should have been a lot more help, but perhaps I've just given you more homework."

"Not at all. You've been very generous with your time. You've given me a lot to think about, and I appreciate that."

As soon as she turned to walk to reception, I sprinted to the end of the hallway and crouched around the corner. I held my hair back so not even a strand of my tell-tale red was visible, and I peered around.

A couple of minutes later, she reappeared, walking back to her office.

With Cassius.

CHAPTER TWENTY-FIVE

I WAITED IN a café opposite the convent, my gaze trained on the front entrance for Sister Innocenta. At least I knew Cassius wouldn't turn up as he was with Ishani at Sotheby's.

It was nearly 8:55 a.m. I'd pretty much run from Sotheby's. While I waited, I texted Sunny to make plans to meet up again.

> Me: *Any word about Cassius and that Grecian frieze?*
>
> Sunny: *Yes! Apparently he's gone over Mother Superior's head to the bishop! Says he's willing to pay more for it now his sister has died!*

That meant I had to discover the significance of that frieze before he was successful. If Cassius had his way, and it seemed like he normally did, that would be soon.

I was just about to text Sunny back when Sister Innocenta appeared through the huge wooden doors, a distinctive black-and-white figure sweeping down the stairs, her stiff wimple framing her already flushed face, clutching her cloth shopping bags. Squinting, a hand over her forehead, she scanned the street. For Cassius maybe? No sign of him.

I froze. There *was* a man at the corner, waiting expectantly. Tall, big. Was he the guy who'd chased me? Maybe? It was hard to tell because it had been nighttime and dark, and after I saw him across the road, I didn't see his face again, only heard him. Was he following me or Sister Innocenta? Would he notice or recognize me? The throb behind my eyes intensified as I shoved my handbag higher up my shoulder. If this was the man who'd chased me, I *had* to get Sister Innocenta to tell me what she knew. We were all in danger now.

I paced behind her, waiting until she was swallowed up by workers holding coffees, women in black burkas, and schoolchildren. She couldn't protest too much with this many people around.

I caught up to her.

"Sister, keep moving," I hissed. "I think there's someone following us."

Tucking her head, she sped up, black veil flying, her robes swishing angrily from side to side. "Maybe they are following *you*, not me. Go away. You are trouble, and I don't want any more of it." Puffing and agitated, she strode off even faster. I was trotting beside her now. Maybe Cassius was speaking the truth when he said she'd trekked the Himalayas.

"Please. I know something is going on at the convent. Turn left." I tapped her elbow.

She shook her arm as if I'd grabbed her. "That's not the way to Sainsbury's."

"Turn left into the lingerie store."

I grabbed her elbow and steered her into the pink, black, and mirrored La Perla, one of the most exclusive lingerie stores in London. I'd wandered in one day thinking I'd surprise Declan that night, but seeing the prices—£900 for a corset, I'd decided he'd be just as surprised by knickers and a bra from good old Marks and Spencer's.

I pulled her straight to the counter, where two sleek young women, both dressed in nude bodysuits and stilettoes, were comparing their white nail polish. I had a small moment of unease taking Sister Innocenta through this kind of place. She looked around, unfazed, seeming curious rather than scandalized. It wasn't anything she hadn't already seen, considering the carvings on the frieze. And she had a life before this, and who knew what that life was besides scaling mountains?

"Excuse me. Can we run out of your shop's back entrance?" My voice was unsteady. "There's a scary man following Sister. She's had issues with him before."

Confused, they glanced at each other, then at Sister Innocenta, who was equally wide-eyed, her cheeks even rosier from our rushing down the street. It was clear she was a real nun, and this wasn't some sort of scam or wild cosplay.

"Nun fetish?" one asked. The other curled her lip. "Bloody creep, I know the type. Shall I call the police on him?"

Oh no, I shouldn't have said that. The last thing I wanted was for the police to turn up. What would Barb say to that scenario? I'd become the story rather than the one reporting on it.

Sister Innocenta looked distraught. "No police, please."

"We'll talk to the police when we get back to the convent," I promised.

I glanced back at the street. No sign of him, but he might have been hiding off to the side, waiting for us to come out.

One of them grabbed my hand and led us through the stockroom, weaving our way around naked forms stacked in bizarre positions. She unlocked the back door.

"Run to the right, then left." She pointed. "It's kind of a maze of mews houses that no one knows about."

We jogged along the back streets until we turned left into a cobbled street of mews, typically built in the seventeenth century to house horses.

We slowed down, and I pulled Sister Innocenta into an alleyway. Collapsing against a wall, we each caught our breath.

Sister Innocenta stared at me, still panting. "I'm not talking to you."

I had to gain her trust.

I repeated what the caller told me about the shipment and how I'd confirmed it was Sister Modestia on the phone. I told her about the Russian man who had knocked on the phone booth calling about "your brother" and had then walked away with her.

Hearing this, she dropped to her knees, her face buried in her thick black skirts. "Oh, poor Sister." She sobbed. "Poor Sister."

"Who was that man?" Crouching beside her, I held a hand on her shuddering back. "What do you think happened? How did she know about the shipment?"

She shook her head. "None of us know."

Disappointment racked my shoulders. She still wouldn't help. I rubbed her arm.

"Sister, do you think she was killed?"

Her jaw set, she glared at my hand on her arm.

"Sorry." I dropped my hand. "It feels like no one wants to help me find out what happened to her. Not even you, her friend."

"How dare you!" Her mouth screwed up at me in contempt.

"I do dare, Sister." I stood up abruptly, and she followed more slowly. I was so upset that I turned her first words to me around on her. "How do I know you were her friend? This is all starting to worry me. You could be part of all this, whatever it is."

She rounded on me and seized my shoulders. Her eyes boring into mine, she shook me. "I loved her." Her voice was hoarse, like she wanted to shout but knew she wouldn't. "How can you say that?"

"Answer me then." I was frustrated with her too. I scanned around, nervous about being seen with a crying nun and the possibility of someone coming to check. We were in an alley, but anyone could walk by. "Do you think she was killed?"

"Yes!" She dropped her hands from my arms. Terror pulsed in her blue eyes, liquid with tears.

"Why?" I didn't shout it at her, but I was passionate, insistent.

She fixed me with a look. "If I tell you that, I will destroy all our hard work." She swiped at her eyes. "Don't worry about the convent, don't go there. What is most important is that you write a story about this drug shipment. Find out who is behind it. Otherwise, she died for nothing."

Was she using the drug shipment to distract me from whatever was going on at the convent? Why?

"I promise I will be at the port when the drug shipment arrives," I said. "Is it connected with whatever I saw at the convent?"

I could see the moment in her face when she withdrew from me. A chaos of emotions hurtled through me, searching for a way to get through to her.

"I can't say more," she said. "I don't know you. I don't know who you are with. Maybe you are with her brother."

"Cassius?" I spat out. "I'm not with him. I've barely met him." But I had been seen with him, and now I owed him a favor. I searched her face closely, looking for some tell-tale sign that she knew. But how could she? Did they even get the newspapers? "Why? Are you concerned about him?"

"Stay away from him. That's one thing I'm going to tell you. I still don't trust you. Even if Sister Modestia tried to contact you, that doesn't mean you're a good person."

Not a good person? *What?* Sister Modestia had chosen to give me a tip-off. I was doing this to find the Sister's killer. What did I have to do to convince her? It was almost like her fear of Mother Superior was greater than her desire to help me.

"But, Sister, don't you see? I *have* to deal with him because you won't talk to me. I'm doing this all to find out if Sister Modestia was killed. Can I trust anything he says?"

An older blonde woman in pearls emerged from the house opposite and strode toward us. "Everything okay? I heard shouting. Should I call the police? An ambulance?"

Shit. That was the last thing we needed here. I had to calm things down and move us both onto another street.

Instead of answering her, Sister Innocenta looked up and down the street, as if getting her bearings. Was she going to make a break for it?

"Yes, all good. We're friends, just talking," I said.

The blonde woman waited for a while, nervously fiddling with her pearl necklace.

Finally, Sister Innocenta nodded, which I supposed the blonde woman was waiting for. The woman gave a stiff smile and walked back inside her house, casting us a troubled glance.

I sensed we didn't have much time before she returned or made the call.

"Should we head back to the convent?" I asked.

Sister Innocenta agreed, and we walked until we hit a busy street.

"Cassius told me he loved Sister Modestia and that she was like a mother to him." I tried to stay close as we made our way through shoppers and tourists. "Was that true?"

Her flushed face hooked with interest, but she seemed to battle with herself over the mention of his name. "I suppose he did love her in his way. She tried to protect him when they were growing up. She talked about playing in a room behind the walls. They also used to hide there when their father was on a drunken rampage. They were very afraid of him."

"*A secret room?*"

"It was part of the original castle, built in Henry the Eighth's time. The family was at constant risk of being arrested for practicing Catholicism, which back then was a banned religion. The room was called a priest hole. But even once she and Cassius were grown, she worried about him still—recently, a great deal."

Wow, that was a lot. He seemed very reliant on his sister. Then there was the secret room. I wasn't sure if it was linked to his sister's death or the information she knew about the drugs, but it was very interesting. And she'd worried about him lately—what had he been doing that was a concern? "Worried in what way?" I asked Sister Innocenta.

"That his entire goal seemed to be saving the castle and his way of life."

My brain scrambled, trying to reassemble the reality of Cassius. His sister's comment to Sister Innocenta was at odds with how I'd perceived him. How he'd just blown himself up with his peers by giving me this story about his club. But it didn't make sense for me to start arguing with her.

"When is the funeral?" I asked. "I just talked to him, and he said the convent was organizing the whole thing."

She gave a noise of disgust. "He's lying." Her voice was forceful and confident, and she crossed her arms. "There were no directives in her will as to what happened after she died. Cassius stepped in. The police released her body from the morgue." Her eyes filled with tears, her mouth wrangled with pain. "He's already had her body transported to Westminster Crematorium." She crumpled, devastated, at her last word.

"What?"

A vast panic made me clutch her shoulders tight. A group of schoolkids bumped past us, but I barely felt their elbows, barely registered their raised voices. The most important evidence I had—her body—had been destroyed. And this was proof Cassius was outright lying to me. "When did you find this out?"

Stepping back abruptly, she shook her shoulders to get rid of my hands. "Mother Superior rang the morgue this morning.

They were reluctant to speak with her, as legally, they can't release information to anyone but him. As you can imagine, Mother used the nun card."

"Sister, this is bad news." My face dropped into my hands.

This was the first hint that Cassius was trying to cover something up. All the blood seemed to drain from my body, and I swayed in the busy street, shoppers bumping me to get past.

She used my shock as an opportunity to take off. I followed her at a distance, sensing that was all I was going to get out of her today, until she turned into the convent.

Now we would never know if Sister Modestia had been poisoned.

CHAPTER TWENTY-SIX

HURRYING TO WORK through the avenues of Kensington Garden, the protective canopy of the ancient oaks did nothing to calm my nerves. Instead my brain tried to ram against this massive dead end in the case.

Unless we found the man who killed Sister Modestia and he confessed, how could we show she was murdered? I no longer questioned whether she had been killed. Given Sister Innocenta's reaction, I felt fully committed to that theory now, especially as the two women seemed friends. Whether it was the convent or Cassius telling lies, I still wasn't sure. I tended to believe Sister Innocenta, but the fact that they were accusing each other proved her death was suspicious.

My phone pinged with a text.

> Cassius: *I have another story for you. This one is in your wheelhouse. I think you know what that means.*

I sat down on a park bench to concentrate, the vast Round Pond at my feet. The water rippled with white swans, regal and serene above the surface but furiously paddling through the murky depths.

Cassius. His name struck a chill through me now that I suspected he was lying. How could I trust him as a source? I was suspicious of why he was giving me these stories. Did he somehow know what I was investigating, and he wanted to keep tabs on me? Or was he using me to get back at all the people he hated or had grudges against? That would usually make me worry about the veracity of the Toff's story he'd given me yesterday evening, but none of the facts had been challenged.

I knew I should play along. The fact remained, I still needed a big story. He'd mentioned my wheelhouse. Did he mean it was a crime story? Even if it wasn't a good story—and he'd already proven himself a good source with Toff's—I wanted to keep in touch with him because of his sister. My plan was to keep the channels of communication open, and I'd decide on whether or not I wanted this story when he told me about it. Still, I had to be wary of him.

> Me: *Sounds intriguing. And thank you again for today's front page.*

I'd already texted him a link with my thanks. He'd replied with a thumbs-up. A man of few words and one emoji.

> Cassius: *I'll text you later where to meet tonight.*

Ugh. Meeting him at night filled me with a sick, cold anxiety. I immediately called Declan, who was in the car with Sephy. I wanted to be up-front with him about everything, but also because I couldn't figure out where to meet.

"Hello? Everything okay?" he asked immediately. "I've got you on speakerphone, and Sephy's in the car with me."

The thought of her made me smile. I pictured her sitting in the front seat, dressed in one of her many pairs of wide jeans, teasing her dad about his driving and everything else he did. I realized I'd missed her, and I couldn't wait to hear about her surfing and her stories about her aunts and cousins. "Hi, Sephy." She said hi back. "Declan, you better pull over so we can talk." I felt awful about making him stop during an arduous six-hour drive so I could give him information. But he'd wanted me to keep him updated. Still, I expected he was not going to be happy to hear about me meeting with Cassius.

"Okay, I'm taking you off speaker now," he said. As he did this, I could hear Sephy beside him asking what the emergency was. He told her it was a work thing.

"I'm outside the car now," he said. Traffic roared in the background. "Sephy can't hear. What's up?"

"Hi, sorry to interrupt your drive. I just wanted to let you know that Cassius called and said he's got another story for me. Sounds like a crime story this time."

"A *crime* story?"

I told him what Sister Innocenta had said about Cassius being the one who ordered his sister's body to be cremated. Cassius had accused the convent of doing it.

"Sounds like the Sister is telling the truth," he said. "I believe her—what motivation does she have to lie about this?"

"Yes, I tend to agree." But still, I needed to hear what Cassius had for me. "I don't want to meet him in public or at night—but where should I meet him?"

He groaned. The scuff of his feet kicking the gravel filled my ears.

"Fuck. Isla, why are you even considering meeting him? Haven't we been through this? You got a story from him, and it worked out okay. But he's a snake and has an ulterior motive. It's either that he wants to get together with you. Or—I just don't know what it is."

My chest constricted with disappointment, even though I agreed with his assessment. Cassius had just given me a good story. That could happen again. Some of my sources in the past had been people with questionable motives or people who hadn't always operated in a straightforward, honest way in their own businesses or their private lives, but that didn't mean they didn't have information. "I'm not in a good position. I can't afford to ignore his calls."

"Yes, you can." His voice was strained, as if he was stopping himself from shouting. "You can do what you want. Ignore him. Or just tell him you can't do this story because— No, you don't even owe him an explanation. You can't take this man on all by yourself."

"Declan, I'm going to meet him. I need a story, and he *has* a story." My stomach tightened—I'd left out my true reason to keep the connection, so I could investigate Sister Modestia's death.

"No, Isla—"

"You wanted me to tell you everything. Well, here it is. I'm telling you. And if you don't want to help me, I'll just work it out for myself." I rubbed the soreness around my wound, the constant reminder that I *wasn't* telling him everything. I squirmed inside. It was hard to reconcile that with what I'd just said to him.

I listened for his answer. It didn't come.

"Declan, I'm hanging up now."

He cried out, frustrated. "I don't like this. *I hate this.* But I do want you to keep talking to me." He gave a huge sigh. "He has some offices in Belgravia. Text me as soon as you get there, just before you walk in. I'll text you five minutes later when you're seated in his office. Make sure you answer that text and let him know, so he knows I'm keeping an eye on him. His offices should be the safest place during the day. Although, Isla, a caveat—I don't believe any place is safe with this guy."

Still, I breathed out, hugely relieved that Declan was helping me. "I agree that no place is safe, but I'm willing to take the risk." I heard his intake of breath. "Thank you for this, Declan. I love you."

"Okay then." His voice was tight. He was trying to hold back his outright anger. I waited for him to say something affectionate, but he quickly ended the call so he could get back on the road.

I texted Cassius: *Can we meet at your offices in Belgravia during the day?*

If he suggested dinner again, I'd just have to decline him flat out. I'd suggest a time tomorrow, but I had to be careful. There was a fine line between being tenacious and begging. I couldn't let him think I was so desperate that he could walk all over me.

> Cassius: *Yes, I'll text you as soon as I get a break in my meetings.*

My heart sank. I was worried enough about him suggesting dinner. Meeting him at his offices didn't seem great either. But surely there would be other staff around?

> Me: *Great. I can get a black cab and be there within ten minutes.*

I zipped my phone into my bag and strode out through the gilded gates of Kensington Garden, along the busy high street and into my office. All through the day, Cassius kept giving me times, then canceling. I kept Declan updated, and, of course, he got more and more outraged on my account that Cassius was mucking me around. I'd intended to visit Tilbury Port in Essex again, still trying to find a way in, but I was worried about the cell phone reception. Instead, I was stuck in my office seat, researching the shipping line. And with so little distraction, I felt the aching around my wound more. I checked and found the cell phone reception at the emergency clinic was good, so I kept my appointment. The nurse had just injected around my wound to stop infection when Cassius texted at 6:45 p.m.

> Cassius: *Can you come now?*

A sick thud hit my gut. I knew now he wasn't going to make it easy on me. But I had to agree. It was never a good idea to put off a meeting with a source until the next day. He was so busy, he might even put it off for a week, and I needed this story now.

Me: *Yes, I'll be there by 7.*

During the cab ride, I texted Declan my location.

Declan: *I'm back home from getting Sephy. I'm driving to you now and parking around the corner. Please keep texting me!*

I was relieved he was going to be there, though I wondered if it was an overreaction on his part. And I dreaded facing him when I was done with the meeting.

When I stepped out of the cab, I looked up at the grand Regency façade. The whole building was dark.

CHAPTER TWENTY-SEVEN

THE DOOR OPENED before I even knocked. Cassius filled the threshold, wearing tortoiseshell glasses and a dark suit with a purple silk tie. He greeted me with a smile and a handshake. Businesslike. Good.

"Sorry about all the back-and-forth today. Fridays are always frantic." He took off his glasses and rubbed his eyes as though they were strained and he was exhausted, like he'd been genuinely too busy for me.

I gave a slight smile. "That's okay. I appreciate you making the time."

He loosened his tie, looking pleased. He was very close, his wide shoulders looming over me, his face angled towards mine. To get us moving, I glanced down a dark hallway and indicated, *Should I go first?* Only one light shone above us. He ushered me through the hallway and into a huge office that smelled of new leather and was barely illuminated by a desk light. My heart sank. My leg was so sore and my throat ached. Cassius moved closer. If he reached for me at all, I didn't stand a chance. It would have been better if I'd asked him to meet in public.

"May I take your coat?" He held out a hand to hang it up. I quickly took it off, sat down, and folded it over my lap. He frowned and moved to the silver bar cart at the side of the room. "Gin and tonic? Champagne? New Zealand sauvignon blanc?"

"Thank you, but honestly, I'm fine."

He tapped his teeth together and poured himself a Scotch, dropping in ice from the bucket. Swirling his drink, he moved back to me.

"You okay? You seem to be limping."

Holy shit. He was the only person today who'd mentioned this.

He stared at my thigh exactly where the bite was.

Dread—swift and primal—flared in me.

Did he know? Was he aware I'd hidden in the Serpentine that night? Was he telling me that he knew?

I lurched back in my chair. He flinched, and his mouth turned down.

"Do you mind putting some more lights on?" I said. He scowled at my request but stood up and flicked on the main switch at the wall.

"I also promised Declan I'd let him know when I'm here." With a bit of a show, I reached inside my coat pocket and texted Declan.

A muscle pulsed in Cassius's cheek. Without a word, he sat behind his carved mahogany desk.

"Now." He picked up a large piece of paper. "Have you seen this painting?" He started to get to his feet, like he was going to walk around his desk to show it to me. Before he could get close, I reached across his desk and nearly snatched it off him. He flicked up his hands, like I was being rude.

The picture was an old war scene of bloody faces and tumbling horses. I took a breath. I'd seen it before—in our newspaper.

"That's the painting that was stolen from Lord Havistock."

A ping sounded from my phone. Apologizing, I took it out. "Sorry, Declan checking in." I texted him back: *So far so good.*

Cassius sighed. "I have evidence it wasn't stolen—it was a burglary staged by professionals. Havistock is not only getting the insurance payout for the painting, he's also sold it on the black market, so doubling his profit."

I recoiled. "But he's known for being honest and open." Declan was going to be devastated. Lord Havistock was his biggest supporter in the House of Lords, and he was also popular in the House of Commons. It had been quite a coup for Declan to get his support, and others from both houses had followed.

What was Cassius's goal here? To destroy Declan? Or was his real target Lord Havistock all along, and Declan was collateral damage? Did Cassius genuinely want this to come to light? Or did he want to impress me with another story tip-off?

"Why does he need money so badly?" I asked.

"Like the rest of us who own estates, he has shedloads of maintenance and a staff of many. And word is, his bets on the horses got out of hand."

Motivation. A seismic shift rocked the pit of my gut. If this was true, Declan would have to go back to the drawing board and find someone else to be the main champion for his bill. And even if he was successful in finding that someone else, his association with Lord Havistock might tarnish his whole enterprise. I felt sick. Was I going to help destroy Declan?

I caught my reflection in the ornate gold mirror above the bar cart. A flash of red hair and black and white. I felt unbearably conflicted. How much do I trust what Declan tells me about someone? His judgment? Do I trust Declan more than Cassius?

"What evidence do you have?" My tone was harsher than I meant it to be.

His strained look sent a prickle down my backbone.

"I don't like how this"—he waved back and forth between us—"is going. From the minute I let you in, I've felt a tension from you. *You're* the one who suggested my workplace, and I complied with that. I kept you updated all through the day about the time. And now you're treating me like a, well, quite frankly, a creep." He watched his glass as he slowly lowered it onto his desk. "And that's not how I work. Do you have any issues with me? If so, tell me now. I don't have to articulate how many other journalists would be grateful for this story."

My heart thudded. I had to turn this around—fast. "I'm sorry. You're right. I apologize if I seem off. I'm just tired."

"Please, just give me the benefit of the doubt." His face collapsed. This humbled look was unusual for him, a glimpse into his other side.

"Sorry," I said. "Sometimes I'm too skeptical—occupational hazard."

"Okay." He gathered himself. "I have all the invoices and payment slips for the story. I also have a photo of the painting where it is currently held." He barely paused for breath. "I know you saw Sister Innocenta."

Fear shot through my chest.

"What? How?" He was at Sotheby's, five blocks away.

"Do you have to ask that?" Impatiently, he tapped the desk with his fingers. "C'mon, Isla, I've had a long day, and it sounds like you have too."

Blood roared in my ears. Was he just following Sister Innocenta or both of us? The thought ratcheted up my heart until it was beating in time with the pain in my leg. The problem was that right now, I had to give him something.

"I asked about the funeral. She said *you* took Sister Modestia's body from the morgue and transported it to the crematorium."

He gave a cry of outrage.

"She's fucking lying. There's no way I would have my sister cremated. I wanted to bring her home and bury her where she belongs, with the proper ceremony she deserves. I only knew what had happened because I have friends on the board at the crematorium. By the time I heard, it was too late." He dropped his head into his hands. "It was the convent who transported her body there. It was the convent who wanted her body gone."

Slowly, he looked up. I focused on his eyes, dark with pain, and sympathy flowed through me. His emotional reaction seemed genuine and yet, there was how he'd treated Declan. But that was work. Surely a lot of us showed a side at work that wasn't always likable? For years, I was calculated in my career and uninterested in making true connections with people. Or was I just making excuses for him because it was convenient for me?

"Did she hint at what is going on there?" He rested his hands under his chin.

I had to consider my words because I had a duty to protect Sister Innocenta. "No. But she insisted I shouldn't worry about the convent." I felt bad about even giving him this. She was a contact, and I didn't know if he could be trusted.

"Hmm. Did she say anything about me?" he asked.

I decided to test him by giving him a little bit more of the conversation and seeing his reaction.

"She was worried that I was with you. I asked why that was bad. She wouldn't answer."

I'd muffled her message a little, hoping it sounded genuine. I scrutinized every flick of his face. Was he biting?

He looked surprised. "She's trying to divert attention onto me. God knows why."

He would say that, wouldn't he?

"Look, why don't you book another night there?" he asked. "See what you can find."

"Already thought of that. They canceled the booking because they know I'm a journalist." I took a beat. "What are you hoping I'd find?"

He shrugged. "I have no idea. But I just have a bad feeling about the place."

I let that rest in the air for a moment. "By the way, someone said you wanted to buy that Grecian frieze you mentioned to me. Are you still trying?" The tension built as I waited for his answer. I wasn't sure if he'd be angry or worried by my curiosity.

But he nodded sadly. "Yes, even more so, because I want something to remember her by. Apparently, it's an outdoors scene. Bea was very much an outdoors person, loved the cold, fresh air on her face. I intended to place the frieze outside in the garden because I want to remember her that way." A slight smile lifted his lips.

"But didn't you mention the scene depicted is bacchanalian?"

His mouth twitched. "Oh, she had a great sense of humor."

I wasn't convinced. An outdoors person who voluntarily entered a closed community in the center of London? Mind you, Mother Superior had insisted Sister Modestia loved to walk, and maybe she liked to play soccer in the courtyard garden, too. But still.

Cassius paused. His mouth torqued to the side.

"Hmm. Declan is here to pick you up. I wonder why? We weren't finished." He stood up and surveyed me closely. It was like a light had switched off in his angular face, as if I'd displeased him. "We'll have to continue this at a later date."

"Oh? Okay."

How did he know Declan was here? Cassius turned slightly, and I saw he had an earpiece on. It was a small thing, but it made my shoulders stiffen. We were on another level now. Did he have someone feed information into his ear? He must have. How many security guys were out there? He wasn't a celebrity—this security wasn't about keeping fans from bothering him. Did that mean he had something to fear? That kicked my heart into overdrive.

With a flourish of his hand, he indicated I walk to the front door. It was the longest walk of my life. I felt him behind me, close but not touching, near enough to notice the smell of his spicy aftershave. At the exit, he reached in front of me. I startled. He was just opening the door to the street.

"He's not here," I said. There were no lights of a car or anyone waiting. Of course. Declan used to be an undercover cop. There was no way he would be obvious. The unnerving tingling down the back of my neck engulfed my whole body, escalating in a pounding thud. Cassius had a team of people, and there was only me, with Declan reluctantly in the background.

"Here he comes in his family station wagon," Cassius said as lights appeared at the end of the street. Without a smile, he turned to me, his dark eyes dense and unfathomable. "Next time, I can take you home."

He said it like it wasn't an offer; it was a certainty.

CHAPTER TWENTY-EIGHT

DECLAN GAVE ME a frantic hug of relief when I got in the car. I heaved out a breath, warm and secure from being with him. I hadn't realized how much anxiety I was holding just being around Cassius.

Still, Declan clearly wasn't happy about me choosing to take the meeting, even though this time I'd tried to be up-front about it. I suspected he was going to be even more worried when I told him about the tip-off.

"Thank you for coming to get me," I said while he started up the car. "Especially when you've just driven six hours to collect Sephy. I really appreciate it."

"Of course." He seemed stiff and tense, which made me feel worried. "I'm glad you're okay. I want you to call me."

"Where's Sephy?" I was looking forward to seeing her.

"I left her with Chamonix's family. We're meeting them at The Bell, you know the pub across the square from our house? Chammy's doing the open mic. She's written a new song. Do you want to come? Sephy's excited to tell you about her trip."

We were being unnaturally civil to each other. I didn't know about the crowded pub part of it, and I was tired, but I wanted to see her. Probably, too, I wanted to put off the talk with Declan that was inevitable.

"I'd love to come. I want to hear all about her surfing." Missing her was a sharp reminder of Teddy. "Could you call in at Fleur's? I just want to pick up Teddy. I haven't seen much of him." I knew we'd be sitting outside, warmed by patio heaters, in the family area, which welcomed pets.

"Of course." He seemed excited by the idea. "Sephy will be thrilled to meet the little guy."

I picked up Teddy, took a scoop of his food, thanked Fleur, and loaded us back into the car, where Declan made a fuss of Teddy, pleased to see him.

"What did Cassius say?" Declan asked as he pulled the car into traffic.

I'd been waiting for him to ask, hoping we could avoid the conversation until after we got home.

I told him as we wended our way to his house, through streets crammed with Friday night traffic.

"Fuck." Declan thumped the steering wheel. "That guy is unbelievable. He's making it up." His tone was much too decisive. Normally, he was the one who wanted to wait and see, take a step back, let things play out.

I didn't answer as Declan parked outside his house. For Declan's sake, I hoped Cassius was lying, but I couldn't bring myself to dismiss it so easily. He must have decided he didn't want to pursue this tonight because he took my hand, Teddy trotting happily beside us. We strolled across the grassy square as if all were okay with us.

We weaved our way through The Bell, a classic brown-and-gold pub with stained-glass windows, to the garden. Chammy's family of five had saved two seats at a table near the front, and Declan introduced me to everyone. They turned out to be French, chic in assorted jaunty scarves. I gave Sephy a half-hug, not sure if it was too much or not enough. She went in for a bigger hug, and

I was touched by how happy she seemed to see me. I'd worried that she wouldn't want me intruding on their time with old family friends. Both Seph and Chammy squealed over the sight of Teddy, and Sephy insisted he sit on her lap. A comedian had just finished his set. Apparently very crude and not funny. We ordered steak-and-cheese pies and hand-cut chips. The adults ordered ales. I stuck with water. A drink would just make me fall asleep and I was still taking the antibiotics.

"So?" I asked Sephy. "How was the trip?"

Her cheeks were slightly sunburned, and she had a few new freckles over her nose. "Awesome. I learned to surf. Why don't we go back soon and do it together? Surf trip."

"That would be so fun." I clapped my hands. "I'm only a beginner. I'm sure you're much better than me. And your dad, well …" I winked at Declan. He was a terrible surfer, but he'd been a great sport about it when we'd worked together last year. We'd laughed many times about it since.

"Dad?" She made a skeptical face. "We won't be surfing on the same beach as him."

I wondered what she meant. That she knew he was so bad? But how could that be? He'd said Ōhope was his first time surfing. Or was that part of his act being undercover? Well, he might have surfed once or twice before, but he was still clumsy on the waves.

"Seph," Declan interrupted. "Tell her that funny story about your cousins and their dogs."

The other family stopped talking to listen while she told the story. Then they told us cute stories about when the girls were little until the food arrived. While we ate, Chammy's mother described Chammy's school, trying to persuade me to enroll Sephy there too. Declan squeezed my hand, and somehow, I didn't want to remind her that I wasn't the one to make that choice.

While our plates were cleared by staff, Declan patted my knee. "Just remembering about us surfing, both of us seasick," he said softly. "I felt bloody awful but excited because I'd just met you." He gazed lovingly into my eyes, and for the first time in days, I felt happy and hopeful we would see our way through this tricky stage.

Chammy sang a funny, sweary song, which included phrases in French, her first language, about being a teenager and how everything sucked. Her family looked on proudly, feigning shock at the swearing, and laughed and cried at the end. Once she'd finished, she introduced Sephy to the crowd. I looked at Declan, stunned, watching for his reaction. He was surprised too. I squeezed his shoulder with excitement, but I was also nervous for her. Sephy took Chammy's guitar, adjusted the mic, and cleared her throat.

She sang a song she must have composed over her break, about the sea and surfing and starting to find out who you are. It was vulnerable and angsty and sometimes off-key, and it didn't seem to have a chorus, but it brought tears to my eyes. Declan and I linked hands and grinned proudly at her and thoroughly embarrassed her with praise once she returned to the table.

We left the pub at eleven, Friday closing time, and the moon hung joyfully over the rooftops as we agreed to meet next week. It was an ordinary night for them, but for me, magical, two families saying good night to each other and I was part of it. My body felt buoyant, like I could float into the London sky and over the chimney tops.

I want this. I want this life and everything about it.

As we walked across the square to their house, Declan said to Sephy, "Hey, guess what? Isla and I have been invited to a ball. At a castle. We're going to buy her a dress tomorrow morning."

Oh no! I wanted to play down the whole event. I didn't want Sephy invested, as that would make me feel even more guilty. I knew I might not even wear the dress all night because I needed to sneak upstairs unseen.

"Whaaaat?" She stared from Declan to me, grinning with excitement. "That's like something out of a fairy tale. You're going to have so much fun. I want to look up photos of the castle when we get home. I'm coming shopping tomorrow too, right?"

I blocked out my misgivings about this whole shopping expedition and tried to pretend it was what Declan wanted it to be.

"Course you are," I said. "You will be making sure I am bostin'."

"Oof," Sephy said.

"Lush?"

"Argh." She made hair-tearing-out motions.

"Ace, dynamic, tidy, mint?"

Sephy ran ahead screaming, Teddy galloping alongside her, somehow barking gleefully at the same time. Hand in hand, we ran after them, laughing.

CHAPTER TWENTY-NINE

OUTSIDE THEIR HOUSE, I made motions to grab my phone to message an Uber.

"You're not going to stay over?" Declan's happy face snagged, seeming disappointed. I was surprised he'd mentioned it in front of Sephy. It had been a great evening together, and I felt like I was popping the bubble we'd been in. Normally, I wanted to stay, but it seemed too complicated, and I was tired.

I made a tiny motion with my head to Sephy.

"It's okay," she said. "Dad and I talked about it. And talked and talked. You know him."

Now it would seem churlish if I didn't stay over. Especially as we were all shopping together tomorrow. I was keeping my pills in my handbag now and could maintain a regular schedule wherever I was, so there was no real excuse. What did I feel about staying? I longed to curl up next to Declan, but I knew it wasn't going to be that simple. We faced a mountain of discussion, and I anticipated a difficult conversation. At the thought of that, I longed for my own bed.

Sephy got settled into her room with Teddy, who seemed to have cozied up to her as if she were his number one human, the little traitor. My smile over their sweet bond dropped. She really wanted Teddy to stay over tomorrow night with her and her minder while we went to the ball, but I'd already organized he'd stay at

Fleur's just one more time, because I knew I had to witness that 3 a.m. drug arrival at the port.

After all the activity, Declan and I, alone for the first time in hours, stood on opposite sides of his bedroom, quiet. I felt awkward and strangely shy.

We stared at each other. I didn't know about my expression, but his was a mystery.

I tried to hold his gaze with the same inscrutability. I realized I didn't want to talk tonight or overthink anything. Or even think at all. I was exhausted by our back and forth. I just wanted to be with him, feel his lips and the glide of his tongue. Feel his bare skin whisper and grind and slide with sweat against mine. Get back to what we knew for sure about each other.

I walked over to his wardrobe. I slid off my coat and hung it and my handbag on the hooks he'd put up for me. I took out my phone and clicked it into the charger by my side of the bed. I unbuttoned my shirt, took it off, unzipped my skirt. Concerned about showing my injury, I held my hand against the Band-Aid, stepped out of my skirt, and put both in my new washing basket.

He pulled off his jersey and his shirt and took off his jeans and did the same. We took off all the rest of our pieces, keeping eye contact. We stood in front of each other, naked but still not touching. It was surprisingly intimate and somehow nerve-racking.

We were like that for what seemed like ages. His heated gaze skated over my body, a groan sounded from the back of his throat, and closing the distance between us, he wreathed a claiming arm around me, tugging me close. He pressed his entire hard, naked body against me. God, feeling him like this was so good. His mouth brushed mine in light, tender kisses, opening my lips wider until his tongue invaded and stroked mine and we were both moaning. Running a hand down my spine, he lifted me up and laid me down on the bed, covering me with his body, comforting and arousing. We stayed together like that, sighing and kissing, not speaking.

"Just to let you know," his husky voice broke the silence, "these rooms are pretty soundproof. Except for something extreme, like screaming."

"You'll have to rein it in then," I murmured into his lips.

"No, you."

"You."

With a matching hum of amusement, we moved against each other, pressing harder and harder as if we couldn't get close enough, our hands searching, kissing like we couldn't get near enough, deep enough, swallowing each other whole. The slow grinding and rocking and sighing felt like we might have forever after all, until we were both frantic for release. It was hazy and searching, then blaring with sweaty oblivion. What we both needed.

Yet, I was still unsettled. This was only a temporary respite.

Afterward, instead of wrapping himself around me like he usually did before we went to sleep, he turned onto his back, put his hands behind his head, and was motionless except for the rise and fall of his chest, like he was thinking.

He looked so open and inviting, the cut muscles of his biceps and chest, his lashes moving disturbed against his cheeks. It was tempting to trace those indents and bumps, move my body against his, smooth away this uncomfortable conversation, and leave it for another day. But I held myself back because we had to address this. It was just festering away, and things were going downhill.

"Where do you think we are?" he asked.

I breathed out. I needed to be honest and articulate exactly what had changed. My nerves scraped raw at the thought that I was admitting something was wrong with us. It made it feel more real. But I had to do it.

"It feels like there's been a shift. Like you want me to stop taking risks. I'm not talking about what I did with Sephy. I was wrong to take her along. You used to be the one who waited to see how things played out. You kept an open mind. But now it feels like you're nixing my ideas immediately. That's why I've kept things from you."

Relief washed over me at telling him how I felt, even though I wasn't sure I'd expressed myself as well as I would have liked. The stakes were high now, because if he didn't understand and try to change how he was acting—what then?

"I suppose …" He turned to me and traced along my nose. "You have to be able to tell me things even when I don't agree with what you are doing." I wanted to believe this would help. But I wasn't convinced this would change the fact that he was rejecting my ideas and my investigation, and that he was worried about my safety.

I turned my face to him. "Are you going to be okay with hearing things you don't like?"

"I love you," he said simply, holding my gaze. "I don't want any harm to come to you." That made me melt. It came from a kind and gentle place in his heart. And yet, it didn't solve how we would go forward.

"But you can't always be there to protect me."

"I don't want that to be true."

He wrapped his arms around me, and we lay like that for a while. Everything wasn't going to be resolved tonight. But it felt like a start.

Then, I remembered my plan for tomorrow.

CHAPTER THIRTY

"DON'T LOOK NOW," Declan said.

The edge in his voice got my attention. He, Sephy, and I were dodging the Saturday morning crowds on New Bond Street looking for my ball dress. I'd been here just a couple of days ago at Sotheby's, so now I knew the street well. Sephy was excited about the masked ball and how I should look, and I was calming her expectations. We were about to enter the store where I normally bought my clothes.

"It's Cassius," I said.

The mysterious duke was swaggering toward us, head and shoulders above the other pedestrians, dressed in another iteration of the trench coat-and-cashmere outfit, this one all in navy. I was pleased that I had another opportunity to study him in action and try to understand him. A sweep of disquiet put my guard up. I was with Declan, who distrusted Cassius and felt humiliated by him.

Also—what on earth was Cassius doing in London, two hours from his castle, when he had five hundred guests arriving that evening?

Declan gave him a cursory wave. Cassius didn't wave back. He just smiled. But unless I was mistaken, he smiled only at me, laser-focused. I dropped my head, embarrassed by his attention, especially since Declan and Sephy were watching him being oversolicitous. Maybe he knew, and that was why he did it—to somehow get back at Declan.

"Here he is," Cassius said once he got closer. He held out a hand to Declan, but not to shake his hand. "The man who buys only one cupcake."

Declan's jaw tensed like he was struggling hard not to show Cassius how much he was affected. Sephy looked confused. I suspected she would be upset if she knew her father was being taunted.

"Your Grace." Declan nodded. "Lovely to see you as ever."

"Told you before, McDermott," he said, irritated. "You don't have to call me that."

I jolted in surprise. What did that mean? Maybe Cassius had stipulated Declan could call him by his first name. But why? So he could pretend they were friends?

Cassius turned to Sephy. "Isla, who's this? Surely you're much too young to have a grown-up daughter?"

Sephy looked pleased at being called grown up. Declan went slack-faced. Despite the fact that I teased Declan about it, the age difference between us was not great, and I was sure Cassius was playing it up. And maybe even emphasizing that Sephy was not mine.

"She's mine. My. Daughter. Your Grace, this is Seraphim. Sephy, this is His Grace, the Duke of Cheltenham."

Sephy's eyes went wide, transfixed by Cassius. "Oh, you're the one with the castle. You're having the ball." She put a hand to her mouth. "Shit, I was supposed to say 'Your Grace.'" She'd probably learned that at her boarding school, especially if some of the students were titled. My lips quirked up in amusement at her honest response, though I suppose some parents would have corrected her on the swearing.

Cassius rocked with laughter. Leaning down, he said, "No, you and your dad don't have to." What did he mean? He'd just said something similar to Declan, so he was trying to drive home the point. He shook Sephy's hand. "Delighted to meet you, Seraphim. What a beautiful name. The highest-ranking angels—well done, you."

She gave Cassius a look of surprise and respect. He knew his angels. Not many people knew the meaning of her name. I wondered about his reaction. He might be pandering to Sephy, like he sometimes did with me.

"Who gave you that name?" he asked.

Glowing under his attention, she looked up at Declan. "My mother? Right, Dad?"

Declan smiled at her and nodded. His face dropped as he caught Cassius's face.

Because Cassius's expression was more than knowing. His white teeth flashed a gloating half-smile, and his dark eyes glinted. My mind leaped frantically. Could he know about Sephy's mother? No way. *Could he?*

He took us all in. "Saturday morning shopping?"

Sephy grinned and bounced on the heels of her Doc Martens. "Yep. Dad's buying a dress for Isla for the ball. Your ball."

"Oh?" Pointedly, he peered over our heads at the store sign. He repeated the name, a chain store, firmly midmarket and my usual territory, as if confused we were shopping there. "Oh, well." He shrugged slightly and gave me a smile of commiseration. "Carry on then."

I drooped slightly as I watched Cassius saunter back toward his vintage black Rolls, which was waiting for him, parked on a red line. Wait—did he stop when he saw us? Or … *was he still following me?* It would explain why he was here rather than overseeing preparations for a huge event at his castle. Was that attributing too much importance to myself? It assumed he was suspicious of me. Or he knew a lot more about what I was doing.

I glanced at Declan and Sephy and my heart dipped, noting that their high spirits had deflated like popped balloons.

Sephy curled her lip. "I thought that guy was cool at first, like in *Bridgerton*, but he's actually a dickhead."

"Out of the mouths of babes," Declan said bitterly. "Dickboi Duke."

"Don't do it, Dad." Sephy rolled her eyes, but her mouth twitched with amusement despite herself. She gave her father a longer look and seemed to see his bitterness, unusual for him, and her forehead furrowed in concern. I cupped his shoulder.

Declan scanned across the road and brightened. "That's it. C'mon." He grabbed our hands, looked both ways and pulled us across the road.

"This is your dress." Triumphant, he held out a hand to the window display.

It was stunning, with rose gold sequins on the strapless top and a full fifties-style tulle skirt. Sexy and yet romantic. I sighed dreamily.

But.

"No, Declan." I shook my head and tugged him away. "This is the sort of store that offers you free champagne and those stupid macarons."

"Yeah, what's the deal with those things?" Sephy asked.

"Don't get it." I shook my head. "Taste like colored cardboard."

"Just try it on." Declan pulled us through the doors. "I want to see it on you."

Sure enough, as soon as we entered, the saleswoman offered us champagne, sparkling water, and macarons from a silver mirrored tray.

Declan plucked a glass of champagne from her tray and handed it to me. I sipped it and put it down on a glass table. It tasted funny. Anyway, I shouldn't be drinking with the antibiotics I was taking.

Declan gave me a surprised look.

"Don't want to spill on anything, you know how klutzy I am," I explained.

In the dressing room, I slipped on the dress gingerly, trying not to smudge my makeup on it or catch the zipper.

Standing in front of the mirror, I saw the gold complemented my bright red hair. And holy shit, my boobs looked amazing. Must have been the way the bodice was cut. Or maybe, instead of my weight going onto my arse, it was finally landing up top. Whatever, it was working miracles. The girls were right up there, front and center, looking very ready for the ball. Ouch, and they were kind of tender too. I squirmed a little in the bodice, trying to get comfortable. Was it the sequins? I searched inside the fabric. No, it was all lined with soft silk. I must be getting my period. Was I? Hmm. I couldn't remember. I'd think about that later. I slipped on the high-heeled shoes provided for customers and stepped out.

Declan stared. "You look beautiful." His voice was tight, his pupils dilated, his eyes transformed into a lush, grass-after-the-rain green.

All that dazzling emotion radiated from his body to mine, filling me with a euphoria that sparkled around the edges. I'd never loved him more than at that moment. Not because I was in a princess dress and looking my best, and he'd said I was beautiful—that was an easy moment to get a rush of feelings. But because it made me remember all the mundane, everyday times he'd said it too and seemed to mean it, even though I knew I was looking average or just blah. It was easy to see the fineness in him—everyone saw it. But he saw goodness and light in me when I failed to see it in myself. He was my person, and I was his. A heady swell of gratitude rushed through me that I was lucky enough to find him. I had to do everything I could to hang on to us.

"You do, Isla." Sephy stroked the skirt. "This dress is so cool on you."

"Thank you, Sephy. That means a lot to me." I gave her a goofy grin.

"I want to buy it for you," Declan said.

I searched for the tag and found it sticking into my armpit. I gasped. There were too many numbers.

"Declan. No. That's too much for one night." Like journalists, cops weren't paid handsomely, and I knew in the new role he'd created for himself, he'd taken a pay cut. He had a mortgage and Sephy to support.

He shrugged. "Working in Parliament, there'll be a surprising number of balls for us to attend. And endless fundraisers." His lips tilted at the corners. "The dress will practically pay for itself."

I opened my mouth to protest.

"It's decided," he said.

Sephy squealed and clapped her hands.

"Okay, if you're certain I'll wear it again." I twirled.

Sephy fluttered my skirts with her fingers. "Isla, I can do your hair and makeup … I mean, if you like?"

I looked at her. "Oh, Seph, that would be awesome." She flinched slightly at my shortening of her already-shortened name. Too familiar. "I've seen your smoky eye, or is it a crease cut? Should I call you Seraphim or Sephora?"

She snorted at my weak joke, a hint of relief in her eyes. I smiled. I might be getting better at this. Most of the time, I had no idea whether I was doing or saying the right thing in my interactions with her. But just then, I saw that she needed me to be a safe, dorky adult in her life, not a mate.

Back in the dressing room, I couldn't get the zipper down.

I poked my head out. "The zipper seems to be stuck. Declan, can you call a salesperson?"

"I can try," Declan volunteered.

He came in and, focusing on my back, eased it back and forth until it gave.

"Oh, phew." I breathed, holding the bodice against me modestly.

In the mirror, he gave me a steamy body scan and stopped at my chest, almost startled.

I want to show him what he can never have.

"Satisfied with the revenge boobs?" I teased him.

"They are fucking spectacular." His voice was low and raspy. "And right now, I don't want to waste one second thinking about that wanker."

He gave me a chaste kiss on my bare shoulder. Then, his hands on my hips, he trailed warmer kisses up to my neck.

Breaking off, he gave me a molten glance that buckled my knees. "I better get out of here," he said decisively.

I hung up my sparkly fairy-tale dress and pulled on my crumpled jeans and striped shirt that had slipped onto the carpeted floor, reality setting in. *He was my person and look what I intended to do.* The sequins on the dress seemed to flash accusingly, and I flinched. The first chance I got, I'd have to swap this dress for something anonymous so I could slip upstairs at the castle.

On the bus back to Declan's house, I texted Shay. I'd texted or called her most days, and I felt terrible I couldn't visit, but she had her mother there, and she was happy with all her help. I promised her that after the two-week deadline, I'd be there so much she'd get sick of me.

Shay: *How's it going with Sephy?*

Me: *I made the big mistake of dragging her along on a story. Declan's not happy with me. But otherwise she's coming around. I think we might be becoming friends.*

Shay: *Oh, Isla, I love this for you. Who would have thought?*

Me: *I know. A ready-made family.*

Shay: *Next you'll be telling me you're pregnant.*

Me: *Don't hold your breath. I'm far from that stage. Like, Alaska far. If it ever happens.*

Shay: *Ooookay.*

Me: *Ha. That's what Sephy says.*

Shay: *Same as the kids. Still got it.*

Me: *Mm-hmm.*

CHAPTER THIRTY-ONE

THAT AFTERNOON, I stared anxiously at the bright blue sky as Tabitha's old Volvo bumped along the motorway. I was counting down the minutes until we arrived at the castle tonight after getting changed at Tabs' parents' house.

My clanging nerves weren't because I was looking forward to being at the ball with my friends, sharing the excitement of being inside a castle, or even enjoying the sight of Declan in a tux. I was frantic with how much I had to accomplish before Declan arrived—how to get upstairs and search around the castle without getting caught. What would happen when we arrived? Would I even have a chance to look around? I still didn't know what I was looking for besides the vague *Something to do with Sister Modestia.* Looking for a needle in a haystack seemed easier because you knew it was there.

I was wearing jeans and a T-shirt, my hair and makeup done by Sephy. We'd decided on half up, half down, and my neck felt stiff, my fingers itchy from trying not to fiddle with it, and also the sense that I was betraying her as well. We were entering the Cotswolds, and I was worn out by Tabitha's insufferable Peregrine, who'd decided to ride with us after all. He was forced to sit in the back because I got carsick, which meant there was no escape from his prattling about etiquette.

"There are so many signs that the castle was built in 1510 during the reign of Henry the Eighth," Peregrine said. "If you look up when we arrive, you'll notice its four turrets are reflective of that era in that—"

I couldn't hear any more about the turrets.

"They were one of the few titled Catholic families of that era, weren't they?" I asked.

"Has the little Kuwu"—he imitated my accent to say Kiwi—"been googling again?"

"Peregrine, you are such a bloody tosser sometimes." I wasn't usually rude to him, for Tabitha's sake, but she liked it when I talked back to him because she was too sweet to do the same. "Cassius told me they were Catholic."

"Isla, you simply cannot call him Cassius like that in front of anyone." He smiled gleefully and tapped his nose. "And yes, you're right. Supposedly it was modeled on Malahide Castle in Ireland. Actually, Isla, could you ask him this question, just not when I'm around? There was a rumor about a room behind Cassius's castle walls where his forebears used to hide."

A room behind the walls?

I sat bolt upright. That lined up with what I learned about Cassius and his sister going behind the walls to play or hide from their drunken father. Now I was more determined to sneak upstairs to try to find this hidden room.

We'd reached the Cotswolds, weaving through ridiculously cute little chocolate box villages with thatched cottages, green pastures, and stone churches. We arrived at Tabs' parents' home, a romantic but crumbling manor house with bleating and barking animals and tools and hay bales strewn everywhere.

"My bebe." Penelope, her mother, strode to greet us, clad in gumboots, a headscarf, and a ripped Liberty blouse. We got out, garment bags in hand. She reached for Tabs. "Thank gosh you've made it back safe from the big bad city. I do worry with you down there, you know. Terribly."

She turned to me. "Darling Isla. You look more beautiful every time I see you. Love looks wonderful on you, darling. Now, where is that handsome suitor of yours, Declan?"

Penelope treated me and Dec as if we were characters in a fairy tale from a land far away.

"Hello, sir. Hello, ma'am." Peregrine stiffly shook Montgomery and Penelope's hands. "Exciting times, eh?"

Tabitha's parents always looked a bit bewildered by Peregrine's pronouncements.

My lips twitched with the welcome amusement, a short break from my trepidation about this evening.

We all took showers. Tabs and I wore old-fashioned shower caps loaned by her mother, who, like my mother back in New Zealand, seemed to never throw anything out. I also kept my face out of the spray, as Sephy had done my makeup with a cat eye and contouring I'd never be able to replicate. Tabs and I got changed in her bedroom. I wanted to be more excited about tonight, but I missed Declan, and I had to be "on" as soon as I got to the Castle. I'd need to find a way to slip upstairs without resorting to climbing the grand staircase I'd seen in stock photos, in full view of everyone at the ball. And once Declan arrived, my investigating would be over.

"Oh." Tabs was surprised when she saw me. She was dressed in a red satin Grace Kelly-style dress with high red pumps, her hair spilling from the top of her head. I knew I looked underwhelming in a black sheath I'd ordered from a chain store. I'd also stuffed my mop into a black snood, to downplay its bright-red color. Sephy's hairstyling was ruined. My mask was also plain black. "Very elegant and understated. But I thought Declan bought you a gold dress? He sounded thrilled about seeing you in it."

Oh, God, yes, he'd said that on the ball's group chat.

I intended to change into it later, just before Declan got to the party. I'd have to leave my bag somewhere in the castle and change in the loo. Which was all going to look a bit odd.

"It's kind of itchy, gave me a bit of a rash, so I'm going to change just before he arrives."

"Oh, what a shame. I have loads of slips you can wear if that would help?"

"I don't want to risk it. I wore it at home, and it gave me welts on my chest."

She looked puzzled but was too polite to pursue it. "Don't you just hate that when the dress isn't lined? And that's an expensive store too."

"Don't say anything to Declan."

"Of course not. He's so sweet, he'd be crushed. But how will you know—"

Slam. The door opposite us shook the whole house.

"What the?" Tabs fumed. "Tim fucking Langston. That's the builder. No one slams a door like him."

That was funny. Tabs rarely swore. Furious, she bustled out to the opposite room, which was under construction. I'd never seen her like this. Even at work, she was unruffled. Just because I was intrigued, I followed a bit behind her.

She faced him, bristling, her hands on her hips. "Tim, we spoke about a bathroom in every bedroom. What happened in this room?"

Her red satin dress gleamed with her every move. He faced her, his powerful legs apart in tan work pants topped with a tool belt slung low on his hips. His arms crossed tight over his plaid shirt, which clung to his muscled arms and chest, the sleeves rolled up to show his huge, tatted forearms. He watched her with a bemused look, his thick brown hair sticking up all over the place, smudges on his face.

"We did speak about that, and I'll repeat what I already told you," he said. "It's impossible in an old place like this."

She tipped her chin. "That's for me to decide. I've done the drawings, and I want you to stick to them."

"Your drawings are just pretty pictures like the ones you did in kindergarten, but they don't work in reality. Maybe you could write a story about this?"

"I'll remind you I was a trained architect before I became a journalist, so don't give me that bullshit. And speaking of kindergarten, you're still the same pigheaded ass you were then. Build it as I've drawn it."

"Yes, milady." He doffed his imaginary cap.

She moved closer to him, poking his chest with her finger. "No, no, no, you don't. You don't get to do that bloody routine. Follow my drawings. Final."

She turned to leave, so incandescent with rage that her shimmering blonde waterfall arrangement had dropped around her shoulders. This was a side of Tabs I'd never seen. She was known at work as being the peacemaker and almost always avoided conflict. Some staff, unfortunately, saw her as a pushover and took advantage. I thought she could flex her muscles more. In conferences, the editors were always surprised when she came up with a page-one or page-three story, even though she did it regularly. Advertising for her section paid the salaries for half the newspaper staff. She had a lot of power. But she never used it.

"Hey, Tabbycat," he rumbled out.

She rounded on him, her dainty red peep-toe to his scuffed, steel-capped work boots, and jerked her chin up to his amused face.

"Stop calling me that stupid name. It's my five-year-old name, and it's very belittling, which you very bloody well know. What? What now?" She was seething, her face screwed up, hands fisted at her sides.

His eyes traced down her red dress. Then burned into hers.

"You look absolutely gorgeous." He said it softly, genuinely.

Her face melted.

"Tabbycat," he murmured.

"Oooh," she fumed. "You're impossible." Fists thrown over her head, she stomped out.

He laughed as she slammed the door behind her.

"Wow," I said, once we were back in the bedroom.

"Yes, I know." She touched her hair, realizing her waterfall hairdo was now more of a puddle. "Argh. You heard that? He's *such* a wanker."

"No, I'm talking about the sexual tension. He is smoking hot, Tabs. And you two together are fire."

"What?" She shook herself, incredulous, like she didn't know what I was talking about. Turning to the mirror, she cursed him under her breath and tried to fix her hair, muttering about the time she'd wasted in a hairdresser's chair, and he was responsible for that too.

The look he gave her. The burn in his eyes. I missed Declan so much that I ached all over. His eyes, his arms around my waist, his funny asides, how we'd swap knowing looks, smiling at how much we had to talk about afterward. Peregrine. This house and all the animals, Tim the Builder and Tabs' fight, why she didn't ditch Peregrine and take up with Tim.

Me: *I miss you so much. I love you. I wish we could talk right now.*

He wouldn't see this until he was out of the meeting. Probably not until I was at the ball, but it might look rude to keep checking my phone.

I sighed, my heart heavy. Our timing was all wrong these days.

CHAPTER THIRTY-TWO

"JEEZ, WOULDN'T WANT to be responsible for cleaning these tiles." I was referring to the vast black-and-white checkered flooring in the castle entry. "It's a veritable football field."

"Isla." Peregrine pursed his lips in chagrin.

"Sorry, I'm a pleb."

The two of us were silenced as a crush of elegance transported us through the entry—men in tuxes and beautiful women in fabulous gowns, their necks dripping with diamonds. It was like a fashion magazine had exploded.

Despite my nerves, I grinned. This crowd cram was perfect. Just what I needed. Now the staff at the entry couldn't announce our names. I could stay low-key and unnoticed by Cassius.

The sea of glossed and coiffed heads was overseen by life-size marble statues of naked men and women. I thought of the glamorous art dealer Ishani Ali and her funny aside about seeing too many scrotums in her work. I liked her, but was she helping Cassius with something dishonest?

Beyond, beckoning, teasingly offering the answer to all my questions about Cassius, was a wide, twirling staircase. It was too early to guess when I'd be able to sneak upstairs, but this staircase seemed far too public and exposed.

One of the women on the first step lifted her eye mask and waved. It was Sunny. She rushed up to me, her blue-lidded eyes shining with excitement.

"This is my girlfriend, Shikha." A tiny woman with silver piercings grinned at me, her glittery cheeks flashing, her long hair bouncing. They both looked stunning in puffy eighties-style gowns in neon. "Why are you hulking around that overnight bag? I thought you were staying over? Surely you're not driving all the way back to London tonight?"

Smiling ruefully, I said we had to get back to Sephy. I felt horrible about lying to my new friend.

Before she could ask more, I introduced the two women to Tabs and Peregrine. There was much hand-shaking and complimenting each other's outfits. I'm sure they had to stretch it for mine, which was so plain I worried I might stand out after all. I asked one of the waiters where I could stash my overnight bag—his white-gloved hands carried my scuffed-up tote reverentially into the library next door, as though it were the luggage of the King, me following, embarrassed.

Back at the entrance hall, the others already had glasses of champers in their hands, and Tabs handed me mine. We all strolled into the massive ballroom, oohing and aahing.

I placed a hand on Tabs' arm. "You should see the fainting couches in the library. They have these cool touches of punk."

She fluttered her eyelashes. "I love how you notice interiors. I wish you would work with me. You know you could be visiting and writing about these sorts of homes all the time."

Before I could think about that, the four of them pointed out the changes and discussed how last year, the ballroom had been a bit paint-peeling and drab. I hadn't seen it before to be able to compare, but I'd researched old photos.

The walls of the ballroom were intricate, with cream-and-blue moldings and gold mirrors, the ceilings dripping with Italian chandeliers. Potted ferns surrounded high cocktail tables, with large French doors offering glimpses to the formal gardens, including animal-shaped topiary, the stone chapel, and the vine-covered medieval ruins beyond the lake. The splendor and history of this place was mind-blowing. Cassius must have generated a lot of money to remodel it.

I took a sip of champagne to calm my nerves. It tasted off. I put it down. That was two glasses now—no, three, counting the one at the dress store. Maybe I'd just lost my taste for champagne? The five of us gathered around the table with the best view of the outside gardens.

"Oh, for the love of God. No." Peregrine stared at a group in the corner and swiftly looked away. "Chap yonder must be crying inside."

"What is it?" I asked breathlessly, ever nosy.

"He's wearing"—he sucked in a breath—"*white tie.* It specifically said black tie. He's at three o'clock. Looks like a rugger player. Tails and white dickey. Can you imagine? Must be bloody mortified."

In fact, the guy looked happy and pleased with himself, holding a large beer in his white-gloved hand, swishing his tails joyfully like a merman, his huge chest puffing out the white dickey. He broke into rollicking laughter at something the elegant woman beside him said. *Hey. I know that guy.*

"That's your builder, Tabs," I said. "What's his name again?"

Tabs peered around me and tsked. "Tim fucking Langston."

Peregrine turned up his nose. "Your builder? *Trade?*"

I rolled my eyes, and Tabs elbowed him sharply. Sunny and Shikha gave me a look like, Is he for real?

Tabs gave a grunt. "That outfit is his great-grandfather's. Who was a butler between the wars. He's rubbing it in, as usual."

Because he seemed fun and because I wanted to see him interact with Tabs again, and maybe a little to annoy Peregrine—oh, there were so many shit-stirring reasons I wanted to get him over—I waved to him. Grinning, he waved back. He looked straight over my shoulder and mouthed *Tabs*, lowered his mask, and gave her a wink. A satisfied glow bloomed in my little matchmaking heart. I turned to see her reaction. She rolled her eyes and huffed.

"Isla, no!" Peregrine fussed. "For God's sake. Don't lure him over here. We'll be tainted by his embarrassing outfit."

Tabs screwed up her big blues at him. "Perry. Would you stop being so … so … *you* for one night."

I'd never heard her so exasperated with him. She was usually so patient. I wondered whether her heated altercation with Tim fucking Langston had only served to make her more frustrated with Peregrine.

Tim held up a finger.

"Looks like he'll be over in a jiffy," I reported back to them.

Peregrine blanched, and, casting around the room, nodded to a group on the other side. "Some of our chums want to say hello. You'll excuse us, won't you?" He dragged Tabs over with him.

Sunny, her girlfriend and I hurried through the doors outside. We let loose with snorting, folding-over-yourself laughter, the thousand years of history that stretched in front of us—the geometric gardens, the ruins, the baroque fountains—stoically ignoring our silliness.

Sunny nudged her girlfriend's elbow. "What did I tell you?" She turned to me, shaking her head. "Why is it every time I see you, it's chaos?"

"Bloody colonials." I grimaced. "What can I say?"

That made us laugh even more.

"Isla," a deep voice called from behind. I jumped. I turned. Cassius.

Oh God, I'd fucked up. I'd left it too long.

CHAPTER THIRTY-THREE

HE WAS A daunting mountain of tux, topped with raven hair and glowing skin.

"Oh, you look magnificent," he said.

Surely I looked like a mafioso's widow? I couldn't take him seriously.

He smiled, looking deep into my eyes as if we had a secret. "How clever to do the matte black when all the other women are doing shiny color."

Was he being sarcastic? Or was he telling me something? That he knew I was trying to hide?

"Thank you so much for inviting me. What a beautiful place, er, house, ah, castle you have here." I was embarrassed by my struggle for the right word. But I had a thought. I hoped it might make him underestimate me.

He gave an amused laugh and offered me his elbow. "I'd love to give you a tour and have you meet my friends." Panic pounded in me, swift and sharp. I pictured him showing me around from room to room, introducing me to his friends, stopping at each group to chat about something. That could take ages. I imagined what it would be like if I was at his side when Declan arrived. My heart stopped. That couldn't happen.

"Thank you, but I have some friends over there." I nodded to the two groups. "I was just dashing to the loo."

"Yes, I'll show you."

I stiffened, on edge. Did he know what I was up to? Was he deliberately interrupting my plan? What host leads his female guest to the bathroom? Especially one who had five hundred people to get around?

He ushered me through the arch and around to two wooden doors that had *W* and *M* on them, respectively. I went to open the door. Hands in pockets, he stayed where he was. Oh no, he wasn't going to wait here for me, was he?

"Don't let me keep you from your guests," I tossed out a bit starkly. He gave me a good hard stare—was he annoyed at being dismissed? Maybe he was just used to women, everyone, wanting more of him, not trying to brush him off?

With a few blinks, he turned on a heel and headed back to the ballroom.

The bathroom was as big as my flat, with vast expanses of marble and elegant pink sofas. How much money had he spent in its entirety? Mind-blowing.

I listened at the door. He wouldn't come in here, would he? My heart thumped. I couldn't get a bead on this guy.

I emerged after a proper amount of time to find Cassius wasn't there. Phew. I peeked through the arch into the ballroom. There might not be another time to disappear. I was going to find something about Sister Modestia, and I was going to find that secret room.

Shoes in hand, I bolted upstairs. I stopped for a second and looked around for cameras. None that I could see. I knocked and stepped into a huge bathroom with a copper bath and modern art. God, was that a Lichtenstein? I opened a few drawers. They were empty except for new razors and spare toothbrushes, one used.

Was this *his* bathroom? I ran my hand along the walls, pressing at intervals. Nothing.

But would the secret room be located behind a bathroom? It had to be accessible any time of the day or night if the family was at constant risk of being arrested for practicing a banned religion. That meant it was more likely accessed from a bedroom.

I crept through the adjoining door. It had a modern four-poster bed, masculine but comfortable. Still, it was pristine, no clothes cast around, so I had to wonder if it was a guest room rather than Cassius's. To make sure, I opened a few drawers. Nothing. All his clothes must be stored in a walk-in wardrobe. I opened the bedside drawer—expecting what? Secret papers? Condoms? The top drawer contained my story about Sister Modestia's death. And a sheath of old papers. I flicked through them, noticing the dates. They were letters still in sealed envelopes from him to his sister. He'd stubbornly used her old name, Lady Beatrice Devonport, and they had been sent back, some quite recently. Was he sad about that? The fact that he couldn't communicate with her? Or was he bitter that his sister hadn't wanted to read his letters or that Mother Superior insisted they were sent back to him unopened? How funny to keep letters that he had sent as though that was one of the few connections with her and he couldn't let go.

A *tap tap tap* sounded from the bathroom. Heels clicked on the marble floor. I'd left the adjoining door open. The sounds of water. *Fuuuck.* No, no, no. Someone was in the bathroom. Where could I hide? He had to have a walk-in wardrobe. Where was the door? I couldn't see it anywhere. Desperate, I slid under the bed. I heard a woman's hum. Using his private en-suite bathroom was a bit proprietorial. It must be someone who expected to end up in this room at the end of the night. Which might mean she would feel comfortable with wandering into his bedroom too. Holding my breath, I listened to her leave and close the bathroom door, the click of her high heels on the stone floor. Click, click down the stairs. Then silence. I whooshed out a breath.

I opened the bottom drawer of his bedside table. Another sheath of papers, this time yellowed with age. I read the first page. It was a child writing to Cassius. I flicked it over to check the sign-off signature. A well-tutored Bea with a little bee beside it, hearts on the antennae. He'd called his sister Bea. My heart broke a little. He was a devoted brother to keep her old letters. Tap. Tap. Footsteps, high-heeled shoes on the stairs? Women's voices, this time more than one. For God's sake, use the downstairs loo.

I couldn't stay here any longer, even though I was finding interesting documents. If I wanted to keep searching without being discovered, I had to get away from the carnival that was his bathroom. I needed to run to the other end of the hallway. Shoving the letters back in, I closed the drawer, tiptoed out, and, making sure the hallway was empty, I sprinted to the other end. Thank goodness for the rugs on the stone floors.

Puffing, I ran into the last room. Large, curved windows revealed rolling hills, which should have made it light and airy, but it was stuffy and too warm, and unlike the rest of the castle, it hadn't been modernized. It was a nursery room for two, set up with a chalkboard, two chair-and-desk sets, twin beds, and children's books lined up in bookcases. I touched one of the tiny chairs, scratched and old but polished. But it wasn't a playful room. It was a museum, preserved in an almost creepy way, as if it were dusted every day, but no one was allowed inside. It didn't seem like a place that was waiting for new children to play or learn. There was a fireplace with a mantelpiece that displayed framed photos. Each featured a little boy and his older sister at different ages, and in each one, she had her arm around him protectively.

A gold-and-silver container sat in the middle of the arrangement of framed photos, about the height of a hand. It was so shiny it stuck out, lacking the patina and age of the rest of the room. Something deep in my years of training set off a distant alarm bell.

Checking the door, I approached the container. I reached out for it, grasped it, and pulled it off the ledge. Argh. My hands dropped. I'd almost let go of it. It was much heavier than I thought. What on earth was inside? Jewelry? With both hands tight around it, I brought it up to me. I unscrewed the lid. Inside was a clear plastic bag containing what looked like sand, sealed with a twisty tie. Sand? Maybe sand from their holidays as children? I inspected the texture more carefully through the plastic.

It was gray dust. No, not dust.

Ashes.

This was a burial urn.

I recoiled, almost dropping it. Lowering to a crouch, I set down the container. I turned up the lid. Westminster Crematorium. It *was* ashes, cremains. I recognized that name. It was the crematorium Sister Innocenta talked about.

Were these Sister Modestia's ashes?

Sealing the lid again, I turned the container upside down. Six initials. *BAOAAD.* Sister Modestia was listed in Debrett's and Who's Who as Lady Beatrice Anastasia Octavia Aurelia Athena Devonport.

These *were* her ashes. Oh God. I felt a cold hand clutch at my throat and squeeze hard, cutting off my breath.

Cassius said he had no jurisdiction over her body following her death.

Sister Innocenta claimed Cassius had had his sister's body cremated.

Sister was right. *Cassius was lying.*

And I was in his house, snooping. And no one knew I was up here.

A muffled noise came from behind the fireplace. Bats? Mice? Ugh. At the thought it might be mice, a sick nausea blasted through my torso. But I couldn't hear squeaking or scuttling. A hand over my mouth, I listened again. Murmurs, but I couldn't make out the words.

It was *human* voices. A sudden notion hit me. Was it ghosts? This place was one thousand years old. Wait a minute—ghosts? I mentally slapped myself for even going there. Stop this. I was freaking myself out. Was I just hearing other people moving through the castle? Or was it the secret room Peregrine and Sister Innocenta had talked about? It made sense that one of the entries, or maybe the only entry, to the secret room was from the nursery. The children hid in the room when their father was on a rampage. Wasn't that what Sister Innocenta had said?

I felt a burst of hope and determination. I might have found the secret room, even though I had no clue how it tied in. I started pressing the walls, looking for cracks, trying to find a way to gain access.

A door slam punched from the hallway. I jumped out of my skin. If I got caught in here, what would I say? That I was looking for the bathroom? But that only worked if it wasn't Cassius. And then what would he do? A thought shot through my mind. These walls were thick. Screams for help would be muffled.

Jumpy with nerves, I hurried to the door and peered around. Cassius turned into his bedroom. My knees buckled. He was here. Snatching up my heels and checking down the hall, I ran straight out and down the staircase. Pausing at the bottom, I slipped on my shoes.

Without looking up, I took a step and hit smack into something hard.

CHAPTER THIRTY-FOUR

I LOOKED UP. It wasn't a wall—it was Declan's chest.

"Oh, God, Declan. You've got to stop giving me frights like this," I said. "What are you doing here?"

He put his hands on his hips. "What were you doing *up there*?"

I took a second to see that he looked incredible, his crisp white shirt showing off the sharp edges of his jawline, his black tux jacket sitting perfectly on his square shoulders. He was clean-shaven, and he smelled gorgeous, like the ocean and the promises of nighttime.

"What time is it?" I asked, knowing I hadn't answered his question.

A line formed between his eyebrows. "Around ten. I put pressure on everyone to finish writing up the bill so I could get away for this. Where on earth were *you*?"

"Just looking around, waiting for you to arrive. I don't know that many people here." I felt horrible about lying, but I had to. Everything was good again between us. Another rift, another fight—what would that do to us? Would this be the lie that broke us? Maybe he wouldn't notice I wasn't wearing his dress? Maybe I was worrying about nothing.

He ran a thumb under his bottom lip. "I saw Tabitha as I came in. She said you disappeared soon after you arrived, and she was worried about you. A woman with her called Sunny introduced herself as a new friend. She also said she met you at the beginning of the evening and hasn't seen you since." He lowered his voice. "Isla, tell me you haven't been snooping around."

Heavy steps pulled my eyes upward. Cassius walked slowly down the stairs, focused only on me. No, no, no. He was so obvious, making it look like there was something between us, and I was complicit. Was he doing it to piss off Declan? Because it was working. Out of the corner of my eye, I clocked that Declan's face was rigid. His jaw muscles pulsed as he watched Cassius stare at me.

"Good evening. Welcome." Cassius turned to Declan when he reached the bottom step. He came up behind me and placed his hand on my shoulder. He murmured very close to my ear, "Isla, are we having a little trouble here?"

In a flash, Declan lifted Cassius's hand off my shoulder, stepped between us, and steered me away from him. "This isn't your business," he said to Cassius.

Cassius looked flustered. Catching himself, he grunted as if unconcerned about Declan. "Supper will be served soon."

As I watched Cassius saunter away, a brick weighed on my heart. Declan tensed up, and the strain filled the air between us. I had two thoughts. First, did Cassius hear me up there? Had he seen me at all? Then, this did not look good.

"We weren't up there together, I swear," I said, my heart in my mouth.

Pressing his lips together, Declan stared at me as if he was trying to work out whether I was telling the truth. Then his brows raised, as though he suddenly remembered something else. He ran his gaze up and down me. My pulse spiked.

"Where is your dress? The gold one. Why aren't you wearing your new dress?"

"I—I."

Should I say I spilled red wine on it? That a houseguest of Cassius loaned me this? No, that drew in Cassius.

I held my breath, thinking.

He took a minute while my gaze roamed around my face. Was he searching for an answer that he wanted to believe? Then he looked like he didn't have any hope. His chest heaved up and down. He seemed utterly crushed.

"Oh God. You deliberately didn't wear it because you intended to snoop around this place." His face dropped further. "You were never going to wear it."

"That's not true." My jaw tightened. It *was* true, and my lying about it churned my stomach.

He looked around. I did, too, to make sure we were alone.

"Isla, do you know what would happen if that man found you? Or one of his staff? I told you he's bad news. No one can hear you up there. What on earth were you expecting to find?"

I lowered my voice. Should I share my plan with him? But wouldn't he be negative, just like he'd been all along? I didn't want to block him out. I wanted to include him in my decisions and my experiences, and I wanted his advice and help. "I told you what Sister Innocenta said about the room behind the walls. What if whatever is behind these walls links all the things I know?"

His crushed face turned to anger. "So much for our solid, dazzling front." He spat out the words. "You didn't want to come to this ball with me. You just wanted to get into the upstairs rooms."

"I *did* want to come to the ball with you. And, of course, I also wanted to get into the upstairs rooms. It's my job."

"Why didn't you tell me this when we were shopping for your dress?"

I felt sick about how much money he'd spent on me. "I told you not to buy the dress." Oh, God, no, that was wrong. I flashed a hand through the air, trying to wipe away my words. "Sorry, I mean, thank you for buying the dress. I *loved* that you did. But it was too expensive, and I told you that."

God, that *still* came out all wrong. *What a mess, what a horrible mess.*

He closed his eyes. "So, now I'm in the wrong for buying you the dress." He raised his arms. "Fuck me. Honestly, I don't know how to answer that. You've stumped me. You've lied to me so many times I've lost count. And you've made a fool out of me twice now. I just don't know what to do." He let his hands drop to his thighs with a slap. "I do know one thing. There's no point in staying. I'm headed home."

His breathing went shallow, and he ran a hand down his face. He seemed thoroughly fed up, embarrassed and angry.

Looking at him, I felt a deep tenderness. His turmoil and pain were ripping my insides apart. I wanted to save our relationship; that was the most important thing in my life, and I didn't want to lie anymore. I wanted to explain everything. I knew I was abandoning my chance to investigate here further—though Cassius had seen me walking down from upstairs, so I'd have to be doubly careful. I had no other choice.

"I'll come with you," I said.

It would add an hour to my journey to the port instead of traveling direct, but I had to do it.

He breathed in and out. Shrugged. He was such a good guy that no matter how angry he was with me, how much he didn't want to see my face for a while, he couldn't leave me behind.

I collected my bag of clothing from the library. While Declan got the car, I found Sunny, Shikha, Tabs, and Perry nearby in the ballroom and gave them a weak excuse for leaving so suddenly about not feeling well. They all offered their sympathy, but none of them believed it. He pulled up to the front, and I climbed in with him. I made a pact with myself to be calm.

I told Declan about what I'd found.

"Okay, so now you have some evidence to bring to the police." His knuckles whitened on the wheel. "Let them deal with him. And let them deal with the port too."

"That Cassius lied about cremating his sister? How could I go to the police with that? That's not enough, Declan. You must see that."

The car's tires spat out the gravel as we made our way through the shadowed grounds.

"What about the port?"

"I owe it to Sister Modestia to go tonight. And I still need this story. I can't just give it to the police and hope they follow it up when, at that time of the morning, they're short-staffed." My solar plexus went rigid, strengthening my resolve. I was exhausted and upset, but I had no other choice. I had to do this.

He shook his head.

"Do you know for sure Cassius is dangerous? What do people say about him?" I asked as we rode down the long driveway, the somber half-moon hanging over the trees.

"Everyone is scared of him, Isla. If you disagree with him, cross him, he comes after you."

"He sounds like an arsehole and a bully. But have you heard of any instances where he's dangerous?" In my heart I knew I was hoping to find something to justify still going to the port.

"The word is that people disappear around him. Staff, for instance."

I immediately thought of the cook. Goosebumps snaked along my arms. Cassius had mentioned that his cook had disappeared. We passed under the eerie stone archway and it was a relief to get off the estate.

"But is there any evidence?" I asked. "Do the staff just leave? Any instance where the cops have turned up to his door?"

I asked, even though I'd just found evidence that he'd lied about cremating his sister's body and there were no consequences for him.

He huffed, annoyed. "We both know it's not just people who have interactions with the police who are dodgy. But okay, I'm going to dig around and get you evidence that he is more than just a bully, that he's dangerous."

A ray of optimism burst through my chest. I was immediately happy that we were working together. But I was confused as to why he'd volunteered to help. Then, because my mind always went in that direction, suspicious—why was he agreeing to get involved, even if it was to prove me wrong? Maybe he'd accepted that I wasn't going to quit and he'd realized that it was better for both of us if he tried to help in whatever way he could. Because he seemed to be coming around, I thought it was a good time to try to push it further. I also wanted him to see that although I was touched that he was worried about me, his previous job was always unsafe.

"Thank you. But also, Declan, I know you're saying this because you are worried about me and you don't want me to be in danger. But every hour of every day of every year you worked as an undercover cop, you were under threat. You've just retired from that role at the age of thirty-nine. So that's what? Fourteen years of being undercover?"

He nodded.

"But you're saying to me I shouldn't take any risks."

He challenged me with a hard look. "Isla, I had a whole team under me, backing me up. I was a trained professional. My investigations were official. I could call Interpol and the local police if things turned nasty. You are acting on your own with no training in this kind of thing. You don't even have developed self-defense skills. And you haven't even pitched this story to your editor, so I'm the only one who knows you're working on it."

My heart sank. But it was important we keep talking, and maybe I could still make him understand. "Dec, I worked with you for two weeks in Ōhope, remember? I knew if something went down, there was no one close enough to save you or me. Okay, we had those cops stationed outside the house for a couple of nights, but the other time you called backup, they were an hour away."

He stared at me in between watching the road. I saw something closed off in his expression that made me think I wasn't making progress in getting through to him.

"And you have a daughter who depends on you," I said. "I have no one."

He sucked in a breath. The tension was painful. I hadn't meant it like that. I touched his arm, wanting to take it back. I felt terrible that I'd said that to him.

His jaw flexed. "How can you say that? You have me. And I hoped you felt like you had Sephy too. I hoped that eventually you would think of her as a daughter."

Did I think that was a possibility? I wanted to, but I just couldn't totally see it yet.

"But how can I when you don't trust me with her?"

"I never said I didn't trust you."

"You said you shouldn't expect to leave her with me." This was a weak response, as I'd already admitted to being wrong about taking her along to a job, but still, it had hurt.

"It's early days. That will change."

I sighed. After that, we just went around and around the same argument. About halfway home, we lapsed into an exhausted but tense silence for the rest of the way.

The arguing started again as soon as we got out of the car.

On the doorstep, Declan stood in front of me. "You're not going to the port, right?"

"I have to. If I don't, Sister Modestia's murderer will go free, her death was for nothing, and all those drugs will be released onto the streets." I pushed the front door open.

We both quieted at the sight of the childminder watching TV on the sofa. She seemed surprised to see us because it was only 12:30 a.m. She said she'd thought we'd be much later.

Declan checked that Sephy had a good night, thanked the childminder, paid her, and saw her to her car.

I hoped the whole interaction might calm him down, but by the time he came back inside, the fresh night air had made him only more agitated.

He strode up and down the living room rug as I hung up my dresses and changed into dark yoga pants, a thick jersey, and sneakers. "I cannot get my head around what you did tonight." His voice was getting louder and louder. He faced me, hands on hips, his eyes flashing. "Isla, tell me you're not going to see *that man* again."

"Why are you asking me this? It just makes it so much harder for me. I've got to do what I need to do. We've talked about this." I had to find justice for Sister Modestia, and that involved determining whether Cassius was connected to her death in some way. It wasn't that I was putting my job above Declan. I shouldn't have to choose between them.

"What I feel doesn't figure in any of your calculations," Declan said. "Our relationship doesn't figure in it. This is the third time we've talked about this. You've made a choice."

You've made a choice.

I did a double-take at those words. It was like he was emphasizing that I was choosing the story over him. Which I wasn't. I loved him. The knot in my gut burned. I wanted him to support me. But I had to move forward even if he didn't.

"And it's the third time I've said the same thing about him," I said.

A creak sounded upstairs. I glanced upward at the ceiling. Had we woken Sephy? Had she heard us? I didn't want her to hear us fighting like this. It was too early in our "getting to know each other" for her to see me at odds with her father.

He looked tired. "I'm going to leave you to do whatever is important to you, whatever you have to. I can't stop you—you've made a choice."

I squirmed, my blood curdling in my veins. Those words again. Like a signpost, portentous, like this was a turn in the road for us.

He swayed on his feet.

"Okay, I'll call an Uber." I had to leave by 1 a.m. The drive was an hour and a half, and I needed extra time to find a vantage point to watch the ship unload.

I didn't know whether I should even kiss him on the cheek. He was normally so affectionate.

"Text me when you get home." He trudged wearily up the stairs.

I felt hollow and wrung out. I was so tired I could sleep on my feet, but I had a long night ahead of me. I couldn't think about our relationship now. We were going to be fine once I got this story. And tonight might be the final step.

This tension would be over.

I grabbed my small backpack and packed my handbag, jacket, and binoculars.

When the Uber said it was a minute away, I stepped outside and waited.

Something shuffled above me. A bird? I glanced up to the first floor. Declan had his curtains and windows closed. Sephy stood at her open window. Was that melancholy I saw lingering in her dark outline, or was she just listening to music? I waved at her, but she didn't wave back.

CHAPTER THIRTY-FIVE

A PRIUS DRIVER stuck his head out the window.

"Isla?" he called. I nodded. "You want to go to Steptoe and Daughters junkyard, next to Tilbury Port in Essex?"

"Yes, thanks, that's the one."

During the hour-and-half-long journey, I vacillated between churning over Declan's anger and disappointment and feeling ill about the vagueness of my plan. I had to find a place in the junkyard from where I could watch the ship being unloaded without getting caught. But how did I even get into the junkyard? How would I know which container the drugs were in?

The driver came to a stop. I checked the time on my phone: 2:30 a.m. I had half an hour before the ship came in.

"Sure you're okay by yourself in the dark?" He seemed concerned as I slid out of the back seat. "There's nothing here."

"I'm sure."

Watching him drive away, I wasn't quite so confident. Gulls circled overhead, and the smell of petrol and fishy brine caught in the back of my throat. Tall ships punched into the black skyline, reminding me that I knew nothing about them.

Oh God, this is it.

A suffocating alarm seized my throat, making it hard to breathe. It was pitch black outside the junkyard, with only one light on the high fence illuminating a sign with missing letters. Next door at the port, the lights beamed big and blinding, stadium bright. I counted at least four cameras along the front. I was protected from sight by a row of prefab buildings along the fence line. I couldn't see into the port, but they didn't have a good view of the junkyard either. I had to get to the waterfront, half a football field away, to get a better view when the ship came in.

My head rolled back to survey the junkyard fence. It seemed more than three times my height, maybe twenty feet.

I crouched and tried to push up the chain fence to sneak under. It wouldn't stretch far enough. *Shit.* I was counting on that. What now? I had to climb it. If I fell, minimum, I'd break some bones. My heart thrashed around wildly.

I ignored my aching thigh and grabbed onto the fence with both hands, stabbing the toe of my sneakers through the triangle-shaped wires. Okay, one more. Lift. One more. My hands were killing me. I had to go on. Hand, hand, hold, move the toe of your shoe. Oh God, this was agony.

Eventually, I was near the top. That was the worst of it. Clutching on with two hands, I did a precarious hoist of one leg over. I shoved my toe hard into the fence on the other side. Wobbling, I reached over and fixed one hand. Then the other leg. *Don't look down, don't look down.* Descending was easier.

I dropped to the ground and looked around. Amid the piled-up junk was an old office on the port's fence line. It was midway to the waterfront. Scrambling over the junk to reach the office, I peered into the windows to make sure no one was here. A voice broke the air. I ducked behind the office. I had a good view of the waterfront at the port, about a basketball court away now, workers milling around. I sat there, churning with nerves, until it was nearly 3 a.m.

A huge ship appeared down the river. The shrill blast of its arrival seared into my brain, and a pressure mounted behind my eyes. It glided to a halt. Within seconds, workers in safety vests appeared on the many deck levels, flinging ropes and shouting out to each other and the workers below. How would I know which container had the drugs? Maybe there would be a definite sign, like they loaded the container into a completely different truck. What was I going to do when it was unloaded? Take photos? Yell out? Call the police?

"Hey-hey." A man at the port cupped his hands around his mouth. "Oi, you," he hollered. I crouched. Did he mean me? But surely he couldn't see me?

"What the fuck are you doing?" he yelled.

I leaned out from the shed with my binoculars. But he wasn't facing me. I didn't think he could even see me. He was tall and big, dressed all in black, but he didn't have on a safety vest like the other workers. Was he one of the team waiting for the drugs to be offloaded?

"Hey-hey," he called.

I shuddered. Those words reminded me of someone. Why did they make my heart beat faster? That Russian guy behind the phone booth, asking Sister Modestia to come out. He said, "Hey-hey." Then something about "Your brother."

From the corner of my eye, movement flashed. Someone was wandering along the junkyard's waterfront. It was a girl dressed in black with long dark hair. How did she get in here without me seeing? She must have scrambled over the fence quickly while I was hiding behind the office. She switched from foot to foot, impatiently looking around. She turned at the man's voice.

Something about that swing of the hair and how she held the knees of her jeans.

Blood rushed to my ears. Oh my God—

Sephy.

What the hell was she doing here?

CHAPTER THIRTY-SIX

I SQUEEZED MY binoculars tight against my face. My hands shook so hard that everything in front of me was blurry.

My breath shuddered out. *Focus.*

Clenching my hands to stop the shaking, I fixed my sights first on Sephy and then around her. Oh, God. The big man dressed all in black ran toward her from the port side. I had a few minutes, at least. He'd have to climb the fence. There was no way. The fence for the junkyard was high, but it was shoddy and amateur. The chain-link fence on the boundary was at least two stories high, with barbed wire woven all the way through and long spikes at the top and bottom. He stopped at the fence, pulling down his black balaclava to cover his face. Why? This was not good. He fiddled with the fence in front of him. Was he unlocking a gate? *Shit.* He was going to get through.

Not Sephy, no! He wasn't going to get anywhere near her. My heart slammed against my rib cage. I would die before I let him touch her.

My raw terror slowed everything down. I was aware of a few raindrops that fell on my head and a slight groan from the ship listing at the docks.

With an unnerving clarity, a peek of the tall man's red checkered shirt surfaced from under his black hoodie. He pressed his ear, spat out something. Frustrated, he yelled over his shoulder. Another man, shorter, stockier, but also dressed in black ran toward him.

"Sephy!" I screamed. "Sephy!" Through the binoculars, I could see her look around, confused, then back at the men who were coming through the gate. She peered into the darkness, looking for the person attached to the voice. She was very close to the water. Too close. My mind raced.

They could push her in, and no one would see.

I ran toward her, scrambling over the junk. One foot slipped on something slimy, and I jerked to the side, trying to right myself. I splattered on the ground. Argh. I'd badly scraped my knee. I was doing this all wrong. I had to call the police, now. Breathing heavily, I got up and pulled my phone from my back pocket. My fingers fumbled with the buttons. *Stop.* Taking a deep breath, I punched out "2" for the local police. I'd keyed it in during the Uber ride. A ringtone sounded, then the crack of an answer.

"Essex Police—what is your emergency?"

My eyes never left Sephy.

"Isla Joyson here. I'm at Steptoe and Daughters junkyard next to Tilbury Port in Essex. Two big men from the port are running toward my stepdaughter. She's only thirteen years old. I don't know what they will do with her. They look very angry. Can you get here as soon as you can? We are not safe."

"Dispatching now," she said.

I held on to the phone, listening for an update, as I ran toward Sephy, sliding and half-tripping over all the junk, while the operator called for two cars, four officers, to come and get us.

"Why are you at the junkyard?" the operator asked.

"I'm a journalist," I puffed out, still scrambling toward Sephy. "I was investigating a tip-off that there are drugs on one of the ships. I think Sephy must have followed me."

Covering the phone, I screamed Sephy's name again. She flung herself around.

"Who's that?" she yelled into the night.

"It's me, Isla!" I waved my arms, trying to get her attention.

"Isla," she called back.

"The police are coming," I yelled to the men. "Leave her alone."

They pushed through the gate. One of the men pointed at me. I couldn't make out their faces, just the outline. The shorter man pulled down his black balaclava. He took something out of his back pocket and into his front pocket. It glinted silver in the moonlight. They powered toward me. *Keep coming.* Despite the sight of these men heading my way, relief swamped me. At least they weren't going for Sephy. I intended to stay where I was, act as a decoy.

"Run!" I yelled at Sephy. "Call the police again. Dial 999."

She headed away from us—to the other side of the yard. Good girl. Good tactic. I stood still, sweat pouring down my back. The men ran toward me. Closer, hands fisted. I waited for them, not trying to escape. Still, the big man slammed into me. *Ooof.* The force of his body against mine whiplashed my head so hard I almost vomited. I doubled up, my head sinking to my knees, fear and panic driving into me.

"What the fuck," I punched out, trying to keep him from me. Had he knocked some of my teeth out? I put my finger to my mouth. Then my fingers were no longer in front of my face, and my shoulders were killing me.

The other one had yanked my arms up my back.

"Shit," I screamed. A whooshing soared through my ears. I bellowed from the pain in my shoulders. Was he going to break my arms? That was what it felt like. I couldn't stand another second. Then he released me. *Phew.*

The tall one stood in front and pushed at my chest. My torso shivered with revulsion. His hand was on my chest, not farther down, but I didn't trust he wouldn't go there. They were masked, anonymous. Clearly, they did this for a living. Life had no value for them, and they certainly didn't respect me. I didn't trust they would stop at beating me.

"Who the fuck are you?" Another shove from the tall man. His wide lips dripped with contempt. He was terrifying, but I had to notice something about him. His eyes, through the opening in the balaclava, were a watery blue, his skin damp and pale. One finger glinted. It was a ring, but it had a sharp point.

I had to give them something—they weren't going to mess around.

"I'm a journalist. I'm here to write a story."

"What about the girl?"

"She just followed me. She's only thirteen. She's my, um, stepdaughter. She doesn't know anything." The image of her made me angry and strong. I would do whatever I needed to protect her from these men.

A metallic point scraped my cheek as he slapped me. I knew this wasn't his hardest effort. My face smarted. I felt liquid run off my cheek. Blood? He'd cut it. With what? His ring?

"What are you writing about?" He had an accent. Slavic. Russian? Like the guy who stood outside Sister Modestia's red phone booth. Was he the same guy?

"My source told me something about the ship that just came in."

His meaty hand shoved me again, knocking me back against the other guy. "What? Just say it. Stop fucking stalling." He was so close to my face I could smell the coffee on his breath, the diesel on his jacket.

"The police are coming," I spat out. I was hoping they would drop my arms and run.

"All the more reason to tell us quickly. Otherwise, we'll shoot you and toss you in the water." He patted the breast of his jacket with his spare hand, showing the outline of something bulky.

I gulped down air. "It's about what's in one of the containers."

Slap. My cheek stung with the scrape of sharp metal. "Stop trying to be a fucking hero. Say it."

"It's—"

Lights flashed into the sky, and sirens screamed into the night. My heartbeat nearly exploded. The urgent sounds and rotating light got closer and closer. How far away were they?

"Let's take her." The man behind me looped his thumb and forefinger around the back of my neck and squeezed. "She knows something."

CHAPTER THIRTY-SEVEN

THE TALLER MAN considered me with a blank expression. "Hmm." He spread his palm over my face and inspected me through his fingers.

My life depended on the decision of a man who thought nothing of me.

He flicked at my forehead. "Nah, she'll slow us down. We've got work to do."

A punch landed on my back. I fell forward, hitting an old tire and clanging my head on the metal rim. "That's what you get for fucking us around." A hard boot kicked my shoulder. I seized up into a ball, my hands over my head, trying to protect myself. The scream of sirens got closer.

"Fuck. Let's get out of here." They took off through the side gate to the port and were gone. The relief that they could no longer touch my body was overwhelming. My eyes pricked with hot, angry, emotional tears. The police were close, but still, I worried about Sephy.

I got up, my head pounding. Whimpering from the pain, I hobbled toward the main gate. This time, the climb was excruciating, every movement so painful that I cried out. By the time I jumped to the ground, I was sobbing with frustration and sheer exhaustion.

Holding one arm, I shuffled toward Sephy. She was head down, glued to her phone. She looked so young and defenseless, illuminated by a pool of lamplight, dressed in her high-tops and baggy jeans. Thank God she was okay. “Sephy,” I said.

She ran to me, calling my name and we hugged. I broke down in tears, my chest bursting with gratitude and relief that she was safe.

“What did they do to your arm?” She shivered. “What happened to your face? I called the police again like you told me. Sounds like they’re near.” The siren got louder and louder. A swirling sea of overwhelming relief eased my limbs and my rigid neck, reducing the stabbing pain of my headache.

“Let’s call your dad.”

I reached into my back pocket for my phone and pressed “1.” I was still on edge, glancing around me. I couldn’t let my guard down for one second. We weren’t safe until the police car arrived.

No answer. I called again.

“Isla?” Declan was groggy. Warmth spread through my body at the sound of his voice, comforting me. Then I braced myself for what was coming. He paused, as if he was looking at his alarm clock. “It’s so late. No. Early in the morning.”

“Declan, I’m at Tilbury Port in Essex. Sephy is here with me. She followed me here. I saw two men chasing her, and I called the police. She’s fine, a bit shaken. The police are coming.”

“What? What are you talking about?”

I repeated it with even more urgency. Now I could hear him typing. “Where will they take you?” he said.

“Probably to Tilbury Police Station. I’ll confirm once we’re in the car. Okay, they’re here. I have to go now.”

“No. Stay on the line; keep me on speaker. Just keep the phone in your hand. I’m getting dressed and driving there now.”

Two police cars screeched to a halt. One person got out of each, a younger man with glasses and a tall woman with black box braids. The two drivers stayed in the car.

“What’s going on?” the woman asked. “Where are the two men?”

"Can you just get us out of here?" I asked. "I'll tell you what happened on the ride to the station. I just want to get Sephy out of danger."

If Sephy wasn't here, I would have told them the whole story, pleaded with them to get the gates opened, to search for the two men, and to inspect the ship, even though it was unlikely they would legally be allowed to.

The younger cop looked to the woman for guidance, like she was his superior. "Shouldn't we be searching for them? Two tall men? No other description?"

"One was tall and big; the other was shorter, stockier," I said. "Both were wearing black clothes and balaclavas, no safety vests. The tall one was wearing a sharp ring and a tartan shirt underneath and had blue eyes. Both had Slavic accents, maybe Russian." I groaned, frustrated. "That doesn't seem enough. I wish I had more for you. I'm sorry."

"Okay, we'll go on that," said the woman. "There should be footage showing your altercation."

"Thank you," I said. "I want to help as much as I can, and I'll stay as late as I'm needed. But my priority is to get Sephy as far away from here as possible, back to the station to safety."

"Officer," the policewoman said to the younger cop, "I'll take them back. See if you can view the videotapes on-site."

She bundled us into the back, got in the passenger seat, and told the driver, a young policewoman, to head back to the station.

After I confirmed the station's exact address with her, I went back to Declan on speaker.

"Hey, it's me. Police arrived. We're both okay."

"I heard it all. Thank God. Sephy, can you say something?"

"Hi, Dad, we're riding in the back of a police car," Sephy called into my phone. She had a childlike enthusiasm to her voice, and it made me feel worse about her being here.

"Hello, sweetheart, are you okay?" His voice was low and comforting with so much love in it, but strained, as if he was struggling to keep his anxiety from her.

"Yes, I'm all right. It was just really scary with the big men. Isla looks like shit, though."

My chest hurt that she was worried about me, and she shouldn't have to be.

He gave a long groan. "Oh, God. Okay, sweetheart, I'll be there in an hour."

"Okay, Dad." She got a little teary. My heart tore for her since she'd tried to show so little emotion before. "I love you, Dad. I was just— I didn't mean to get in trouble."

"Love you too. I'm sure you haven't done anything wrong, sweetheart. I'm sure you're not in trouble. Don't worry about any of that. Just stay calm. I'm going to sort everything out. Isla, just keep me on speaker, would you?"

I pressed my eyes with a shaking hand to still the tears. "I'll try to. I have to talk to the police now. I'll tell you everything when you get here. Honestly, Sephy is fine, and so am I."

He grunted, frustrated. "Just keep me on speaker. I don't understand what's going—" He let out a loud groan. "Can't you just— Shit. Well, they can't interview Sephy without me being there. Has someone called the paramedics?"

"Yes, sir, we're just about to do that." The policewoman in charge, in the passenger's seat, turned around. I read her name badge. Sergeant Gisele Sweeting.

"Thank you, Sergeant Sweeting," I said, so Declan knew her name too.

"Okay, good, thank you, I heard that." Declan was breathless, obviously running around the bedroom and getting changed. "The paramedics can make a preliminary examination of Sephy with Isla present unless there are emergencies, but please wait for me to get there for a fuller exam."

"I'm okay, Dad. No one hurt me. My clothes just got a bit ripped from climbing over the fence, but it's not an emergency."

"Climbing over the *fence*?" His voice was raised. The click of typing filled the air. Was he looking at an image of the fence? "Seph, you could have been badly injured." He blew out a breath. "Call me as soon as you get to the station."

"Okay, I will, Dad."

"Love you, sweetheart. Can you pass me to Sergeant Sweeting?"

"Love you too," we chorused back.

Sephy passed the phone.

"I give permission for you to give her medical treatment, but I want to be there for the police interview. Thank you, Sergeant," Declan said.

"Understood, sir." She handed me the phone, and I went to speak, but he'd ended the call. Sephy was his first concern, and she should be. He'd made his anger toward me obvious.

I stared out the side window as we pulled away. The two other policemen stood, motioning to the port guards to open the gates. As we drove past to turn around, I saw that a team of men was unloading a container onto the tarmac with lightning speed. A huge van was waiting; its back open, a ramp already in place. We'd be gone by the time it sped through these gates.

They were going to get away with it. And now they knew I was onto them.

CHAPTER THIRTY-EIGHT

"SO, THIS TIP-OFF—why didn't you tell the police?" Sergeant Sweeting smoothed her braids.

They'd wrapped us in foil blankets and handed us sweet tea and food. Paramedics had given Sephy a short exam that showed she was okay, except she might need something for the shock, and they had cleaned up my injuries. I was giving my police statement while Sephy was being looked after, and I'd explained why I was at the junkyard.

"I didn't think that was enough evidence," I said. "I would have been laughed out of the door or ignored. I wanted to keep investigating."

Admitting that, my forehead felt damp with sweat, and my cheeks burned. I felt desperate to crawl out of my skin. I thought about the lying I'd done and that I had put Sephy in danger again.

"The tip-off is not enough evidence to get a warrant," the Sergeant said. "But maybe the police could have started to build a case. And you were trespassing on that property. To be honest, you could be charged for both wasting police time and trespassing. Sephy could be charged for trespassing too."

"Oh God. No." I hadn't thought about that. My stomach plunged to the floor of the frigid gray room.

She clicked off the tape.

"It will be up to our boss when she gets in later this morning."

I sank into myself, crushed. Instead of tenaciously trying to stop illegal drugs from being distributed throughout the country, finding a link to the death of Sister Modestia, proving that she was murdered, I might be in court for breaking the law. And Sephy might be too. I imagined Declan's face, his reaction. There was no way he was going to be calm about this. He was going to be devastated. He was going to hit the roof.

Instead of gaining ground on the case, the drug ring was tipped off now, and it was extremely unlikely they would channel any more drugs through this port or even by means of this ship. I had completely wasted Sister Modestia's tip-off. I had let her down, let myself down, let Sephy and Declan down.

Sergeant Sweeting indicated we'd finished. I pictured my editor's face. Instead of bringing her a great story, I might be in court being reported on by other journalists. I'd already experienced my career falling apart over a story mistake the previous year. The possibility that this might happen again filled me with a deep, dark despair.

My thoughts were interrupted by the policemen who had stayed back at the port to try to find the two men who'd attacked me.

"No sightings of the men," one of the policemen said. "They definitely weren't security. We have requested video recordings of that area."

I nodded and dropped my head. That meant they were still out there, and there was nothing to support my side of the story.

"Thank you," I said. They disappeared to their offices. I was grateful they were taking this seriously. But I had no doubt that the recordings would be erased or blurred.

We walked out to the main office, me gingerly, aching. A commotion of voices rattled from outside. Declan? I froze at the thought of facing him, his fear and disappointment.

In the burst of his entry, he looked like safety and home and everything I needed and loved in that exact moment, dressed in his huge, favorite old black jersey. My heart twinged hard, and I longed to rest my face against his neck, his large, capable hand on the back of my head. Sephy cast off her foil blanket and threw herself at him, sobbing. I ached to do the same but held myself back so he could concentrate on Sephy. The doors opened again, and behind him appeared two women, one in a police uniform, the other in scrubs. It looked like they'd arrived with Declan.

Over the top of Sephy's head, which was burrowed tight against his chest, Declan introduced the two women to the room. They were friends he'd worked with for years. One was a police officer who worked in victim support, the other an emergency nurse. I was numb, swaying. He'd barely tried to catch my eye. A ringing sounded in my ears. I didn't hear their names.

"Lisa?" Sephy turned from where she was glued to Declan, her head burrowed into his chest. "Is that you?"

Lisa was petite, with a short brown pixie haircut under her police cap and a sweet rosebud-lipped smile. Was this the Lisa whom Sephy had mentioned when I first met her? The Lisa whom Declan had dated but failed to tell me about? Why had they split up if they were this close? Obviously, there were no hard feelings if she pulled herself out of bed with one call for help.

"Yes, it's me." Lisa held out her arms. "Oh, Sephy, it's so good to see you again."

Sephy stepped into her, and they hugged, both squealing with delight. Declan smiled fondly at their entwined forms. The sounds ripped through me, trailing an emotion I couldn't immediately name. It was jealousy, green as emeralds, but shameful rather than shiny. Envious of how delighted Sephy was to see her and of how easy, fun, and established their relationship clearly was. Had Lisa greeted Declan like this? With the close hugs and the squeals?

I turned my attention to Declan's other friend, dressed in scrubs, who was taking everyone in with a pensive scratch of her cheek. She had one of those immediately likable faces. But those long coral fingernails. How did she do injections and get a stent in with those long nails?

Bolts of tension cracked through my scalp.

I know those fingernails. I know that face. God, it was—

She saw me. Her face flashed with recognition.

"Islaaa," she called, moving toward me with outstretched hands. "Declan just gave me your first name, so I didn't realize it was you. It's Isla Joyson? Hello. Nurse Milly Monroe. I never remember ER patients' names, but you were so memorable. We met at St Mary's Hospital in Paddington."

Nononono. How was this happening? My shock must not have shown on my face.

"That night you fell into the Serpentine," Nurse Milly said. "Well, of course you remember, you poor thing. How *is* that bite?" She grimaced. "That was truly the most horrifying story we heard that night. All week. I just hate rats, so that would be my absolute nightmare."

The room spun around and around. I braced a hand on the desk in front of me. Maybe Declan hadn't heard? I held my breath, willing myself not to cry out. How many people lived in London? How many nurses? In all of London, how was I in a room with someone who'd given me medical assistance after I'd waded into the Serpentine? An event that I was specifically trying to keep from Declan.

"Wasn't that just awful—" She turned to Declan. Saw his confused face. Swiveled back to me. Registered my horrified face.

Silence descended hard and hollow.

Her mouth dropped, her eyes rounded. Her expression told me that she'd remembered something else about that night. Maybe that my emergency contact was not Declan, and I'd obviously kept it from him from the start.

"Oooh, shit," she said, biting her lip. "I just assumed … my big mouth. That was a breach of confidentiality. I'm so sorry."

Ohgodohgodohgod. My face burned so hot my hand flew to my cheeks to cool it. I mouthed, *It's okay*. It wasn't her fault. It was my fault.

My eyes roamed Declan's face, trying to latch onto his gaze, trying to say I'd explain this all later.

But his eyes turned hard, and his frown deepened.

CHAPTER THIRTY-NINE

SERGEANT SWEETING CLEARED her throat. "Mr. McDermott, now that you are here, we can take Sephy's statement."

She spoke as if my bite hadn't been mentioned. There were now five police officers in the room, including Lisa. I noticed because now this was bigger, and this wasn't about my investigation. Inside me, something wild and useless grappled to make a plan but flailed instead. This was all out of my control.

"Yes, go ahead." He glanced around at all the people in the room, which jolted them to return to patrol or their offices. Declan and Lisa moved their chairs closer to Sephy. Nurse Milly sat close by. I was the farthest away, holding a cup of sweet tea. "Sephy, would you be more comfortable in a room with just the four of us?" Declan said.

I looked around at the empty office. And realized what he was saying. He was asking her if she wanted to give her statement without me present. Why? Was I the enemy here? My lungs deflated.

She gave her one-shoulder shrug. "It's fine. Of course Isla can stay." She said it with warmth, and it made my throat tighten with gratitude and fondness. She didn't realize how much trouble I was in, not like everyone else in this building. She might think differently of me after she realized.

"It's okay to go ahead now." Declan nodded to Sergeant Sweeting.

She clicked on a tape and gave her own name, the police station, and the time, date, and full names of all five of us, and Declan and Sephy's address. "Interview with Seraphim McDermott, aged thirteen." She took a breath. "Sephy, what happened tonight?"

Sephy took a deep, trembling breath. A burning singed my nerves. I'd put her in this position. Declan squeezed her shoulders and whispered something.

"It was late, but I woke up. I heard Dad and Isla fighting. Like they've been doing a bit lately."

I caught my breath. Had we fought so much that she'd noticed? She looked at me and sent me an apologetic wince.

I gave her what I hoped was a reassuring smile that said, *Just tell them like you heard it, it's okay.*

"It sounded like Isla was having an affair, and Dad was mad about it. He asked her to stop seeing the man, but she said no." She looked down.

My face flared hot with shock. Was this as bad as it sounded? I did a quick audit of their body language. Declan scrubbed a hand over his face. The sergeant, Lisa, and Milly the nurse gave me a quick glance. My stomach curled with embarrassment.

Sergeant Sweeting hummed her encouragement for Sephy to go on.

"Then, through my window, I heard her leaving. She was outside with her Uber driver. She gave the driver directions to the junkyard next to the port in Essex. I recorded the name into my phone as soon as she said it. I thought that confirmed what I suspected, but I wanted to be sure. I assumed she was meeting the man there because it was so far away."

She had a vivid imagination. Like me. I watched Declan's throat move around a hard swallow. Shame pulsed through me. Her conclusion was logical. Again, she'd shown her mind worked like Declan's, someone who'd been a successful undercover agent. Our behavior had obviously led her to these conclusions. A depressing thud landed in my chest.

She gave me a small smile. Did part of her worry about me having an affair come from wanting me in her life and thinking she was losing that? If so, I was touched.

"So I took an Uber, and got there and climbed over the fence. Then I was very confused. Why would she meet someone there? At a junkyard? I wandered around, trying to find her. I was at the front, looking over the water when I heard someone yelling to me. A woman. I turned around and saw it was Isla. Then she yelled at me, *Look out.* I saw this big man coming toward me through the fence to the port. I assumed it must be a security guy and he'd be mad at me. I'd talk my way out of it. Then there were two of them. That's when it dawned on me—this was bad. I remembered another day when Isla was scared. We were at Parliament Square, and she was investigating that nun's drowning. Then I thought—was this connected to the dead nun? That didn't explain who these men were. Isla seemed terrified of them."

She started breathing heavily and brought a shaking hand to her mouth. Declan put his arm around her, squeezing her. Watching her go through this distress, reliving her fear, my heartbeat hammered violently in my ears.

"Take all the time you need," Sergeant Sweeting said. "Do you need to take a break?"

Sephy shook her head. "No, I'm okay."

She took a deep breath. "Isla yelled at them to leave me alone, said she'd called the police. They looked around, saw her, changed direction, and ran toward her. Then she screamed at me to get out of there. Run for the front gates. Run and don't look back. I sprinted to the other side of the junkyard as far away from those men as I could get, and then I ran along the fence to the entry. I didn't look back, just like she said. But I heard more yelling coming from them, first the men, then Isla. I was really scared for her, but I scrambled over the fence and waited at the front like she asked me to."

Her lip trembled, and she seemed close to tears. My body felt like it was turning inside out at her emotions. She was so frightened. Of course she was. She was a young girl.

"She asked me to call the police again, and I did. It seemed like I waited for ages, but it was only five minutes. She turned up looking bad, her face all bruised and bleeding. I saw the lights of the police arriving, sirens on. I looked at Isla and asked her what happened to her face. But the police pulled up in a screech, and the doors opened and they ran to me."

Sephy turned to me. "So did you fall over?" Her forehead smashed into a V, like something occurred to her. "Shit, Isla, did they beat you up? Or push you down or something?"

Declan stared at her, then at me, like he couldn't believe what he was hearing. I noticed that Lisa wasn't looking at either of us. She was watching Declan.

As though her life was about to change.

CHAPTER FORTY

"PROBABLY BEST IF you just drop me home?" I said to Declan as signs for London popped up on the motorway. The hour drive had been silent, me nodding off in the front; Sephy sleeping in the back.

"I know you're tired." He glanced at me from the driver's seat, his hands smoothing the wheel, his expression unreadable. "But I'd like to talk."

He didn't *seem* angry. He wanted to talk. Maybe it was all going to be okay. Outside, the sunrise glowed through the window, casting a strip of light across him. The car clock showed that it was 5:30 a.m. I even thought I heard a bird chirp optimistically. Maybe we'd just go straight to bed, and when we woke later today, it would be all right, and it wouldn't feel like everything had gone horribly wrong.

Inside his house, Declan caught my eye. "Isla, I'll just be a moment. Could you wait while I get Sephy settled?"

"Night, Isla," Sephy called as they trudged up the stairs.

"Night, Sephy," I replied with a wobbly smile. "I'm so sorry about what happened. Have a good sleep."

Declan sounded reasonable, but maybe that was only because Sephy was listening. He wouldn't want to frighten her or worry her further. I had no idea what he was going to say to me, but every second waiting on that sofa felt like an hour.

Once he got back downstairs, he sat in a chair opposite me. My relief exploded into dust. Not a good sign. He was always so tactile in any situation, always wanting to get physically closer. His face hardened as he pulled himself upright.

Tiredness and disappointment radiated from him as he met my eyes. "How did you get the rat bite?"

My throat was so tight that I could barely talk. He'd caught me out in a lie tonight—not exactly a lie, more like not telling him something frightening and important. Of course he'd been embarrassed by it because it was in front of people he knew, respected and trusted, and who respected him.

Waiting for my reply, he bit the inside of his mouth.

"That night I left you—" I said.

His lips pressed into a hard line.

"I headed for the street behind the convent. I watched the back of the convent from a stairwell on the other side of the road. A man started loading young nuns into his truck. He saw me. He spoke on his phone, and he must have alerted another man at the end of the road. I ran into Hyde Park, but the second man chased me with his dog. I hid in the Serpentine so the dog wouldn't find me. It worked. But while I was in there, something bit me. I walked straight to Paddington Hospital. That's where your friend met me."

My chest loosened at the relief of getting it all out. And yet, hearing myself recount it out loud—waiting in the dark outside the convent, being chased by a huge man and a dog, hiding in the lake—it all sounded bizarre and extreme. But I hoped that he was thinking, *I can see why she'd do that. That's how I'd respond in that situation.* Maybe I was also hoping he might find some humor in this wild scenario.

He made a sound in the back of his throat. A deep groove formed on his brow. "Isla, I'm really sorry about what those men did to you tonight. That must have been awful to go through."

Now that I was sitting for a minute, safe under his worried gaze, for the first time I thought properly about the experience, and I felt the force of their huge hands all over again. My face ached from the slap. My chest pounded from the shoves, and the feel of his hand imprinted like a burn on my skin. What would have happened if the police hadn't come so quickly? They would have killed us both. We'd have vanished without a trace.

I struggled to speak. Then I said, "I was just trying to distract them from Sephy."

He stared into space, his breathing shallow, like he was fearful. For Sephy's safety? It sent a painful ache into my head. Finally, he looked up at me, and what I saw made the lining of my stomach turn to acid.

"Last night, when you told me you were going to the port, I tried to persuade you not to. I was worried what could happen to you. Then I said I was going to leave it up to you to do what was important to you. You made that choice. You chose your work over us."

My gaze tracked his every move, absorbing his changes of expression and trying to find some solace in what he was saying. Where was he going with this? He looked me straight in the eye but with a terrifying distance, sending an awful hollow thud into my gut.

"We need some space," he said.

I recoiled, blindsided.

His voice was reasonable, but there was a cutting edge.

"Until you can be completely honest with me, I can't have Sephy around you." His eyes were open, but the light in them had shut down. To me, anyway. "I brought her home to get her away from bad influences. And now you are being a bad influence."

You are a bad influence.

Misery churned my chest raw.

"Declan, I admit the day I took her to Parliament Square on a job was very poor judgment, and I really regret that. I didn't tell you about the bite. That was … I'm so sorry. But tonight, Sephy followed me. How could I have stopped her if I didn't know?" I shook at his unfairness.

He observed me calmly. My mouth went dry. Oh God. Had he already made up his mind? Is this him breaking things off?

"She admires you. I can see it. That's why she followed you. I cannot have that sort of danger in her life."

"I would have never put her in danger. I need this story because I need this job. I have to make my own way. I can't depend on anyone else. I called the police as soon as I realized she was there. I had no thoughts about that being the end of the story." I dug down deep and dragged it up, voiced my worse fear. "I still need the story because, quite honestly, now I don't know that we will be together in the future—you could leave at any time. You would still have Sephy, but I'd be left with nothing."

He drew back, a shocked look on his face.

"That hurts me the most." His voice cracked. "You don't fully trust me to take care of you or to be there for you."

That wasn't true. Was it? God. It was. Because of everything that had happened in my past, I couldn't let myself depend on him.

He searched my face, seeming to battle himself, like he was looking for evidence that he was wrong about me.

His eyes flickered with decision.

"What are we even doing here?" He shook his head, exasperated. "I think it's time to take a break. *You* need space to think about whether you want to be with me and Sephy." His voice was calm and even now. "*I* need space to take care of Sephy."

"Of course I'm committed," I said, pressing my palm to my chest.

His eyes still seemed far away, and my heart pounded with urgency. I had to make him understand. "I love you, and I care about Sephy. I want to be with both of you." My growing attachment to

Sephy made this even harder. God. I might never see her again if we broke up.

He bit his lip. "Everything you do says the opposite."

Tears threatened and I willed them back. "That's just not true. Tonight, I called the police immediately. My first thought was to make Sephy safe. And when the police arrived, I just wanted to get her out of there."

He seemed unmoved by my arguments. "She shouldn't have been there in the first place."

My gut wound into a thousand knots. It was hard to say this, but I wanted the truth, and I had to go there. "It feels like you're saying we should split up."

He made no rush to comfort me or contradict me. He took a deep breath, distanced still, his face devoid of emotion.

"I'm saying we both need time apart to decide what we want."

Every emotionless word scraped and scratched at my open nerves.

I shuddered in another breath. I had to ask the next hard question. "How much time are you talking about?"

"As much as it takes for us both to be sure."

I felt devastated, then angry. Everything he said was hypocritical, but I knew not to use that word outright.

"It feels like you only want me if I don't take on police stories—but you know I can't do that. I know there are risks, but for all of Sephy's life, you've been involved in extremely dangerous investigations."

His eyes wavered, defensive, and his mouth was tight. "She was always safe with her nanny or my sisters or in boarding school. I never took her to work with me."

"But, Declan, this is the first time in Sephy's life that you don't have a risky job. And you even told me back in Ōhope that some bad guys turned up to her school once."

His jaw pulsed, as if angry I was using a confidence against him, but he couldn't say anything to counter it.

"And, anyway, once I get this story, I'll have a good chance at getting the big job. I can move on. This push will be over. It will be the end."

"But now this story is dead. So you need another story." He sounded worn out, which was understandable given the night we'd had, but also cynical, which was not like him. "And let's be honest, even if you get it—c'mon, Isla—there is always going to be the next story. And you are always going to be willing to do whatever it takes to get it. You will not let this be the end."

I sat, my chest bound, my eyes welling with tears, trying to think of something that would save us. But there was nothing more either of us could say.

Without another word, he stood up and climbed the stairs to his room. He switched off the stair lights, leaving me to wait by myself in the lonely glow of the lamps. I pulled out my phone and messaged for an Uber.

The downstairs felt empty and eerie with the weight of one harrowing question. Was it over for us?

CHAPTER FORTY-ONE

"SORRY ABOUT WHAT happened early this morning, Isla," Jack said.

He appeared behind Fleur as she opened the door to hand over Teddy. I'd texted while leaving Declan's to make sure they were awake at seven in the morning.

What? Shock flared through me.

How the hell did he find out so quickly?

"How many people know?" I couldn't ask him not to report it.

"Only me, I think. And that's only because I have a good contact out that way. I won't take it any further. It will come up on the local police blotter, maybe just as a disturbance at the junkyard. But it only takes a keen young journo—" He gave a rueful smile. "Just like we once were—to ask more questions, and someone's going to see it for the unusual incident it is, involving a minor. And then it might be reported locally, and later it might even make its way up to Barb."

Barb was going to hear, eviscerating any drop of credibility I'd tried to scrape together. I'd had my career destroyed before when I made that mistake on a story last year. Would I lose it all again?

"Thanks for telling me, Jack."

"Honestly, let me know if there is anything I can do." He seemed genuine and that made me even more tearful.

I had to contact my editor before she heard about this from someone else.

I thanked Fleur profusely. Frustration and embarrassment coiled in my throat. The number of nights she'd had Teddy was ridiculous. I was making a complete hash of my life, even down to caring for the dog I loved. I'd have to hire a dog minder if this was to go on, and I hoped it wasn't for too much longer. My body and my spirit just couldn't take it.

Back home, I immediately called my editor and told her everything that had happened. I admitted that a rival journalist already knew the details. "I wanted to learn more about the story before I talked to you."

"Yes, I can see that." She took a deep breath. "Look, you must be exhausted. It might be better to lie low until we know what course of action the police are going to take. Just rest today at home."

I drew a bath and soaked in it, inspecting all my bruises, marinating in my misery. I glanced at my phone. Mum had sent an email, overjoyed that I was coming home for such a long visit. This only added to my gloom. I needed to return to New Zealand at Christmas showing I was a serious journalist who continued to break stories and was not simply coasting on the success of my piece about Janey's death. I felt very far from that.

I sank under the water and resurfaced, pressing my wet hair away from my face. It had been such a bad day. And it wasn't even nine in the morning. It could still get worse. I could be charged for trespass and wasting police time. Sephy could be charged. I was absolutely not going to be moving in with Declan, so I still needed a story to get the promotion.

I'd lost the drug story. Did that mean Sister Modestia had died for nothing? I pitched around in the unfairness and misery. Enough. I could do something. I heaved myself out of the bath. No more wallowing.

I drained the bath and shook myself into action. I would keep trying to find out who killed Sister Modestia—I owed that to her. Somehow, I knew Cassius had information that would shed light on some or all of this. I wanted to get behind those walls at the castle. I had to secure another interview with him. He'd said he had a story for me, though, after the ball, I wasn't sure whether he'd caught me snooping around his home. I had to achieve something today, drag one positive thing out of all this mess.

After I dried off and slipped into fresh pajamas, I texted Cassius. My goal was to get back into his house, but I didn't know how.

> Me: *I'm interested in meeting up to talk more about your story. Somewhere private.*
>
> Cassius: *I'm still at Tewksbury. Do you want to come up for dinner tonight?*

Surprise and relief shot through me at his invitation. Replaced by a squirming suspicion. He'd immediately suggested his place to meet—that was too easy. He didn't know I wanted to snoop around his house again, did he?

I needed to sleep. And dinner, nighttime, was dark and added more danger.

I consulted the train timetables.

> Me: *Lunch tomorrow would be better for me. I can leave on the 9 a.m. train to Cheltenham and Uber to Tewksbury.*
>
> Cassius: *I can send a car for you instead?*

I'd allowed him to buy me a drink at his club because nonmembers couldn't pay, but generally, as a journalist, we couldn't accept anything free. Traveling in his car would have been a good chance to pump the driver for information, though that went both ways, because then Cassius would know for sure I'd asked the questions. It was time to emphasize professional lines and make clear this was not a social call.

> Me: *Thank you for the offer, but no worries, I'll take the train. I'm thinking I'll be there about noon tomorrow. I'm looking forward to it.*
>
> Cassius: *I'll inform the gatehouse and the staff.*

I texted an agency to look after Teddy tomorrow. It wasn't how I'd wanted to do this, allowing someone into my flat to look after him without interviewing them first, even though they were supposed to be experienced and trustworthy, but it seemed that everything in my life was rocketing messily out of my control.

I swallowed all my medications, inspected my wound, which seemed better, and rubbed ointment into my bruises. My cheek was bruised from the slap and cut from that man's ring. I'd have to slather on some pretty thick makeup to hide it from Cassius.

I climbed into bed, slammed-against-a-wall tired. I didn't want to think about tomorrow just yet. I didn't want to think of anything. Teddy grunted and curled closer to my face. I normally didn't let him sleep on my pillow, as he was forever making noises and adjusting his limbs through the night. But today, I craved the comfort of his little self.

But now that I was still, everything silent, my brain went into overdrive. Images of what happened at the port, of what could have happened to Sephy and to me, of Declan's devastating words, flashed through my mind. One tear trickled down my face, then a steady stream until I was sobbing into my pillows. I couldn't imagine my life without Declan, but I knew I had to do this story, for Sister Modestia and for myself. And now it seemed like her friend, Sister Innocenta, wanted me to do this story too. Eventually, it felt like all the moisture had left my body through my eyes.

I fell into the sleep of the heartsick, disturbed and desolate.

CHAPTER FORTY-TWO

I WOKE, BLEARY-EYED, at four in the afternoon and checked my phone. There was a voice message. Declan? My breath caught, hoping it was him.

With a sick feeling I reminded myself that we were on a break. Or was it the end? My heart dragged. I couldn't think about this. It was from a phone number I didn't recognize. They'd called at 10:05 a.m. Maybe one of our readers. I had to listen. I played it. It sounded like a phone booth at the beginning.

"Isla, this is Sister Innocenta. I want to talk. I'll try you again tomorrow at the same time."

Damn. I'd missed her. I called the convent, but when I heard what I recognized as Mother Superior's voice, I burst out with, "Wrong number." How many of those calls could I make? I consulted the website and noticed the convent's hours were 9:00 a.m. to 5:00 p.m. I'd try again in an hour, just before they closed for the day.

I'd have to delay my train journey tomorrow to make sure I was at home and had good reception for Sister Innocenta's call. Or should I scout out the call boxes around the convent to try to meet her before then? Maybe she was being followed? That wasn't a good idea. I called the convent again at 5:00 p.m. Mother Superior answered. "Wrong number," I blurted out again. While I was feeding Teddy, I debated texting Cassius. I was worried about offending him, but I had to talk to Sister Innocenta.

> Me: *Something came up. I'll arrive more like 1 p.m. tomorrow. Sorry for the change.*
>
> Cassius: *No woz. Life happens.*

No woz. That was what my Kiwi friends texted when we communicated on WhatsApp. It was a very laid-back answer for him, even though I wouldn't have flattered myself that I knew the usual "him." An unsettling chill cut through me. Why did I always feel like he knew everything that happened to me? If that was true and I wasn't just paranoid, how on earth was I ever going to get the better of him? It was me against him and his staff of … well, who knew the numbers?

I fed Teddy and took him out for a walk around the garden square opposite. After ten minutes, I felt like I couldn't take another step. What was wrong with me? I'd slept enough to make up for last night. But I was still so tired. I trudged back to the flat, Teddy in tow. At least his sitter tomorrow would give him a good run around. Back home, I cuddled Teddy in bed and set the alarm for seven tomorrow morning.

Lunch at one of the loveliest stately homes in the country. Wave after wave of anxiety crashed through me. How could I get what I wanted without Cassius discovering my plan? Or did he already know?

CHAPTER FORTY-THREE

I WOKE TO the buzz of my phone. Panic set in immediately. God, had I slept in? Teddy lifted his head. I checked the time—it was only six o'clock. What was going on? I answered the call.

"Isla. Sister Innocenta here. I haven't got much time. I heard what happened to you yesterday. I'm so sorry."

Wait, did I hear her right? I was dizzy from the early hour. I rubbed my eyes, trying to wake up. "Who told you?"

"I haven't time for that. Mother Superior could come in any minute. I know where Cassius is hiding things. It's called a priest hole, just like the one at Malahide Castle in Ireland. Like I told you, it was built in Henry the Eighth's time so priests could conduct Mass behind closed doors. Just like Malahide, the key is a ring in the wall."

Goddammit. I propped myself up on my elbow, annoyed. She had mentioned a secret room and then Peregrine said something about Malahide Castle, and I hadn't properly followed it up.

"You pull the ring around one of the angels' feet that are carved into a wood-paneled wall in the nursery. But be careful. Once you press the ring back down, you can't open the door from the inside." Hmm. I remembered how Cassius knew Sephy was named after the highest-ranking angels.

"But what's behind the wall? What will I find there?"

"She's coming. I can't talk more."

Click. She was gone.

CHAPTER FORTY-FOUR

"EVERYTHING ALL RIGHT?"

Cassius's gaze roamed my face as we lounged at our table, set up on the stone-paved terrace outside his castle's library. I pretended to be absorbed by our view of the magnificent formal gardens.

No wonder he was asking whether I was okay. I was banged up from what happened yesterday at the port. This morning, before leaving the house, I'd slathered on the foundation, but the cut from the guy's ring still showed.

"Yes, all good," I said perkily, taking a sip of water from my glass. I missed my mouth, squeaked, and dabbed at my shirt. "Just had a weight fall on me at the gym." Sweltering, I plucked at my high-collared red shirt. I'd worn it with my pink pantsuit, even though it was unseasonably warm for England, to cover the worst bruises on my arms, legs, and neck.

"Just that I heard you and Declan had broken up. I hope the ending was amicable. I mean to say, I hope these bruises were not the result of some altercation? I'm sure he was devastated, poor chap."

"*What?* God, no." Anger spiked down my backbone. I was shocked by what he suggested about Declan. I watched his face carefully. Was he just provoking me? And how did he hear that? Surely Declan hadn't spoken about this with anyone? Had Cassius listened in somehow? "Declan respects women way too much to do that." I hoped he would drop the subject. It also occurred to me that he saw me as single. Declan and I were taking a break, but I didn't consider myself single.

"I'm sorry. I didn't mean to upset you. Yes, he does love women, doesn't he? He has a lot of women friends. I've noticed them coming to visit him at Parliament."

That galled me—what was he suggesting? *What are you doing, Isla? Don't let him get to you.*

"Just that I'm concerned about you."

I tamped down my anger. "Thank you for your concern." I raised my hands to the view. "Look at this. I mean, Cassius, it's impressive, all this beauty, these gardens and rooms." I was burbling now, still angry and unsettled. I had to focus. How on earth did he pay for all this? That might be the link to everything I know about the story.

"Thank you. It's a labor of love."

"Does it ever get too much? The staff, the upkeep, the responsibility. I mean, I know Lord Havistock has one hundred thousand visitors a year just to keep his place funded."

He grimaced. "Yes, and clearly he still can't make it work without stealing one of his own paintings."

Maybe. But still, how did *Cassius* do it?

"Have you ever thought of letting visitors through?"

He scoffed. "God no. Turn this place into a fucking zoo like my contemporaries have done? I mean, one of my friends literally has a zoo with giraffes and monkeys. Ghastly. Another friend must vacate his private rooms every weekend to allow for exclusive tours. It's not enough that they're milling around your front lawn, picnicking on their Tesco-bought ham-and-cheese sandwiches. They're also in your bedroom, making comments about how they'd never pick that wall color. Ugh."

He was shocked, maybe regretting his emotional rant, which was so impassioned it was genuinely disconcerting. But he'd shown himself. What he thought of his fellow peers and their efforts to embrace commerce to keep their castles going as if he shouldn't have to stoop so low. Maybe this was what I needed to put all the pieces together, even though I couldn't see right now how it made anything clearer.

"But it's a way to keep these places going," I argued. "How do *you* manage it?"

He curled his fingers, surveyed his impeccable nails, and gave me a smug, Cheshire cat smile. "Good investments."

"Well done. You're good with business and money." I was flattering him, trying to provoke a genuine response.

"Good with money?" he spat out. "*Business?*" Clearly, he was not flattered. It seemed like he didn't want to be seen to be interested in either. As if he shouldn't have to work at it—a glimpse into the true depths of his arrogance. "No, I've been brought up to be a leader, to take on the responsibility of my position, and provide for the people who've been like family to me for decades. Nothing to do with money. It's loyalty and destiny derived from centuries of history."

We were getting somewhere. He'd pretended to me on first meeting that he'd reluctantly taken his place as a peer, and yet now he was talking about it as if it were a God-given birthright. Declan had been right about him. Cassius hadn't remotely explained how he'd paid for the remodeling, let alone gotten this place to tick over.

I turned my mind to what I was here for. To sneak into the secret room. At some stage of this lunch, I'd have to excuse myself and say I was going to the loo. I'd have only a few minutes. I wondered if he was going to try to follow me again. I needed a backup plan.

A butler had just brought our bowls of gazpacho when angry voices invaded from inside. Cassius dropped his casual mask and looked concerned. This was going to be interesting.

"Sir. Sir. I must ask you to leave."

"I've had just about enough of His Lordship or whatever the hell he calls himself. I'm going to tell him *exactly* what I think of him."

A red-faced man in work boots and a safety vest strode from out of the library to our table. A butler trailed worriedly after him. What was going on? Were we in any danger from this man? I angled myself out of the man's path, discreetly slid my chair away from the table, and placed my soles firmly on the ground, ready to flee.

The man flapped some papers in Cassius's face. Cassius recoiled and batted them away.

"My name is Sam Cochran. I am your contractor. I've done two million pounds worth of remodeling on your property. We have met countless times. I sent these invoices to you seven months ago, then four months ago, then a month ago, and every day this week. And I've made thousands of follow-up calls to your office with no response." His voice was shaky, and he breathed in slowly. This poor man was at the end of his rope. I almost spoke up for him but held myself back. In the end, I could help him more by staying quiet and listening. "Because I'm an honest and businesslike man, I've already paid my staff. I've already paid the yard for your tiles and wood and stucco and"—he paused to wave the papers around the property—"everything that made this place look how it does now. And I am about to go bankrupt because of you."

What was going on here? He was desperate and emotional, but everything he said rang true. Cassius kept an impassive face, but the cords on his neck distended red and furious.

The butler stepped up. "I'm sorry, Your Grace. I told him to leave it until after lunch. But he wouldn't take no for an answer."

Cassius nodded to his butler. "Thank you, Williams." He turned to the man and gave him his full attention. "Mr. Cochran, can you come back later? As you can see, I'm having lunch with a friend."

That was dismissive. Mr. Cochran stamped his foot and slapped the papers against his thigh. "I will not come back later.

I want my money now. I did the work. I put myself into debt to pay my workers and my bill at the yard. I want us to go to your office, and I want to see with my own eyes you transfer money into my account. I'm fed up with this arrogant Mr. High and Mighty treatment."

I swallowed hard. I felt for him. He made Cassius sound like an arrogant asshole. Cassius didn't pay his bills, and this poor man was about to go under. Was Cassius not paying his bills because he didn't have the money to start with? Or had he run out of money? Or had he planned never to pay them? Whatever his tactic, he spent money he didn't have, and the tradespeople in town had suffered for it.

Cassius surveyed him with equanimity, though a pulse in his cheek betrayed his anger. "There's obviously been some misunderstanding."

"There's no misunderstanding. I know for certain you paid Tim Langston for all his caulking and painting." Tim Langston. That was Tabs' builder and friend, whom we'd also seen at the ball. "No doubt because you play cricket with him, and you don't want all your cricket mates knowing you don't pay local tradespeople."

Cassius stood up so suddenly that his wrought-iron chair fell backward and clanged onto the stone terrace. The butler righted it. "Mr. Cochran, follow me to my office. I would only be too pleased to correct this. Believe me when I tell you, I wasn't aware of this, and I apologize profusely. This is not the way I operate. I agree it's been a very difficult situation for you, and maybe I can also compensate you extra for your trouble."

Mr. Cochran's high color diffused from his face, and he started to look appeased. "Well, okay then. Maybe it wasn't your fault. Yes—let's get this sorted."

"Isla." Cassius rested his hand on my shoulder. I slightly jumped at his touch, then calmed myself in order not to give anything away. My shoulder was still sore and bruised from being assaulted. "I'll just be a minute."

I nodded to Cassius and gave Mr. Cochran a sympathetic smile. He ran a questioning eye over me. The butler exited with them, leaving me alone.

I waited and waited. I drank a half carafe of water and attacked the breadbasket and butter while scanning all the doors to the inside and debating trying to look around. The butler reappeared.

"Ms. Joyson, I'm sorry to say His Grace will be delayed a little longer than he expected. It will be at least another fifteen minutes. He said to go ahead and eat without him."

I tried to look slightly concerned for Cassius, but I was secretly thrilled—here was my chance. "Not a problem." I checked my phone. Cassius would be back around 1:45 p.m. I took a second to think and grabbed my handbag. "I might just nip to the loo."

"Yes, of course, madam. I will show you the way."

I waved a hand. "Don't worry, I know it from the ball."

I headed inside and tried to shrug him off by turning right. Apprehensive and tense, I moved quickly. Once I was sure he was out of sight, I turned around, retraced my steps, and took the back stairs to the nursery, the way I knew that didn't involve using the main staircase. I took deep breaths to calm my shaking body, but it wouldn't still. I hadn't a clue where Cassius's office was, but I hoped it wasn't on the second floor with his bedroom and the nursery.

My neck stiff from straining to hear footsteps, I tiptoed to the nursery, keeping a close watch for staff. My gaze flitted around the room and landed on the angels carved into the wood paneling. I froze. What was that? I could hear a dull murmur. But the sounds weren't outside the room or in the hallway. They were coming from behind the wall. The sounds were louder than on the night of the ball when I'd thought they might be bats or mice. And they were more distinct. I listened harder. They were voices. *Women's* voices.

Why were they in there? I pressed an ear to the wood paneling. It was a dull, flat noise, not joyful.

Were these women in the secret room? Of their own volition—or imprisoned?

I flinched. Oh God.

I scanned the wood paneling. Five boy angels fluttered through the clouds. I traced my finger over the first one's feet. Nope. Nothing on the second or third one, either. The fourth angel, the smallest, was the lowest. *Of course.* He had to be low enough for the children to reach. The pads of my fingers felt the slightly raised surface of a ring. Lifting it out from the wall, I pulled. The panel spun on its axis. A yelp escaped me. I slammed my hand over my mouth. Oh my God! Wow, it was real. It worked. Despite my fear, I felt an initial rush of wonderment, like I was in a fairy tale. But no. This was a horror story.

I checked my phone: 1:35 p.m. I could only investigate for five minutes—I had to be back before Cassius returned at 1:45 p.m. Leaving the door open for good measure, I checked over my shoulder and crept through.

The first thing I saw made my blood run cold.

Cassius was a lot more devious and twisted than I imagined.

CHAPTER FORTY-FIVE

IN THE STONE corridor, propped casually, arrogantly against the wall, as if no one would ever find it, was Lord Havistock's oil painting. I whipped out my phone from my bag and snapped some photos.

The war scene of screaming soldiers mounted on rearing, wild-eyed horses had a thickly daubed texture. I crouched, running my fingers over it to make sure it was an oil rather than a watercolor. I should inspect the signature to make sure it wasn't a copy. I drew my eye to it but I didn't have that level of expertise. I couldn't spot a copy and it could be a very good forgery. After carefully turning the painting around, I checked the back and took more photos. There was another signature and the date, 1750. The board on the back was yellowed with age. Cassius might have stolen this art piece and accused the owner of doing the same. But had he done something much worse? A murmur of women's voices edged toward me. I had to keep going.

I ran my hand around the back of the door for the lever that closed it. *None.* Of course. There could be no escape. I shuddered. I had to leave the door open.

I crept along the wall, the women's voices louder and louder, trying to figure out what they were saying. It was hard to believe Cassius was not doing something bad here. Now that I was closer, the women's voices were strained and low, as though they were in fear. I steeled myself to see something horrible and painful. How would I see into the room without them seeing me? As I got to the end of the corridor, I spotted an opening on the left. As I got closer, a flash from a mirror caught my eye. It was strategically placed to allow me to see into the room while staying hidden in the dark corridor. A device obviously set up by their captors. From what I could see, it was an airless, windowless room built entirely of stone and lit like a surgery with standing lamps. The room was filled with women, about twenty of them, seated around tables. The women seemed to be of different nationalities, speaking at least three languages that I could pick out immediately. Some were wearing headscarves, but they were dressed in matching gray sweatsuits. I thought they may have been brought from their countries and forced to change clothing when they got here.

In front of them were weighing machines and calculators, and they were marking forms. They were weighing out white and brown powdery substances—cocaine? meth? fentanyl?—which they were then pouring into clear baggies and sealing. Where had this come from? Were these women in here voluntarily? The atmosphere was depressed; the women tense. It didn't seem like they'd chosen to be here. And if they had, why were they working in this particular room? Was Cassius keeping them here, imprisoned in this airless hole?

Oh God. This was so much worse than anything I'd imagined.

My hands clammy, I pulled out my phone and took a photo. The sound of a vacuum cleaner blasted from the open door. The women picked up their heads. I ducked back. *Shit, I hope that photo comes out.* I rehearsed an excuse for if I was caught. I might pretend that I thought this was some sort of cottage industry, and I'd wondered what they were making in here. That was weak—there was no excuse. It was obvious what I was doing. I should let Declan or someone else know where I was—in case I didn't get to leave. But there was no time. I headed back the way I had come.

I pushed the door closed. It was so heavy. It must have been easier somehow when the children did it. Maybe Cassius had weighed it down. The door shut, and I felt relief I was back in the nursery. But then I felt lightheaded and nauseated. It must have been from the exertion. The vacuum cleaner got louder. I needed to get out of here, find Declan, and together we would contact the police. If only I could stop swaying.

I tried to take a step. The room went blurry. The noise of the vacuum cleaner was deafening. I felt myself moving from side to side. A pain seared through my head.

Then nothing.

CHAPTER FORTY-SIX

"YOU FEELING OKAY now, my love?" A middle-aged woman with short gray hair, wearing a gingham uniform, was standing over me. My first thought was she had hit me on the head. My gaze flew to her hands. But she wasn't holding anything, and her blue eyes seemed kind. "You fainted."

I was crumpled on the floor. I tried to sit up. My head hurt. Had I banged it when I fell? I flopped forward.

She laid a soft hand on my back. I looked up at her. "That's weird. I've never fainted in my life." My stomach seized and I thought of lunch. Had Cassius slipped me something? But I hadn't eaten the soup yet. He could have put something into my water. But if he'd tried to drug me, wouldn't it have hit me immediately?

The woman crouched beside me. "I'm the head housekeeper, Mrs. Wilbur. Here, put your arm around my shoulders, and I'll help you down to the kitchen and get you something to eat and drink. Maybe I should call His Grace first."

I took in a sharp breath. No. Not him. I couldn't explain why I was up in the nursery. What would he do if he knew? I wouldn't put it past him to do something violent. He would get away with it. Maybe he had done it before. I stilled her hand with mine. "Thank you, Mrs. Wilbur. Please don't bother him. I'll just come down to the kitchen and then head home. I was just looking for the loo, and

I must have fainted. I haven't eaten all day, and we were just about to have lunch." This wasn't true. I'd drunk half a carafe of water and eaten nearly a whole breadbasket with butter, so that couldn't have been the reason. Maybe it was because I was out in the heat dressed in a suit?

She helped me across the hall to a discreet doorway that led to a lift down to the kitchen. I was worried about running into Cassius and eager to leave. What would I tell him if I saw him? Just that I felt ill. I'd leave out that Mrs. Wilbur had found me in the nursery. But I couldn't imagine she'd omit this detail if asked. I'd just have to use the "looking for a bathroom" story. I started planning who I would contact first to save the women.

The huge, stainless-steel basement kitchen was filled with steam and incredible smells of roasting meat, savory sauces, and sweetness, and it was bustling with cooks cutting, frying, and baking. It made me wonder how and when the women ate. Did they bring food to them up there? Or did the women come down here? Either way, the staff had to know about them. What had Cassius told them about why they were kept in the secret room? I scanned their faces, but none of them wanted to catch my eye. What did they think? Were they in on it too? Was Cassius paying them off, or did they just keep their mouths closed because they were afraid of him?

Two butlers loaded up plates and dishes. I counted the cooks—five of them. Cassius needed five cooks just to feed himself? Supposedly, they also fed all the staff. Oh yes, and he still had his guests, however many there were. All the staff stopped what they were doing and turned to me, silent.

"It's His Grace's lunch guest, Ms. Joyson," Mrs. Wilbur said, addressing all of them. I guessed that it was code for *Watch what you say in her presence*. "She fainted upstairs." There was a collective murmur of *So sorry, ma'am*. That statement didn't seem to make them less tense, but they went back to their work.

She sat me down at an old wooden table that looked like it might be original to the castle, and fetched me a glass of water, which she placed before me.

A young man dressed in a chef's uniform came over. "Can I get you something to eat, Ms. Joyson?"

"This is Freddy, the new chef." Mrs. Wilbur sat down next to me.

I was dying to drink the water. Just one sip. My throat was parched, and my head pounded. I slid my hand around it, feeling the coldness and the condensation, but stopped myself from taking a drink. I felt terrible, shockingly bad. My limbs ached and I was bone weary. My stomach seized at the horror of what was going on in this place. Now I'd witnessed it, I wanted to leave as soon as I could and talk with Declan about a plan to get these women out and have Cassius arrested. But I knew this might be the only time I could question the staff without Cassius within earshot.

"You did a wonderful job of the ball." I hadn't stayed to eat the food, but Sunny had texted yesterday, worried, checking up on me, and said it was a "gastronomibus."

"Thank you, ma'am." He bowed slightly, deferentially, and I waited for him to say more. Maybe he was afraid to. Since I'd gotten here, all the staff in this castle had seemed tight-lipped and circumspect.

"I heard the old cook left after four decades. Do you keep in touch with him? Is he still local?"

His face drained of all color. The rest of the staff in the background raised their heads and swiftly lowered them again. His eyes shot to Mrs. Wilbur.

"Henry?" she said. "We worked together all those forty years. God rest his soul." She turned to the young chef. "Freddy, could you bring our guest some chicken soup?"

"What happened to him?" I asked. "Someone told me he disappeared, and it didn't seem right."

"We don't speak of him." Clearly battling to keep her composure, she leaned over me with a closed-mouth smile. "Now. Why do you think you fainted?"

Should I be more afraid of being in this kitchen? Was she in on this, whatever it was? Was Freddy? Were all the staff? Maybe I should get out of here as soon as I could. "I don't know. I feel ill and tired and just weak."

She let out a breath. "Ms. Joyson, forgive the familiarity, but all those symptoms? They remind me of something."

"What?" Was she going to confide about how Cassius drugged people? "Please say anything you need to. You are not overstepping. You are helping me."

Then she did something utterly surprising. She positively beamed at me.

Her lips quirked a little. "Are you sure you're not pregnant?"

CHAPTER FORTY-SEVEN

EACH CLINK IN the kitchen rang excruciatingly loud in my eardrums. Steam from a pot on the stove billowed in slow motion toward the ceiling. The scent of the roses on the table hit the back of my nose with an overwhelming sweetness. I fought to bring myself back to my body. She was trying to divert me.

One of the butlers set a tray on a table in front of me. It was covered with a pristine white napkin, beautifully laid out with a china bowl of soup that smelled like chicken, a shiny spoon, a folded white napkin, and brown bread steaming hot from the oven.

I turned to her. Her face was expanding, balloon-like, and she seemed to be swaying from side to side. It felt like ten years since she spoke.

"Me? Pregnant? Oh, that's not even slightly possible." Panic setting in, I tried to remember my last period. But my brain was too foggy. I'd work it out later. Or was she just making fantastical suggestions to mess me around? Clearly, there was nothing more I would get from her. "Look, thank you for the soup, but I think I should just head home."

She seemed disappointed. "I'm sorry, was that intrusive? I know not to say anything personal to guests. Please don't let me upset you. I think you should eat and have a lie-down. I have a room that is freshly made up. You'll feel much better after something to eat and a rest."

I swallowed. I pushed away my glass of water. That sounded terrible. That sounded like maybe I'd never walk back out these doors again.

She stood up and reverted to a formal stance, hands folded, head bowed. "Very well. I'll call the driver and ask him to take you to the station. Or would you prefer he drive you all the way to Notting Hill?"

She knew where I lived. Her kind blue eyes turned piercing and calculating. She was standing way too close. I had to get out of here.

"Just to the station." I pulled out my phone and fired out a text. "I'm messaging my boyfriend that I'm leaving now, and he can pick me up at the other end."

She raised her eyebrows in disbelief. Surely she didn't know I no longer had a boyfriend?

"Declan, I have to see you." I was calling him from the train after he hadn't replied to my text.

The car ride from the castle to the station was tense. I'd rather have taken an Uber, but I wanted to put as much distance between Cassius and me as I could. With every inch of that distance, I felt like I'd abandoned the women trapped in that room. How frightened they must be. I kept looking back in the car, and even when I seated myself on the train, I watched for any movement. I didn't feel safe.

Declan paused on the end of the line. "I saw your text. Isla. It's too soon to talk. We need to leave it for a while. I'm sorry—"

"No, it's nothing to do with us. It's about"—I looked around me and cupped my phone— "Cassius. It's about the painting. I've seen it."

He took in a breath. "What? The Lord Havistock painting? Where did you see it?"

"At the castle."

A moan reverberated from the back of his throat. "*Isla.* Oh God, you didn't go and see him? By yourself?"

My silence indicated that I did.

"Fuck. Are you okay?" he asked.

"Yes, I got out of there early because I fainted. Can I come around and talk about the painting and something else I saw today? Something much worse."

"You fainted? God. Are you feeling okay now? Yes, of course you can come around. I'll pick you up outside Paddington."

I spent the rest of my train ride processing what I'd found out, going back and forth on my conversation with Cassius and what I'd seen there. Physically, I still felt nauseated and exhausted, but utterly relieved I was out of that castle.

Climbing into Declan's car, feeling the shelter of his kind smile and seeing the anguish in his eyes was painful. I couldn't just collapse into his strong, protective arms and stay there as long as I needed. I wouldn't feel the comfort of his large capable hands smoothing my hair, his lips kissing the top of my head, freeing me to fall apart and shed the pretense that I was still coping. "Shhh, I got you. I got you," he'd say. "It's okay. I'm here. It's okay now."

We pulled out into traffic. My gaze instinctively sought out snatches of his familiar profile, his straight nose and sharp cheekbones, and I had to clasp my hands together to stop myself from reaching out. His muscled arm under his short-sleeve polo shirt flexed on the wheel as if he knew I was watching him. I didn't get to reach for him and touch him, and it hurt to remind myself that I might never get to do that again. How did I ever get to this place where I was so close to him but so alone?

Even though, quite possibly, I could no longer look forward to being with him again, I knew for sure that I trusted and respected his judgment above anyone else's. He was the one whose help I wanted to analyze what I'd seen and form a plan of how to take Cassius down.

"Are you ready to tell me what happened?" he asked.

I told him about what I'd found at the castle. His lips drew tighter, and the tendons on his neck pulsed with anger, but he listened, silent.

Finally, I asked, "What do you think?"

"Probably just what you are thinking." His tense face showed he was still angry and worried, but his tone was calm and in cop mode. "He stole that painting because he needs the money for the castle, and he wants to take down Lord Havistock because he's a narcissist who constantly wants to flex his power. He is trafficking those women and importing those drugs."

I nodded, appreciating the confirmation. "Now we need to call the police." I wanted to charge in and get everyone out.

"Wait a minute. We can't just go barreling in there, guns blazing. We have to go through the proper channels. Otherwise we put ourselves and the women in more danger, and we won't make the charges stick."

I nodded reluctantly. I knew he was the voice of reason.

"First, we need to deal with you fainting. I'm worried about that, especially after that bite. Maybe there's some sort of internal infection? What about I ask Milly—you know, my nurse friend—to come here and give you a medical?"

I was genuinely touched by his concern. My mind wandered back to my fainting at the castle and Mrs. Wilbur's question, but I steered myself away. I didn't want to think about it. Still, I couldn't afford to be ill. I had to get this sorted. "Okay, okay."

He made the call from the car.

Inside the house, I felt like a stranger forensically scouring his home so I could torture myself about it later. It smelled like him.

At the door, I glanced down on the entry table at the pile of mail. On the top was an intriguing letter. The address read *Count Declan McDermott*. The return address was a Swedish embassy.

"I know, isn't it a crack-up?" Sephy said, thumping down the stairs. "He gets that joke mail all the time. Hi, Isla."

Shyness clenched me, stopping me from rushing up to her. Should I hug her? She answered my question by jumping down the last few stairs and launching a hug on me. Ooh. A surprise, but a nice surprise. She gave Declan a look. They'd obviously discussed what happened. He answered her look with, "Isla's here about work." That should have made things easier on me, but I hated that he'd had to have that talk with her.

"I was going shopping with Chammy anyway," she said. "Oof. Isla, that cut looks sore. And I'm sure you have some bad bruises. Sorry, maybe I shouldn't have mentioned them."

My heart melted at her concern. But I didn't want her to worry about my injuries, so I tried to play it down. "Only surface injuries, nothing really."

She left just as Declan's nurse friend Milly arrived, dressed in her scrubs and carrying a medical bag. We greeted each other, and we both thanked her for coming so quickly—again.

"Isla, you pretty much need your own traveling nurse," she joked. She took my temperature and my blood pressure as I sat on the sofa. Declan hovered protectively, commenting that the readings seemed high. "How are you feeling after that awful night?" she asked.

"I feel pretty achy and stiff and sore. But today, while I was doing an interview, I felt nauseated and weak, and I fainted, which is why Declan called you. And I feel exhausted all the time, but that's been going on for a while, from before the port incident."

Whether it was an infection or a side effect of all the meds I'd been taking or just overexertion, I needed her to patch me up long enough to keep going and get those women out. Then I'd deal with it.

She turned to Declan. Her face had dropped its casual-friend demeanor, and she had a more guarded, professional body language. "Is there somewhere private I can examine Isla?"

He showed her upstairs, and I followed. I appreciated the privacy, but at the same time, my chest churned at the realization that Declan was leading us to the spare bedroom because he and I weren't together.

She asked me to strip and gave me a gown from her medical bag. I was so exhausted that I fumbled to get my clothes off, seeing it as a hassle and unnecessary. We didn't have time for this. We needed to save the women. But I didn't want to be rude. She examined the bite. "It's starting to heal well," she said, and her body language was relaxed, as though she wasn't worried about it. So it didn't look like an infection, but I couldn't draw her out on anything conclusive. That made me feel better but also added to my confusion.

She did a more thorough internal exam than I expected while asking a million questions about contraception and the last time we'd had sex and when I'd had my last period. I had to stop and think. I just couldn't remember. I grabbed my handbag and tapped into my calendar. The date had been there, but I must have skimmed over it. My period should have come and gone weeks ago.

"Are you thinking it's an internal infection?" I asked from my position on the bed. "Maybe a serious UTI or yeast infection?"

She gave me a pensive look. "Put on your clothes and we'll talk."

After stripping off her gloves, she pushed them into a plastic baggie and folded that into a canvas bag she'd brought with her. I didn't want to get dressed in the fitted pantsuit I wore to lunch, and remembered I had a more comfortable sweatsuit in Declan's bedroom. Excusing myself and hoping he wouldn't mind, I dashed into his room and pulled the pieces from the top drawers that he'd cleared for me. At the thought I'd have to return and empty out his room of all my things, a raw pang throbbed in my chest. I changed in the bathroom in the spare bedroom, trying to put that out of my mind.

"Isla, sit down," she said when I came out. She cleared her throat, looking at her notes and not at me.

Perching on the bed next to her, I rubbed my clammy hands on my sweatpants, worried. Was it something serious?

"Isla, could you be pregnant?"

"Pregnant? What?" Mrs Wilbur had suggested the same thing today. "I'm on birth control pills. That isn't possible."

"The antibiotics I gave you for the bite will mess that up," she said. I was sure it was in the literature they handed me, but somehow, it wasn't at the forefront of my mind at the time. "Anyway, you may have gotten pregnant weeks ago. It explains this continuing nausea you've been having."

I'd had a lot going on, and I was back and forth between my flat and Declan's, and I hadn't decided to carry my pills with me until later. Alcohol tasted funny. My boobs seemed to have grown a full size bigger.

"You should go and get a test now." She leaned towards me. "If you test negative, I think you should see your doctor about doing a battery of tests. These symptoms you've been having are persistent and not normal."

My gut churned, fraught with stress. I could be pregnant? I checked in with myself. What did I think of that? My pulse cranked up higher and higher with the complications that would bring. Declan and I were not together. Would he even want to have another child? He'd certainly never talked about it and I didn't want him to feel obligated to be with me. Would I even want to keep it? The questions clawed at me, overwhelming. I pulled myself up, straightening my spine and rolling back my tired shoulders. This was something I needed to put aside and think about later. I had to follow through with my plan. I needed to get help to those women quickly.

"Thank you for everything." I looked her in the eye. "This is all confidential?"

"Yes, of course. I think you're checking if I'm going to give this away to Declan. I most definitely will not."

I trusted her. Waves of gratitude washed over me at the relief. "Thank you for everything," I repeated.

"You're very welcome."

I stepped carefully down the stairs to where Declan was waiting on the sofa.

His head snapped up, his face a question, but he said nothing.

"It's not certain," I explained. "It could be so many things. I need to take some more tests."

He nodded, but he couldn't keep the worry off his face. I felt off-kilter and unmoored keeping the possibility of such big news from him—but I planned to talk to him about it as soon as we'd saved the women in the castle. I thanked Milly, and she left. Declan insisted on dropping me home, but I called an Uber. I didn't want to be alone at home to think about this. I just wanted to help the women. He was reaching out to his contacts. I was frustrated, but there was nothing more I could do until I heard back from him.

I got home, spoke to the dog minder about Teddy's day and confirmed I'd see them tomorrow. After we said goodbye, I bundled up Teddy and lay on my bed, exhausted and emotional, keeping an eye on my phone for a text from Declan, my nerves frayed with impatience and frustration. Now, unfortunately, I had time to think about the examination. What if I took a test and it was positive? What if, what if… I couldn't think about this now. I needed to press on with the investigation. I'd think about a possible pregnancy later. Even though it was only nine at night, I needed to sleep.

First thing tomorrow morning, I had to talk to Sister Innocenta. I hoped that what I had to tell her would change her mind about speaking to me.

CHAPTER FORTY-EIGHT

I KNOCKED ON the convent door. It was 9:30 a.m., and I'd been waiting on the doorstep since 9:00 a.m. Sister Innocenta hadn't come out. She'd known how to access the secret room. How? Did she know women were trapped there? I needed straight answers from her that I could give Declan to take to the police.

I rapped on the door again.

It opened.

"Yes?" It was Mother Superior. She seemed tired, or maybe she was weary of dealing with me. I hadn't had a good experience with Mother, and dealing with her again put me on edge.

"I have to speak to Sister Innocenta. I need some answers from her and from you. Please let me speak to you both."

"You can't." Her voice seemed flat; her demeanor resigned, not her Mother Superior self.

I sprang forward. "Mother, please. I need to see her now. This isn't about me being annoying and snooping. This could be life and death."

I was desperate to explain everything, but I still didn't know if she was in with Cassius.

"You cannot see her. Now … or ever. She, she—" She spluttered out a sob. "She's *dead.*"

I stumbled backward. My hand flew to my heart.

Sister Innocenta is dead? That can't be true.

Something cruel and icy lanced through my body. I pictured her sweet face.

"What? How? When?"

"Yesterday. She fell off the roof. She must have been climbing and missed her footing."

Now I was angry. I wanted to scream with frustration, call her on her lies, but I knew that would get me nowhere with her. "What on earth was she doing climbing around on the roof?"

Her face was stoic and still, and I knew she was about to embellish her lie. "Maybe she wanted to recapture some of her glory days in the Himalayas."

"When—what time?"

"Around lunchtime."

"Lunchtime."

A sick, terrifying dread landed in my gut.

That was when I was with Cassius. He had made sure he was two hours away. With witnesses. He would never be associated with her death.

"Mother, there's something going on at this convent, and I don't know how, but it seems to be connected with whatever's happening at Cassius's castle. Sister Innocenta told me some things about Cassius, and she was right. I don't know if you're involved, but if you're not, please tell me everything you know so I can move forward with my investigation and stop whatever is happening."

"Sister told you something?" She fixed me in the eyes, her white wimple pinching her skin. "And you found something wrong. Are you sure *you* aren't responsible for her death with this investigation of yours?"

I shook with fury. I didn't know if she was protecting Cassius or so afraid of him that she wouldn't cooperate, but either way, she was setting up the convent for more deaths. I reasoned with myself.

Confronting her about being evasive was a waste of emotion, and I sensed it would put her back up further. Instead, I simply handed her my card.

"Please call me. We don't have much time. Sister Innocenta was brave in telling me what she did, and it looks like she died for it. I don't know what's going on at this convent, but your silence is making everything worse. It means Cassius is getting away with many horrific crimes. I need to make sense of this so I can work with the police and stop him."

Without a word, Mother Superior stepped back into the convent and closed the door.

CHAPTER FORTY-NINE

BACK HOME, I told the dog minder he could go early and I'd pay for a full day. I picked up Teddy, threw myself on my bed, and burst into tears. Poor Sister Innocenta. I didn't know what had happened, but one possibility was that one of Cassius's men came into her room, and she escaped out the window, maybe up the fire escape and onto the roof. Maybe they chased her. They probably did. Did they catch up to her? Push her over? What were those last minutes like? She must have been terrified.

I dialed Declan.

"Isla?"

At the sound of his voice, I hiccupped with sobs.

"What is it? What's wrong?"

"Sister Innocenta died yesterday. I'm sure she was killed. I need you. You're the only person I can trust to help me."

"Oh, Isla. I'm coming now."

I wiped my face with tissues. "Are you in?" I asked. Declan was at the other end of the sofa in my living room. "You know this could ruin your present career if it goes wrong."

His expression was determined. "I'm in. And yes, I understand the consequences. But he must be stopped. Murder, human trafficking, drug trafficking, theft, another murder. Every day this man gets away with something else. I'm going to use all my influence to bring in my old department. We'll need as much backup as we can get when we're at the castle."

We? No, it had to be just me.

I swayed. The nausea again. But first, I needed to be open with him. I had to tell him what Milly, his nurse friend, suspected. I swallowed hard, not knowing how he would react. I suspected if he was upset, he would hide it and just express his support for what I wanted to do.

I took a deep breath. "Your nurse friend, Milly, thinks that with all these symptoms I'm having, it could be a pregnancy."

His face flashed with shock. Without asking about the logistics, or how she'd made this diagnosis, he just stood up.

"C'mon, we're walking around the corner to the pharmacy," he said. "We're going to buy some pregnancy tests."

I was grateful that his reaction was practical and that he was taking action. We had to find out if this was real first. In the end, we bought five tests to make sure.

When we returned home, I unwrapped the tests and took them to the bathroom and followed the instructions. I brought them back to the living room on a small towel. We sat down on the sofa together, elbows on knees, and watched, Teddy on my lap. My heart thumped in my chest, thrown off, not knowing if it was fear or upset or anticipation. His gaze flicked from the tests to my face. Did his knitted brow reflect the worry he saw there?

One pink line. Two pink lines grew longer, more defined, stronger. One pink plus appeared. Until it was real. We stared at the five tests—all positive.

I was pregnant.

Whatever I'd felt before, those moving pink lines had steadily inched joy and excitement into me until I was tingling all over. I was going to have a baby. Shock vibrated through me, and I was quite unable to think about what that meant.

"Okay if I hug you?" he asked. He'd been quiet, not commenting on any of this.

I nodded. I needed a hug. He wrapped his arms around me, and I nearly broke down from the relief and calm washing through me. For just a second, I thought, *This isn't complicated. It's going to be all right.* With a final squeeze, he dropped his arms.

"How are you feeling? What do you want?" he asked. "I'll support you whatever you decide."

"Declan, you're a good guy. I know you will support me. There is one thing: I don't want us together out of obligation. Truthfully, I don't even know what I think about any of this. I just need time."

He nodded. "It's your decision. I'll be with you all the way."

Moving Teddy from my lap onto the sofa, I gathered the tests in a paper towel, threw them into the kitchen rubbish bin and washed my hands in the sink. I turned around.

"But for now," I said, "the most important thing is to bring down Cassius."

He shifted in his seat, taking a moment to breathe and recenter himself. "Okay. Let's talk about how we can get into the castle."

"*We?* But why would Cassius let us both into the castle? It's got to be just me. I'll tell him I'm feeling better and ask if I can call in a rain check on yesterday's lunch. Maybe I should even suggest dinner." The hair lifted on the nape of my neck. Truthfully, I was afraid of facing him alone. I swept a hand across my forehead, and it felt damp from beads of sweat. I was worried about my safety. My chest churned with wariness, holding back my feelings. I could admit that to myself, but I wasn't willing to admit it to Declan.

He crossed his arms, his expression firm. "Isla, you're not going in by yourself." His tone was resolute. "Even if we have police backup, we are doing this together. And I am trusting you to be cautious and follow the plan we agree on."

I nodded and joined him on the sofa, scooping Teddy up and cuddling him. I had been reckless before, and it had affected other people and could have been a disaster. This was not just about me anymore. I had someone else to worry about and to protect.

A realization dawned on me.

Does that mean I've already decided?

I needed to hold off and think about that after we'd taken down Cassius. Back to the plan. How could both of us get into the castle unseen, past scores of staff and maybe even Cassius?

We both fell silent, thinking, and I stroked Teddy on my lap. I picked up my phone and saw Tabs had checked up on me. My chest pinched. She was a lovely friend, and I felt bad for lying to her about leaving the party. I had done so much lying lately. That wasn't how I wanted my life to go on.

But Tabs' text reminded me of Tim.

I turned to Declan. "Remember how I told you yesterday that at lunch with Cassius, this irate contractor turned up to our table? Cassius hadn't paid his bills. The contractor mentioned that Cassius was quick enough to pay this other builder who'd done the caulking and painting because he was one of his cricket mates. That builder is Tim Langston. He was at Tabs' place before the ball. He's one of her old childhood friends. Actually, they're not great friends, but I think it's because they secretly have the hots for each other. Anyway, he seems a decent guy. Could we contact Tim, persuade him to talk his way back in?" I suggested. "Maybe he could pretend he had follow-up work to do in the castle. We could hide in his equipment trolley or whatever it's called. We could dress in overalls, safety glasses, and respirator masks, just in case anyone catches us."

Declan's eyes lit up as I spoke. "Yes, I see. As a sort of Trojan horse. That's a great idea." He opened his laptop. "I'll get a friend to run a few checks on Tim, make sure he hasn't got something in his past."

I considered contacting Tabitha to ask about Tim, but then she'd be involved, and her safety would be at risk.

Excitement pulsed through my body. I felt good about us taking steps and putting a plan in place. We spent the rest of the day researching, making calls and going over details of the plan for the next day. We carefully avoided talking about the pregnancy. I tried to push it from my mind but kept racing back to it. I caught Declan watching me, pensive, which might have indicated he was thinking about it too.

He left for a couple of hours to meet with his old department. Alone, the pregnancy weighed on my mind. I was sure of what I wanted now, but I needed to talk it through with Shay, to feel the comfort of her friendship. I was about to call her when my phone rang. Declan.

"I'm sending you a Zoom link for a meeting with my old department. It's starting now."

I clicked onto the link they'd sent, and on the screen, Declan introduced me to the six men and women present. With something else to focus on, I felt more confident. After we got the go-ahead from Declan's old department, we called Tim on Zoom. Declan sent over forms to Tim for him to sign, and we talked through what we needed from him. He looked different from the ball. Casual, with tousled hair and paint on his cheek. We had to tell him the whole story so he wasn't signing up for something he didn't know enough about. We had to be worried about whether Tim would tip off Cassius, but I was as sure as I could be about his character based on this brief conversation. He was horrified and disgusted. "I've seen loads of instances of Cassius's cruelty and backbiting scheming through the years, but this is next-level evil."

There was the problem of why Tim would be at the castle when the job had already been completed. Tim called Cassius's estate manager to remind him he was coming in tomorrow to redo the walls where the paint was bubbling. The estate manager said he didn't have him scheduled. Tim said he'd call Cassius directly. Maybe worried that the date slippage was his fault, the estate manager gave him the go-ahead. The good news was we had heard that Cassius was supposed to be an hour away, riding in a hunt that day. Our only issue would be if, for some reason, Cassius stayed home and saw Tim. Tim's plan was to say he'd noticed some bubbling on the wall during the ball.

When Tim rang off, Declan asked me to stay on the line to go over logistics. We needed to leave at six in the morning to arrive at Tim's house by eight. He'd load us into his trolley in the back of his van and cover us with painter's sheets. We'd stay there until we arrived at the castle. Once we were in the nursery, we'd open the secret door, introduce ourselves to the women in the room, and take photos of them and the products they were bundling. Then we'd call undercover backup at the hunt to arrest Cassius and the team stationed outside the castle walls to question his staff.

Declan said that because he and Cassius had a history of antagonism, it was important the whole scene was witnessed by his old department so the evidence wasn't questioned. Goosebumps rippled down my arm. I felt good about this plan, eager, especially with so many of us involved. But I was also horribly worried about everything coming together and all the things that could go wrong if Cassius got wind of what we were up to.

"Isla, I'm anxious about you sleeping in your flat by yourself, especially with Sister Innocenta being killed. And we have to leave early. Why don't I pick you up, and you come home with me and sleep in our guest bedroom tonight?"

My knees buckled at his words. He was inviting me to stay in the guest room rather than with him. But of course he would; we weren't together. My chest churned raw at the thought. "Bring Teddy. Sephy and her sitter can look after him."

Despite my nerves about tomorrow and our intricate plan racing around in my brain, along with my anxieties about us, that sounded comforting in its safeness. I texted the dog minder about the change in plans.

That night, I snuggled into Teddy in the spare room. Declan was across the hallway in his bed, which felt wrong, but I put it out of my mind because it was too upsetting. Sephy called out, "Night, Isla. Night, Teddy."

I called back to her, "Night, Sephy."

I could fool myself for a second that hearing Sephy last thing at night would be part of my future, but I knew this wasn't going to be our home life. I'd be living separately. We weren't going to be a family, and that made me feel unmoored. Was it a mistake sleeping here, after all? I concentrated on how warm I felt next to Teddy.

I pictured Declan lying in bed across the hallway from me. I caught a whiff of his scent, a fresh sea breeze and something deeper, his sexy, musky promise of tangled sheets. How his polite, restrained demeanor disappeared on those nights as I felt the weight of his warm hands sliding over my bare hips.

And then I thought about what those nights had created.

I laid a protective hand on my stomach. It would be awkward when Declan and I finally had a free moment to discuss it. Fears and uncertainty about tomorrow flooded my brain. I didn't want to get myself into a violent situation, like at the port, that threatened my pregnancy. Eventually, I fell asleep, but woke up an hour later, shaky and disoriented over nightmares of Trojan horses and being thrown off the turrets and drowned in a moat. I pulled Teddy closer and calmed myself with the thought that Declan would be at my side. We had twenty police trained in these operations to back us up, watching from outside the castle gates, protecting us.

We were ready.

CHAPTER FIFTY

DRESSED AS PAINTERS, Declan and I were on all fours on either side of a covered trolley as we swayed and bumped to the castle's servants' entrance.

It was a ridiculous position. Declan and I would have laughed about it later if we'd still been together, but now it was just awkward and scary. We rose slightly over a workers' entrance ramp, then jolted onto what must be the smooth tiles inside the building.

Fear pulsed through my veins, making me hold on even tighter. I glanced at Declan, and he nodded reassuringly. My stomach felt unprotected, a reminder of the vulnerable and fragile life inside me.

"Morning, mate, I recognize you. Thought you were all done. Why are you here today?"

My breath caught. Shit—stopped already? Who was this? Sounded like a passing butler or someone similar. He didn't sound angry or antagonistic, but I imagined the staff were all pretty frightened of Cassius's ire and worried about doing the wrong thing.

"Tim Langston, contractor, here to remedy the caulking and painting in the main hallway, second floor." Tim's voice was polite and respectful and impressively steady. "The job has been cleared by the estate manager."

"Good-oh, mate. Off you go then."

"Cleared *what* with the estate manager?" said someone new.

I recognized that voice. The damning deepness, the eerie crispness of fathomless authority.

Cassius.

Fuck. I held my breath, clutching the sides of the trolley harder—if that were possible. I couldn't look at Declan. We were one whisk of a painter's sheet away from being exposed, our whole plan scrapped. Cassius could go scot-free. He might have his security men rough us up. Or worse, disappear us. I swallowed painfully around the brick in my throat. I felt sweat break out on my forehead. He had a lot to lose. Everything.

"Sorry, Your Grace," the staff member said stiffly. "I assumed it was all cleared."

What the hell was Cassius doing using the servants' entrance? He was supposed to be hunting an hour away.

"I'll deal with this, Jackson," Cassius said ominously. "Back to the kitchen. And don't let people through so easily again."

I couldn't help it. I grimaced up at Declan, whose face was creased with worry.

"I'm sorry, Your Grace."

Shit.

"What are you doing here, Langston?"

"Morning, Your Grace," Tim said, remaining incredibly calm. "During your ball—great bash, by the way, thank you for inviting me—I discovered the second-floor hallway was bubbling slightly. I insisted to your estate manager that I return—free of charge, of course—to redo it. I'm sorry, it was my apprentice, Taylor, Gen Z, but, of course, I take full blame, Your Grace."

Cassius made some sounds in the back of his throat as he presumably mulled this over. What the hell was he thinking? That he sensed it was all bullshit?

Inside the trolley, the air vibrated with a terrible tension.

"What the fuck were you doing in my private hallway, man?"

He seemed irritated. Almost angry. Was there any good answer to this? *I* couldn't think of one—would Tim? I felt sick. Cassius was volatile and proud, and someone violating his privacy would surely enrage him.

"Showing off my caulking skills to a new female friend, Your Grace." Tim's answer was as light and quick as a seasoned comedian, but also very cheeky. I clenched my stomach. Surely he'd gone too far?

Cassius's uproarious laugh rang through the room. It sounded like relief and a second chance for us. We were still on. Tim had judged it perfectly.

"Okay—on your way. And next time, save your caulking demonstrations until you get home, okay?"

"Yes, Your Grace. I'm sorry for intruding on your private space, Your Grace. That was poor judgment on my part."

"Mmm." A chuckle.

I held my breath as the soft tap of expensive shoe leather on ancient stone floors got more and more distant. Hopefully, Cassius was gone. Our trolley rolled forward. A ping and slide of doors. The elevator? We rolled in with a bump. I desperately wanted to say something to Tim, reassure him and praise him, but we'd discussed this. Cassius could have hidden cameras. No talking until we got to the secret room behind the nursery.

A ping sounded our destination. Doors opened with a slide. Clattering out into the hallway, we moved straight ahead.

"Nursery," Tim whispered. He pulled up the painter's sheets and helped us out. I crawled out clumsily and stood. I stretched, stiff and sore, relieved at being freed from the all-fours position. Without another word, Tim immediately rolled the trolley out to the hallway, closing the door softly behind him.

I looked around the room to see if anything was different from when I was here last. Changes could signal that Cassius was worried about others getting access to this room. Changes might even mean that the women had been taken from here. But no. The urn was still there over the fireplace; the little desks and beds lined up. Declan watched me, his shoulders tensed like he was worried. I suspected he wasn't happy that I was in control of this part of the operation. He was more levelheaded than me. I had no trouble locating the lever this time. Without a word, I pulled on the ring around the angel's foot. The wood door glided open.

He switched on the camera hidden in his bulletproof vest and helped me do the same. Pressing his earpiece, he said, "McDermott. Entering the secret room now. I'll give you the order to enter the castle. Expect it in about five minutes. Over."

This was going to be the tricky part. These women might think we were part of the staff. Why would they trust us? Declan said the fact that I was a woman would help, though presumably, Cassius used female staff to escort them to the bathroom and maybe even to a separate room to have their meals. Declan said he knew several languages if they didn't speak English.

My muscles twitched with nerves. Though we weren't locked in, it still felt claustrophobic.

I pointed to the painting, which was still propped against the wall. Declan examined it and clicked photos with his phone as he described it to police backup. Taking his attention from the painting, he fiddled with the sound and video gear on his bulletproof vest.

He turned to me and jerked a thumb at the entry. We had to go back? Oh no. What was wrong?

Back in the nursery, he said, "I can't communicate with the team. It's the thickness of the walls. We're both recording, but the recordings are not being sent back to the team."

"What should we do?" Surely we shouldn't abandon the operation? But this was too dangerous to do without backup. Had Declan seen enough for him to call them? No, he'd only seen the painting, and neither of us could tell if it was a forgery. My limbs tightened, determined. We had to help the women now. "This is our time. This opportunity might not come again."

"We'll just have to go back in without the link," Declan said. "We'll talk to the women, take photos, and I'll come back out here and give the signal to the team."

I wiped across my damp forehead, relieved we weren't abandoning them. That seemed like a solid plan.

We entered again and crept along the corridor. With a gulp of breath, I stepped out into the room. Like yesterday, they were sitting at tables, measuring out white and brown powder into baggies. Declan stepped out beside me.

The oldest woman in the room, who looked like a sweet grandma with a gray headscarf, noticed us first. She cried out something to the others around her that I couldn't understand. The others raised their heads. They gasped and clutched themselves, terrified. Even though I knew they might be wary, somehow I'd hoped they'd see we weren't with Cassius. I'd pictured us rushing out of here immediately, knowing that the worst of it was over.

I focused on the women, looking for the leader. They kept looking at the sweet grandma, even though they were all speaking different languages, straining to hear what she said.

"Don't be afraid." I tried to catch the older woman's eye. "My name is Isla. I am a journalist. Declan is a policeman. We are good people, I promise." I laid my hands on my heart. "We have come to rescue you." I made a sweeping motion with my arms. "Outside, we have twenty police backing us up."

"Rescue?" In the back, a younger woman with beaded hair repeated my word. The others said it back to her.

Declan asked, "Arabic?" Ten of the women's hands shot up. He repeated what I'd said in Arabic. "Swahili?" Two of them put up their hands. He repeated it in Swahili. Español? Five put up their hands. Mandarin? Three thrust up their hands. My heart soared. This was working. He was gaining their trust. They understood. That meant they'd follow us. We were close to getting out of this place.

Snap. Snap. Snap.

A tiny clicking noise disturbed the air.

The women's faces turned to terror. I swiveled.

Cassius.

CHAPTER FIFTY-ONE

THE SIGHT OF Cassius froze every vein in my body into icy daggers.

His menacing bulk, gleaming eyes, and hard mouth filled the room. He snapped his finger and thumb in one hand instead of clapping. All my hopes exploded with that small sound. Because he was holding a gun in the other hand.

"Oh, very good. Impressing your woman with your language skills, Declan?"

He tipped his gun to Declan's face. I gasped. My heart stopped. Panic strobed through me. We were on our own.

"Turn off the cameras, take off your vests, and slide your guns to the side."

He waited as Declan slowly took off his vest.

I was watching Cassius, but out of the corner of my eye, I saw a flash of movement. Declan launched himself at Cassius. He grabbed at Cassius's gun. Arms and legs punched and kicked amid devastating groans. My breathing torn and ragged, I circled them, my arms thrust out, a piercing shriek inside my brain. How could I help Declan?

The women screamed and crouched against the back wall. With a terrifying roar, Cassius smashed his gun against Declan's face. Crying out, I lunged forward. Cassius shoved me away with his free hand and pulled his gun up, aiming at Declan's head again.

Declan grabbed the gun. A shot fired. Both men yelled. Then, a loud, surprised moan. What happened? Was someone shot? Who?

The gun fell to the stone floor with a clang.

With a shout, Cassius lunged to retrieve it.

Declan dropped with a sickening thud. He lay face down on the stone floor. Blood streamed from the area of his chest. He was unmoving, silent.

Was he—

Oh God, was he dead?

CHAPTER FIFTY-TWO

"DECLAN!" I SCREAMED. I fell on his body.

The thudding sounds of heavy feet came closer. I looked up. A tall man appeared next to Cassius. Black hair, pasty skin, a glint on his finger. Swiftly, he yanked Declan's gun from his side holster. "Shall I put him away, Your Grace?"

"Don't do it," I begged.

But I knew they'd kill him.

Then me. They had to.

But before that, I had to try to do something for these women. My vest was recording this, but the recording wasn't feeding through to the backup team. Before driving here, I'd put my phone on silent and shoved it into my bra. Sobbing, while I was lying down, I slipped my hand into my bra, pulled out my phone, and pressed "3." Sooz. My only hope now was that she answered the phone, pressed "Record," and alerted the police.

"Don't kill Declan," I said. *Sooz, pick up, pick up. Please save us.*

Ignoring me, Cassius pressed his shoulder and winced. "Fucking took you long enough," he said to the man.

"Had to tie down that bloke in the hallway first."

Tim. They knew he was with us, and they weren't going to let him live.

Under me, Declan lay motionless on his stomach, blood pouring from the area of his chest. Panicked, I reached under him to feel his heart and see if he was breathing. I felt only the wetness of blood. *No, no, no.* He couldn't be gone. Then his chest lifted slightly. Hope blasted through me. Thank God. He was still breathing. He was still alive.

"Take her off him," Cassius said. "No rough stuff. Be gentle with her."

Huge hands clamped around my waist. "Get off me," I yelled, holding on tighter to Declan.

Still latched to Declan, I kicked upward at the man.

"Okay, do it," I heard Cassius say.

In one move, the man pulled my hands behind my back and wrenched me upward to my feet, smashing me against his body. I went to kick out, but he slammed his legs in front of mine, caging me into him.

"Don't leave him like this," I pleaded with Cassius as the man held me painfully tight against his steel body. "If he's not dead now, he's going to die. Look how much blood he's losing. Please, Cassius, don't make this worse with a murder."

Cassius pointed his gun at my heart.

"Turn off his camera and take his vest," Cassius instructed the man, still ignoring me. "Take the men and search the house and the grounds. There's got to be more of them if Declan is part of this. I'll take care of her myself."

The man hurried away, looking back at me. Cool relief washed over me until I realized his mouth was strung in a slight, ugly smile. As if he knew Cassius would do worse to me than he could.

Cassius took one step toward me and tipped his gun to my head.

This was it. Terror hammered into my heart and my brain, threatening to close me down. The muzzle of his gun was close, blunt and final, like nothing I could do or say now would change it. I braced myself for the fire, the shot of pain, the end. No. One last thing. I lunged for the entry, for one last hope, to make the recording send.

He grabbed my arm and swung me round to him. "No, you don't. Take off your vest and turn off the recording. Come back into the nursery. Let's see you talk your way out of this one."

CHAPTER FIFTY-THREE

A CLOCK INSIDE this nursery was ticking. Was that the last sound I'd hear?

Cassius loomed over me. I prayed Declan was still alive in the next room. Was he going to die before I got help? How could I do that? I was tied to one of the tiny nursery chairs. How bizarre that I was imprisoned in a nursery, one that threatened the life of my future child.

"Cassius. You killed Declan," I said. "Point-blank."

If Sooz was recording this, I needed her to have all the information I could give, especially if I didn't make it out of here.

He gave a small smile. "In a way, it's all your fault. You just had to keep digging, didn't you?" He cocked his head. "I can't help admiring you for it."

"I also know that Lord Havistock didn't steal his own painting. *You* stole it. My guess is that you pretended to be acting for him and engaged an art dealer to show the painting on the black market."

"Did I? Do you have any proof? I think you'll find my name is not on any transaction. So good luck linking that to me."

"It will be the name of one of your staff, but when this dealer faces charges and prison time, they will testify that it was you in person who approached them and that the money is going into an account that can be traced back to you."

"Interesting." He folded his arms against his wide chest.

"I saw you at Sotheby's that day you visited Ishani. I can't believe she helped you with this."

He sneered. "That goody two-shoes? No way. She wouldn't do anything that doesn't have an official form attached. I always make an appointment with her to cover up that I'm seeing my fence." He looked at me, curious. "Anything else you think you know?"

My heart pounded, hard and urgent. I couldn't mess this up. I had to give him enough but keep him talking. I had to provoke him to answer my questions but not become so incensed that he shot me. "You are trafficking women and drugs in the same container loads, getting the women to bag the drugs up for distribution in the walls of your castle, and then sending both around the country."

He slow-clapped against his pistol, his mouth a sneer.

"Oh, well done you. Feel good about that, do you? Trafficking is absolutely the wrong word. You see, that's where a decent education would put you in better stead to do your job. We were giving them the opportunity to work in another country. We're helping them because their own countries are a war zone or they are on the streets."

A bilious disgust boiled in my chest to think that he was trying to justify his actions. "Maybe you did tell them that—before stealing their passports. And when they arrive at their destination, suddenly the charge for their boat ride is much higher than when they boarded."

He sliced a hand through the air. "Those are details I don't get involved with. Nothing to do with me. Someone else handles that. I cannot, on any level, be blamed if it's executed differently to how I was told. All I know is it's providing these poor women with an opportunity of a lifetime."

His face, almost proud, shut down any argument.

But I was focused on getting him to talk as much as I could.

"You knew exactly what was happening. You had them parceling up the drugs behind the walls in your castle."

"What of it? It's going to happen. You can't stop drugs. Even Declan knows that. That's why he got out of it. Gave up, poor bastard."

I gave him a hard stare, knowing he was trying to get to me and steeling myself to resist it. Instead, I had to concentrate on buying time and trying to get all of this recorded. Declan's team was waiting for an order. He'd given them a timeline of five minutes. But Declan was lying in a pool of his own blood, dying. His team weren't going to get that order. I prayed like hell that, by some stroke of luck or intervention, they decided to enter anyway.

"He gives up on everything," Cassius said. "You know all about that, don't you? He gave up on you without a fight after a pathetic three months. Oh, and don't tell me this namby-pamby nonsense he's doing in Parliament about drugs will achieve anything. It's just a coward's way out, hypocrite that he is. It just gives him a reason to be with his own kind in the House of Lords."

"His own kind?" In the House of Lords? Was he saying Declan had been to school with them or something? Maybe he had.

"Oh, he hasn't told you, has he?" He gave a theatrical stroke of his chin. "Hmm, I wonder why?"

I shook it off. He was just messing me around by trying out all his strategies and throwing out accusations.

"It's such a shame, I liked you. I could have loved you. Maybe I already do. You are headstrong, just like my sister. I made a mistake. I was showing off to her, telling her how well I'd done by raising money to fix up the castle and grounds. I just wanted her to be proud of me. That's all I've ever wanted. But she was suspicious."

A mix of adrenaline and relief surged through me. Finally, I was getting him to confess. "And you killed her for it."

He turned on me, swinging back his palm, like he was about to hit me. I took in a breath, my body rigid. Slowly, he lowered his hand. "No. No, I never killed her."

I was disappointed he'd stopped short. I didn't believe him, and even though he might hit me this time, I wasn't going to back down. "You asked someone else to do it. One of your henchmen. He met her at the telephone booth in Parliament Square, drugged her, and threw her in the Thames."

His head jerked, shocked. "It was nothing to do with me." His tone was outraged, like I'd made a huge mistake. "I can't be blamed."

Triumph pulsed through me. He had admitted to being involved. I had to take this further. Severe, I challenged him. "How can you fool yourself like that?"

"It was a mistake. I suspected what she was doing because I met her every morning for her grocery run. She was clever. Like you. I was trying to persuade her to start an order in the east wing of the castle. She said the castle hadn't been updated well enough." His lips moved in a grim line. "I told her about all the renovations, showed her photos. 'How?' she asked. 'How did you do this?' 'Business investments,' I said. She still looked skeptical."

He shook his head. "I should have been suspicious, but she'd never been interested in anything to do with money or business." He pulled a hand down his face, like he was devastated. It seemed his sister was the only person he completely trusted. "Next week, she said she'd come and look around the castle after all, see if it was suitable. Somehow, she got a special dispensation from Mother Superior. I was so happy. She spent a lot of time with our old cook." He closed his eyes as if to say, *another betrayal.* "He was the one who organized the women's meals. I never let him see the secret rooms. I just brought them down to the kitchen. First day, he thought we were doing a good thing. Only one of them could speak any English, but somehow, our cook must have gathered what they were doing up in the secret rooms. I could see he wasn't happy anymore, but he kept quiet and bided his time. While my sister was here, he must have told her, and the two of them organized an underground railway. They stole the women from us when they disembarked, took them to the convent and then to live elsewhere." He shuddered with anger.

I recoiled violently at his reasoning. *Stole the women from us.* Like he was the victim in this. A cold disgust seized me. How could he have done this? Lied to these unsuspecting women when they were most vulnerable and then kidnapped them, forcing them into a stone hole to package up drugs. Once they'd finished this job, once the next lot arrived, what was he going to do with these women? I gave a full-body shudder at the thought of their fates.

That was who I saw at the convent, the young nuns, the ones who looked as young as Sephy, and the one who seemed to be having an affair. That didn't explain the Botoxed nun, but maybe she was someone from the outside, like the men, helping the nuns. That meant the man who ran after me the night I hid in the Serpentine was part of this underground railway. Or maybe he was one of Cassius's men stationed around the corner. I couldn't think about that at the moment. I had to get more details from Cassius on how this operation worked.

"That's why you wanted to buy the Grecian frieze," I said. "So you could get inside the convent and know for sure?"

"Yes, but by then, they suspected I knew. I could see my sister had changed toward me. I had her followed. I had to, for her own protection. She must have known she was being followed when she went to a phone booth near the convent, because she took off over the parks to use that phone booth in Parliament Square."

"Why that one? It was thirty minutes away."

"She must have remembered it from one of the times our loving pater took us to Parliament to show us off. I remembered it too, and my guy caught up to her. He overheard her talking to you—we didn't know it was you at the time—but after a while, I suspected. He injected her with a sedative, enough to put her out for the two-hour journey back to Tewksbury, her rightful home, so I could talk to her properly."

His breath became ragged. A shaky hand zigzagged through his hair. "The injection had a very bad effect on her. Maybe because she led such a pristine life. She was dead before they got to his car. He waited until night, and threw her in."

What I'd thought happened to Sister Modestia was confirmed. Confidence in my judgment surged through me, followed by a rasping sorrow for her, a moment of painful relief that she wasn't conscious and afraid when she went into the water.

His mouth turned venomous. "When I heard, the same thing happened to him. Except drugs were not involved." He wiped his eyes. "I wanted him to feel her pain, her panic." His mouth twitched. "It was only what he deserved." Justified. Over with. Put out of his mind. Cassius had no more use for him.

Oh God. Now he had no use for *me*. What was he going to do?

CHAPTER FIFTY-FOUR

"THEN, WHEN I met you, I thought you could replace her." He smiled at me. "You seemed to have such strong courage of your convictions. You go for something, and you won't let anything personal stop you. You are willing to sacrifice everything."

His words slammed into me like a brick wall. I had sacrificed Declan and Sephy and a life with them. If he killed me, I would be sacrificing my baby, my new hope.

But wait. He wasn't saying he was going to kill me. He was saying I would replace *her.*

He stepped forward, crouched in front of me, and reached out to touch my hair.

"In that, you are like me."

I shook his hand off my head.

"We're nothing alike."

Instead of being insulted, he gave me a smug smile. Like he had me.

"Oh, but you are. Declan sees it too. That's why he was having second thoughts about you. No. He had a final thought about you—and it was no."

I lost it. My eyes filled with tears. This was unbearable. Was Declan already dead? We'd left without me telling him how much he meant to me, how good he was to me. Instead, I'd fought against him, not trusting him with my plans. I was carrying his child, which would remind me of that every day. If I didn't do something drastic, I might not have any more days.

With renewed determination, I started to make a plan.

It was the opposite of escaping.

"Don't talk about him," I said. "You don't know anything about us."

"I know you've broken up. You're well rid of him. He's small. Why can't you see that we could be *great* together."

I'd tried to drag this out, tried to get him to confess everything on this call I hoped I'd made to Sooz. But I couldn't rely on the idea that the phone call had gone through and that they were coming to rescue us. I had a new plan, and it involved the worst thing possible. He had to put me back into the hole.

I scowled at him. "I hate everything about you. You're the last man on earth I'd want to be with."

But instead of incensing him, his face turned almost fond. Like everything in his life, he'd processed my words how he'd wanted. "Oh, now, that's not nice. I'm wondering if all that anger is just the other side of passion?"

I took another tack. "You like to think you're special, but you are not. You're just a sad person with no friends and no one who cares about you."

He cast me a ferocious glare. That was better than his first reaction. I needed to keep provoking him.

"You know what I realized the night of your ball?" I asked. "People are not frightened of you. They laugh at you. You're like the monster in the castle, but not a tragic one, a comical one."

Now he was incensed, his face red, blown up and twitching. Blood froze in my veins. Had I pushed too hard?

"I don't know why you're saying these things." He snarled with venom and bitterness. "Maybe I should put you in the hole with the women and that dead man who rejected you. See if you come to your senses?"

"It would be better than sitting here talking to you."

Out of the corner of my eye, I searched for something I could hit him with.

"I like the spirit. Just a little too much, Isla. You'll tone it down when you're with me."

He pulled the door open and untied me from the chair just as my eyes landed on a possible weapon. I had just one chance. He stepped back and pulled his gun from his velvet jacket.

"Don't try anything silly," he said.

I swiveled, grabbed the urn from the mantel, and slammed it over his head, knocking the gun out of his hand. He stumbled, still standing. I slammed him on the head again. Dazed, he sank to the ground.

I opened the door again. "Help me," I screamed into the hole. "Help me."

Cassius bobbed his head, disoriented. I dived for his gun and aimed it at him. I'd done this only once before, in New Zealand, and I couldn't shoot the man, even though he was ready to kill me. Returning to London, I'd decided not to do any gun training, hoping I'd never be in that position again. But now, there was a room full of women who depended on me. There was someone inside me who depended on me too.

I fired—into his foot. He screamed, his head rolling back to the ceiling. He could still easily hurt me. I shot again into his other foot. I left his screams to run back into the dark corridor.

Declan was bleeding, unmoving. He might still be alive, and every second I didn't get him help pushed him closer to death. I had to help the women get out. I couldn't slow us down by asking the women to help carry him. It tore me apart to leave him here, but I needed to get him help.

"C'mon. We're going. Freedom." They stood there. "Now."

The younger one in the back moved toward me, calling something to them, agitated. The women turned to the older grandma for her reaction. Was she offended by the younger woman? I hoped my face showed my desperation but also that I was loyal and trustworthy, and I was desperately trying to help them. "Come. Freedom."

The older woman looked into my eyes for a second. I could hear Cassius groaning. Urgently, I begged, "Please, tell them it's okay."

"Okay," she shouted to the women. Relief pumped through me, and I readied my limbs. This was happening. We were leaving, and I was getting Declan help.

Joining hands, we all rushed out of the secret room into the nursery. Cassius crawled toward the door, yelling the names of his staff. We scrambled around him.

Footsteps warned us from the staircase. How many men were coming? Would they be armed?

"Link arms." I crooked my arm, and they understood and linked up. I led with the gun aimed straight in front of me. Together, we surged through the door and down the staircase. There were three enormous men waiting at the entry, blocking it. "Go, go, go," I yelled. "Charge." I sprinted at them before the men had a chance to pull out their guns. Keeping low and nimble, I raced under their arms and around their bodies. The women behind me used their fists and legs, battering their way outside.

"Run," I yelled. We raced down the driveway. The teams were stationed at the end. While we were running, I screamed for them.

Within seconds, three armed cars sped toward us and disgorged police in full bulletproof bodysuits. I closed my eyes in relief that the women were safe. My mind thrashed around with urgency. We had to get back to Declan.

One of the team I met on Zoom found me.

"Isla, what's happened?"

"I shot Cassius in the foot. His men are armed. Three of them are in the entry. Cassius shot Declan." I broke down, unable to get the words out. "He might be dead."

CHAPTER FIFTY-FIVE

"ISLA? FELICITY BARNFIELD here. I just wanted to say, excellent story, brilliant. Wow."

My editor called as I was walking into the hospital, nervous to see Declan for the first time. The clank of medical instruments rattled the air, and the smell of cooked cabbage and cleaning fluids filled my nostrils.

Sooz had received my phone call from the castle, which she'd recorded like the great journalist she was, so she'd got Cassius' confession on tape. She'd called the police, but it had taken a while until they'd confirmed there was a team responsible for backup. By the time they'd communicated to the team to take action, they'd spotted us women running down the driveway. We'd returned to find Declan unconscious, clinging to life, still breathing, but barely. Cassius had shot him in the side, and he'd lost a lot of blood. But they'd gotten him to the hospital in time for a life-saving transfusion and surgery.

"Thank you," I said.

"Look, I know this will probably come as a shock. I'm just going to say it. You didn't get the promotion. The board felt that although you do the one-off, amazing, juicy stories, Sooz is more consistent. They felt there are a lot of consequences to your reporting. You take risks with your own safety—too many, they feel."

I waited to feel devastation, for my eyes to well up with tears. But that emotion never came. The promotion didn't even matter to me anymore and I was genuinely happy for Sooz. She was a rock, and she'd proven that by answering her phone when I'd called from the castle. "Okay, well, thank you, Felicity."

"Isla, great story. You are a star."

As my sneakers squeaked toward Declan's room, I felt a new lightness. I didn't know that I had any more of these investigations in me. I didn't know if I could put my life and other people's lives at risk like that again. I wanted to stay with the newspaper, but I wasn't sure of the new role I wanted for myself. Above all, I needed to feel safe. I put a hand on my stomach and smiled. I was going to have a baby. There was a life growing in me. A new person to meet in the months ahead. It seemed a miracle and inevitable all at once and there was no weighing up pros and cons. It was just a wonderful fact in my life. My heart was so full that I felt like I was going to explode.

One thing was left to do before my happiness was complete. I was determined to win Declan back.

CHAPTER FIFTY-SIX

I WALKED INTO Declan's hospital room just as Lisa was leaving.

I greeted her with a smile as she walked past me, but I felt an annoyed scowl cross my face as she closed the door.

"Hey." His face brightened and his eyes twinkled. At seeing me or just having seen Lisa? His bare chest was partially bandaged, and he was encircled by all sorts of tubes and hooked up to an IV line, a reminder of how close he'd been to dying. Tears gathered, but I held them back. I noticed how he still looked annoyingly buff, and his face, torn and knocked around, remained very handsome. It was hard to accept that I didn't have the right to kiss the parts of his face that didn't look sore and run my fingers lightly over his bare chest. I couldn't even hold his hand.

"Thanks for leaving me behind," he joked.

"We women got it done better without you," I said.

He grinned, then winced, his hand flying up to his bruised forehead. His hard fall onto the old stone floor had left its mark. "Yeah, you did. You do everything better." His tone seemed light, flirty, his eyes sparkling, like he was going to wink at me any moment. Surely not?

"How are you feeling?" My chest tightened.

"Getting better."

"I'm sure you've seen Sephy," I said. "How is she holding up?"

"It was scary at first for her to see me in such a mess. But funnily enough, she only wanted to ask about you."

"Oh, Sephy." I'd call her straight after this. I wasn't sure if that was okay, if that was my place.

His gaze softened, and his eyes flickered down to my belly. "How are you? Whenever you want to talk, I'm not going anywhere."

"Are you sure you're well enough to do this now?"

"Yes, I'm certain. This is a good time."

I took a breath.

"I'm going to keep the baby. I realized early on, when I was worried about my safety, that I'd already decided." I paused. "Also, I didn't get the promotion. My immediate reaction was just I totally get why she made that decision. It didn't even matter to me anymore. I don't want to put myself in that sort of danger again. I still want to write, but I'm not sure about what."

"Oh? Oh." He was clearly shocked, though by which bit of news I wasn't sure. He remained quiet for a while, and I guessed he was processing the new information. "I'm sorry about the promotion. That's interesting about your new direction. And, Isla, I'm happy for both of us about the baby."

A tortured wisp of longing wrapped around me. He was a nice guy. He wasn't going to make me feel bad about us having a baby together but not being together. "Thank you for saying that."

His brows knitted, and his demeanor became serious, a different serious from when he was shocked I didn't get the promotion. He chewed the inside of his mouth, seeming worried. "Isla, I want to talk about us. I want us to sort this out now."

My shoulders hitched. "Is this because of the baby?"

"I do want to talk about what you want for the baby and how I can support you. But I'm thinking we should discuss that tomorrow." He paused. "There's something I've been planning to say to you. In fact, I've pretty much spent hours going over it in my head."

My heart hurt so much it ached to breathe. "Is it about Lisa?"

He seemed calmer than he should have been. What should I read into that?

"Ask me about Lisa," he said.

I pulled farther away from him. Where was he going with this? Was he being deliberately cruel? No. Whatever our issues, that wasn't him.

"Please just ask me. It will explain everything."

I sighed. "Okay, what was the deal with Lisa?"

"Because she was a policewoman, she was very understanding about my hours and me being away for weeks. She doted on Sephy, but she didn't want her own children, which suited me. I love Sephy. She's the best thing I've ever done, but I didn't want more children."

My heart punched the walls of my chest.

Did this mean that deep down, he didn't want the baby I was carrying? That day we'd found out, he'd assured me he'd support me in whatever decision I wanted to make, and he'd embrace a baby in his life. But was he saying he hadn't planned to have any more children? This floored me—but should it? He'd been a single father. Maybe those baby and toddler years had been too hard. We'd never discussed children. Of course we hadn't. We'd been together for only three months.

Was he ignoring the devastation that must have shown on my face? Because he looked like he was going to keep on talking.

"Lisa was extremely neat and tidy and organized and even-tempered and reliable. We all got on well, and everything was easy."

I felt so ill I wanted to run from the room. This was his paragon of female virtue.

"She sounds like the perfect woman for you," I said with more than a trace of bitterness.

This could not get any worse. I wanted to leave. Despite my upset, I stayed. Because he was making clear why he was breaking up with me, giving his reasons. Maybe I had to hear it, even though it was painful, to move on.

"She was." He narrowed his eyes. "Except for one thing."

CHAPTER FIFTY-SEVEN

I WAS BECOMING angry. But still, I was curious about this small imperfection of hers.

"Ask me about the one thing," he said.

Oh my God.

"Fine," I said, furious. "What was the one thing?"

My mind was a painful, mangled mess, trying to guess his worst answers.

He paused. He stared at me.

"She wasn't you."

She wasn't you.

I scrambled to process what he'd just said. His eyes were intense.

"Isla, you're the one I want." He held out his arms.

I took a deep, shaky breath of relief and pure happiness.

But maybe he was leading up to bad news? Maybe I was the one he wanted, but I wasn't good for him. Instead of collapsing into his embrace, I stayed exactly where I was.

"So what you're saying is, I'm messy and unpredictable and hard to be around?" I asked.

His lips quirked, like he was keeping down a chuckle. "You're exactly what I need," he said softly. "Otherwise, my life would become too orderly and contained. But besides all that …"

He motioned me closer. I moved this time. His gaze ensnared mine. Cupping my face with his hands, he tenderly rubbed my temples with his thumbs.

"I love you. I can't fucking do without you." His eyebrows drew together, and his eyes searched mine. "I've been miserable."

I could barely move. "I love you too, Declan." It came out as a breathless whisper.

He touched his forehead to mine. "Look, I know it's complicated because with me, you get a ready-made family."

"I'm arriving with one more."

"I can't tell you how happy I am about that. I thought I didn't want more babies. But I do. With you."

"*Babies?* Plural?"

"Why not? If you want that?"

I stepped away from him, putting some distance between us, because there was one important thing we hadn't discussed. "What about me being a bad influence on Sephy? I mean, I take full responsibility for what I did. I lied to you, and I know I shouldn't take her on a job or expose her to anything dangerous."

He looked down, shamefaced.

"I'm sorry I said that. I believed I was doing it for her. But it was me. I was afraid of not being in control, and I didn't want anything to happen to you, and all that emotion came out as anger. The last thing she needs is to see a man, her father, telling a woman what to do."

I sighed, feeling complete. That was exactly what I needed to hear. "I'm committed to you and Sephy and the baby, to making this life work. I'm going to be a mum." I grinned and squeezed his hand. "No matter how many times I tell myself that, I can't quite believe it. I'm so happy."

"You won't miss the excitement of chasing your stories?"

"My life is going to be exciting in a different way because I don't know what is ahead."

He smiled and brushed my cheek with the tips of his fingers.

"My priorities have changed," I said. "I don't have to prove myself anymore. I'm done with running and being in danger. I'm settling down." It felt like a relief to say that, settling down but not settling.

It was like I'd massaged out the lines in Declan's face. I could see he believed me.

"I want to kiss you, but I can't pull myself up," he said.

I leaned over and, bracing my hands on his pillow beside his head, I put my lips gently on his.

My chest hurt at how good it felt to be touching him. I gently kissed his lips again, his eyes, his forehead.

Then, all the fear and worry I'd kept locked down poured from me.

"Declan, I thought you were dead." One tear dripped down my face, then another. Soon, my shoulders were racked with sobs, and I was drenching his face with my tears. "You were lying on the ground in a pool of blood. I didn't know if you were gone. I see it over and over in my mind, like a terrible nightmare."

He stroked my head, tucking it into the crook of his neck. "Shhh, I got you. I got you. It's okay. I'm here. It's okay now." He patted the bed. "Lie beside me."

Toeing off my sneakers, I edged gingerly onto his hospital bed, taking care not to nudge his tubes. Gently, I burrowed my face into his shoulder and hiccupped with sobs for a while.

"There's something else, isn't there?" he asked after a while, tucking my sodden hair behind my ears. "What is it? You can say anything to me, I promise."

I took a deep breath. "I suppose it worries me. You know, how we had so many issues so soon in our relationship. Everyone says the first two years are the honeymoon period. Then it gets harder."

"Everyone does say that." He shifted his head slightly to catch my attention. "You think it might be portentous, that the writing is on the wall somehow?"

I bit my lip. "A bit."

He turned his face to one side like he had to think about that. Then he … smiled. He shrugged.

He *smiled* and *shrugged* in the face of this thing that others might say sounded the death knell for us.

"Love doesn't have to take a particular course," he said. "It's not some meeting of two soulmates divined in the stars. I don't believe our future is fated either."

"Declan," I said, scandalized. "But you're the romantic."

He gave a small, self-deprecating laugh at his own words.

"I say that, but what the fuck do I know? Our meeting wasn't straightforward, and our future isn't either. Again, we've fast-forwarded. In the first year of our relationship, we're going to have a teenager and a baby. Maybe we just accept the mess and chaos and just keep choosing each other. Maybe everyone has to."

I smiled. Yes, there had been so much uncertainty in our lives together in these past weeks, and I tried to caution myself there would continue to be. Yet, why did I feel so euphorically, giddily happy? So at peace with this? As though this continual choosing was wonderful and my choices weren't hard, they were actually inevitable.

As I started picturing myself hanging up my coat and my bag on those hooks in his wardrobe, folding—well, let's face it, probably just throwing—my clothes into his top two empty drawers, I realized I'd already made the choice to move into that little pastel house with the tiny, well-kept garden at the back.

"You've been honest with me," he said. "Now, I want to be honest with you. There are two things I need to tell you."

He seemed serious. I steeled myself.

"The first thing is that I'm a count."

"You *count*?"

"No. *I'm* a count. I have a title through my father, who is Swedish."

Declan was a count? What? When I heard that word, I pictured some slightly cartoonish guy wearing a white wig with a ruffled shirt and high boots and speaking in a clipped accent. I gazed at his lovely face, took in those familiar planes and his crinkling green eyes. Did it make me think of him differently? It did make him seem more mysterious. I thought I knew him, but I realized I was only starting to understand him. That prospect was exciting, and I hoped I wasn't so transparent that he felt he had nothing else to learn about me.

"That explains the letter I saw. So how does this work? Why is your name McDermott and not something Swedish?"

"It's Blomquist McDermott. Dad took on Mum's last name because they were Irish diplomats. My grandfather was a count in Sweden and owned many thousands of acres of forest and a castle. He was a liberal and gave it to the state. He kept the title, which was passed on to Dad, who passed it on to me. Dad reckoned my older brothers were too idiotic to get it. Not that it means anything. I just get invited to all these silly events I don't go to. But Cassius kept alluding to it, saying I could call him by his family name rather than His Grace. Also, he knew that some historians have even argued that our ranks are similar."

I shuddered at the sound of Cassius's name, a snake of revulsion coiling in my gut. No one was calling him His Grace anymore. "That makes sense now."

"Are you disappointed I've got a title?"

"No, I don't feel any differently toward you." I winked at him. "Might be quite a fun roleplay thing."

"Oh, shit." He bit into his bottom lip. "I'm totally thinking about that now."

I smiled. "What's the other thing?"

"I can surf." He winced. "I'm actually—I'm not going to be modest—I'm really good. Our boarding school was on the coast, and because our parents rarely came and picked us up for the holidays, I surfed a lot. I'm sorry. I was pretending in New Zealand. But I do get seasick."

I groaned. "You were so bad, like those spectacular dive bombs. So bad that …"

"Yeah, you can't be that bad without being quite good."

"Like a rodeo clown."

"Ah," he growled out. "Maybe something sexier than that."

That explained what Sephy said to me the other day about not surfing the same beaches as Declan. "I am really disappointed. I thought I was *so* much better than you at it, and I loved that."

"There are loads of things you are much better at than me." He gave a cheeky grin. "Now let's talk more about this roleplay thing."

CHAPTER FIFTY-EIGHT

TWO WEEKS LATER, I was at Declan's house, starting to unpack some of the clothes I'd brought over. He'd cleared out more of his drawers, and I would bring the rest tomorrow.

While he did some washing upstairs, I went downstairs and started a roast lamb dinner. Sephy offered to peel the potatoes, and I showed her how my mother cut into the tops and coated them with flour to make them crispier.

"Isla, can I say something? Chammy and I were worried that when my baby sister or brother is born, they're going to be very confused."

I did a double-take. I didn't understand. "Confused about what?"

"That I call you Isla, and they call you Mummy."

I smiled that she'd contemplated something that hadn't even entered my mind. "I don't think they can talk for a while. Not sure when. I better read up about that." I noticed that she looked nervous. "You do seem worried."

"It's just … it might be a good idea if we call you the same thing—Mum. What do you think? I just don't want the baby being confused."

My heart dissolved into a gooey, mushy mess. My emotions were all over the place anyway, and at this stage, I was just a pool of myself on the ground.

"Would you like to call me Mum?" I asked.

She squinted as though thinking hard. "Maybe? What do you think?"

"Yes, I'd love that."

I stopped myself. Before she made that decision, Declan needed to tell her the truth about her mother. We'd talked about it again, and he was going to sit her down tomorrow while I was packing up my clothes at my flat. Because knowing how her birth mother had suffered and died, Sephy might want to keep that name for her.

"Honestly, you can call me whatever you like." I winked at her. "Within reason."

She smiled slightly at my joke. "I need to talk to Chammy about it. I'll let you know. Maybe I'll wait until the baby is born. See how I feel."

"Okay, you can do that too, Sephy."

"Isla." She looked horrified. Oh no—had I said the wrong thing? "You're bleeding."

The doctor's rooms were seafoam green, probably to calm patients, but they made me even more on edge. Declan must have felt it, because he squeezed my hand.

"Can you tell me about your job?" the doctor asked. "You're a journalist? Let's start by you telling me about what you've done this month."

I was honest about what I had to do to get this story.

"Holy shit." She looked appalled, then covered her mouth. "Sorry, that was very unprofessional. Can you tell me about your job generally?"

I gave her a quick rundown.

"There have to be changes in your life if you want a healthy pregnancy."

"Are you telling me I have to go on bed rest?"

"No, nothing like that. Everything is okay, but you do need to be careful. You shouldn't work at this level of stress during your pregnancy. You need to be doing something else. I know this is easier said than done, finding a new job for this short space of time. But if you have any questions about what you're taking on, just call me."

"I'll do that."

"Stay home for a week. At home, only light duties."

"You're doing the dishes then," I joked to Declan, elbowing his side. We all laughed.

"And to be safe, no sex for three weeks."

Declan and I stopped laughing. Silence from both of us.

As we climbed into the car to go home, I thought that normally the doctor's advice would be freaking me out. But all I could think was, *I don't want to be doing this dangerous work. I don't want to put myself and my baby at risk.* That was not my passion anymore. I glanced at Declan behind the wheel and smiled at him and smoothed my hand over my belly.

I texted Shay about the doctor's diagnosis. *I'm so sorry!!! I was hoping to come and see you and the bub tomorrow. But I'm supposed to hang around the house for a week.*

> Shay: *No worries. I'll look forward to seeing you next week. Take it day by day on doctor's orders. Good excuse to get caught up on guilty pleasures.*
>
> Me: *Isn't there an emoji for that?*
>
> Shay: *Various fruit and tacos and tongues but you wouldn't understand them. You don't know stuff like me and the kids do.*
>
> Me: *You're so kewl, why do you hang with me?*
>
> Shay: *For charidee, baby.*

CHAPTER FIFTY-NINE

SEVEN DAYS OF rest followed, and the days did not include loads of reunion sex, frustrating Declan and me both. The following week, I visited Shay and the baby, and Declan and I had dinner with Tabitha and Peregrine. Tabs asked me about the doctor's appointment, and I gave everyone a short rundown while Peregrine went distinctly puce.

Tabs patted the table. "Work with me. I can give you a desk job, editing. Mostly. There are some interviews. I'm trying to get more 'how we live now' into our pages rather than just describing rooms with lists of furniture and tiles and paint colors, even though the sales department keeps reminding me that's what brings in the big advertising money."

"That sounds fun." It did. I liked the thought of writing about people's everyday lives, something so very different. It would help me not get antsy. Although, if this feeling was anything to go by, I'd spend most of the months ahead longing to lie on the sofa. "Yes, I'd love to."

Declan couldn't hide his surprise at my enthusiasm. "The most decisive woman in the world."

"Okay, I don't like to mix biz with pleasure, but this interview is first thing in the morning," Tabs said. "Don't worry—if it's too soon, I'll do it."

She pulled her phone out of her bag and showed me some pictures of a Docklands penthouse, filled with macabre artworks and Italian furniture in clashing colors. I asked about the owner, and she told me his name and profession.

"Oh, is this the guy who was involved in that case about developing the Essex coast?"

"I can see your mind turning over," Tabs said.

"I had some theories about that case."

"Aaand she's off," Declan joked. He gave me a worried look but immediately held up his hands. "Sorry. It's your decision."

"If you get anything on him, I can take over if it's going to affect your health," Tabs said.

I smiled. I'd realized that no story was worth risking my health or the baby's.

"I might have to take you up on that," I said.

Despite Declan promising he was going to let me make my own decisions, he beamed.

Peregrine pursed his lips, looking markedly disturbed by our conversation.

"Tabs, darling, just leave that stuff to Isla. You don't want to get mixed up with that horrid man. Stick to the articles you write about the lifestyle swaps. Such fun."

A sharpness flashed in her eyes. "Perry, you're being very patronizing. I'll write about what I want."

I smiled at her. I knew I shouldn't stick my oar between a squabbling couple, but I couldn't help myself. "Good on you."

Even Peregrine knew he'd said the wrong thing and shut up. Maybe she was finally getting to the end with him. Maybe I should even finagle some surprise meetings with Tim, the brawny, silver-tongued builder who was now our hero due to his very brave role in bringing Cassius down.

All in all, it looked like my new stint on the Home and Garden pages might be pretty interesting.

And now that things had settled down—well, slightly—in my home life, I rather fancied myself as a mature Emma doing a little surreptitious matchmaking. A little chaos was a good thing. Didn't even Declan say that? Well, he definitely said something about chaos. I probably don't remember his exact quote because I've got preggers brain. I gave a secret little smile to myself, feeling a bit smug at the thought of this new project.

Declan narrowed his eyes with a now-familiar *Oh God, what the hell are you up to this time?*

Want to read about Isla's baby shower and watch sparks fly between Tabitha and her hot contractor, Tim?
Here's the first chapters of my new romcom.

CHAPTER ONE

Tabitha

The Bell pub, Shepherd's Bush, London, Friday

"WHAT'S WRONG?" ISLA handed me a glass of champers, her red curls glowing in London's golden dusk.

"Everything's fine." I forced a smile. The last thing I wanted to do was cast a pall on her baby shower.

Isla narrowed her eyes at me, skeptical. "I know you too well Ms. Responsible. She who clears the empties at the work booze-up while everyone else gets hammered. For one second, take a break from being the person who looks after everyone else. Let *me* help *you*."

I glanced around the leafy garden of The Bell pub where friends gathered. Isla wasn't showing, even though she was entering her second trimester, but her thirteen-year-old stepdaughter Sephy had insisted on getting a head start on the celebrations and had put herself in charge.

We sat around a table laden with animal-shaped snacks and bouncing with elephant balloons. Isla's closest friends had arrived first. Her old flatmate, Shakayla, in a red jumpsuit, her beautiful baby boy grinning gleefully in her front pack, was laughing with Ishani, dressed in white linen shorts, and Sunny, in purple trousers.

Due to appear soon were Isla's old Kiwi friend, Fleur, our workmates, and Isla's new mum friends from Sephy's school.

"This is your special day," I insisted. "Let's not talk about me."

"It's the first in a series of baby showers apparently. Sephy wanted to have this one at the zoo, and we talked her down. She's keen to try out a number of themes, quite the party planner as it turns out."

Isla smiled at Sephy, dressed in wide jeans and a crochet top. I felt a pang of envy at their special relationship. And Isla's partner, Declan, and she were besotted with each other. Would I ever have that? Since this morning, I felt very far from even a hint of romance, let alone having a family.

"Seriously, Tabitha, I want to know," Isla insisted.

I'd seen Isla's tenacity firsthand. She wasn't going to give up. I took a deep breath.

"Peregrine and I split up," I said.

She scrunched up the freckles sprinkled across her nose. And sighed, like, *Finally*. Peregrine was a stickler for etiquette and a bit of a snob, which was cringing at times, but I had thought he was a reliable, decent bloke underneath his starched shirt and endless scolding about pronunciation. *Had* thought. Past tense.

"So how did you come to that decision?" she asked, tactfully. What she meant was, *What made you finally see the light?*

"It wasn't my decision." My stomach went tight admitting that. "*He* dumped *me.*"

She did a double take. "You. Are. Freaking. Kidding." Then a quiet scream. "This defies the laws of the universe."

A warmth burst through my chest that she thought so highly of me, followed by a knotted twist that she thought so little of Perry. "I'm not kidding."

"How? What? When?"

I wasn't ready to lay out the whole story right now. I needed to stay numb to get through the evening, but I knew Isla the journalist wouldn't let it go until she'd heard the whole sordid tale. "As you know, he'd been doing yoga which I thought was very odd …"

"Yes, you did mention that. I wanted to ask what he'd wear, but I never got the courage. Go on."

"Turns out, he and his female instructor were bending like pretzels in a new partner-yoga class, and apparently, they couldn't stop twisting into each other after class and then took it into the bedroom." Even though I was trying to make it funny, tears pushed at the back of my eyes and my voice cracked. "Not their fault, just 'an inevitable part of the normal exigencies of one's practice,' apparently."

His words. *So* Perry.

Isla's face screwed up, appalled. "Oh God, I'm so sorry, Tabs. That's awful and … bizarre. When did you find out?"

"This morning. I had my suspicions and turned up to his flat at seven a.m. It was full-on *in flagrante*. She is nothing if not flexible." The scene of them on Perry's bed, where I'd slept with him for four years, their arms and legs akimbo, exploded into my mind. And I had no idea how long this had been going on. Anger and nausea made me sway on my feet, and I clutched at the table. This was the first bout of bad news I got today. The second was a couple hours later at my parents' home in the Cotswolds, a full-on building site at the moment.

Isla's eyes flew open wide. She clutched my arm. "Oh Tabs, I wish you'd confided in me about your suspicions. Can I hug you?"

I squeezed the bridge of my nose with my thumb and index finger to stop the tears, but still my eyes pooled. "Better not. I'll just blubber off all this eyeliner. It's okay. I know you didn't like him. You didn't show it, but I knew."

"I, ah, er. As usual you're being nice. I did show it. I never thought he appreciated you, but still, I don't like seeing you hurt like this. That bloody bastard."

Her outrage on my behalf touched my heart. Which prompted me to make another confession. "He told me I was uptight, conservative, and status conscious."

"Whaaat? That's not you, that's him. He's totally projecting. May he be frozen in a downward-facing dog, wearing a footie shirt and cargo shorts for the rest of his days."

I spluttered out my champers. Now I was feeling better. Isla always made me see the silly side of things. I loved having her on my work team. I hoped she stayed. She'd cracked several big, complicated crime cases and I worried she'd get bored with us in the Home and Garden section.

"He said he'd found his free spirit and he wanted to allow himself to soar," I said.

Her mouth dropped. "I picture him soaring into the side of a building."

I giggled again.

"Perry, a free spirit?" Isla said. "I find that hard to believe."

"You're right," I said. "Turns out the yoga instructor is titled, has a trust fund, and holds retreats in the Seychelles, so he is soaring with someone who has jet propellant under her wings."

"So, no wild transformation for Perry, after all."

She'd said it to be nice, but my bottom lip trembled. He was the same old Perry but still, he'd dumped me.

Isla touched my shoulder, like she'd noticed I was affected by her words. "Tabitha, you are a lovely person and a great editor who doesn't know how good she is. And you are hot. You will find someone who realizes how bloody brilliant you are."

Her supportive words straightened my shoulders with resolve. But I could hear Perry's words from this morning, echoing louder.

"I suppose I am a bit stuffy," I said. "Maybe I should lose the pearls."

"Don't change yourself." She held out her arms. "The pearls look perfect with that dress. You look incredible."

I was wearing a red mini with a plunging neckline, a definite change of direction for me. Sunny and Ishani wanted to go out clubbing afterwards, and I'd dressed for the night. A big rebellion, I'd bought the dress on impulse some time ago and never wore it. Tonight I was out to prove that I was not boring. But I kept tugging at the revealing neckline, nervous the double-sided tape was going to give way, and the not insubstantial girls would tumble out into the night.

Isla's gaze flicked to something behind me. She seemed surprised.

"Look who's here," she said.

"Who?"

It wasn't Perry was it? Thinking he could do some groveling? Yuk.

"No really. Turn around. Look. Mr. Goodtimes."

I was confused and eager to see who it was. Mr Goodtimes? Definitely not Perry. A party song playing in my head, I turned.

Oh shit. My heart plummeted. Not him. Not again today, one of the lowest days of my life, and I was showing too much boob and leg to feel secure.

Tim bloody Langston.

He was laughing uproariously, as usual, his brown hair tousled, his annoyingly wide and muscled shoulders flung back, his stupidly chiseled face not as handsome as he thought it was. He wore a fresh flannel shirt and sat at a table full of uncommonly good-looking guys in similar garb, clutching pints. A bouncy blonde woman with a clipboard was hanging over him and … unbuttoning his shirt? How very on-brand. He was such a flirt. I bet they were already sleeping together. Why did that fill me with such rage?

Ishani appeared at our side. "It's your hot contractor, Tabs. That guy is so fun."

Her words soured inside my mind. Was he fun? Or did he always pretend to have fun to annoy me. *Tabs, get a grip, woman.* You're sounding horribly bitter and twisted inside your own head.

"He was so brave," Ishani said. "The presence of mind he displayed that day."

It was true. Tim had helped Isla with a dangerous story. But Ishani's reverence towards him rankled. Had he risked his life? Yes. Saved lives? Yes. Well, all right, he'd been helpful. But his heroism didn't erase the rest of his personality.

Tim brought out the worst in me and I was never sure why. We'd squabbled pretty much continuously after primary school. And now he was helping me convert my parents' crumbling-down manor in the Cotswolds into a themed B&B. Not that I'd chosen him, it was my parents, and they'd given him the upfront payment—my money—before I could object. He had a team of workers, so I was never sure why he was the one who turned up to my parents' house every day.

My parents. Hopeless and hapless and on the bones of their bums, they needed a way to pay for their retirement. I'd designed the B&B to host dating weekends for pet-loving singles looking for their soulmates. "Must Love Animals." I'd come up with that theme when they refused to let go of any of their merry band of animals, which included dogs, cats, chickens, assorted goats and spitting alpacas, and two pigs, all of whom roamed free outside and sometimes—actually often—ventured indoors.

Today Tim had given me my second lot of bad news—he'd found wood rot in the kitchen. He'd told me straight. I'd been rattled but composed myself and told him to go ahead and address it. I'd have to get another loan. Which added to the existing stress. If I didn't make this B&B work, my parents were going to have to move into my tiny two-bedroom apartment with too-close views of King's Cross, which at commuter hour was like the Red Wedding with trains. My parents loved green and space and quiet, and animals foraging in the kitchen, and they were going to be as miserable in my spare room as I was having them.

A commotion shook me out of my thoughts. Tim's table was joined by two men hulking huge cameras on their shoulders, a woman holding a boom, and a scruffy man in an enormous scarf who started gesticulating to them.

"What on earth is that film crew doing with him?" I asked. I wondered if it was one of those funny bits at the ends of the TV news. Tim was the first person a crew would zero in on because he always had a quick quip.

Isla waved to him. He looked over and squinted. His face lit up. He shot to his feet. Wow. I always forgot how huge he was. I could feel my face fall.

Don't come over.

CHAPTER TWO

Tim

OF COURSE I'M coming over.

Her face. God, she was stunning, even when she was horrified—that creamy skin, those full red lips and big blue eyes. I grinned extra hard the way I knew got under her skin. I moved towards her with extra swagger. Did her eyes dip to my thighs and linger there? *Interesting.*

But for once, that annoyed look on her face made my stomach twist. Our banter had always been quite fun. *Banter*? Most of the time, like this morning, when we were going at it about the width of the doors, it was full-on arguing. Usually I enjoyed it, there was a spark of something between us I could never define, but this morning I noticed she was sad. Or maybe after all these years it was wearing me down a bit that she never seemed happy around me. Everyone else thought I was a bloody great bloke. And most times I had to agree with them.

"Hello there," Isla said, giving me a hug.

"What a coincidence seeing you here." I focused on Isla's outfit with all its color and pattern. Because out of the corner of my eye I could see Tabs was wearing a bright red dress which was very low cut. I'd always imagined she had an incredible figure, round and lush with hips that flared, but she'd kept it well covered.

Eyes up, arsehole, I heard my sister Amy say. *She hasn't dressed for you—she's dressed for herself.*

And I didn't need my sister to remind me. I didn't want to be *that* guy. But I did wonder what was going on, what had changed. She usually wore these high ruffly blouses and gathered skirts like her mum.

"Why are you being filmed?" Isla asked.

"Yes, what's going on?" Ishani asked. I'd met her through dinners at Isla and Declan's house. She was staring at the guy on the end of my table. Kingston, I think his name was.

Tabs very pointedly looked away and fiddled with her hair like she wasn't interested in hearing my answer. I was distracted by how it shimmered over her shoulders, bright blonde and mesmerizing. She usually wore it scraped back. Maybe she and Perry were going out to dinner afterwards? Ugh, fucking flaccid Perry. Why did she date posh losers like him? My protective streak fired to the fore at the thought of his constant petty corrections, his undermining comments about her weight, and his dismissal of her career.

Hang on. I'd seen her and Perry leaving for the night while I was working at her parents' house, and she'd never worn a dress like this. An unnerving feeling unsettled my gut. Had she moved on from Perry? To someone who appreciated a body and mind like hers and would treat her the way she deserved?

"I'm on a renovation show," I replied with extra confidence, bracing myself for her scathing reaction. "I'm one of the builders. It's a competition between teams of designers and builders."

"You're on a *reality* show?" Tabitha's upper lip curled.

There it was. I ignored her tone. "Yeah, it's a hoot. We're doing a 'behind the scenes' mates shot, you know, 'getting to know the real guy in his local.'"

"Those aren't your mates."

I shrugged. "Tabitha, you do know telly is not real?"

"And this isn't your local."

"How do you know? Tabs, should I be worried? Anyone would think you were stalking my 'gram."

"You wish."

"I *do* wish." I gave her one of my best smirks.

"You—" A withering look was aimed my way, like, *You didn't win that one, idiot.*

She jolted to her feet and, just like every time she faced me, she threw her shoulders back and slapped her hands on her hips. She was very confident around me. And angry.

Her shiny peep-toe sandals touched my steel-capped work boots. Her face turned up, her glossy red mouth just a breath away from mine. A small growl escaped from the back of her throat.

A rustle sounded from beside me. Shifting my gaze, I could see Ishani move away, seeming a little uncomfortable. Isla stayed, intrigued.

"How did you get on the show?" Tabs asked.

I gave her a relaxed smile as if the force of her confrontation wasn't affecting me. "Auditioned. Like everyone else. They're in the process of finding me a designer to work with, and a project, and we'll be one of four teams."

Tabs glared at me. "I hope this doesn't interfere with your work on Mummy—" My lips quirked at her calling her mother Mummy. A reminder, if I needed it, of her poshness and that she'd been to a French finishing school. In contrast, my grandfather had been a butler. So yeah, a lifetime of serving people like her family. She stopped herself and I was pretty sure it was because she knew I would tease her. "Mum and Dad's place."

"Don't worry, I made that a condition. I'll do the show after hours and on weekends."

"Why on earth are you doing it?"

Her condescending tone niggled me. I suspected I would earn her understanding if I told her the real reason. Why didn't I? Why did I want to be the target of her wrath and scorn? So she would feel bad later when she learned the truth? Or was it that I wanted to confirm to her everything she'd ever thought about me, that I was a superficial idiot who only wanted a good time?

"The fame, of course," I answered finally.

She rolled her eyes.

"Of course," she said. "Just as well we're making the doors at home extra wide— to get your head through."

"Haha. And being on the telly will be fun. You know, *fun*?"

"Are you saying I don't know how to have fun?" she said through clenched teeth.

"Well, now that you mention it …"

I said that to annoy her, but I *could* imagine her having fun. I could imagine having fun *with* her. Far in the past. We'd actually been good mates as kids, playing all day in the fields and streams. Best mates. And there was those two weeks that summer when we were twenty-five. That seemed a million years ago.

"You realize your life as you know it will be over," she warned me, arms crossed. "Blistering feedback, no privacy, a kick-me sign on your back."

"Sounds like one of my rugby games. Anyway, all the dosh will salve any injuries sustained. But thank you for your concern." I rested my hand on my heart. "Tabitha Millicent Amanda Balfour, I am truly touched."

Tabs punched down her fists at her side, which she did a lot around me, widened her big blues and did this indignant little harrumph. It was such an old-fashioned sound that I laughed.

The blonde assistant hustled up—Saffron, that was her name— and put a proprietorial hand on my arm. I noticed Tabs's gaze followed Saffron's hand. My chest expanded with a ridiculous amount of satisfaction. Not totally immune to the Tim Langston charm after all, eh, Tabs?

"Need you back at the table, Tim," Saffron said. "Just want a couple of shots of you laughing with the lads."

The director appeared behind her. "I'm Simon Small-Smythe. Who are you girls?"

"We *women* are Isla and Tabitha," Isla said.

"Cool, cool," he said distractedly. He turned pointedly from Tabitha to me as though refereeing.

"How do you two know each other? That was a lot of tension."

He was saying that like it was a good thing. A niggling sense of worry coiled inside me. Where was he going with this?

"I hope you didn't film that." Tabs cringed, seeming to shift from angry to mortified.

"Ha! You'd have to sign a shedload of forms to get onto *our* show," Saffron said.

"You two seem to have history," Simon persisted.

Not good history, but I didn't want to discuss it with him.

"We went to primary school together, didn't we, Tabs?"

Tabitha scowled at me.

What? It was the truth.

"Clearly you've seen each other since?" Simon tapped his lips.

"Tabitha and I are working together on her parents' new B&B renovation. It's themed 'Must Love Animals' for pet-loving singles who want to find their soulmate. She's a qualified architect and is doing the designs."

Tabs jerked forward, and I guessed it was to counter anything else I added about her skills as an architect. To be fair, I did complain a lot that she wasn't practical, realistic or experienced, all of which was true. Designing houses had been her dream job—as kids she'd bossed me around for hours as we piled up branches, bricks, and stones to make little homes. But she hadn't stayed at the architecture firm for long. I never understood why.

Simon and his assistant looked at each other, their eyes shining.

Why were they so interested?

Simon sighed happily. "You two have the sort of chemistry you can't get even from actors. I want you to work together on the project you already have. Win-win. We will of course pay you. And there is prize money for Best Design in Quickest Time."

No no no, I wanted to yell. I need this gig and I need to win the prize. I did not want the complication of Tabitha sniping at me every second, questioning my judgement and competence. She will slow everything down.

"Tabitha already has a full-time job—she is the Home and Garden editor at the *UK News*," I said.

Tabitha was quiet. She didn't say, *Don't speak for me* like I expected. She was frowning, like she was thinking very hard. I would have thought she'd be irritated by the suggestion and completely dismiss the idea. But no. My breathing went sharp, on edge. Surely she wasn't truly considering it?

"We schedule around you both," Simon said. "You already work together on the house, so we'll just film then. I don't see why we can't start tomorrow."

My heart missed a beat. *Tomorrow?* No, this could not happen.

"Forms signed, of course," Saffron added.

Panic stabbed at my insides. Tabitha was going to mess this up for me. I took a breath and tried to sound reasonable. "But we don't get on."

"Precisely," Simon said. "You two are quintessential telly."

"What is the payment for taking part in the show?" Tabitha finally spoke.

My heart leaped into my mouth. She was considering it.

He told her the number. She gasped.

Yeah, it was a lot, but surely she didn't need money? She had family money. A bottomless pit of it, the way her parent spent.

"And what is the prize amount if we win?" she asked.

He told her.

She rolled her head back. "Aaaah," she said.

CHAPTER THREE

Tabitha

MY MIND WAS ticking over. They would film us while we were together anyway. The payment would pay for the wood rot and what I owed Tim for the second half of the remodel. If we could win, it would also pay for six months' breathing room while the B&B started up.

"Yes, I'd love to," I said, my stomach clenched. Everything about this was not me. I didn't even like that I had a picture byline at work. Not that I ever checked. "This sounds like a great idea. I'm in."

Tim's huge grin dropped. It was almost worth it to witness that.

Ignoring the look of shock on his face, I arranged a time for all of us to meet at my parents' house and exchanged phone numbers. I said I had to get back to the party, shot them my most poised smile, and returned to the baby shower table.

I half-listened to Ishani and Sunny talk about an event at a new restaurant. I realized I wasn't as hungry for the details as I would have been. Had I started to weary of the buzz and bustle of London? I'd surprised myself that I'd started to look forward to coming back to the peaceful rolling hills and honey-colored stone of the market town where I'd grown up in the Cotswolds. Surely I'd never want to live here full-time though? That reminded me of Mum and Dad. My stomach buckled with conflict over the decision I'd just made. My parents would hate having cameras and strange people in their house. They loved chaos but only when it came to animals. It also meant that I'd have to become a different person for a while.

"Hello, everyone." Declan walked in, kissed Isla on the cheek, and set down Teddy, their little white dog, who greeted us like, *Hi, hi, hi, I love you.*

Sephy wailed. "Dad, I said no boys. And that means Teds too."

Declan made a sheepish face. "Just popped in to say, call me when you're ready, and I can walk you home." He and Isla looked into each other's eyes.

Sephy took us all in. "See what I have to put up with? The gooey eyes all day long. Dad take Teddy and go. I've got games planned."

Declan paused at Tim's table to talk, snatching proud glances of Sephy setting up the games. Catching Isla's eye, he winked. Chin on hand, she gazed lovingly at him as he left.

Sigh.

I noticed Ishani and Sunny conferring. They went to chat to Tim and returned, looking very pleased with themselves. They're up to something—what?

"Hey, Tim is coming with us to the club," Ishani said. "Maybe some of the other guys too." She blushed a little.

I pictured my evening with him at the club. What I needed tonight was to forget about my sorry life, drink too much, dance with abandon, and find someone to flirt with. Things I'm not very good at. I didn't need Tim hovering, critiquing my amateur moves.

"He says he's heading home to the Cotswolds after, and he can drive you too," Sunny said.

I glanced at my overnight bag at my feet. Currently, during the remodeling, I was staying weekends at my parents' house in the

Cotswolds. But there was no way I was spending more time with Tim than I had to.

"Oh, that won't work," I checked him sipping his beer, relieved to have an excuse. "He's been drinking. I'll just take the train."

"He's drinking alcohol-free beer. The others confirmed," Ishani said. "All good."

Ishani and Sunny were trying to set me up with Tim, I could see it. And I knew *his* reason for coming to the club and driving me back to my parents' house, a two-hour journey. He was going to persuade me to *not* do the show. Well, tough. I need this show. I need the money for my parents.

"Guys, don't do this," I pleaded.

"What? I'm not doing anything." Ishani swapped innocent looks with Sunny. "Are *you* doing something?

"Me?" Sunny flung up her hands, mock-offended. "I am most definitely not doing something."

I groaned inside.

What have I got myself into?

Keep reading for the first chapter of *Things Not Seen*, Jody Brettkelly's next novel, a standalone mystery in which a humor writer accidentally witnesses a sinister cloning experiment, forcing her to take her family on the run from an international agency who wants them dead.

SNEAK PEEK

THINGS NOT SEEN

CHAPTER ONE

I STEPPED ONTO our stone patio and tipped back my head to enjoy the rare sun-drenched serenity of a London morning.

A splashing sound snagged my attention.

José, the cleaner next door, was pouring a bucket of his sudsy water over the dahlias. Uh-oh. Sarah won't like that. She was serious about her greywater system. I hoped for his sake that his cleaning products were Sarah-sanctioned. Although, she loved this new guy.

He glanced up with his soulful brown eyes. "Good morning, Mama."

Small for a man, he had dark skin, curly black hair, and a beard. My heart twisted a little to see how his worn jeans and company T-shirt hung on him, making him appear thin to the point of ill-nourished.

"Morning, José."

A single raven, as though sent from Sarah, swooped ominously around her white Victorian mansion house, which backed onto the biggest private garden square in London. Nine idyllic acres. I drank in the lush green lawns and ethereal willows. Beyond, the storybook gravel paths wound around a tennis court, play structure, and rose garden. Rumor was, the producers of *Notting Hill* had considered this garden square for their movie, but it was too vast, the mansion houses too huge to be relatable.

Which is a roundabout way of saying I lived in one of those mansions too.

Funny to think Jonny and I started out on the other side of our garden square in a tiny rental flat. It was dark and moldy, so I don't know why I smiled at the thought of that place, and a warmth sifted into my belly.

We'd made that short but seemingly insurmountable journey across this garden square on our own. Truthfully, my salary as a lifestyle journalist then columnist with a couple of piss-take books, like *Wild Sh*t Shar Comes Up With* and *Healthy Gut Hangovers*, only got us through the iron gates. It was Jonny's job, something that involved running office blocks of people and shedloads of money, which had wheelbarrowed us slowly but surely across the manicured grounds.

I wrangled a cup of black coffee from our ridiculously complicated coffee maker and, not for the first time, thought about how happy I'd been when it broke, and I'd had to drink instant. I popped my head into the butler's pantry, and always perfectly organized, with its white walls, pristine shelves with cans facing the door, it was a sight that calmed my day. It was a bit of a museum because the kids weren't allowed in there—their cereal spilled from huge drawers near the fridge.

Settled at my laptop on the kitchen table, I gazed around at the cabinetry in different shades of blue and green, the black-and-white tiling, and the peach-colored floral wallpaper. Miss Havisham if she were a cheerleader, I'd told the designer, who only did the job because, for some reason, she thought I knew food writer, Nigella Lawson. I took in the riot of color and patterns and exhaled a stressed sigh. Was it just a bloody big mess?

I waved away my out-of-sorts thoughts and made myself focus. Work. I scanned the online celebrity news. What the hell have you beautiful people done overnight that I can parlay into a scathing/inspiring/touching column?

Out of the corner of my eye, I spotted a blur of black lettering flashing through the kitchen.

"Allegra! What the—did you get another bloody tattoo?"

My seventeen-year-old daughter flounced away. Everything about her gave me the middle finger, from her flying black hair to the soles of her Doc Martens. And she'd cut the hem of her expensive tartan school uniform again. And frayed it. Ooh, it actually looked good, dammit. But *not* the tattoo.

She turned, the Ally fume gathering on her face, ready to gaslight me with her own indignation. I glared down to check the details of the blur of calligraphy.

She had *Fuck the Patriachy* tattooed on her forearm.

Arrgh! *Whatwhatwhat?* Anger spiked through my veins. Again? Last year, she'd shaved her head—thank God it had grown back, lesson learned. Then she'd pierced her nose and upper lip. And now this. Why did she do it?

I took a deep breath and calmed myself. Three quick thoughts tangled with one another in my head. First, I agreed with the sentiment but was furious that she'd cut something so indelible into her young skin. Second, she was going to be in huge trouble with her Catholic school. Not that we were at all religious—I wasn't even certain I believed in God—but it was the best school in walking distance I could get them into without knowing Nigella. And third, there was always the voice of my therapist: *allow her to feel the consequences.* Well, *she* can deal with the school. There. So why did I still feel like crying?

"Shar," she spat out. There was something scathing in store for me. She always called me that when she had a scorcher. "Check your judgment, *woman.* It's my body. I can do what I like."

She stared at me like I was an alien and smoothed her middle-parted hair, which I guessed was deliberately greasy for her grunge look. I focused for a second on the line of her exposed scalp. Something about that parting was heartbreakingly vulnerable, leaving her small head open to the world without protection. I wanted to hold my hands over her young scalp and shield her. My heart swelled and pressed against my rib cage with so much love for her I could barely breathe. Was she in pain? Was that why she had this tattoo done? I couldn't bear to see her shouldering that alone.

Still. "Please call me Mum. And—no! Because you're using our money and you're too young. Who did this? I'm going to give them a piece of my mind. It's illegal to tattoo anyone under eighteen."

"Chill. I'm nearly there."

"Not until the end of the year." I took another look at her arm. "Shit." Utter horror roiled in me—and then a creeping glee. No, I shouldn't even think that. A good mother would never say, "serves you bloody right, kid," in this situation. *Would they?* "It's misspelled. It's missing an 'r.'"

She glanced at her forearm. Something flashed across her face—panic?—before she righted herself. "Can't you let go of your upper-middle-class, white-woman expectations?"

"Of spelling? No."

She gritted her teeth. I knew what was coming. "Perfect Jeremy wouldn't have done it. That's what you're thinking, isn't it?"

"Dude." Jeremy appeared at the door, his navy school jacket hooked on a finger, his white shirt and tie untampered with, his forearms un-inked. At sixteen, he was one year younger than Ally, but he towered over her, had Jonny's brown hair and my dark eyes and was easy, hardworking, and sporty. As my best friends always told me, he made us look like really good parents. I wanted to take pride in that, but suspected, as I'm sure they did, that it had nothing to do with us—he'd come out that way.

Even Ally relaxed her face. Usually, one of his "dudes" calmed her. Jez had a quiet authority, like Jonny. Ally snorted in my direction as if she knew what I was thinking. For the millionth time today—and we hadn't even had breakfast—she rolled her eyes at me. "See you after school, *I suppose.*" Like there was some debate about her returning home.

She stomped through the house and slammed the door shut.

"No eggs, toast, cereal?" I muttered to myself. "Have a nice day, darling."

Jeremy hugged me. "Sorry, Mum." I hugged him back, feeling guilty. I should be the one comforting him. *I* should be *his* rock.

"Thanks, Jez. All good." I squeezed his hand. "What's on the agenda for you today?"

"Usual. Practice, school, a meeting, work." He was being included in some meetings at school because he was probably going to be head boy eventually. I looked into his kind eyes, and what I saw there worried me. It was a still, fathomless sadness. Real. It was not something I'd imagined as I might have done with Ally.

"You don't have to do all this, Jez. Quit your job. You can, you know." He'd started out volunteering and had worked at the old folk's home down the road for three years. "There's a power in walking away. Quitting is perfectly acceptable now, even encouraged." I'd done a review of the book about how we should quit more, and found it freeing in principle, but I wondered if I could ever leave any path I'd started on.

"Nah, I like work." He smiled. "I like the oldies and the other staff. We all have a good laugh."

That made sense because he always arrived home with exceptional stories. He hugged me again and walked to the front door before I realized he'd only said it was work he liked. What was going on with him?

Now I'm not angry but I'm very, very worried.

Should I call Jez's teachers? His friends' parents? I made one of my usual lists in my head. An "Is Jez Depressed?" task list. No, Jez and depressed didn't go together in the same sentence … did they? I started to google all sorts of things, and my heart rat-a-tat-tatted into the force of a machine gun.

Pressing a shaking hand on my forehead, I paused. I needed to talk to Jonny first—otherwise I'd spin myself out in all sorts of directions. Was it a girl Jez was keen on at school? Or a boy? Or both? I considered sending him a TikTok link that demonstrated how I would happily accept what he had to tell me. Something like, "Mum, I've got some shocking news for you. I'm gay/queer." "Honey, I'm so happy for you. Now, what would you like for dinner?" But Ally and Jez had both warned me in the past that my link-sending was passive-aggressive.

Hoping to divert myself from the overwhelming anxiety, I got up and walked through the French doors and outside to the patio again.

Was José talking to the dahlias?

He looked up at me and smiled. There was something about him. Sweet and approachable and understanding, even though I'd barely spoken to him yet. I wanted to walk down my stairs and lean over the rose-clad wall and confide in him about how mean Ally was to me and how worried I was about Jez. Totally inappropriate offloading. I'd never do it.

"Everything okay, Mama?" he called.

I warmed from my heart to my toes. I loved that he called me Mama. It sounded like I was a fun, together person, almost not about being a mother. And yet, I'd always intended to be a good mother, and somehow, it was like he recognized that too.

Fuck it.

I strolled down the stairs and leaned over the wall. I told him about my interaction with Ally and how Jez seemed so sad.

"Oh, Mama, that's hard," he said.

"It is."

My heart softened and a bright euphoria filled my chest, and for the first time, I really understood that expression about being seen, which I always thought was a ridiculous, made-up thing. I rested my eyes happily on the garden.

Wait.

Those dahlias he was talking to? They were two feet higher.

Preorder: *Things Not Seen*
jodybrettkelly.com

ACKNOWLEDGMENTS

So many thanks to developmental editor Dawn Alexander for ushering this book into being with humor, myriad ideas for how to climb out of various plot holes, and 20/20 vision. Thanks to James Gallagher for his close, sensitive and practical eye, and to Lisa Grant for her careful reading. Thanks to Renell Judais for her experienced and sharp editing. Thank you so much Jessica Snyder for continuing to guide me through the indie author process.

The book Shar refers to is *Quit: The Power of Knowing When to Walk Away* by Annie Duke.

Thanks to my husband, Kevin, for his endless patience and honest reactions while listening to me talk about the book and read it out aloud.

ABOUT THE AUTHOR

Jody Brettkelly grew up in a tiny beach town in New Zealand. But instead of surfing, she spent most days indoors, reading about murder most foul.

After qualifying as a barrister, she decided to cross the courtroom to the press gallery and became a radio journalist.

When she fumbled the word "hospital" five times, in the worst example of newsreading in the history of broadcasting, she took to print journalism.

That proved to be her happy place, and she worked in London for fifteen years as a journalist for national newspapers. Amazingly, considering "hospitabitible-gate," she also appeared on television and radio.

After moving to California, she worked for regional magazines and newspapers, but now, if she's not writing tales about curious women who just won't give up, she's enjoying outdoor adventures with her husband and four grown kids, taking each day, one(ish) Aperol spritz at a time.

To learn more about my characters, upcoming books, and various shenanigans, sign up for my newsletter at *jodybrettkelly.com*

Printed in Dunstable, United Kingdom

68166555R00201